Forever Right Now

a novel

Emma Scott

Acknowledgments

The writing of a book is a solitary endeavor, until the moment you send it to the first person to read the words. Then it suddenly becomes too unwieldy for the author to carry alone. I am forever grateful to the following people who helped me haul this book over the mountain and into the world. I could not have done it without them: Angela Shockley, Joy Kriebel-Sadowski, Kathleen Ripley, Jeannine Allison, Sarah Torpey, Suanne Laqueur, Jennifer Balogh-Ghosh, and William Hairston.

To Tom Ripley for his legal expertise, I thank you so very much. And while I stand by my research and his advice, I did take some liberties and exerted creative license over certain aspects of California custody law. Don't kill me.

To the bloggers, readers, and amazing people of this community who make it possible for me to do this job. Thank you.

To Grey, who literally saved me from disaster. Thank you for your kindness, your time, for being there for me at one a.m., and *especially* for that last read-through. With love.

To Melissa Panio-Petersen, who keeps me sane while I write the words, then she wraps the words inside a beautiful cover. Thank you for sharing your time, talent, and artistry, and for being the winner of World's Most Thoughtful and Hilarious Human, six years running.

To Robin Renee Hill for all the reasons, and a thousand more I can't remember but I'm sure we talked about them in an email somewhere, and it probably ended with you sending me an eyeroll emoji. <3 you more than all the babka.

And to every single member of Emma's Entourage. Words cannot express how much you mean to me, how I'm so grateful to all of you each and every day. Thank you for being there, my Blue Ribbon Stalkers. I cry more tears of joy than you know for what you do for me. Thank you. <3

Playlist

Sex and Candy, Marcy Playground
Down, Marian Hill
One More Light, Linkin Park
Tightrope, LP
Open Your Heart, Madonna
You and Me and the Bottle Makes Three Tonight, Big Bad Voodoo Daddy
Cheek to Cheek, Ella Fitzgerald
In the Mood, The Glenn Miller Band
To Wish Impossible Things, The Cure
Muddy Waters, LP
Cell Block Tango: Chicago the Musical, Kander and Ebb
Only Hope, Mandy Moore

Dedication

To those fighting secret battles, don't let your light go out. This one is for you.

Forever Right Now

a novel

Act One

Coincidence of Opposites (philosophy): a revelation of the oneness of things previously believed to be different.

Prologue

Sawyer

August 15, 10 months ago

I barely heard the doorbell under the pounding music and the laughing conversations of a hundred of my closest friends. Jackson Smith jerked his head at me from across the room, a shit-eating grin on his face. He was dressed as Idris Elba's Roland the Gunslinger, to my Man in Black. Across the crowd of costumed guests—each dressed as a villain from movies or comics—he mouthed the words, *Your turn.*

I widened my eyes and inclined my head at the beautiful redhead in the Poison Ivy costume beside me. She was a second year at Hastings, asking me for advice about which professors were the hardest in Year Three, my year, but I don't think she was listening. Her gaze kept drifting down to my mouth.

Jackson shook his head and made eyes at the pretty Nurse Ratchet beside him, then held up his hands in an exaggerated shrug.

I sighed at my best friend, and scratched my eye with my middle finger.

"I gotta get that," I told Poison Ivy. I think she said her name was Carly or Marly. Not that it mattered. Her name wasn't what I wanted from her. I flashed her what my friends called my trademark panty-dropping smile. "Save my spot?"

Carly-or-Marly nodded and tilted her own approving smile back.

"Not going anywhere."

"Good," I said, and the way our eyes met and held was like a pact being sealed.

I'm going to get laid tonight.

I shot Jackson a triumphant smile, which he answered with a two-finger-gun salute. I laughed and wound my way through our place.

Jackson, myself and two other guys lived in a rented Victorian in the Upper Haight neighborhood. There were no frats at UC Hastings College of the Law, so our three-story house had become the next best thing. Our parties were infamous, and I was happy to see this one was no exception. Guests swayed to "Sex and Candy" playing on Jackson's state-of-the-art sound system. They smiled at me, thumped me on the back, or leaned in to shout drunkenly above the music that this Evil-Doer party was "The Best Party Ever." I just smiled back and nodded.

Every party of ours was "The Best Party Ever."

I opened the door; a charming smile and an excuse on my lips should it be one of my neighbors complaining about the noise. My smile dropped off my face like a mask and I stared.

A young woman with dark hair tied in a messy ponytail, strands falling loose to frame her narrow face, stared back at me. Her eyes were shadowed and bloodshot. She wore faded jeans, a stained shirt, and she struggled under the weight of an enormous bag on her shoulder. Old alcohol oozed out of her pores—the stench of someone who'd got plastered the night before.

The vision before me warred with a hazy memory of this same girl, wild and laughing next to me at a bar; tossing down drinks like they were water; kissing me in a cab. The taste of vodka and cranberry came to my lips, and then her name.

"Molly...Abbott?"

"Hi, Sawyer," she said, and shifted a baby in her arms.

A baby.

My stomach tightened and my balls tried to crawl back into my guts. The hazy memory became stark and vibrant, with brutal clarity.

A little more than a year ago. A summer trip to Vegas. A kiss in the cab had led to a drunken night of lustful tumbling on Molly's bed in her tiny apartment and a half-heard assurance that she was on the pill. And then I was inside her without a fucking care in the world.

The words fell out of my mouth. "Oh shit."

2

Molly barked a nervous laugh and shifted the huge, overstuffed nylon bag on her other arm. "Yeah, well, here we are," she said, and stood on tiptoe to peek over my shoulder. "Having a party? Looks epic. Sorry to just show up like this but…"

I stepped into the hallway and closed the door behind me. The music and laughter cut in half, became distant. My eyes darted to the baby bundled in a faded blanket with yellow teddy bears on it, stained and grimy. My heart panged against my chest like a heavy drum.

"What… What are you doing here?"

"I was in the city," Molly said, swallowing hard, her eyes not meeting mine. "I wanted to introduce you."

"Introduce me…"

Molly swallowed again and looked up at me as if it took effort. "Can I come in? Can we…talk? Just for a minute. I don't want to ruin your party."

"Talk."

Shock had turned me stupid. I'd been valedictorian of my class at UCSF, now a straight-A law student at Hastings, reduced to repeating the last thing I heard like a parrot. My glance darting to the baby whose face was bundled out of sight.

Introduce me. Holy fuck.

I blinked, shook my head. "Yeah, uh, sure. Come in."

I took the bag off Molly's shoulder and my own arm dropped at its weight. I hefted it over mine and hustled Molly through the evil-doers, into my bedroom off the kitchen. The room was dim, and I flipped on a light. Molly blinked, glanced around.

"This is a nice room," she said. She had dirt on her jeans and one of her jacket pockets was inside out. Her costume wasn't evil nurse or witch, but homeless girl with a baby.

"The house is great. Huge." She sat on the edge of the bed, hefted the baby in her arms. "You look good too, Sawyer. And you're going to law school, right? You're going to be a lawyer?"

I nodded. "Yeah."

"I read on your Facebook page you're going to work for a federal judge when you graduate. That's a big deal, right? That sounds like a really good job."

"I hope so," I said. "I don't have the job yet. I still have to graduate. Pass the bar exam and then he has to choose me."

I had a mountain of pressure already. My glance darted to the baby again and my throat went dry.

"That sounds good, Sawyer," Molly said. "You seem like you're really doing well."

"I'm doing okay." I heaved a breath. "Molly...?"

"Her name is Olivia," she said, shifting the baby. "That's a good name, right? I wanted one that sounded...smart. Like you."

My stomach was tied in the tightest of knots and my legs were itching to run out the door and not look back... Instead, I sank down on the bed beside Molly, like a magnet, drawn to the bundle in her arms.

"Olivia," I murmured.

"Yes. And she *is* smart. Advanced. She can already hold her head up and everything."

Molly pulled the blanket from the baby's face and my damn breath caught in my throat. I saw a rounded cheek, tiny, pouty little lips, and eyes squeezed shut. Molly's breath was tinged with booze, same as mine from the 'special punch' one of my roommates had made. But Olivia smelled clean, like talcum powder and some unidentifiable sweet smell that was probably reserved for babies.

"She's pretty, right?" Molly said, glancing at me nervously. "She looks just like you."

"Just like me..."

Outside my door, the party was blaring but muted. Young people laughing and drinking and probably hooking up...just as I had thirteen months ago.

"Are you sure she's...?" I couldn't say the word.

Molly's head jerked in a fast nod. "She's yours. One hundred percent." She bit her lip. "Do you want to hold her?"

Fuck no!

My arms fell open and Molly put the baby in them.

I stared down at Olivia, willing her little features to become recognizable. A clue or hereditary whisper that she really was mine. But she looked nothing like Molly or me. She was just a baby.

My baby?

Molly sniffed and I looked up to see her smiling at Olivia and me. "You're a natural," she said softly. "I knew you would be."

I stared down at the baby and swallowed a jagged lump of every emotion known to man.

"H-how old is she?"

"Three months," Molly said. She nudged my arm with her elbow. "Remember that night? Pretty wild, right?"

My head shot up. "You told me you were on the pill."

She flinched and tucked a lock of hair behind her ear. "I was. It didn't work. That happens sometimes."

I stared, incredulous, and then my gaze dropped back down to the baby in my arms. She stirred in her sleep, her little fist brushing her own chin. One half of the impenetrable confines of my heart battened down like a storm was coming, shoring up defenses, building walls because this *can't be happening.* The other half marveled at this baby's tiny movements like they were minor miracles. I felt like laughing, crying, or screaming all at once.

"I almost didn't come here," Molly was saying. "I just wanted you to meet her and so...here we are."

"Are you in the city? Do you have a place...?"

I wondered if Molly needed to move in with me, and the reality of the situation was like a bucket of ice water. I still had another nine months of law school. I had the bar exam to take and pass—the *first* time—if I had any prayer of getting the clerkship with Judge Miller. The clerkship was my ticket to my dream career as a federal prosecutor.

"What the hell, Molly. I can't...I can't have a *baby*," I said, my voice rising. "I'm twenty-three fucking years old."

Molly sniffed. "Oh really?" She crossed her arms over her chest. "You *can* have a baby, Sawyer. If you can fuck, you can have a baby. So that's what we did and that's what we have."

I gritted my teeth and spat each word slowly. "You told me you were on the pill..."

She stared back and I knew it was useless. Saying those words over and over wasn't going to make the baby in my arms magically evaporate. The pill may have failed or Molly may have been lying about taking them, but in the bleary, booze-soaked memories of that night, there had been one second where I told myself to put on a condom like I always did, and that time I didn't.

"Fuck," I whispered, and a terrible sadness gripped me as I stared into Olivia's little face. Sadness for all of the fear and anxiety wrapped up with her in one tight bundle. I took a deep breath. "Okay, what happens now?"

"I don't know," Molly said, her fingers twitching in her lap. "I just…wanted to see you. To see how you were and let you know that she's yours. I've made a lot of mistakes in my life. I'm still making them." She smiled wanly. "But you… You're a good guy, Sawyer. I know you are."

I frowned, shook my head. "I'm not. Jesus, Molly—"

"Can I use your restroom?" she asked. "It was a long drive up."

"Yeah, sure," I said. "Down the hall, first door on your left."

She sucked in a breath and bent to kiss the baby on her forehead, then quickly rose and went out.

I held Olivia and watched as she woke up. Her eyes fluttered open and met mine for the first time. They were blue like Molly's, not brown like mine, but I felt something shift in me. One tiny tear in my fabric, the first of many that would eventually lead to a complete unraveling and remaking of me into someone I'd hardly recognize.

"Hi," I whispered to my daughter.

My daughter. Oh Christ…

Sudden panic tore through the shock and fear. I jerked my head up and glanced frantically around my empty room, to the huge bag on the floor, to the empty space where Molly had been sitting. My breath caught in my chest at my brain's slow realization of what had happened.

I tore off the bed with the baby in my arms, and hurried to the living area where the party was going on full blast. The noise frightened Olivia and her cries spread through the party like a fire hose, dousing everything until the music shut off. All talk and laughter dampened down to nothing. I glanced around the room, searching for Molly and found only slack-jawed stares and snickers. Jackson gaped with a million questions in his eyes. My other roommates stared. Carly-or-Marly's sexy smile had turned into one of bemused pity. I barely registered any of it as my eyes found the front door, left slightly ajar.

Oh my God…

In between Olivia's growing cries, someone snorted a small laugh. "This party is *so* over."

Chapter 1

Darlene

June 15, present day

The music began with a lone piano. A few haunting notes, then a young woman's soft, clear voice.

I began on the floor, barefoot in leggings and a T-shirt. Nothing professional. No choreography. I hadn't meant to come here, but I was passing by on the street. The space happened to be free and I'd rented it for thirty minutes before I could talk myself out of it. I'd paid with shaking hands.

I shut out thoughts; let my body listen to the music. I was rusty; out of practice. My muscles were shy, my limbs hesitant, until the beat dropped—a tinny high-hat and uncomplicated techno beat—and then I let go.

Are you down...?
Are you down...?
Are you down, down, down...?

My back arched into a back bend, then collapsed. I writhed in controlled movements—my body a series of flowing shapes and arches and undulating flesh and sinew, swaying to the rhythm that simmered back to the piano and the singer's voice—haunting and lonely.

Are you down...?

The pulse increased again and I was up, crisscrossing the studio, leaping and dragging, spinning three turns, my head whipping, arms reaching up and then out, grasping at something to hold onto and finding only air.

Are you down…?

Muscles woke up to the dance, aching, complaining at the sudden demands. My breath was heavy in my chest like a stone, sweat streaking between my shoulder blades.

Are you…?

Are you…?

Are you…?

It dripped off my chin as I collapsed to my knees like a beggar.

…down?

I sucked in a breath, the faintest of smiles pulling my lips. "Maybe not."

On the subway back to the dinky studio apartment in Brooklyn I shared with my boyfriend, my pulse wouldn't slow down. Sweat was sticking to my back under my gray old man sweater. I had just danced. For the first time in more than a year. A tiny little step that was a mile wide; it covered so much empty distance.

Today, I stepped into the humid June of New York City. Three years ago, I'd stepped off the bus at Brooklyn Metropolitan Detention Center after a three-month stint for misdemeanor drug possession. A year and a half after that, I OD'd at a New Year's Eve party. Rock bottom.

I hadn't danced in all that time—it felt wrong to allow myself to do something I loved when I'd been polluting my body and mind. But Roy Goodwin—the best parole officer in the world—had helped me take the steps necessary to shorten my parole. I'd have mandatory NA meetings for another year, but otherwise a clean slate. And I was nearly finished getting an esthetician's license and massage therapist certificate.

And today, I danced.

Things were getting better. I was getting my shit together. And

Kyle...I could fix things with Kyle. We were going through a rough patch, that's all. A rough patch that had been going on for two months.

My hopes deflated with a sigh. Just this morning, it took three tries to get him to answer to his name. Lately, his smiles were full of apologies, and he had a detached fade in his eyes. I'd seen it before. There'd be no big drama. No epic fight. Just a disappearing act. Maybe with a note or a text.

Despite the heat, I shivered and walked faster, as if I could outrun my thoughts. I wondered—for the millionth time—if I were trying to hold on to Kyle because I cared about him, or because I couldn't stand the thought of letting another relationship slip through my fingers.

"It's not over. Not yet," I said as my combat boots clomped down our block.

This time I wasn't going to fail. Not again. This time I could do something right. I'd been clean for more than a year, and with Kyle for longer than that. My longest relationship. I wasn't a fuck up. Not anymore. I'd hold on tighter, if that's what it took.

On the third floor of the shabby walk-up, I opened the door on 3C, and stepped inside...and nearly tripped on the duffel bag. Kyle's duffel bag. It was stuffed so full, the zipper looked ready to burst. I shut the door behind me and looked up, squinting, as if I could minimize the pain of what I was seeing.

Kyle was at the small kitchen counter writing a note. He set down the pen when he saw me. Slowly.

A note, not a text.

"Hey, babe," he said, hardly looking at me. "I'm sorry, but I...."

"Don't," I said. "Just don't." I hugged myself at the elbows. "You weren't even going to tell me?"

"I...I didn't want a scene." He sighed and ran a hand through his shaggy blond hair. "I'm sorry, Darlene. I really am. But I can't do this anymore."

"Can't do what?" I shook my head. "No, never mind. I don't want to hear it. Not again."

Again, I'm not enough. Not good enough. Not funny or pretty or something *enough.*

"Didn't hold on tight enough." I murmured.

"Darlene, I do care about you, but..."

"You're sorry, *but.* You care about me, *but.*" I shook my head, tears choking my throat. "Go if you're going to go, but don't say anything else. You're just making it worse."

He sighed and looked at me imploringly. "Come on, Dar. I know I'm not alone in this. You feel it too. There's just…nothing left in the tank, right? The engine's grinding and grinding, and we're hoping something will catch and spark back up again. But we both know it's not going to happen." He sighed and shook his head. "It's not you. It's not me. It's us."

I opened my mouth to speak. To deny. To scream and curse and rage.

I said, "Yeah, I guess."

Kyle sighed again, but this time with relief. He came to me and I hugged him tight; tried to absorb the feeling of his arms around me one more time. I inhaled him, to hold on. Then exhaled, and he slipped away.

He moved to the door and I stepped back toward our tiny kitchen.

Kyle hefted his bag onto his shoulders. "See you around, Dar."

I kept my eyes averted and then squeezed them shut at the sound of the door closing. The click was as loud as a slap.

"See you around," I murmured.

"Are you sure you want to do this?" Zelda asked. The screech of an incoming bus lurching into the depot nearly drowned her words, and a light summer shower sprinkled diamonds in my friend's long, dark hair.

Beckett, her fiancé and my best friend, towered over her. Instinctively, he leaned in slightly, to shield her from the elements. I don't even think he realized he was doing it. A frown pulled his mouth down. Worry made his blue eyes sharp.

"I'm sure," I answered Zelda, hefting my heavy-as-shit backpack higher on my shoulder. A porter came and took my green army duffel to stow it under the bus. "Whether or not I'm *ready* to do this, is another question."

"Are you ready to do this?" Beckett asked with a small smile.

Zelda nudged him. "Smart ass."

My gaze went between them fondly…and with envy. Zelda and Beckett were living their happily-ever-after, publishing their comic books, and busy being madly in love. Jealousy bit at me for what they had; a kind of love that seemed impossible for someone with my history. But I wasn't leaving the city to find someone, I was leaving someone behind. The old me.

Leaving Zelda and Beckett was scary, but because they were my best friends, I knew they would not fade away to the background of my life as I left New York.

"Holy shit, I'm leaving New York."

"Yes, you are," Zelda said. "Not just leaving the city, but going clear across the country." She pursed her lips and fixed me a look with her large green eyes. "Tell me again what San Francisco has that Brooklyn doesn't?"

The chance to start over where no one knows me as a former drug addict.

"A job, an NA sponsor, and a six-month sublet," I said, mustering a smile. "No fear; if my new city chews me up and spits me out, I'll be back in NYC by Christmas."

"You're going to do great," Beckett said, pulling me into a hug.

I clung tight. "Thank you."

"But call if you need anything. Any time."

I hid my fallen smile against his jacket. I was never the person someone called when they needed help. I was the call-er, never the call-ee.

But I can change that.

Zelda took her turn with a hug that smelled like cinnamon and ink. "Love you, Dar."

"Love you, Zel. And you too, Becks."

"Take care," Beckett said. The rain became more insistent. Beckett shielded Zelda with his jacket.

"Get out of here before I cry," I said, shooing them.

They started away and when they were out of sight, I stepped into the rain and turned my face to the sky.

There was nothing like New York rain. I let it baptize me a final time before I stepped on the bus, praying I would step off in San Francisco, clean and new.

Turns out, there's nothing cleansing about a three-day bus ride.

Three thousand miles of road later—most of which was spent with a little old lady snoring on my shoulder—I stepped off the Greyhound into sharp, early morning San Francisco sunlight. It was more gold and metallic than New York's hazy yellow, and I stretched in it, welcoming it. I let it infuse me, imagining it was a beam of golden light that was going to fill me with mental fortitude and the willpower to be a better version of myself. The sun's warmth didn't magically turn me into one of Zelda's comic book superheroes, but it felt good anyway.

After the porter emptied the underbelly of the bus, I found my huge army duffel and slung it over my shoulder to join the weight of my purple backpack. I walked out to the bus plaza and searched for a transit map to show me the way to my new neighborhood. My eyes landed on a young guy leaning against a cement pillar, scanning the crowd. He was Hollywood-handsome; an actor playing a greaser from the 50's with his gelled blond hair and chiseled jaw. He wore a white T-shirt, jeans, and black boots. All he needed was a cigarette tucked behind one ear and a pack rolled up his sleeve. He caught sight of me and pushed himself off the pillar with his shoulder.

"Darlene Montgomery?"

I stopped. "Yeah? Who…? Are you Max Kaufman?"

"That's me," he said, and offered his hand.

"Aren't you a little young to be a sponsor?" I asked, my gaze roaming over his broad, muscled chest, then up his handsome face and piercing blue eyes.

He's way too hot to be my sponsor. Lord, have mercy.

"The powers-that-be seemed to feel I have experience enough to be of some help," Max said. "I started down the path of turpitude early."

I grinned. "Advanced for your age?"

Max grinned back. "First in my class at juvie."

I laughed, then heaved a sigh. "Dammit, you're adorable."

"Say again?"

I planted one hand on my hip and wagged a finger at him with the other. "Let me just tell you straight off the bat that I have sworn off men for a year. So no matter what, nothing is going to happen between us, got it? If I call you up crying and desperate some night, you have to stay strong, okay?"

Max gave an incredulous laugh.

"I'm only half kidding," I said. "I'm not presuming you want to jump in the sack with me, but I can guarantee you I will have at least one lonely night, and you're ridiculously good-looking. A bad combination."

Max laughed harder. "I can tell I'm going to love this assignment already. But your chastity is safe, Darlene, I promise. I'm gay."

I narrowed my eyes. "A likely story."

"Scout's honor."

"Fine. That's a good place to start," I said, "but that doesn't mean you're not going to get that phone call, that's all I'm saying."

Max chuckled, shaking his head. "I think I can handle it." He offered me his arm and I hooked mine in it. "Let's see your new digs."

"You're my official San Francisco welcome wagon?"

"Brought to you by Narcotics Anonymous and the Justice Department."

I harrumphed. "Three meetings a week is excessive, isn't it? I've been clean for a year and a half."

"Not up to me," Max said. He glanced down at me. "You know you can't skip any, right?"

"I won't," I said. "And while I might have a lonely night or *ten*, that doesn't mean I'm going back to using. I won't. Not ever."

Max smiled thinly. "Good to know."

"I know, I know," I said. "You've heard it all before."

"Yep, but it's a good place to start."

We stepped out into San Francisco and I turned my gaze all around, taking in my new city. The street sign on the corner read Folsom and Beale. The letters were black on white, instead of New York's white on green.

"Brand new," I murmured.

"What's that?" Max asked.

"Nothing."

From the bus depot, Max led me underground and we took a Muni train—San Francisco's public transit system—deeper into the city. Compared to New York's subway system; the red, green, and yellow snakes on the transit map looked simple.

"This doesn't look too bad."

"The city is only about seven by seven miles," Max said, holding on to the overhead bar, as the Muni train screeched underground to my sublet in a neighborhood called the Duboce Triangle. "Big enough to feel like a real city, not so big as to get lost in."

"That's good," I said. "I didn't come here to get lost."

"On the contrary," Max said. "You came here to find yourself."

"Ooh, that's deep."

He shrugged one shoulder. "It's the truth, isn't it?"

I nudged his arm. "Are you on the clock already?"

"Twenty-four, seven. I'm here for you whenever you need me. I know how hard it is to start over." Max scratched his chin. "Or even just to keep going, come to think of it."

I smiled as warmth spread through my chest. "Did you have someone like you as a sponsor when you were recovering? I hope you did."

Max's clear blue eyes clouded up a bit, and his smile tightened. "Yes and no." The train screeched to a stop. We were above ground again and the day was brilliant. "This is you."

We exited the train, and Max tossed my army duffel over one shoulder as if it were nothing, while my overstuffed backpack felt like it weighed a thousand pounds.

"I hope it's not a far walk," I said.

"What's the address again?"

I told him and he led me west along Duboce Street.

"This is a nice neighborhood," Max said. "You found a place here?"

"My friend said it was the last rent-controlled Victorian in all of San Francisco."

"Your friend is probably right," Max said. "In most parts of the city, the words 'rent-control' bring about fits of disbelieving laughter." He grinned. "And then crying."

"Then I won't tell you what my rent is."

"Bless you."

"So when you're not spending every waking hour being my sponsor, what do you do?" I asked.

"I'm an ER nurse at UCSF."

"Really? You weren't kidding. You are an around-the-clock lifesaver."

He shrugged nonchalantly, but his smile told me he liked hearing that. "And what about you? Do you have a job lined up?"

"Indeed," I said. "Massage therapist by day…"

"Yes?" Max said into my silence. "Usually there's another half of the sentence."

"I used to dance," I said slowly. "In my old life, if you know what I mean."

"I do," he said. "Old life, drug life, new life. The life cycle of recovery. So did dance survive the drug life to re-emerge in the new life?"

"That remains to be seen," I said with a small smile. "But I have hope."

Max nodded. "Sometimes that's all you need."

We walked along a row of Victorian houses, each tucked between another, in a variety of colors. I glanced down at the address on my hand, then up to a cream-colored three-story wedged between a smaller, beige house, and one the color of old brick.

"That's the one," I said, pointing to the cream-colored.

"You're kidding." Max stared. "You're going to live *there*? By yourself?"

"The studio on the third floor," I said, hefting my backpack. "It's really pretty, isn't it?"

"*Really pretty*?" Max gaped. "That house is *rent-controlled*?"

"There's that word again. Are you going to laugh or cry?"

"Cry." He whistled through his teeth. "What you have here is a unicorn eating four-leaf clovers while shitting rainbow turds in the shape of winning lottery numbers."

I laughed. "Well, it's only for six months, and then I have to give it back and find a new place."

"That'll suck," Max said. "After this Shangri-La, you're going to be shell-shocked at how the rest of us plebes make it in SF."

"That's easy, I'll just shack up with you."

He laughed. "Maybe. But I could be outta here in a few months. Maybe sooner."

I sagged. "What? Noooo. Don't say that. I like you too much already."

"Nothing set in stone, but I have a potential job transfer to

Seattle in the works." Max smiled down at me with warmth in his clear blue eyes. "I like you a lot, too. I don't think I've ever made a friend faster."

"I don't like to waste time," I said with a grin. "Want to come check out my unicorn?"

"So I can be more jealous? Some other time. In fact..." He pulled his phone from the back pocket of his jeans and checked the time. "Oh shit, I gotta run. My shift starts in twenty," he said. "But I'll take your bag up."

"Nope, I got it." I took it off his shoulder and dumped it on the sidewalk.

"You sure?"

"I carry my own weight, bub."

"Okay, then." Max offered his hand. "Good to meet you, Darlene."

I scoffed at his hand and gave him a hug. His arms went around me and I felt his broad chest reverberate with a chuckle.

"Mmmm, you smell like bus."

"Eau de Greyhound."

He pulled away, still grinning. "I'll see you Friday night. At the Y on Buchanan Street. Room 14. Nine o'clock, sharp."

I pursed my lips. "Friday night? Ugh."

"Disappointed?" He held his hands out and started walking backwards to the bus stop. "Cry it out in your rent-controlled penthouse."

I laughed and hefted my army bag with a grunt, and stepped up to the house. The Victorian really was beautiful, and perfectly maintained. My key turned in the lock and I stepped inside a tiny entry.

I was no architect, but I could tell the house had once been a *house* and was now cut up into separate flats. I peeked around a wall that no sane homeowner would put in the entry, to see a tiny laundry room with one coin-op washer and dryer. On the other side of the hallway was a door with #1 on it. A potted plant and welcome mat with bright colors adorned the threshold. Faintly, I could hear what sounded like Spanish music and the sound of children's laughter.

I dragged my army duffel up the one flight of stairs to an awkward landing—also a new construction to give the second floor some separation. The door on this floor was marked #2 and had no welcome mat or plant or décor of any kind. Silence on the other side.

I continued up one more flight. The ceiling was lower and angled, and door #3 opened on a tiny studio. Bed, table, chair, kitchen and postage-stamp bathroom. My friend in NYC who had arranged this sublet for me said the owner—a gal named Rachel who worked for Greenpeace—had cleaned the place out of everything but sheets, towels, pots and pans. It could not have been more perfect; I didn't need much.

A slow smile spread over my lips, and I shut the door behind me. I headed to the window where I had to duck my head a little at the sloped ceiling. The view stole my breath. Rows of Victorians lined up on the hill, and over their roofs, the city spread out before me. It was a different kind of city than New York. A quieter city; with colorful old buildings, hills, a green rectangle of a park, all cradled in the blue of a bay.

I sucked in a breath and blew it out my cheeks.

"I can do this."

But after a three-day bus ride, I was too tired and overwhelmed to think about conquering a new city just then. I turned to my borrowed bed and collapsed face down.

Sleep reached for me at once, and music drifted into my scattered thoughts.

I danced.

Are you down...?

Are you d-d-d-down...?

I smiled against my borrowed pillow. It smelled like laundry soap and the person who actually lived here. A stranger.

Soon it would smell like me.

Are you down, down, down...?

"Not yet," I murmured, and slipped into sleep.

Chapter 2

Sawyer

Study Room #2 at UC Hastings College of the Law was silent but for the turning of pages and keyboards clacking. Students sat together in stuffed chairs, barricaded behind laptops and headphones.

My study partners, Beth, Andrew and Sanaa were on couches and chairs in our circle, bent over their work, nary a joke or smartass remark among them. I missed Jackson, but the bastard had the nerve to graduate one quarter ahead of me.

The relentless overhead fluorescents seared my tired eyes and made the text on the page in front of me blur. I blinked, focused, and took a mental snapshot of a paragraph of California Family Law Code. With the image firmly in mind, I put pen to a page in my notebook and wrote what I saw in my own words. To lock them down.

When I finished my notes, I leaned back in my chair and let my eyes fall shut.

"Hey, Haas," Andrew said, a millisecond later. I could hear the smug smile color his words. "You going to sleep through the rest of the hour?"

"If you'd shut up, I might," I said without opening my eyes.

He *hmphed* and sniffed but didn't rejoin. Jackson would have given me a smart-ass remark back and we'd be off to races to see who could out-insult the other. Andrew was no Jackson.

"This Family Law exam is going to kill me," Andrew groused.

"Someone quiz me."

"Section 7602?" Beth asked.

"Uh...shit." I heard Andrew tap his pen on the table. "It's right there..."

I smiled to myself. My focus was Criminal Justice, but since a certain Evil-Doer party ten months ago, Family Law had become my unofficial minor.

I mentally scrolled through my Family Law code photo album to section 7602, and recited, "*The parent and child relationship extends equally to every child and to every parent, regardless of the marital status of the parents.*"

Silence. I peeked one eye open. "Sorry. It's one of my favorites."

"I'll bet." Andrew snorted and took up his laptop. "Okay, let's see what else you got, Haas."

The others leaned forward with interest. It was a novelty, what I could do. Very little escaped the mental darkroom in my mind; names and faces, years-old memories down to the smallest detail; even whole pages of text—word for word—if I read them enough times. I don't know how I ended up with a photographic memory, but thank God I did, or I'd never have made it through these last ten months. Not on three or four hours of sleep every night.

"What other section is applicable to Section 7603?" Andrew asked smugly. He was kind of an asshole. I think he thought he'd feel better about the incredible stress of law school if he stumped me. I never tried to make him feel better.

"Section 3140," I said. I was kind of an asshole too.

"In 7604, a court may order *pendente lite* relief consisting of a custody or visitation if...?"

"A parent and child relationship exists pursuant to Section 7540 and the custody or visitation order would be in the best interest of the child."

"Why do you even bother coming here?" Andrew groused and shut his Mac.

"To give you the answers," I said.

The women snickered while Andrew shook his head and muttered under his breath, "Arrogant prick."

"You're wasting your time, anyway," Sanaa said to him. "Sawyer's memory is infallible." She shot me with a knowing smile.

"I'm sure he could go for days."

I didn't miss the double meaning behind her words, and the invitation behind her eyes. My body went warm all over, begging me to reconsider my rule. Sanaa was beautiful and smart; a new addition to our group when Jackson and another friend graduated last quarter. But I could've told her the same thing she told Andrew. She was wasting her time. My days of hooking up with random women were over with a capital O.

Beth didn't miss Sanaa's approving smile at me. She rolled her eyes at all of us. "We should name this group Dysfunction Junction." She checked her watch. "Come on. It's time to go."

We gathered our shit, stuffing notebooks and laptops back into bags, and chucking our empty coffee cups. I shuffled out of the room after my study group. Beth was right. Even in my mind, these people weren't my friends. I didn't have too many of those anymore, but I looked at Beth with her severe hair and Andrew with his shirt buttoned up to his ears and tried to imagine them at one of our epic Evil-Doer parties. I tried to imagine *me* at another Evil-Doer party and couldn't do it.

"Something smell bad, Haas?" Andrew asked.

"Nah," I said, blinking as we stepped into the sharp June sunlight. "Just remembering some ancient history."

"You probably have the Classics memorized too. Got some *Odyssey* up in that steel trap of yours?"

I met his gaze steadily.

"Speak, Memory—
Of the cunning hero,
*The wanderer, blown off course time and again...*Sounds like you, Andy."

"Shut up. And don't call me Andy."

Sanaa hid a smile in her coat collar. "See you all Monday," she said to the others, then moved to stand beside me. "You're so mean to poor Andrew."

I shrugged. "I've never met a guy with zero interest in hiding his short-comings."

"He's just jealous. He struggles to get this stuff down and it's all so easy for you."

I could've laughed at that if I wasn't so damn tired.

"So." Sanaa tossed a lock of silky black hair over her shoulder.

"Any weekend plans? I have an extra ticket to The Revivalists at the Warfield tomorrow night."

A couple of mild excuses came to me, but I was too tired to bullshit too. "I'm out of commission. No social engagements for me until graduation and the bar exam."

"That doesn't sound healthy."

I shrugged and tried a smile. "Thanks for the offer, though."

"Okay," she said, with her own smile that barely contained her disappointment. "See you Monday, then."

"Yep."

I watched her walk away and the weariness hit me.

It did that sometimes, like being punched in the gut. The late nights and sleeplessness, stress and anxiety; it all bowled right into me. No beers with the guys. No dates with hot study partners. No sex, no parties...

"Suck it up, Haas," I muttered into the wind as I began to walk. "This is what you signed up for."

At the Civic Center Muni station, I got onto the J line for Duboce Triangle, and slumped against my seat. The train wasn't crowded with rush hour commuters yet. Friday was my one early day; no late classes. I was usually home by four, instead of five or six.

The rumble of the train beneath me lulled my tired eyes closed. The Family Law code seemed projected onto the back of my eyelids—an unpleasant side effect of eidetic memory. The more I committed something to memory, the greater the chance it would stick with me forever.

...when one parent has left the child in the care and custody of another person for a period of one year without any provision for the child's support, or without communication, that parent is presumed to have abandoned the child...

Those words I would never forget, and the gentle gyrations of the train took me back to last August. Ancient history. I wasn't tired, then. Not yet.

The drab building with the Department of Family and Child Services sign loomed across the street. The sky was overcast; a chilly wind swept over me as I held the bundle in my arms more tightly. It didn't feel like summer, but like a cold winter was about to set in.

"Tell me again what happens when I turn her in?" I asked.

Jackson gave me a wary, side-eyed glance. "They'll try to track Molly down."

"I tried that and got nowhere."

"Then the baby goes into foster care."

"Foster care." I glanced down at the sleeping face tucked in the blankets. My arms were getting tired. Olivia was small, but holding her on the Muni, then the three-block walk was rougher on me than any workout at the Hastings gym. I would have taken an Uber but I didn't have a car seat.

I had nothing.

"It's the best thing," Jackson said for the hundredth time since the party, six days ago.

"Yeah," I murmured. "The best thing."

He gave me a dimmer, sympathetic version of his mega-watt smile. "C'mon. The light's green."

He nudged my arm to walk but I didn't move. My feet were rooted to the corner.

I cast my gaze over the busy city streets. The wind whistled through the cement buildings that rose up all around us, cold and flat and gray. I tried to imagine walking into the CPS building and handing the baby over to some stranger. It would be so easy. She felt so heavy with the weight of the years that lay ahead, and all I had to do was set her down and walk away.

But already Olivia felt melded to my arms; to myself.

"I can't."

My friend's smile stiffened then crumbled away. "Christ, Sawyer."

"Molly entrusted her to me, Jax. Olivia's mine."

He stood, gaping at me. Then he shook his head, and turned in a circle on the street corner, arms out. "I knew it! Give me a prize, folks, I fucking knew it."

He stopped and faced me.

"I knew six nights ago. After the party. Everyone was gone and you were sitting on the couch, sitting in a mess of beer cans and Solo cups, feeding her a bottle like there was no one else in the world. So is that what you're going to do? Raise her? You're going to raise a baby, Sawyer?"

"I don't know what I'm doing, Jackson," I said. "But this feels wrong. Being here feels fucking wrong."

Jackson pressed his lips together. "So you keep her? How? With what money?"

"My scholarship fund is—"

"Just enough so you can go to school and pay rent," Jackson finished. "It's not enough to pay for childcare. And that shit is expensive."

"I'll figure it out. I'll get a job."

"You're going to upheave your life. For what?"

"For what? For her," I snapped, inclining my head at the baby.

"She's not—"

"Shut up, Jax," I said harshly. "Molly abandoned her, and in one year from now, the law will say she did too. I looked it up. I can put my name on her birth certificate. Molly should have done it, but a year from now, it won't matter."

Jackson stared at me for a long moment.

"You have to graduate, Sawyer, and you have to pass the bar— the first time—or your clerkship with Judge Miller? You can kiss it goodbye. You'll lose that job and everything you've worked for."

I clenched my jaw. He was right about that too. I'd laid out the stepping-stones of my life so clearly and concretely. Graduate Hastings, pass the bar, earn a clerkship with Judge Miller, then begin my own career in criminal prosecution, maybe a run for district attorney. Who knew where I could go from there? I glanced down at Olivia and realized I wanted those things just as badly as ever.

But I wanted her too.

More than that, my goals would mean exactly shit if I achieved them with the mystery of her life trailing me wherever I went.

Jackson read it all in my eyes. He ran a hand over his close-cropped hair. "Sawyer, I love you, man, and I get that you think you're doing what's best. But as hard as you think it might be? It's going to be a million times harder than that."

"I know."

"No, I don't think you do. My mother had to work three jobs, one for each of me and my two brothers. Three jobs just to keep food on the table for us, and a roof over our heads, and never mind doing something like law school."

"But she did it, and now her youngest son is finishing law

school," I said. "She's proud of you. I'd like to think my mom would be proud of me too."

"She would be, man," he said quietly. "I know she would be."

I clenched my teeth against the old pain, locked it down deep. A drunk driver had killed my mother when I was eight years old. If I tallied all of the things I thought she might be proud of me for, my full-boat scholarship to Hastings was pretty much it.

Jackson sighed, shook his head. "I don't know."

"Olivia's mine," I said. "That's what I know. I have a responsibility to take care of her."

Jackson's stiffened expression softened, and the faintest smile tugged the corners of his mouth. "I must be living in bizarro world."

"I'm right there with you," I said. I felt a tightness around my heart unclench, and a swamp of unfamiliar, strong emotion nearly drowned me.

My daughter.

"So you going to help or what?" I said, gruffly. "Someone once told me this single-parenting shit is hard."

"There's that exceptional memory of yours again." Jackson grinned, then his face fell. "You'll have to move out, you know that, right? The other guys aren't going to do any Three Men and a Baby. Kevin's already panicked that we're losing street cred."

"I'll find a new place."

Jackson stared at me a few moments more, then blew air out his cheeks and laughed. He lifted the baby bag off my shoulder and slung it over his. "Christ, this is heavy. You are one crazy bastard."

I eased a sigh of relief. "Thanks, Jax."

"Yeah, yeah, just don't call me at two in the morning asking me about whooping cough or... what are they called? Fontanels?"

I laughed but a gust of cold, SF wind tore it away.

I hefted the baby in my aching arms, held her tighter to me. "Come on," I told her. "Let's go home."

I woke with a start when my chin touched my chest, and blinked blearily. The Muni was screeching to a stop at Duboce. I shouldered my bag and got off, and walked the block and a half to the cream-colored Victorian in which I rented the second-story flat.

I passed the first floor door where Elena Melendez lived, and shot it a small smile, then dragged my tired ass up to the second. In my place, I took off my jacket, hung it on the stand and tossed my bag under it. I veered left, straight to the kitchen to put on a pot of coffee, then to the living area, to my desk by the window. The clock read 4:42 pm. Technically, I still had eighteen minutes to myself.

I slumped in the chair and closed my eyes... then opened them again.

I didn't want those minutes, I wanted my girl.

I headed downstairs, taking them two at a time and knocked on #1. Hector, Elena's five-year old, opened the door.

"Hey, Hector," I said. "Can you tell your mom I'm here?"

He nodded his dark-haired head and retreated. I heard from inside, "Sawyer? Come on in, querido. She's ready."

I stepped inside Elena's flat that smelled like warmth, spices, and laundry soap. It was a tad cluttered, but not messy. Homey. A family lived here. Elena—a plump, forty-five year old woman with thick dark hair in a braid down her back and large, soft eyes—was bending to pick Olivia out of the playpen.

I smiled like a dope when Olivia's little face lit up to see me. Her blue eyes were bright and clear, and her wispy dark curls framed her cheeks that were rounded with thirteen-month old baby chub.

She reached for me. "Daddy!"

Not Dada or Dah-yee, but Daddy. All syllables. My stupid heart clenched.

Elena handed her over with a soft smile, and Olivia wrapped her little arms around my neck.

"She had a good day. Ate all of her peas."

"You did? Were you a good girl?" I kissed Olivia's cheek and then fished in my pocket and pulled out my wallet. Olivia made a grab for it, and I gave it to her after I pulled out a check. "Thank you, Elena."

"Always my pleasure, Sawyer," she said, pocketing this week's pay. She reached out and gave Olivia's little wrist a tug. "See you Monday, little love."

I took my wallet out of Olivia's hands—and mouth—and shouldered the diaper bag. "Say bye-bye."

"Bye-bye," Olivia said.

Elena clasped her hands over her heart. "Already so smart, this one. Like her daddy."

I smiled. "Come on, Livvie," I said. "Let's go home."

Chapter 3

Darlene

The alarm went off at the ungodly hour of 5:30 a.m. I dragged my ass out of bed, started the coffee pot in my little kitchen, then swayed with my eyes closed under the shower spray in my tiny bathroom. I had never been much of an early-riser, but a friend of a friend in NYC had pulled a gazillion strings to get me a job at a posh spa in the Financial District. The pay was worth getting up for, but *God.*

"Is this what being responsible feels like?" I muttered as I dropped the shampoo bottle for the second time.

After showering, I sipped coffee in the kitchen, wrapped in my towel with another turban'ed around my hair, marveling that the sky outside my window was still dark.

Being responsible, I decided, sucked ass.

But after the initial sluggishness passed, I felt more awake than I had in a long time. Ready. The day was dawning on my new life, I decided, and I didn't even care if that sounded cheesy. It felt good.

I dressed in beige skirt, men's button-down shirt, thigh-high maroon socks, and my black combat boots. In the bathroom mirror, I put on the usual dark shadow and heavy liner around my blue eyes, gold hoops in my ears, and tied my long brown hair in a ponytail. I still looked like my New York self.

I couldn't decide if that was good or bad.

Outside, I pulled on my favorite old man sweater and shouldered my purple backpack. The sun was finally climbing out of the sky, and the sheer early-ness of the day was palpable. The street was quiet. Asleep.

An app on my phone told me I needed the J train to take me to the Embarcadero Muni station. Twenty minutes later, I emerged in a neighborhood of condos, modern loft space, and shops with a view of the Bay. My map said the Wharf, and all the fun touristy stuff was just around the corner so to speak, another ten minutes by train. This neighborhood felt quiet, and I wondered if I'd have enough clients to keep me afloat, or if I'd need a second job.

If you get a second job, you won't have time to start dancing again.

I couldn't decide if that was good or bad, either.

Turns out, I needn't have worried. Serenity Spa was a pretty, sleek storefront that screamed *expensive*, and was bustling with clients inside, even at 6:45 a.m.

My supervisor, Whitney Sellers, looked to be in her mid-thirties, with strawberry blonde hair and hard blue eyes. She eyed me up and down with a furrowed brow.

"*Darlene*, right?" she asked, as if my name didn't taste right in her mouth.

I nodded. "Yes, hi. Nice to meet you."

She reached a hand for me to shake, hard and short.

"I wouldn't get attached to this place," she said. "Turnover is high. I'm up to my neck in hires and fires every week. You start in ten minutes and you need a uniform." She appraised my outfit. "Badly."

She gave me a pair of white yoga pants and a soft, white button-down shirt with short sleeves. I changed in the employee bathroom and checked myself out in the mirror

"I look like a nurse," I told Whitney when I came out for her inspection.

"That's the idea," Whitney said. "You work in healthcare now, massaging for the therapeutic well-being of our clients." She arched a brow. It seemed eyebrows did most of the talking around here. "Well? Go. Your first client is waiting."

It took me all of three minutes to determine that the serenity of Serenity Spa was reserved for the clients. For a place that catered to luxury and relaxation, every employee there looked like they were stressed to the max.

"Do you like working here?" I asked one of my coworkers in the break room after my first appointment was done. The gal gave me a strange look.

"You must be new." She sighed and rubbed her shoulder. "It's like kneading dough all day, but what other job can you say you can make this much per hour?"

Selling X at a rave, I thought but did not say.

Serenity Spa was the elegant business of my new life, and I vowed to never go back to the old. I was going to keep myself as clean and pristine as my new uniform. But by the time my shift was over, my arms felt like they weighed a hundred pounds each, and my shoulders and forearms were screaming.

"I just have to get used to it," I muttered to myself on the street. It was like a new dance routine. At first, your body was sore as the same muscles were worked over and over again, but I'd adjust. No, more than adjust. I'd conquer.

The clang of a cable car sounded, and I watched a sailboat glide across the Bay. A smile spread over my lips. "I did good today."

And then my gaze landed on a post on the corner beside me, covered in bills and flyers; someone offering guitar lessons, a lost cat sign…and flyers for an independent, modern dance troupe that was having a showcase at a theatre in the Mission District in a few weeks. They were holding auditions. One spot. A female dancer for the ensemble.

I bit my lip. The cable car was rounding the corner, going the opposite direction from where I needed to be. If I jumped on, I might get lost, but I was feeling brave that day.

The car made its stop and I went for it. As I did, my hand snaked out to grab a phone number tag from the bottom of the dance flyer. I stuffed the scrap of paper in my pocket, and jumped on the car to who-knew-where.

After a late afternoon doing touristy stuff at Pier 39 along the Wharf—and eating chocolate from Ghirardelli Square to celebrate me in my new city—I navigated the buses and trains to get back home.

Duboce Street was bathed in twilight copper, and the beautiful houses, fronted with trees and flowers, looked idyllic. Like a postcard for San Francisco. I grinned and pulled out my phone and took a photo of the cream-colored Victorian.

I live here! I typed in a message to Carla, my sister, and attached the photo.

No response.

I told myself she was busy with family stuff, or having dinner. It was seven o'clock in New York, after all.

On the first floor in the Victorian I heard voices. The door to #1 was open, and a middle-aged Hispanic woman stood in it, talking to a young man. The guy looked to be about my age. He cradled a toddler on his hip with one hand, held a briefcase in the other, and wore a diaper bag slung over his shoulder. He had short, dark blond hair with soft, loose curls, sharp brown eyes fringed with long lashes, a square jaw, and a broad mouth that was currently turned down in a stiff frown...

I could have kept mentally appraising his attributes for days, but in the space of a second, my brain had tallied up the sum of his parts and came to the very definitive conclusion that he was fucking gorgeous.

Seriously? Do not *tell me Mr. Mom is my neighbor.*

He and the Hispanic woman both stopped talking when they saw me. The woman's face broke out into a warm, welcoming smile. The guy stared at me with a mixture of alarm and disdain.

"Who are you?" he demanded rudely, shifting the diaper bag higher on his shoulder while hoisting his little girl in his other arm. Six feet of hotness in a rumpled suit, glaring at me with suspicion in his dark eyes.

The woman swatted his arm lightly. "Sawyer, be a good boy."

"I...I'm your new neighbor?" I said. It sounded more like a question; as if I needed this guy's permission to *live*. I straightened to my full height. "I'm Darlene. I just moved in upstairs. I'm a dancer. Well, I was. Had to take some time off but I'm going to get back into it soon...ish." I put on my friendliest smile. "I'm a massage therapist now. Just got my license and..."

My words died under Sawyer's withering stare.

"A dancer. Fantastic," he said bitterly. "Just what I always wanted. Someone leaping and thumping above me, waking my kid up and disturbing my studies at all hours of the night."

I planted my hands on my hips. "I can't dance in a dinky apartment, and besides..."

Words failed me again as the sharp planes and hard angles of Sawyer's face melted when his daughter—I guessed her to be about a year old—clapped her small hand over his chin. Sawyer's gaze softened, and his broad mouth turned up in a smile—a beautiful smile I was sure he saved only for his little girl, and one so full of love that, for a moment, I could hardly breathe.

"It is *very* nice to meet you, Darlene," the woman interjected. "I'm Elena Melendez. This is Sawyer, and his little angel is Olivia. They live upstairs."

"Me too," I said. "Third floor, I mean. Obviously," I added with a weak laugh. "The studio?"

"You're subletting for Rachel, yes?" Elena smiled. "She's such a nice girl."

"And *quiet*," Sawyer added, earning himself another swat from Elena.

"Yes, I'm subletting for six months," I said. "Rachel's doing a Green Peace tour."

Elena beamed. "Welcome to the building."

Sawyer took his little girl's hand off his chin, gave it a kiss, then grunted something unintelligible as he brushed past me to go upstairs. I got a whiff of cologne and baby powder, and the strangest sensation ripped through me. It was as if every sexual and maternal molecule in my body ignited in response to Sawyer's masculinity and the sheer *babyness* of his little girl at the same time.

Oh my God, cool your jets, girl. He's probably married and is definitely kind of an asshole.

Except to his daughter. Over Sawyer's shoulder, Olivia watched me and smiled.

I waved at her.

She waved back.

"He's really a very nice young man," Elena said with a sigh, watching Sawyer round the corner.

"I'll take your word for it," I said, easing a sigh of relief that Sawyer had taken the strange tension—and his arsenal of potent pheromones—upstairs with him. "His death-glare could cut diamonds. His daughter's a cutie, though. How old?"

"Thirteen months," Elena said. "I've been babysitting her since she was an infant, and I love every minute. I'd do it for free but Sawyer insists on paying the 'going rate.'" She leaned in conspiratorially and whispered, "I tell him *my* going rate because it's much less. My pleasure to help him. He works so hard. Every day, all night."

"What does he do?"

"He's studying to be a lawyer," she said proudly. "Very close to being done too."

I scuffed my combat boot on the thinly carpeted floor. "What...um, what does Olivia's mom do?"

Tell me he's happily married. Have mercy.

"She is not in the picture," Elena said quietly.

"Oh? That's...too bad."

"Sawyer has never mentioned her and I don't ask. I figure if he wants to tell, he'll tell but he's sealed up tight. Like a drum. He has a heart of gold, that one, but so serious. All the time, so much stress. I worry about him." She smiled warmly. "I tell him his handsome face was meant for smiling, but he saves those for Livvie."

"I noticed."

Elena gave my hand a pat. "And what do you do for work, Darlene? Massage therapist, you say?"

"Yes," I said. "I started today."

"A massage therapist. Isn't that something?" Elena's smile widened and her glance darted upward, to the heavens or Sawyer's apartment. "Dios trabaja de maneras misteriosas."

"What's that?"

"A guess. I tell you later."

A little dark-haired girl with large eyes appeared at Elena's hip. She put her hand on the girl's head. "This is Laura. She's two and I have a son, Hector, who is five. My husband works late but you'll meet him someday."

I smiled and waved at the little girl. "You really have your hands full."

"I do," Elena said, "or else I'd invite you in like a proper neighbor and make you dinner. But I have to get these two in the bath."

"That's so sweet of you. Another time, maybe?" I said, and I meant it. Elena was like a prototype for the ideal mother, and a wave of homesick with a side of lonely washed over me. I had a sudden urge to sit on her couch, rest my head on her shoulder, and pour my guts out to her.

You are being extra ridiculous right now. No one needs to know anything. Not here, in your new life.

"Speaking of dinner," I said brightly, "I should get going. I haven't done any shopping since I got here except for the essentials: coffee and tampons. Where's the closest grocery?"

"There's a Safeway and a Whole Foods. Both are a short walk up 14th, then cross over to Market."

"Perfect. Thank you so much, Elena."

"Of course, querida. I'm very happy you're here, and I believe Sawyer will soon come to feel the same."

I blinked and laughed. "I'm pretty sure he'll forget all about me. In New York you can go months without talking to anyone else in your apartment building."

"Ah, but this is not an apartment building, is it? It's a house. A home." Elena's smile was like warm bread. "You'll see."

Chapter 4

Darlene

Back in my place, I changed out of my clothes and put on some yoga pants, and a black, dance camisole. I figured my best bet for keeping ahead of massage-soreness was to stretch out every night.

I sat on the floor in my little living area, between the couch and TV stand, and began a mini-routine, but I didn't get very far. My cupboards were bare and I was hungrier than I realized. I threw on my gray sweater, my boots; shouldered my purple backpack, and headed out.

On the landing in front of #2, I hesitated. Did Sawyer need anything? It couldn't have been easy to get to the store often with a toddler.

My hand rose to knock but I mentally reiterated how I'd sworn off men for an entire year. No need to torture myself in the meanwhile.

Or you could be mature about it and be helpful. Grown-ups do that.

I knocked softly on the door. No answer.

"Welp, can't say I didn't try."

I turned on my heel and hurried down the rest of the stairs.

Outside, the twilight was golden and perfect, and the air felt warmer than I expected. Before I'd left New York, Becks had told me there was a famous saying about my new city—that the coldest winter ever spent was a summer in San Francisco. But it was the middle of

June and no hint of the chill wind I'd been warned about. I added the warm night to my mental tally of all the things that were good about being here. It was a small thing, but if I thought for longer than a second about Becks or Zelda, or my family, the loneliness would seep in. And if it got too bad, I was apt to do something stupid.

I'm done with that shit, I told myself. *I'm brand new.*

I concentrated on the city as I walked. My neighborhood of Victorians quickly gave way to commercial towers and shops along Market Street, which I'd deduced was a major vein in the network of the city. Whole Foods appealed to my will to eat healthy, but Safeway appealed to my scrawny bank account. But as I perused the aisles with a basket on my arm, I decided I was better off finding a bodega. Supermarkets, like everything else in SF, were expensive as hell.

I rounded an aisle and crashed basket-first into my new neighbor, Sawyer.

"It's you," I said softly before I could regain control of my brain that had become momentarily paralyzed at the sight of him.

He'd changed from his suit to jeans, a hooded sweatshirt over a green T-shirt, and a baseball cap. He was pushing Olivia in a stroller, and the carry-space underneath was filled with fresh fruit and vegetables.

Up close, he was even more ridiculously handsome but tired. So, so tired.

"Oh," he said. "Hey."

"I don't think we were *properly* introduced." I stuck out my hand. "Darlene Montgomery. Your new upstairs neighbor who will *not* be—how did you say it? *Prancing and jumping* at all hours of the night?"

"Leaping and thumping," he said, not smiling. He gave my hand a brief shake. "Sawyer Haas."

For a moment, I became lost in the deep brown of his eyes and my words tangled on my tongue. I sought refuge with the toddler between us and knelt in front of the stroller.

"And this is Olivia? Hi, cutie."

The little dark-haired girl watched me with wide, blue eyes, then arched her back and pushed at her tray with a squawk.

"She doesn't like being cooped up for too long," Sawyer said. "I try to get through this quick. On that note..." he added pointedly.

I stood up quickly. "Oh, sure, of course. See you back at the house."

His brows came together and he frowned.

"That sounded weird, right?" I said with a short laugh. "We're virtual strangers but also practically roommates. Isn't it funny how two things can be so opposite and yet completely true at the same time?"

"Yeah. Weird," he said tonelessly. "I have to go. Nice meeting you. Again."

He pushed off, wheeling Olivia away, the sounds of her frustration trailing after. I heaved a sigh and watched him go.

"Nice talking to you."

No, that's good. Let him go. You're working on you.

I perused a few aisles, filling my cart with cottage cheese, lettuce, ravioli and pasta sauce. I was reaching for a packet of coffee filters which happened to share space with the baby food when I heard a child's fussing growing louder one aisle over. Olivia was on the verge of a full-blown meltdown. Below her screeching came Sawyer's low admonitions asking her gently to hold on, they were almost done.

I bit my lip and scanned the colorful rows of brightly-colored baby food packaging. With a *woot* of triumph, I found a box of zwieback toast biscuits, and hurried around the corner.

"Hi, again," I said. "I think maybe she could use a food diversion."

"We're fine, thanks."

Olivia squawked loudly, as if to say, *No, father of mine, I am distinctly not 'fine.'*

I bit back a smile. "Can I help?"

Sawyer took off his baseball cap, ran a hand through his loose, dark blond curls, then put it back on with a tired sigh. "She finished all of her strawberries and I don't want to feed her a bunch of crap baby snacks."

"How about one good one?" I held up the box of biscuits. "Talk about old school. I can't believe they still make these. They're like dog bones for babies."

"*Dog* bones?" Sawyer took the box out of my hands and scanned the ingredients. Or at least I think he did—it took only a second before he handed it back. "Yeah, looks okay but..."

"Great." I opened the box and tore apart the plastic bag inside.

"What are you doing? I haven't paid for those," Sawyer said, then muttered, "Guess I am now..."

"You won't regret it." I offered Olivia an oblong piece of the toast and she reached for it with one chubby little hand. "My mom gave my sister and me these things when we were little," I said. "They take some serious slobbering to turn into mush, and that'll give you time to shop."

Sawyer peered into the stroller, which had gone quiet as Olivia happily worked on the biscuit.

"Oh. Okay. Thanks," Sawyer said slowly. He took the box from me and tried to make room under the stroller amid the avocado, turkey slices, pineapple, peas and squash.

"Are you on a raw food diet?" I asked.

"That's all for her," Sawyer said.

"What about you?"

"What about me?"

"Do you eat food?"

"In theory," he said. "I have a date with aisle twelve, actually, so if you'll excuse me..."

I scanned the aisle markers. I found twelve and wrinkled my nose. "Frozen dinners? That doesn't sound healthy. You prepare all this fresh food for her but none for yourself?"

"I don't have room to carry a whole lot more," he said. "I'll be okay, thanks for your concern..."

"I'll help," I said. "What do you want? I'll carry it for you."

Sawyer sighed. "Listen...Darlene? That's nice of you to offer, and thanks for the crackers, but I'm good. After she goes to bed, I'll throw something in the microwave and hit the books." He stopped, shook his head, perplexed. "Why am I explaining this? I have to go."

He started to walk away and I was tempted to let him. He was kind of a jerk, but that was probably the exhaustion. I tried to imagine what it would be like taking care of an entire little human being all by myself. It was hard enough taking care of one adult me. I decided to set aside Sawyer's gruffness (and his ridiculous attractiveness) and help the guy out. Be neighborly.

"You're being so silly right now," I called after him.

He stopped, turned. "Silly?"

"Yes! I'm right here. Let me help you." I crossed my arms. "How long has it been since you've had a really nice meal for yourself?" He didn't say anything but stared back at me.

"That's what I thought," I said. "Come on. I'll make you

something."

"Now you're going to cook for me? We met eight seconds ago."

"So?"

Sawyer blinked. "So…you don't have to cook for me."

"Of course I don't *have* to. I want to. We're neighbors." I peered at the aisle markers again to get my bearings. "I was going to make tuna casserole. Mostly because it's the only thing I know how to make. How does that sound?" I squatted beside the stroller. "Do you like casserole, sweet pea?"

Olivia smiled at me over her biscuit, and kicked her foot with spastic baby joy. I smiled back and straightened.

"Olivia said she would love some casserole."

Sawyer looked at me with a strange expression on his face. I gave the sleeve of his hoodie a tug.

"Come on. Looks like fish is this way."

Sawyer hesitated. "I'm not going to get out of this, am I?"

I cocked my head, frowning. "Why would you want to?"

He was still frowning, but he pushed the stroller after me. "I'm just not used to people doing things for me. Elena does enough already. I feel like a charity case."

"You're not a charity case," I said. "One dinner isn't going to kill you."

"I know, but I'm juggling a hundred balls in the air and if someone reaches in and grabs one, it's going to throw me off." He covered his mouth with the back of his hand as a jaw-cracking yawn came over him. "Shit, I don't know why I just said that. I don't even know you."

"That's the benefit to talking," I said. "Getting to know someone. A revolutionary concept, I know."

He rolled his eyes and yawned again.

"You really do burn the midnight oil, don't you?" I said. "Elena told me you're studying law."

"Oh yeah?" he said. We'd arrived at the meat section. He picked up a package of rib eye steak, then tossed it back with a sigh. "What else did she tell you?"

I selected some fresh tuna and put it in my basket. "That you have a heart of gold but you're stressed out all the time."

His head came up, alarmed. "What? Why…why did she say that?"

"Maybe she thinks it's true. The second part looks like it, for sure. As for the first?" I shrugged, then gave him a dry smile. "The jury is still out."

"Ha ha," he said dully. He glanced at me, then looked away. "Are you always this blunt?"

"I wish I could say honesty is the best policy, but it's more of a lack-of-filter situation."

"I noticed."

"Says the guy who began our acquaintance with *Who are you?*" I said, with a laugh.

Sawyer stopped and stared at me like I was a puzzle he couldn't figure out. My pulse thumped a little harder while under his sharp, dark-eyed scrutiny. I cleared my throat, and cocked an eyebrow.

"Take a picture, it'll last longer," I said with a nervous laugh.

Sawyer's eyes widened in surprise and he shook his head. "Sorry, I...I'm just really tired."

He moved ahead of me and I watched a pretty young woman check out Sawyer, then Olivia, then Sawyer and Olivia together. I could practically see the hearts in her eyes. Sawyer was oblivious.

"So you're in law school," I said, catching up to him.

"Yeah," he said. "At UC Hastings."

"Oh, is that a good school?" I asked, then froze. "Wait. It just hit me. You're going to be a lawyer?"

"Yeah?"

"Sawyer the Lawyer?"

He groaned. "Please don't call me that."

"Why not? It's cute."

"It's childish and stupid."

"Oh, come on." I scoffed. "Surely you can see how cute it is. Such a funny coincidence."

"Yeah, one I haven't heard a million times," he muttered. "Anyway, I'm going to be an attorney, not a lawyer."

"What's the difference?"

"If you finish law school, you're a lawyer. If you pass the bar and are licensed to practice, you're an attorney. I'm going to be an attorney."

"Sawyer the Attorney doesn't have the same ring to it." I fished my phone out of my backpack. "Wikipedia says the terms are practically interchangeable." I shot him a grin.

He sighed, and a tired chuckle escaped him, one that seemed to surprise him. He gave me another perplexed look.

"I've never met anyone like you," he said. "You're like a..."

"I'm like a, what?"

Our eyes met and held, and despite the perpetual supermarket cold, I felt warm in Sawyer's gaze. His stiff expression loosened, the tension he carried on him eased slightly. He was locked up tight, this guy; but for that handful of heartbeats, I saw him. A thought slipped into the crevices of my mind.

He's lonely.

Then Sawyer blinked, shook his head and looked away. "Nothing," he said. The tension came back—I could feel it like a prickly force field around him—and I was locked out again. "Let's get out of here before your magic baby biscuit wears off."

I smiled and followed after silently, while internally I was dying to know what he'd been about to say.

Maybe nothing good, I thought. That was likely; I didn't know when to stop talking and got all up in people's business.

But that warm feeling in my chest—in the general vicinity of my heart—didn't go away. Sawyer had been about to pay me a compliment, I was sure of it. Nothing boring or bland—he was too smart for that. But something extraordinary, maybe.

A compliment that didn't sound like a compliment but it was, because it was made only for me.

You're the one being silly now, I thought, and walked with him to the checkout. But it seemed that I'd traveled three thousand miles, and the deep longing to have someone see *me* trailed after like a shadow I would never shake.

Chapter 5

Sawyer

We walked home together, Olivia and I…and my new neighbor.

How in the hell did this happen?

Mere hours ago, it had been a typical Friday. While the rest of my friends and fellow law students were out drinking or partying to blow off the stress of Third Year, I was going to make dinner for my daughter, play and read with her before bath time, then put her to bed and study until my eyes gave out.

And now…

Now, Darlene Montgomery was going to cook dinner for me.

Mental alarms and whistles were going off, telling me this was a bad idea. I didn't bring women home anymore, and yet I'd caved so easily. I chalked it up to my fatigue and her energy. Darlene must be a flexible dancer, I thought, because she slipped past all of my usual barricades and defenses, bending and contorting herself through a field of red laser beams like a ninja in a spy movie.

One dinner. That's it.

Twilight had fallen, coppery and warm, as we walked. Darlene talked nonstop about the differences between New York and San Francisco. I thought it would drive me crazy but I liked listening to her. She had a pretty voice, and my conversations these days consisted mostly of cajoling my kid to eat her peas, or listening to law students bitch about finals.

My eyes kept stealing glances at her.

In the grocery store, my photographic memory had taken an entire reel of just her face. She was a collage of striking features—a wide mouth, large eyes, full lips, high cheekbones, dark eyebrows—not one aspect insignificant.

Here, under the yellow of the streetlights, her eyes were deeper blue and full of light. Over her lithe frame, she wore a bulky sweater, but it didn't conceal what she was. She *looked* like a dancer—slender but with lean muscle, and she walked with an easy grace, despite the heavy black combat boots on her feet.

"So what's with the boots?" I asked. It was the most harmless part of what she was wearing.

"Protection."

"From what?"

"Not from. For. For my feet," she said. "I'm a dancer—or will be again soon, and my feet are a precious commodity."

"What kind of dance do you do? Ballet?"

"When I was little," she said. "But I'm into modern dances and capoeira. Have you heard of capoeira?"

"An Afro-Brazilian martial art that combines elements of dance, acrobatics, and music, developed in Brazil at the beginning of the 16th century."

Darlene stopped. "Well, look at you, Encyclopedia Brown. Are you a fan?"

"I read something about it once."

"Once? Do you always remember something you read once so precisely?"

"Yes."

I felt her gaze on me and glanced over to see an expectant look on her face—the kind women wear when the guy has said or done something that obviously requires further explanation.

"I have an eidetic memory," I said.

"A what?"

"Eidetic—photographic memory."

"Get out!" Darlene swatted my arm. "For real?"

I nodded.

"So you can remember long strings of numbers, or... what you were wearing on January 24th, 2005."

I shrugged. "It's pretty strong."

"Well…how strong is it?" Darlene demanded. "On a scale of one to you-should-be-on-*The Ellen DeGeneres Show*?"

"Not sure what Ellen's requirements are. Eight?"

Darlene was staring at me with wide eyes. "Wow. You've got a mega-mind. That must help with law school, yeah?"

"Yeah, it does," I said. "I probably wouldn't be graduating on time otherwise."

"Very cool," Darlene said.

I could feel her gearing up to quiz me like Andrew from my study group and cut her off at the pass.

"Anyway, you're getting back into dancing?" I asked. "Just in time to be my upstairs neighbor? Lucky me."

She grinned but it wilted quickly. "Not sure yet." Her fingers toyed with a tiny scrap of paper from her sweater pocket. "I've nearly thrown this away a hundred times since this afternoon."

"Is that your fortune?"

"It does look like that, doesn't it?" she said. "Who knows? Maybe it is. It's a phone number for a dance troupe, but I'm not sure if I'm going to call it."

"Why not?"

She shoved the paper back into her pocket. "I've only been here a few days. I have a great place, a job. I'm not sure what I'm doing yet. I sort of came here to start over again."

"Why? Are you on the run from the law?"

It was a joke, but Darlene's eyes flared and she looked away.

"No, nothing like that," she said quickly. Her smile looked forced. "I kind of like how no one knows me here. It's like the proverbial blank slate and I can write whatever I want on it."

I nodded, at a loss. The conversation had taken a turn for the personal and that was forbidden territory. I didn't have the time to dive deep into anyone; I was barely keeping my head above water as it was. I was heavy and anchored down, dragging myself through the days until one year was up and Olivia was safely all mine. The exhaustion was like a suit of armor, but Darlene…She seemed weightless—as if she wore combat boots to keep her from floating away. She smiled constantly, laughed easily, and she swept into my life at a grocery store like it were nothing.

She's the exact opposite of me in every way.

A short silence fell, that lasted all of three seconds.

"Anyway, tonight, I'm your chef," Darlene said.

"You don't have to…"

She stopped and planted her hands on her hips. "I've seen *Law and Order*. Are we going to, what's the word? Where you argue over the same thing a second time?"

"Relitigate."

"Yes, that. Are we going to relitigate dinner tonight?"

"I'm just not used to—"

"Overruled, Sawyer the Lawyer," she said. "I'm going to make dinner and you're going to let me or I'm going to tell Elena on you."

"Jesus, you're a pain in the ass, you know that?"

Darlene grinned. "That's just another way of saying *persistent*."

I rolled my eyes and bent to check on Olivia. She was still happily munching on the little biscuit and babbling. She grinned over a mouthful of mush at me. I grinned back.

Holy hell, I love that face.

I straightened to see Darlene watching me, her eyes soft, and I realized I was still smiling like a moron. I reverted back to neutral, took the stroller handle and started pushing.

"You're so sweet with her," Darlene said. "How long has it been just the two of you?"

"Ten months," I said. My jaw stiffened. I never talked about Molly if I could help it. I had an irrational fear that even saying her name would call her back from wherever she was, to try to take Olivia away from me.

My shoulders hunched in anticipation of the next questions; more personal questions that I hated. But Darlene must've gotten the memo since she didn't say anything else about it.

At the Victorian, I carried the stroller with Olivia in it up the three steps while Darlene unlocked the front door. In the foyer, she glanced at the flight of stairs leading up with a frown.

"Do you carry the baby and the stroller up a whole flight of stairs?" she asked.

"No, I take Olivia up, then come back for it." I shot her a dry look. "Hence, the-not-buying-a crap-ton-of-stuff to carry."

"Such a man." Darlene sighed. "I'll help. Stroller or baby?"

I hesitated. The stroller was heavier and bulkier but the alternative was Darlene carried Olivia. I scrubbed my chin.

Darlene gave me a tilted smile. "I won't break her, I promise. Or

I can take the stroller," she added quickly. "Whatever you're comfortable with."

"Oh, *now* you're concerned about what I'm comfortable with?" I asked with laugh. "That's a first."

She grinned and rolled her eyes. "Such a crank. Pick."

"The stroller is heavy," I said slowly. "If you don't mind taking her?"

"Mind? Not in a million years."

She knelt in front of Olivia and moved the tray aside, undid the mini-seatbelt.

"Hey, sweet pea. Can I hold you?" Olivia's little face split open with a smile as Darlene lifted her up and cradled her easily on her hip. "Is that a yummy cracker? I bet it is. Can I have some?"

She pretended to bite at the biscuit and Olivia squealed with laughter.

The alarm bells were screaming now as I folded up the stroller and carried it up the stairs, Darlene following after. At my door, I fumbled for my key, acutely conscious of Darlene's presence behind me, like a low heat against my back. A sliver of something electric slipped down my spine. I hadn't brought a woman back here since I moved in.

Darlene isn't a woman by your usual definition, she's a neighbor. And you didn't bring her back; she somehow finagled her way in.

My body didn't give a damn how she got there, only that she was.

I opened the door and set the stroller against the wall just inside, then shut the door behind us. Us. Three of us.

Don't get soft now. One dinner, strictly neighborly.

"She's precious." Darlene handed Olivia back to me, and then slipped out of her backpack to set it on the kitchen counter. "And this is a nice place. Much bigger than mine. Two bedroom?"

"Yeah."

"I've never seen a baby-proofed bachelor pad." Darlene tilted her chin at the coffee table that had a protective slab of rubber on each corner. "Super cute."

I started to tell her my place was the furthest from a bachelor pad as you could get, but my words died.

Darlene had taken off her ratty old sweater and tied it around her slender waist, then rummaged in my cupboards. She was wearing a black dancer's top with straps that crisscrossed her back. I became mesmerized by her lean muscles that moved under her pale skin, the elegant line of her neck, and the sleek cut of her arms as she reached up on a high shelf for a pan.

I suddenly had the urge to see her dance. To see her move the way the lines of her body hinted she could.

And just like that, ten months of celibacy came crashing into me. The blood rushed to my groin, and *going soft* was suddenly the least of my worries. I coughed to conceal a sudden groan that nearly erupted out of me.

"You okay?" Darlene asked over her shoulder.

"Sure. Fine."

This is a bad idea.

I started to put Olivia in her playpen but she fussed and squirmed out of my arms once she saw where she was headed. I set her on the floor instead, and watched her toddle straight to the kitchen, to Darlene.

"What are you doing down there?" Darlene cooed. "You want to come up here and help?" She scooped Olivia up and set her on her hip again, holding her one-armed. "Now, tell me, where does your daddy keep the baking pans?"

I watched a beautiful woman hold my daughter in my kitchen, talking easily to her, making her laugh. An ache—a thousand times more potent than any sexual frustration—rose up from a deep place in my heart. It felt like hundreds of emotions I'd been keeping locked down were suddenly erupting out all at once: what I wanted for me, for Olivia, what she had lost and what I was working for to keep her. They were all spilling out of me like a bag of marbles, and now I had to scramble to put them all back before I fell on my ass.

"This wasn't a good idea," I said.

Darlene was making a silly face at Olivia. "Hmmm?"

"I can't do this."

"Do what? Eat dinner?"

"Yes," I snapped. "I can't eat dinner. With you. And I can't have you over here all the time, helping me out or playing with Livvie. I can't."

Darlene's expression folded and I hated myself for stealing the light out of her eyes.

"Oh."

She carefully set Olivia down and Olivia immediately squawked to be picked up again.

"Shit," I said, running a hand through my hair. "This is exactly why I didn't want any help. Because one thing leads to the next and before you know it…"

"Before you know it you're eating a decent meal?" Darlene said with a weak smile.

"It's not that." I ground my teeth in frustration.

Darlene waved her hands. "No, you're right. I'm sorry. It's your place. Your privacy. I do this a lot. I get *involved*. I moved here to work on me." She shouldered her backpack and took Olivia by the hand to walk her to me. "I have a lot of work left to do."

"Darlene…"

She bent down to Olivia. "Bye-bye, sweet pea." She raised her head and flashed me the tattered remains of her brilliant smile. "Have a nice night."

The sound of the door shutting made me flinch. The room suddenly seemed a little dimmer. Quieter.

Olivia was tugging on my jeans. "Up," she said "Up, Daddy."

I picked her up and held her. She smiled at me and I bottled up my spilled emotions but for one. My love for her. She was the only thing that mattered.

"Come on," I told her. "Let's have some dinner."

Darlene had the tuna in her bag, which she'd taken with her in her hurry to escape. I gave Olivia avocado, cubes of turkey, a hard-boiled egg, and another one of those biscuits Darlene had introduced me to. After, I bathed Olivia, and read *Freight Train* to her about ten times until she was yawning instead of saying, "Again!"

After I put her to bed in her small bedroom, I set up my study materials at the desk in the living room. The clock on the wall said it was eight-fifteen. I went to the fridge to find a frozen dinner. My stomach growled for damn tuna casserole.

Now that Livvie was in bed, guilt churned my empty stomach.

You didn't have to kick her out.

I had a thousand good reasons for keeping my private business private, and yet being an ass to Darlene was like saying 'fuck off' to someone after they said they hoped you have a nice day.

I leaned my head against the freezer. Now I'd have to apologize.

I hated apologizing.

A soft knock came at the door. I whispered a prayer to any god that would listen it wasn't Elena coming to tell me she had a conflict sometime next week and couldn't babysit.

I opened the door to Darlene. She had a plate of food in one hand covered in aluminum foil. Steam wafted up in little tendrils, carrying with it the scents of warm noodles, mushrooms and tuna.

Dammit, she's beautiful.

The images stored in my perfect memory were dull copies compared to the real thing. I crossed my arms over my chest as if I could put a barricade between us.

"Hi, again," Darlene said. "I am not here to make you feel bad, or barge in again, I promise." She thrust the plate of food toward me. "This is a peace offering *and* a parting gift. A promise that I won't get up in your business."

I took the plate. "This is a lot of casserole."

"You insisted on paying for it back at the store, and I know you'd never cook it yourself." Her radiant smile was back. "You can eat what you want now and have leftovers tomorrow."

I stared down at the food in her hand. A simple apology and a thank you was all it would take, and then I could close the door and get back to my life. My stressed out, anxiety-ridden life.

Darlene tilted her head. "Okay, so…I'm going to go. Good ni—"

"Olivia's mom abandoned her ten months ago," I heard myself say. "My buddies and I were having a party and she showed up and just…left her. She left Olivia without a mom."

"Oh no," Darlene said softly. She wilted against the doorjamb. "I'm so sorry."

"Yeah, so, it is what it is, but…that's why I don't bring anyone here. I don't have time for a relationship with anyone, and I don't bring anyone over casually. Not even friends, really. I hate the idea of Livvie having strange women in her house. It's hard enough for her without a mom. I don't want to confuse her."

"I get it," Darlene said.

"It's probably stupid or overprotective but… She's starting to call Elena 'mama.' She hears her kids call her that and I…I don't know what to do."

Darlene's smile was soft and she reached her hand to pat my hand awkwardly for a moment, then pulled it away.

"I think you're great with her. And she's obviously very happy with you."

"Yeah, well..." I ran a hand through my hair. "So listen, this is dumb. Olivia's sleeping. Come in and help me eat this."

Darlene grinned and shook her head before I finished my sentence. "Nope. I have my rules too. I'm working on me, remember? Trying to, anyway."

Her cell phone chimed a text and she pulled it out of her sweater pocket. Her face went pale.

"Shit. I have to go," she said. "Um, I have a meeting. It's a...a work meeting in, oh hell, thirty minutes. I totally forgot."

I frowned. "A work meeting at nine on a Friday night?"

"Yeah, bummer, right?" Darlene laughed loosely. "So I can't stay to eat anyway. I'd be neglecting my obligations. I'm trying to be responsible to myself. No distractions."

"Right," I said, my chest feeling heavy. "No distractions. Well, thanks again for the casserole."

"No problem," Darlene said. She chucked me on the arm. "See? Not so bad, right? We don't have to be BFF's but we don't need to be strangers, either. Neighbors."

"Yeah, I guess that could work."

"Good," Darlene said, her smile widening, as she walked backward down the hall. "Okay. Bye." She flashed me a little wave, spun on her heels and raced downstairs.

"Bye."

I shut the door, and leaned against it for a few seconds, more tired than before. The entire night I'd been swept up in Darlene's energy. I'd felt more awake than I had in a long time, and now I was sagging again.

Friend or stranger.

Aside from Jackson, I didn't have a ton of friends anymore, and didn't have time for them anyway. I didn't have time for anything. 'Neighbor' fit somewhere in between 'friend' and 'stranger.' Darlene could be there.

I couldn't put her anywhere else.

Chapter 6

Darlene

"Oh my God, this is going to *suck*," I moaned.

I was hanging on to Max's arm as we made our way into the YMCA. My heart was racing after my mad dash from the parking lot. Praise be to Uber, I'd made it on time to my first NA meeting.

Praise be to Max's reminder text, I added but didn't say aloud.

"What's going to suck?" he asked, frowning. "The meeting?"

That too.

"No," I said. "My new living situation. It's going to be a true test of my sexual willpower."

"Sexual willpower," Max mused. "That's one I haven't heard before."

He looked exceptionally handsome in jeans and a black T-shirt under a black leather jacket, but I noticed my observation of him had changed. He was gorgeous, no question, but his eyes were light blue instead of brown, and his hair was perfectly straight with no soft curls.

He's not as attractive in the same way because you know he's gay. That's all.

I gave my head a shake. "I'm a warm-blooded American woman," I said. "I have needs. Urges. Like, a lot of them, and yet I've relegated myself to a year's worth of celibacy. A *year.*"

"Unrealistic expectations are failures waiting to happen," Max said.

"Is that in your Sponsor's Manual?"

"It's the title," he said, shooting me a small smile. "Anyway, I thought your plan was to stay out of a relationship for a year. Not to go full chastity."

"I can't do one without the other," I said. "It's my addiction, too. Not sex, but filling the emptiness with something that makes me feel good. And being with a man…that makes me feel good. The sex and the touching and the morning afters. God, I love the morning afters."

I glanced up to see Max smiling at me with amusement. I flapped my hand. "But then I get attached and try to make something out of nothing, and it all slips through my fingers. I'm back to square one, only with another failure under my belt."

"Mmmkay," Max said. We stepped inside the linoleum and fluorescent hallway of the Y where our footsteps joined the soft clopping of other people headed toward their respective groups. "So what brought this sudden revelation on?"

"The unbearable hotness of my new neighbor."

"Oh…? Do tell."

"He lives below me. And he has a little girl, and I don't even care. I thought that would be a total turnoff but it's not. The way he cares for her only adds to his ridiculous sex appeal."

A small voice in my head whispered that Sawyer was attractive in a hundred different ways, but his extreme good looks was the only one I'd let myself admit.

We stepped inside the meeting room. It looked to be a small group, only fifteen chairs sat facing a podium. I glanced around at my fellow recovering addicts. They ranged from young like Max and myself, to the oldest, who looked to be in his mid-sixties. In a corner was a table with coffee and donuts, and a woman, with dark hair and a tired but warm smile, who was setting out napkins and paper cups. Angela, the program director, I guessed.

We headed for the snack table. Max gave Angela a nod and a smile of greeting, and leaned in to me. "I think you need to be careful."

"Of what?" I asked, perusing the donuts. "Aside from the hundred million other things I'm trying to be careful of…?"

"This guy—your neighbor—has a kid?" Max said. "If you start anything with him, that's two relationships you'd be having, not one. And the one he has with his daughter is always going to be the most sacred."

"I told you, there will be no relationship, sexual or otherwise, for one whole year," I declared. I chose a bear claw and poured a Styrofoam cup of black coffee.

A year. God, that felt like a prison sentence too. The image of Sawyer's handsome face, smiling at his little girl, rose unbidden in my mind.

"And even if I wanted to pursue something, it couldn't be with Sawyer," I said quickly, as if I were casting a spell to banish him from my thoughts. "He's got too much going on with Olivia and his studies to be with anyone."

"This Sawyer is a student? Please tell me he's not in high school."

I swatted Max's arm with a laugh. "Don't be gross. He's at UC Hastings," I said proudly. "He's going to be a lawyer."

"Sawyer the Lawyer?"

"This is why I love you, Max."

"So he has no time for relationships."

"Correct! So that's good, right?" I said, taking a huge bite of donut. "He has no time, and I have to get my shit together." Crumbs spilled down the front of my shirt. I brushed them off irritably. "It would just be easier if he weren't so damn hot. And smart. And funny. He's grouchy as hell too, but only on the surface. It's like he turns this certain face to the world, but when it's just him and Olivia..."

"Whoa, whoa, whoa," Max said. "How do you know all that about him?" He gave me a stern look. "Are you hanging out with the guy who already said he has no time for you?"

"Jeez, when you put it that way." I rolled my eyes. "Yes, we hung out. Once. Tonight. I ran into him at the grocery store. The poor guy is living in frozen dinner hell. So I cooked for him."

"You *cooked* for him?"

"Tuna casserole. It wasn't as sinister as it sounds."

We took seats toward the back of the group. Max wrinkled his lips.

"I'm serious, Dar. If you want to succeed at being sober, or at finding your own self, or whatever it was you came out here for, then you have to give yourself a chance."

"I am."

"You moved in two days ago and you're already having dinner

with the guy."

"I did *not* have dinner *with* him," I said, and busied myself smoothing my napkin on my lap. "I cooked for him, true, but we...decided it was better if we kept things strictly neighborly."

I glanced up quickly to see Max watching me. I suddenly felt naked, as if my stupid little half-truth was tattooed all over my skin. I thrust my chin out.

"I'd never have told you about him if I knew you were going to freak out."

Max frowned. "I just don't think it's a good idea to put yourself in a situation that is only going to get more intense."

"We're not even *friends*, Sawyer and me. Not really."

"And you're okay with that?"

"Of course. Sure. Why wouldn't I be? I'm not going to be the same idiot I was in New York who gets attached to the first guy who's nice to me. I'm *not*."

Max inclined his chin to the podium where Angela was standing, bringing the meeting to order. "Tell it to them."

"We have someone new with us tonight," the program director said. "Will everyone please give a warm welcome to Darlene."

The group turned in their seats and gave me a smattering of applause.

Max nudged my elbow. He'd finally exchanged his gloomy grimace for an encouraging smile. "You're on. Let's see what you got."

I moved to the front of the room. I hated this part. Getting up and telling my story to a bunch of strangers. I know it was supposed to make me feel a sense of solidarity, and to keep confronting what I had done and what I was; to speak it out loud so I couldn't pretend like it never happened. But it just felt like telling the story of my weakness all over again.

"Hi, I'm Darlene."

The chorus returned with, "Hi, Darlene."

Ugh. So stupid.

Briefly, I sketched my history. Three months in jail for possession, parole, an overdose at a New Year's Eve party, more parole, and finally freedom but for mandatory meetings three times a week.

"And how do you feel being here?" Angela asked when I moved

to take my seat.

"Good. Great. Happy to be here in a new city. Starting over where everything is new. Except, for here. NA meetings are the same no matter where you go, right?"

I laughed weakly. No one else did.

When I'd slunk back into my seat, Max's frown looked etched in stone.

"Didn't your mom ever tell you if you keep making that face, it'll freeze that way?" I whispered as another gal, Kelly, was taking the podium to continue a story she'd begun last session.

"Later," Max said and nudged his chin at Kelly. "Listen."

After the meeting, a few other group members introduced themselves and shook my hand. Two younger gals and one nervous-looking guy offered to hang out some time and grab coffee. I declined politely, blaming work. I'd already decided that the only time I was a recovering addict was when I was in this room. The old Darlene was here. Everywhere else, I was brand new.

I gathered my backpack as Angela and Max talked near the podium. They both glanced at me at the same time, like parents trying to figure out what to do with their problem child.

Let them, I thought. *The past stays inside these walls. That's what anonymous means. No one has to know. Sawyer doesn't have to know...*

Why he should pop into my thoughts—again—irritated me. Being here irritated me. I stood up and headed for the door, feeling as if I were being chased by the ghosts of everything I was trying not to be anymore.

Outside, Max still hadn't shaken his frown.

"I take it you were not impressed with my debut?" I said, trying to keep my tone light.

"You sounded like you were reading a grocery list," he said.

"What you mean? I told my story."

"That was more of a plot summary. Point one: I did drugs. Point two: I got caught. Point three: I did more drugs."

"Yeah? And?" I snapped. "Look, to be honest, I don't really feel as if there's much more to tell. I got clean and have been clean for a long time." I squared my shoulders to him. "I'm never going back. I hit my rock bottom and I came out the other side. End of story."

"You hit rock bottom?"

"Yes."

"When?"

"Weren't you listening? When I OD'd at a New Year's party a year and a half ago."

"You said that happened but you didn't talk about what rock bottom meant for you. Or what it felt like."

"How do you think it felt? It sucked! But right now I feel good. Why should I talk about all the bad crap when I've gotten past all that?"

Max crossed his arms over his broad chest. "So you're just here because the court has ordered you to be?"

I sighed. "I'm not going to fail, Max. That's what my family is expecting. But I'm better than I have been. I have my massage license, a good job, a fresh start. I have to hope my worst days are behind me, right?" I grinned weakly and slugged him in the shoulder. "I'm going to prove my parents wrong, you'll see."

Max's expression softened. "I can't tell you how to recover, Dar. That's a long dark road that each addict takes on their own. As your sponsor, all I can do is point out the road signs you don't want to miss, ones that I've passed myself."

"And?"

"And from my pseudo-professional opinion, I don't think you've passed as many as you think you have."

I started to argue, but then snapped my mouth shut. That's what addicts do. They *talk* about how they're not addicts anymore. But I was recovered. Actions mattered more than words.

"Then I'll prove you wrong, too."

Chapter 7

Sawyer

"Let me get this straight," Jackson said, pressing the bar up and holding it. Sweat ran down his temples to the bench beneath him. I stood over him as a spotter.

"This new neighbor of yours..." He eased the bar down to his chest. "She's hot, funny, great with Olivia, so—*naturally*,"—he grimaced and pushed the weight up—"you kicked her out."

I helped him set the bar on the rack, and he sat up, sucking in air.

"It wasn't quite like that," I said.

My best friend fixed me a look. Hastings gym was never crowded this early in the morning on a Monday, he had nearly the entire place to himself in which to lecture me uninterrupted.

"I love you, bro, but you have lost your ever-loving mind."

"Come on, Jax, you know my deal." I went to the tricep rope machine. "What the hell was I supposed to do?"

"Is this a trick question?" Jackson moved to a rack of hand weights. He hefted a forty-pounder in each hand and faced the wall mirror. "Forget your deal, and ask her out. Or take her to bed. Or take her out and *then* take her to bed."

Take Darlene to bed.

Instantly, there she was in my mind's eye; naked and curled against me, her dark hair spilled over my pillow, her brilliant smile muted in the soft light of morning.

I shook my head, irritated.

"You can't have a one-night stand with a person who lives in the same building as you. That's madness."

"And something beyond a one-night stand is impossible?" Jackson said, his eyebrows raised.

"Yes. If it goes south—which it will—I'll have to move."

He chuckled, then narrowed his eyes. "Hold up. If the whole situation with the lovely Darlene is hopeless, why tell me about it? Because you want me to talk sense into that thick skull of yours, am I right?"

Shit.

"Wrong," I said. "I told you because it was newsworthy. She's a new person in my building." I heard how stupid that sounded and kept talking as if I could bury the words with more words. "And we're not compatible anyway. We're too different. She's..."

Weightless.

"She's not serious," I said. "And I am."

"Understatement of the century," Jackson muttered. "So she's fun? You need fun. You're in desperate need of fun."

"What I need is to graduate, then pass the bar. Besides," I added in between reps, "she's not interested in dating. She said she moved here to *work on herself,* which is code for, 'I'm a young, hot girl who doesn't want to hang out with a guy and his toddler.'" I pressed the ropes down, hard as I could, my muscles screaming. "She's going to go out. Party. Have dates. I don't have the time or funds for either one, never mind the mental energy to put toward a girlfriend."

"Hold the phone." Jackson's triumphant smile was blinding. "In all the *five years* I've known you, you have *never* used the word 'girlfriend' in my presence."

"Because I've never wanted one."

"*Wanted*? Past tense?" Jackson said through the strain of bicep curls. "The plot thickens."

I rolled my eyes. "I don't have girlfriends and I'm not doing casual hook-ups around Livvie. And I can't ask Elena to babysit more than she does already so I can take someone out. I don't see Olivia enough as it is."

"That's noble, my friend. And stupid," Jackson said. "You need to blow off steam before you have a mental breakdown. Remember Frank? In our second year? All the guy did was study. Got busted snorting rails of coke between classes to stay awake."

"I'm not going to do drugs, for fuck's sake. I have a kid."

"Not saying you are, but the pressure of law school breaks people down. And you're buried."

"I've got it under control."

Jackson looked like he was going to pursue it, but he stared at me for a moment, then went back to his reps. "So what does this Darlene do?"

"She's a dancer."

"Ooh, so she's flexible. Bonus."

I shot him a dirty look. "The dancing's a side thing. She's a massage therapist."

Jackson dropped his arms and glared at me through the mirror.

I stared back. "What?"

"She's a *massage therapist?*"

"Yeah? So?"

"Jesus, man, have you lost your game entirely? Tell her you're stressed out—not a lie— and that she can practice on you. Do you need me to think of everything? Hell, if you won't date her, maybe I will."

The sudden rush of blood to my face shocked me, and the rope slipped out of my hands. The weights *clanged* on the rack.

"Wow, easy there, tiger," Jackson said. "I was kidding. Possessive, are we?"

"What? No...fuck, I'm just tired. I've got a few more weeks of law school, the bar, and in two months, I can petition to get my name on Olivia's birth certificate. Until then..." I shrugged and grabbed the ropes again.

"Nada," Jackson said. He heaved a sigh. "Okay, then. But don't blame me if your dick shrivels up and falls off from lack of use."

"I'll keep that in mind."

Jackson grinned. "How's everything else? How's your scholarship fund holding up?"

"It's going to run out just in time for my first clerkship paycheck to come in," I said. "Of course, I have to actually *get* the job."

"A minor detail," Jackson said. "And Olivia?"

"She's perfect."

"No sign of Molly?"

"No." I pressed down as hard as I could. My triceps burned.

"How's the job at Nelson and Murdoch?" I asked before he could ask me anything else. "It's been two months. Have they made you partner yet?"

"It's only a matter of time," Jackson said, resuming his reps.

He'd been hired straight out of Hastings, before the notice came in the mail he'd passed the bar. I was only half-kidding about his new firm making him partner so fast; Jackson was a genius tax attorney, but I'd never say it out loud.

"But for real, tell me about your shot at the clerkship with Miller," Jackson said. "Has your competition cracked yet?"

"No, but I got this," I said after one last pull. I let the weights crash down and leaned against the machine, sipped from my water bottle. "We have a progress report this afternoon. Judge wants to make sure we're both on track for finals and the bar."

"Are you?"

I snorted. "Of course. I can see the damn finish line. The last thing I need is to get sidetracked by—"

"A beautiful massage therapist with dancer-flexibility who's great with your kid and lives ten feet away from you?" Jackson batted his eyes at me. "Solid plan, Haas."

I laughed despite myself. "Shut up, Smith, or I'll remind Hastings you haven't returned your gym card."

I showered, changed, and went to two classes—Advanced Legal Research and Analysis, and American Legal History, then took the Muni home. I'd enough time to grab a fast lunch, change into a suit and tie, say hi to Livvie at Elena's, then head to the Superior Courthouse for the progress meeting with Judge Miller.

I'd just opened the front door of the Victorian when I heard a commotion by Elena's place. She was coming out with her phone in one hand, Olivia cradled in her other arm, all the while gently guiding a sniffling Hector into the hallway. The little boy was holding his elbow and tears streaked his face. His little sister, Laura, followed behind looking nervous.

I rushed over and took Olivia out of Elena's arms. "What

happened?"

"I was just going to call you on the way to the ER," Elena said with a sigh of relief. "I think Hector broke his elbow." She gave him a stern look overlaid with worry. "He jumped off the couch—again, though I told him a million times no—and landed funny."

"Oh damn." I knelt in front of Hector. "You okay, buddy?"

He sniffed and nodded, his little mouth stiff with repressed tears.

"Brave man." I ruffled his hair and straightened. "Let's go."

"No, no, we'll be fine. The Uber car is coming," Elena said, then put a hand to her mouth. "Oh, and you have your special meeting today..."

"Don't even think about it."

I walked them to the front door, and held it open for them so that Elena could help cradle Hector's arm as they walked. The car was already pulling up to the front of the house. I helped Hector into his seat and buckled him in while Elena took care of Laura.

"We're fine," Elena said from the backseat. "You stay. Maybe a friend can watch the baby?"

"I'll figure it out. Shoot me a text when you know he's okay."

"I will."

I stood on the sidewalk with Olivia patting the top of my head and giggling as they drove away.

The prospects of making my meeting vanished down the street along with that car, and I wondered if I'd blown my chance at the clerkship. Roger Harris, the other candidate was probably camped outside Judge Miller's chambers with a box of cigars at that moment, the little ass-kisser.

My mind scrolled through a mental rolodex of people I could call, last minute, but even if one were available, getting to me in time was impossible.

"Shit," I muttered.

"Shih," Olivia said.

"Is that Sesame Street's word of the day?" asked a voice behind me.

I turned and blinked. Darlene was practically glowing under the blazing afternoon sun in her white spa uniform.

"What happened?" she asked. "Where was Elena running off to?"

"Hector broke his elbow," I said.

Darlene put a hand over her mouth. "Oh, no, the poor little guy. I hope he's okay." She bent toward Olivia. "And what are you doing, sweet pea? Just hanging with Daddy?"

Olivia cooed laughter, and Darlene started to touch her hand but pulled it back and straightened quickly.

"Sorry," she said. "I know you'd prefer I...*not.* But I can't help it. She's too cute for words." She cocked her head at me. "Are you usually home this early?"

"No, I'm not," I said, carving a hand through my hair. "I came home to change for a meeting with Judge Miller. I'm a clerkship candidate. If I miss it, I could be sincerely screwed."

"Scrooo," Olivia said and kicked her foot for emphasis.

"And I've just taught my one-year-old daughter two curse words in the space of a minute."

Darlene laughed. "You won't miss your meeting. I got her." She gave me a look when I hesitated. "*Really?*"

"Darlene..."

"Look, I know the score, but you need help and I just happened to have a cancellation that brought me home early." She grinned. "I'll teach her the word 'babysitter', I promise."

I rubbed my chin. "Are you sure?"

"Of course. Happy to." Her eyebrows rose. "Are *you* sure?"

No, I was not sure. Not by any stretch. Darlene was a natural with Olivia—I didn't doubt her babysitting abilities. But already, I was having a hard time keeping my eyes off of her and my thoughts in line around her. It was only going to get worse the more we came in contact.

My inner alarms blared.

Judge Miller! Because of Darlene, you aren't going to miss this meeting after all. Do not fuck this up!

I shook my head. "Yeah, yes, of course. Thanks." A sigh of relief that began in my feet gusted out of me. "Yeah, thank you."

In the Victorian, Darlene ran up to her place to change out of her uniform, while I put Olivia in her playpen and threw on gray suit pants and white dress shirt. Darlene knocked, then peeked her head in while I was tying my tie in the living room mirror.

"You decent?"

"Yeah, come in." I glanced at her through the mirror, then quickly away.

Darlene had changed into leggings and an oversize white shirt that came down to mid-thigh. It wasn't anything fancy, but it draped over her lithe body, somehow highlighting her elegant lines and soft curves just as perfectly as if she were wearing skin-tight clothing.

You haven't been laid in ten months. She could be wearing a bag and you'd get hard.

I cleared my throat and sought sanctuary behind my desk. "So...emergency numbers are on the fridge," I said, pawing through papers and throwing those I needed into my briefcase. "But honestly, if anything happens, call 911 first, me second."

"Got it," she said. Olivia was squawking to be picked up. Darlene lifted her and set her on her hip. "Oh, but I don't have your phone number."

I scribbled my number on a piece of paper and moved to hand it to her. "Write yours down," I said, and shrugged into my suit coat I'd set out on the desk chair.

Darlene put pen to paper as Olivia played with her hair, then she frowned. "Wait. You can't take my number with you; I need to keep your number. Let me get my cell; I'll punch yours in."

"No need," I said. I picked up the paper and took a mental snapshot of Darlene's phone number, then handed it back. "Got it."

Darlene's smile was ridiculously beautiful. "Mega-mind strikes again."

I leaned in to kiss Olivia on the cheek, and caught a whiff of Darlene's perfume and the faint scent of massage oil.

"Call for any reason," I told her and hurried to the door. "I'll be back in an hour and a half. Two, tops."

"No problem," Darlene said. "We're good, aren't we, sweet pea? Say bye-bye to Daddy."

"Bye-bye, Daddy," Olivia said from where she was securely fastened to Darlene's slender hip, both of them smiling at me and waving.

My stupid perfect memory took a snapshot of that too.

Chapter 8

Sawyer

My competition, Roger Harris, stood at attention outside the judge's office at the Superior Courthouse, looking impeccable and put-together while I flew in with sweat slipping between my shoulder blades and my tie flying over my shoulder. I'd made it with a minute to spare. Roger glanced at his watch and gave me a smug nod in greeting.

In his office, Judge Miller went over our Hastings curriculum progress, results from latest finals, and read the mock briefings he'd assigned us since the last meeting a month ago.

Judge Jared Miller was a kind man but he never gave compliments or reprimands; his poker face was legendary in and out of the courtroom. He nodded with equal fervor—hardly any—at both Roger's and my progress.

"Your final assignment before I make my decision," Judge Miller said, regarding us both. "Write a brief regarding a personal incident in your lives and how you would handle it as prosecutors. That's it. Until next month."

I blinked then eased a breath. I'd been expecting something difficult, but this was easy. I knew already what I'd write about and what I'd say.

My mother. I'll write about my mother.

"Mr. Haas, may I speak to you a moment?"

Roger's eyes flare in panic before he recovered himself. I returned his smug smile earlier with my own. "Of course, Your Honor."

Judge Miller sat behind his desk without his black robe looking less like an acclaimed federal judge and more like a grandfather. Framed photos of his family lined his desk and hung on the walls beside degrees and honors from various universities. An 8x10 of what looked to be a granddaughter the same age as Olivia, shared wall space with a certificate of appreciation from the San Francisco Police Officers Union. He'd removed his tie and loosened his collar, then sat back in his seat, regarding me.

"Your finals are in the next two weeks," he said.

"Yes, Your Honor."

"No real chance you won't pass with flying colors."

"I hope not, Your Honor."

"And you're registered for the bar in Sacramento next month."

I nodded. It had cost me a small fortune and I'd had to tutor other law students after Livvie had gone to bed for two weeks but I did it.

"All set."

He nodded. "I like you, Mr. Haas. I think you're a brilliant lawyer."

I fought to keep my face neutral. "Thank you, Your Honor."

He's made a decision. He's going to give it to me. Holy shit, all that work and struggle and long nights.

"On paper," he said.

My body stiffened. "Thank you." It almost came out sounding like a question.

"Your brief today was impeccable; not a precedent missed, every argument meticulously researched. It was better than Mr. Harris's in that regard. But do you know what his briefing had that yours lacked?"

"No, Your Honor."

"Life."

I frowned. "I don't understand..."

"You have a little girl, do you not?"

"Yes. Thirteen months old."

Judge Miller smiled and inclined his chin at the photo on the wall. "My granddaughter, Abigail, is about that age. She's a joy." His smile tightened. "I want to give you the clerkship, Mr. Haas, but if I had to choose today, I would pick Mr. Harris."

My galloping heart stopped and plummeted to my knees. I straightened my shoulders, determined to take this like a man, but my mouth had gone dry.

"I'm sorry, Your Honor," I managed. "I don't understand."

"As I said your brief was impeccable. Scholarly and purely academic. Which is understandable as you are an academic at this stage." He leaned his arms on his desk, fingers laced. "In the course of preparing this brief, did you consider *Johnson v. McKenzie?*"

I scanned my mental catalog and pulled up the case.

"That was…an appeal," I said, mentally reading. "The defendant's sentence was reduced due to good behavior and programs completed during prison time. I don't see how that's relevant…"

"It's relevant," Judge Miller said, "to a brief concerned with the overcrowding of prison populations. You argued, strongly I might add, for the strict use of mandatory sentencing and unequivocal upholding of the Three Strikes law."

"Yes, Your Honor," I said. "Those are the laws."

Judge Miller nodded. "Nowhere in your brief did you make any stipulation for the defendant's rehabilitation or his continued education in the prison system."

"I wasn't aware that you were asking for me to take a position on such things," I said. "I was merely providing the appropriate laws pertinent to the matter at hand."

"Yes, and you did it brilliantly. You *are* brilliant, Mr. Haas. I have no question or doubt that you would make an exceptional prosecutor. And to be perfectly frank, I'd rather *not* work with Mr. Harris." He pursed his lip. "He's a bit of a bore. But I'm concerned that you see only the law; the words on paper, and not the lives behind them."

I straightened to my full height. "I don't understand, Your Honor. The law is the law. Isn't our duty to uphold it as it is written?"

He held my gaze, lips pursed. "Why do you want to be a federal prosecutor?"

For my mother.

"Justice," I said. "The punishment should fit the crime, and the criminal *should* be punished."

"And leniency?"

"I…I don't know," I said. "I don't know that personal feelings should interfere with this kind of work."

Judge Miller sighed. "I've seen your type before. Full of piss and vinegar, as my father would've said. More concerned with being right than with being fair. You are not a coldhearted man. I can see that in you. But feelings, Mr. Haas, are what make us human. And humanity should be the beating heart of justice." He leaned back in his seat and reached for some papers on his desk. "That is all."

I left Judge Miller's chambers feeling as if I had just been sucker punched and then doused in ice water. I had no idea what he was asking of me. In the deep catalog of California law codes I had committed to memory, there wasn't one mention of emotions or feelings. That's why I liked law. It was black and white, right and wrong.

On the Muni home, I racked my brain for a way to give the Judge what he wanted.

Life.

But my mother was dead. Killed by a drunk driver when I was eight years old.

I gripped the Muni bar hard as the train screeched into a tunnel and the windows went black, as if it were taking me into the dark heart of my worst memories.

Blue and red flashing lights fill the foyer with garish color. Clown colors, from a nightmarish carnival. A knock at the door. I step into the hallway behind my dad. Emmett tugs on my pants. He's only four, but my little brother's smart. He knows something's very, very wrong, and he's scared.

Like me.

I'm so scared I can't breathe.

"Mr. Haas?"

My dad's head bobs. "Yes?"

"I'm very sorry but there's been an accident."

Dad staggers back a step then clutches the doorjamb. His knuckles are white. The red and blue lights spin around and around. Their sirens are off, but the sound is deafening. Screaming. Ripping the black of the night, tearing through my father and brother and me like a banshee; shrieking with sinister glee that nothing will ever be the same again.

The Muni train surged into daylight and I blinked the horrible reverie away. The memory retreated slowly, never far from sight and always crystal clear in my perfect memory.

The defendant—my mother's murderer—had been jailed for alcohol-related incidents twice before, and was driving with a suspended license. But it didn't matter. The judge used discretion. *Discretion.* I fucking hated that word. The driver was released and three weeks later, he killed my mother. He was sentenced to twenty-five years but what the fuck did that matter? He'd already put my mother to death and given my father, brother, and I life sentences.

And none of it needed to happen.

My hand on the Muni rail tightened again until my joints ached. The senselessness of it gnawed at my guts whenever I thought of it for too long. I turned my focus on what I could do as a prosecutor, instead. Sought sanctuary, as I always did, in the law.

But Miller's lecture in his office had me scared shitless. If I didn't give him what he wanted—life, in a briefing about senseless death—I'd lose everything.

I was still pondering these questions when I walked up to the Victorian. In my flat, Darlene was at the kitchen table, sitting next to Olivia in her high chair, feeding her a snack of cubed cheese and grapes that Darlene had cut in half.

"Hey," she said brightly. Her beautiful face like a ray of sun I basked in for a moment. "Elena came by. She said Hector did break a bone but it was a clean break, no surgery needed."

"Good, good," I said. "Glad to hear it."

"How was your meeting?"

Catastrophic.

"Fine."

I leaned over Olivia's high chair from behind. "Hey, baby. Having a snack?" I plucked a piece of Jack cheese from her tray and ate it.

"Cheece, cheece," she said, and I watched her tiny fingers pick up the white cube and bring it to her mouth.

I looked up to see Darlene watching me. She quickly averted her eyes.

"She's got a great vocab," she said, brushing a curl of Olivia's hair out of her eyes. "She's a smarty, aren't you, sweet pea?"

"Would you mind hanging out for one more minute?" I asked. "I want to change out of this suit."

"Knock yourself out."

In my bedroom, I changed into my evening uniform of flannel sleep pants and a white, V-neck undershirt. I grabbed my wallet from my suit on the bed, and pulled out a twenty dollar bill. In the kitchen, Darlene was wiping Olivia's face with a cloth, and saying something to make my daughter laugh.

Jackson's words from this morning came back to haunt me. Darlene was beautiful, fun, and great with Olivia.

Why not ask her out?

It seemed like such a simple thing, but I was on the verge of losing my clerkship. Aside from studying and classes, I was going to have to devote even more time to Judge Miller's final assignment to ensure I gave him what he wanted.

The tiredness fell over me like a heavy coat.

I have nothing to offer her.

Darlene removed the tray from Olivia's highchair, and set her down on the floor where my daughter made a bee-line for the wooden blocks scattered on the carpet by my desk.

"We were making towers," Darlene said. "I'll clean those up."

"No, it's fine. Here." I held out the twenty. "I don't know what your going rate is but…"

She was already shaking her head. "Nope. I owe you from the other night. I was so pushy, and I still feel bad about it."

"What? No. Take it."

Darlene ignored my money and knelt beside Olivia. "Bye-bye, sweet pea."

"Bye-bye," Olivia said. She stacked a wooden block with letters on each side on top of another that was covered in numbers.

"So smart, this girl." Darlene popped back up with a breathy exhilaration. Her eyes were impossibly blue. "I should go."

"Darlene…"

Her phone chimed a text. She fished it out of her bag. "Oh, that's Max. He's a friend. I told him I'd meet him later, so yeah." She shouldered her bag and headed for the door.

Max. Okay.

I followed Darlene to the door to open it.

Max is the guy who's going to ask her out if he hasn't already because you won't.

"Such a gentleman," Darlene said as I held the door for her.

"You should take the money," I said stiffly. Almost harshly. "You saved my ass today so…"

I held out the cash again but Darlene pushed my hand away and held on for a moment. Her fingers were soft and warm on mine.

"Your money's no good here. We're even."

A short silence fell, and my mind—so full of every goddamn thing I'd ever seen and read—had no words.

"Goodbye, Sawyer the Lawyer."

She let go of my hand, her smile softer now, and turned to go. Half a second later, she stopped and spun back around.

"I changed my mind. I know how you can pay me for today."

A small laugh erupted out of me, despite myself. *God, this girl.*

"How?"

"Last Friday, at the grocery store? You said that I was a…" She held her hands out.

I blinked. "A what?"

"That's just it. I don't know. You never finished your sentence."

I thought back to that night, that moment. "Oh, yeah."

"You remember, right? Your mega-mind has it?"

"Yeah, I have it but I'm not sure you want to hear it."

"Try me."

"Well, I was going to say you're like a human tornado."

"Oh," Darlene said. Her face fell, the light in her eyes dimmed slightly. "I'm like a twisty windstorm that destroys everything I touch?"

"No, not at all." I rubbed the back of my neck. "I didn't say it then because I thought you'd take it as an insult. And saying it now, it *sounds* like an insult. But it's actually—"

"A compliment?"

Her light was back and she was standing so close to me.

"Yes. I meant, you're like this whirling ball of energy that sweeps people up so they…can't help getting caught up in you."

"Oh," she breathed. "They can't?"

I can't.

I was leaning over her, my shoulder against the doorjamb, and she was right there, her breath on my chin and her eyes so blue with light and life.

Darlene is full of the life Judge Miller wants. I'm the machine that has to keep going and going until there's nothing left of me.

I straightened and smiled faintly. "Thanks for taking good care of Olivia, Darlene."

Darlene's smile was brilliant and her words, seemingly innocuous, hit me right in the chest and sank in.

"Thank you, Sawyer, for the lovely compliment."

Chapter 9

Darlene

I went back to my little place with a smile on my face that made my cheeks hurt, and a warmth in my chest that wouldn't quit. Max's text said he wanted to grab dinner before the NA meeting tonight, so I jumped in the shower. After, I did my makeup in the mirror.

Can't help getting caught up in you.

My cheeks turned pink without blush, and my eyes looked bluer than I'd ever seen them.

I pointed my mascara wand at my reflection. "Stop right there. You are doing great at this responsibility stuff. Don't mess it up now."

But visions of Sawyer Haas looking devastatingly handsome in his suit, tangled with those of him looking deliciously sexy in his pajamas. And his compliment, like a song stuck in my head, played over and over, except I didn't want it to stop.

It was only going to get harder to mind my own business, I thought, as I put on my usual smoky eyeshadow. My attraction to Sawyer was bad enough, but his little girl was an angel too. Watching her smile and hearing her talk or build block towers or even eat her 'cheece' were like special little gifts, the kind of mini-joys you never knew you wanted in your life until you had them.

My reflection's smile slipped.

Back off, girl. He's got too much going on and you...

"I'm working on me."

Another tiny thought whispered that maybe part of who I was here in SF might have something to do with Sawyer and Olivia, but I bottled it up quick.

I grabbed my old gray sweater and headed out.

Mel's Drive-In on Geary Blvd was a hopping, 1950's style hamburger joint that pleasantly assaulted the senses with its red and white décor, chrome details, and posters of the movie *American Graffiti* on every wall. The air smelt of French fries and milkshakes. On the jukebox, Chuck Berry sang about a country boy named Johnny B. Goode.

"I'm in love already," I said, plopping down across from Max in a red-upholstered booth.

"With Sawyer the Lawyer?"

The question shocked me so much I nearly knocked my silverware into my lap.

"What? *No.* With this diner! It's super cute." I shot Max a dirty look. "Why on earth was that your first thought?"

Max held up his hands. He looked like he'd stepped out of one of the *American Graffiti* posters himself, with his gelled hair and black leather jacket. "You wear your heart on your sleeve, Dar," he said with a grin. "I took a shot."

I wrinkled my nose at him. "Well, I'm not. I've been in love hundreds of times. I know what it feels like. It's not like that with Sawyer. It's...not the same."

Max raised his eyebrows.

"Never mind." I flapped my hands at him. "There is no 'with Sawyer' anyway. I babysat for him earlier today, and left his place without making a fool of myself." I held up my hands. "And here I am."

"Here you are, looking radiant," Max said, a dry grin on his lips. "Hence, my supposition that it was Mr. 'the Lawyer' who was responsible."

I rolled my eyes. "Oh, stop. I met the guy a few days ago. Even I don't fall that fast."

"Right. You need a week, minimum."

I chucked a sugar packet at him, as a waitress wearing a 50's uniform with a cap on her head appeared. Her nametag read *Betty.*

Betty put a pen to her pad. "You ready, hon?"

"I'll have a jack cheeseburger—extra pickles—fries, and a Coke with three cherries in it," I said, and gave Max a scolding look. "And bring him something to put in his mouth before I get mad."

Max laughed, and ordered a bacon cheeseburger, fries and a root beer.

"I thought you were all for me *not* getting involved with someone," I said when Betty had gone.

"I don't know," Max said with a wistful smile. "I have my own good days and bad. Today wasn't great. Your happiness seems more like something to boost up instead of tear down with a bunch of warnings."

My heart ached a little, and I reached my hand across the table to hold his. "What happened?"

"Nah, it's nothing," Max said, smiling thinly. "I'm the sponsor. I'm supposed to have my shit together."

"The meeting's not until nine," I said. "You're not on the clock yet."

"I'm always on the clock."

"I just smashed the clock."

He chuckled, then heaved a sigh and sat back in the booth. I put my hand in my lap and listened.

"My parents caught me with a guy when I was sixteen. So nine years ago. They didn't take it well, especially considering they hadn't known I was gay. They disowned me, kicked me out." He shook his head, his blue eyes heavy. "God, my life is such a cliché."

"It's not," I said. "It's what happened to you. Go on."

Max toyed with his fork and waited while Betty set down our drinks and hurried off again.

"I'd met this guy. Travis. He was a little bit older than me, in college at the University of Washington."

"Seattle?" I asked. I popped a cherry into my mouth. "Is that where you're from?"

Max nodded. "Travis was a good guy, too. He was good to *me*. Never tried anything; was willing to wait until I got older. We were both new to actually living as ourselves. We weren't in a hurry to experience everything all at once. We just wanted to be together."

"What happened?" I asked softly.

"My parents freaked out. They told Travis if he came near me they'd have him arrested for statutory rape, even though we hadn't come close to actual sex. But it scared him. His first relationship with a guy and he's being threatened with jail. He broke it off with me and I was devastated."

Max wrenched himself from his story to look at me.

"I don't know if I should be telling you this."

"Why not?" I asked. "We're friends, aren't we?"

His smile flickered over his lips. "Yeah, we are." He took a sip of root beer, wiped his mouth on a napkin. "Not much left to tell, actually. My parents' concern about me being 'violated' by Travis was utter bullshit. They just wanted to punish him. And me." He managed a grin. "My parents were trapped in another era. *This* era," he said, indicating the restaurant. "You walked into their bedroom half-expecting to find twin beds, instead of one."

I smiled for him, while inside I braced myself for something terrible.

"They forced me to break up with Travis, and then kicked me out of the house anyway."

My eyes widened. "You were sixteen?"

He nodded. "I had no job, no place to live and a shit-ton of anger." He lowered his voice, toyed with his straw. "I hooked up with some other homeless guys and they got me into selling drugs. Selling quickly became doing. I felt like I was carving up my soul into little pieces. I got caught a bunch of times, went to juvie a bunch of times. It's so movie-of-the-week."

"How did you survive?"

"I don't know, to be honest. I hitchhiked down here and fell in with a new set of bad guys. They sold more than drugs and convinced me I could make a lot of money if I did the same."

"You mean... prostitution?"

He nodded. "That's drugs for you. They make you think fucking terrible ideas are really good ideas."

"Or even better, not think at all."

Max lifted his soda in mock toast. "Anyway, I was seventeen, and got busted one night. The cop was a good guy. Instead of taking me to the station, he took me home, let me crash on his couch. I thought he was a perv with ulterior motives but I was too high to care."

"But he wasn't a perv," I said.

"No. He got me cleaned up, got me in the program, helped me get my GED, then nursing school after that. All of it. I'd be dead without him." He shook his head, his blue eyes cloudy with heavy storms of memory. "It's funny how someone can be a better dad to you than the one who shares your blood."

"Where is he now?" I asked.

"He died a couple years back," Max said. "Myocardial infarction."

"A what?"

"Heart attack." He smiled a little. "Sorry, I take refuge in medical terminology. Easier to take sometimes."

"I'm so sorry. But I'll bet he was really proud of you," I said with a gentle smile. "Is that why the shitty day? Were you missing him?"

Max shrugged. "No, no reason. It just happens sometimes, doesn't it? Like the weight of your personal pain is hiding in your psyche, and something will trigger it to jump with claws out."

"What triggered yours?"

"A lamppost," Max said with a rueful smile. "This morning on the way to work, my bus broke down. I got off to walk the rest of the way, and took a street I hadn't been on in a long time. And there's a lamppost there, papered up in flyers and graffiti. When I first came to SF, that was the street where I sold myself for the first time. That night was black, except for under that light, and I held on to that lamppost so tight. I can still feel the rough cement under my palm. The first car pulled up. The window rolled down, and I remembered thinking, *Don't let go of this lamppost. If you hold on, you'll be safe.*"

I nodded, a lump thick in my throat. "I know how that feels."

"But I let go and I got in the car," Max said. He twisted his soda around and around, leaving wet rings on the table. "This morning, I saw that lamppost and the rest of my day's been half here, half in the past." He smiled faintly. "Seeing you so happy did not suck."

I tucked a lock of hair behind my ear. "I planned it that way."

Max chuckled and the sadness hanging over him lifted. By the time we'd finished our food, it had dissipated completely, and he was laughing again.

After dinner, we headed out to catch a cab for the Y, arm in arm.

On Geary, near the diner, was an AMC movie theater. I sighed loudly.

Max looked down at me, in full sponsor mode again. "What's that for?"

I nodded my chin at the theater. "Don't you wish we could blow the meeting and go see a flick? Eat popcorn and forget everything for a little while?"

"Of course," Max said. "But forgetting is the first step down the road toward relapse. You lull yourself into thinking the pain of addiction is asleep forever, then something wakes it up and you're fucked."

"I don't get it," I said as a cab pulled up. "Isn't forgetting a good thing? Like, why do I want to relive the shitty past, instead of all the good stuff now?"

"Forgetting is pretending it never happened," Max said. "You need to remember and remember and remember, until it has no power over you anymore. Someday, I'm going to walk up to that lamppost and all of the memories will still be there, but they'll be a part of who I am. Instead of having a shitty day, I'll smile and think of how it was a piece of my past, but not the sum of it."

We climbed into the cab and on the entire ride to the YMCA, I tried to imagine my overdose at the New Year's party as something I would ever smile about. Or how I'd tell someone—*Sawyer*, my heart whispered—what I was and it wouldn't make me feel like curling up and dying inside for shame.

Impossible.

At the Y, we headed up the lamp-lit stairs with a thin crowd of people. I hunched deeper into my sweater and my hand curled around the dance troupe's phone number in the pocket. Calling it sort of felt impossible, too.

Inside, the meeting began and I chose not to share that night. My brain was too full of thoughts and words and feelings; Max's story and Sawyer's compliment for me, all tangled together.

Afterward, Max and I walked out into a warmer-than-usual San Francisco night.

"You didn't talk tonight," he said.

I shrugged. "Didn't feel like it."

Silence.

I sighed. "I'm doing really good, Max. Working, paying rent…"

"Are you dancing?

"I'm still…limbering up."

Max glanced down at me. "Lonely?"

I bit my lip. "Maybe. A little. But I sometimes wonder if that's my default setting."

He nodded, a soft smile on his lips. "The loneliness of the recovering addict. I get it. I have it too." He jerked his thumb to the Y behind us. "You should talk about it in group."

"I want to talk about it with you."

"I'm here."

I heaved a breath. "I used to think I was needy or clingy, the way I stuck like glue to the men in my life. But I just want to love someone. It's so simple and yet feels so impossible at the same time. And yes, I know, I'm supposed to be focusing on me, but isn't that the whole point of working on myself? To become worthy of love?"

"Everyone is worthy of love," Max said. "But it starts with loving yourself first. That sounds like cheesy, clichéd shit, but it's true. You have to know you can be good for someone else. Not just to fill up that hole in yourself, but to give."

"I know, but it seems like, in the past, I've done all the giving. I'm the one who holds on and they don't."

"Are you holding on because you love them, or holding on because the alternative is being alone?"

I frowned, opened my mouth to speak, then shut it again. Finally, I huffed a sigh. "You're wise in the way of life, O Max."

"I know," he said, puffing his chest out. "That's why I'm the sponsor."

I laughed and tucked my arm in his as he walked me to my bus stop.

"Have you told him?" Max asked after a minute.

"Told who, what?"

Max gave me a look. "Have you told *your neighbor* where you are tonight? Where you're court-ordered to go three times a week?"

"No," I said. "Why would I?"

"Are you ashamed? I know it's hard, but don't be. Or don't let it rule you, it'll just cause more problems in the end."

But if I never tell, there will be no end. Only beginnings.

Max gave my arm a squeeze.

"We're all made up of strengths and weaknesses, every one of us. You have strengths. Plenty. Getting clean is a strength. Picking yourself back up again after you fall, that's a strength."

"I don't feel strong. Not yet. I feel like…"

"What?"

I sniffed and wiped my eyes with my sleeve. For some stupid, unknowable reason I was on the verge of tears. "He'll hate me, Max."

"I'm more concerned about *you* hating you."

"I don't…"

"Addicts lie, Dar," Max said gently. "That's one of our defining characteristics. You'll always be an addict. You'll always fight that battle. But fight it with your best, most honest self, if you want a chance to win." His smile was sad and knowing at the same time. "It's too easy to slip if you don't."

At the Victorian, I crept up the stairs past Sawyer's place like a burglar, sure that his door would swing open and he'd loudly demand where I'd been, or that he'd see right through me without having to ask. The evidence was all over me, inside me, and coming out through my pores—the scent of cheap YMCA coffee and shame.

I flinched and hurried into my studio.

Inside, I dumped my bag on the floor, and stretched out on my tiny couch under the window. It was a loveseat, hardly big enough for two; beige with reddish swirls of flowers. Gerber daisies—my favorite—and roses.

Outside the window, the night sky deepened. San Francisco was a quieter city than New York, and the silence felt thick and stifling, like a blanket on a hot night. I felt restless.

I had to keep myself busy. I jumped off the couch to make chocolate chip cookies for Hector. While I stirred the batter, everything Max and I had talked about floated in and out of my thoughts. All of his warnings and advice sounded so wonderful and smart and helpful, but as if they were meant for someone else. Someone far worse off than me. Things were fine as they were without anyone here knowing, especially Sawyer. He might need me again, for Livvie, and hell would freeze up before I *ever* brought anything bad near that little angel, so why worry him?

A twinge of something unpleasant settled in my stomach. The same uneasy feeling I'd had as a kid, where I'd done something wrong and it was only a matter of time until I got caught.

I put the cookies in the oven and let the door slam shut.

"It was too damn hot in here, that's all," I muttered. I started to take off my sweater and my hand found the phone number in my pocket again. I sat up and contemplated the ten digits.

Actions, not words.

I picked up my phone, then hesitated at the time. Ten-thirty on a weeknight. But I'd already wasted four days.

"They probably already found someone," I said as I punched in the numbers.

"Hello?" a man's voice answered.

"Yeah, hi, sorry it's so late. I'm calling about your dance troupe?" I twirled a lock of hair around my finger. "I was wondering if you still needed someone?"

"*Yes,*" the guy said, then lowered his voice. "Yes, we are still auditioning dancers. Are you available tomorrow?"

I pulled my sweater sleeve over my hand and bit the cuff.

This is really happening, if you have the guts.

I squeezed my eyes shut.

"Yeah, I am."

Chapter 10

Darlene

In the break room at Serenity Spa the next day, I changed out of my uniform and slipped a black leotard and spandex dance shorts on under my sundress. My stomach was twisted in knots and my arms felt heavy from the day's massages.

This is stupid, I thought for the hundredth time as I left the spa. I was ridiculously unprepared for this dance audition, and certain to fail.

Is that why you agreed to audition in the first place? A voice in my head sounding suspiciously like Max wondered. *So you can say you tried without really trying?*

"Oh, hush," I murmured, and gnawed on the cuff of my sweater the entire bus ride to the studio.

I arrived at the San Francisco Dance Academy with thirty minutes to spare. The woman at the front desk told me a space had been reserved for the audition but was open now if I wanted it. I paid $15 to jump in early and warm up.

The dance room had a mirror covering one entire wall, with a barre running along its length. Golden sunlight streamed in from the high windows, and spilled across the wooden floors. A sound system with a tangle of cords sat against the wall under the windows beside a couple of simple wooden chairs and a few wooden rifles. I picked up a rifle and gave it a spin. Maybe someone was rehearsing the finale to *Chicago,* one of my favorite musicals.

If I let myself envision my perfect show, it was *Chicago*. I wasn't the strongest singer, but I could hold a key. I wanted to play Liz, the inmate who killed her husband because he wouldn't stop popping his gum. "The Cell Block Tango" was my dream performance, but instead of preparing and training for a major role, I was winging an audition for a tiny, independent dance troupe that advertised on a lamppost.

You aren't even prepared to dance for a tiny, independent dance troupe that advertises on a lamppost.

"Stupid." I put the prop down and sat on the floor.

My eyes kept glancing at the door as I stretched. Any second now, it would open. The director I'd spoken to on the phone would walk in and I'd make a ginormous fool of myself. But I kept stretching and breathing, waking my body from its hibernation. I wanted to get up and run, but at four-fifteen, the door opened and I was still there.

Greg Spanos was a tall, dark-haired guy; early thirties, dressed all in black. He was followed by an artsy-looking gal in glasses and streaks of blue in her hair.

"I'm the director and choreographer of *Iris and Ivy*," he said, shaking my hand. "This is Paula Lee, the stage manager."

"Hi," I said with breathy nervousness. "Hi. Nice to meet you. I'm Darlene."

I watched them size me up, certain that the fact I was utterly unprepared was written all over my face.

"A moment, please," Greg said.

He and Paula carried two chairs from the side of the room, and set them up on one end, their backs to the wall mirror. With no table, they rested their folders on their laps and endeavored to look professional.

"Whenever you're ready."

At the sound system against the wall, I plugged my phone in and hurried back to the middle of the room. I'd barely taken my position on the floor—lying on my back as I had in New York—when the music started.

"The music is the language and your body speaks the words."

My first dance teacher told me that when I was eight years old, scowling in a pink tutu. I hated the tutu and the ballet flats on my feet. I wanted to be barefoot and raw. Even then, the *something* inside me that wanted to dance was a fierce energy that I loved to feed. I'd given it everything—my sweat and tears; aching muscles and sprained ligaments. It was there, that urge to sing for the world with my entire self.

Until I'd ruined it with drugs. Dirtied it. Soiled myself so that dancing while the X or the coke surged through my veins felt like a violation of that pure energy.

But I'm here now.

I closed my eyes and let the first notes of the music seep into my bones and muscles and sinew; I listened with my body. When Marian Hill sang the first lines, my back arched up off the wooden floor, and then I was gone; lifted up by the soft words and gentle piano, then sparking to life when the techno beat dropped.

I forgot everything else and lived between each note, moment to moment, feeling everything I wanted to feel without thinking or stopping myself. I let my body speak for the music and there was no shame, in these words. No loneliness.

Only myself, and I was alive.

I collapsed to my knees, arched back, and lifted one arm—grasping at air—as the last note on the last word faded away to silence.

One heartbeat. Two.

I looked through a few tendrils of hair that had come loose from my ponytail. Greg and Paula were staring at me, then bent their heads to confer. A bead of sweat slipped down my temple, and I realized the twisting feeling in my stomach was gone. My pulse pounded from the dance, not nerves, and I suddenly didn't care if they wanted me or not.

But they did.

"You have…" Greg exchanged a look with Paula, "quite a lot of natural talent."

"Pure, raw talent," Paula said, nodding.

"Thank you," I said, breathlessly. "Thanks so much for saying so."

Somehow, I wasn't crying.

"Have you, auditioned anywhere else?" Greg asked slowly.

"I just moved here last week," I said. "I saw your flyer and took a shot."

They exchanged knowing looks again, laced with relief.

"Opening night is closing in," Paula said "We'd prefer not to have to recast so late in the game. We need full commitment to rehearsal, which is every night, six to nine p.m. and some afternoons on the weekend."

I bobbed my head. "Of course, absolutely. But I'll have to cut out early Monday, Wednesday, and Friday. There's a place I have to be at nine. But it's not far from here. Fifteen minutes?"

"I suppose," Greg said. "If it can't be avoided."

"It can't," I said.

"Fine," he said. "There's no pay," he added stiffly. "This is a labor of love. An independent piece of art, not a commercialized package of glitz and sequins."

"It's raw," Paula said. I guessed she must like using that word. "Stripped down and real. No pretense."

"Sounds great, really," I said. "Perfect."

"Good," Greg said, offering his hand. "Welcome to the show, Darlene."

Outside on the street, I sucked in air. "Holy shit."

It had been almost four years since I'd danced in front of an audience. Four years. I tried to tell myself it wasn't a big deal; *Iris and Ivy* was a far cry from a big dance company. But it was a huge fucking deal. I'd begun to wonder if the dancer version of myself was gone forever, still locked up behind bars even after the drug-addict had been released.

But it's still there. Me. I'm still here.

I dug my phone out of my purse and stared at it, my thumb hovering over the contacts. I called up my parents at their house in Queens. The answering machine picked up but I didn't leave a message. I needed voices. A live person. I scrolled down to my sister.

She picked up on the sixth ring, sounding harried and distracted with just one, "Hello?"

"Hey, Carla, it's Dar."

"Oh hey, hon. How are you? How's Frisco treating you?"

"It's going great here. In fact, I have the best news—"

"Are you keeping your nose clean? Staying out of trouble?"

I winced. "Yes. I'm doing really great, actually. I auditioned for a dance company—a little one—and you'll never believe it, but they hired me. There's going to be a show in a few weeks—"

Carla's voice became muffled. "Sammy! Sammy, get off the couch!" She turned her mouth back to the phone. "That dumb dog, I swear…" Her breath hissed a sigh. "Sorry, what? A show? Good for you. Are they paying you?"

I hunched my shoulders, as if I could contain the excitement that was fast draining out of me. "I'm not doing it for the pay. It's mostly for the experience. It's been four years—"

"Uh huh. Well, just don't go and do something crazy and quit your spa job over it."

I frowned. "No, no, of course not."

"Good, because you know how these things go."

I slumped against the wall. "How do these things go, Carla?"

"Sammy! I swear to God…" She huffed a sigh. "Sorry, what?"

"Nothing. So I called Mom and Dad but no answer."

"It's Bridge night. They're at the Antolini's."

"Oh yeah. Bridge night. I forgot."

"So listen, hon. I've got a roast in the oven for tomorrow. The cousins are coming over for Aunt Lois' birthday and I've got a million things left to do."

"Oh, okay. That sounds fun."

I imagined my sister's house bustling with my loud family; kids bumping into adult legs as they chased each other around the living room, while Grandma Bea screeched at them to stop "rough-housing like monkeys at the zoo."

I smiled against the phone. "I wish I could be there."

"Listen, you got a good thing going with that spa job. Keep it up. I'll talk to you soon, yeah?"

"Yeah, sure," I said. "Bye, Carla. Love you."

"Love you too, hon."

The phone went quiet.

My thumb hovered over Beckett's number but I didn't feel like talking on the phone anymore. I thought about shooting Max a text to ask him to meet me somewhere, but he was working a double shift at UCSF Medical Center and wouldn't be home until dawn. People passed me on the street and I had a crazy urge to reach out and grab one by the sleeve and tell them I was going to dance again.

The faces were all strangers.

I went home.

At the Victorian, Elena's place was bustling with muffled talk and laughter. It was six o'clock; they were probably getting ready to sit down to dinner. On the second floor, Sawyer's place was quiet. He was probably heating up some crappy food for himself while taking care to make sure Olivia ate the good stuff.

In my place, the silence was stifling.

I threw open the window in the living area but the neighborhood was quiet too; sleepy under the falling twilight. I tried the TV, but it was too loud, talking at me. I shut it off and contemplated the rest of my night. Hours stretched before me.

I had the makings of another tuna casserole in my cabinets and fridge; the only thing I could cook.

My stomach voiced its approval of the plan but a terrible claustrophobia was sneaking up on me, sucking the air out of the room. I needed someone. People. A face and a voice and a kind smile when I shared my news.

I stripped out of my dress and took a shower, keeping the water lukewarm.

As the water fell over me, I replayed my conversation with Carla. I didn't expect my sister to go into hysterics of joy at my news. But in the eyes of those who knew my past, my accomplishments were always going to be tempered by how close I might be to fucking them all up.

The loneliness of an addict, Max had said.

I stepped out of the shower with my heart beating like a heavy metronome in my chest, counting out the seconds. The exhilaration of my dance morphed into fear. The kind that whispered that I wasn't good enough to dance anyway, and how much easier would it be to lose myself for a few hours in manufactured happiness? Wouldn't it be better to feel pretend-good than to feel like this?

"No." My voice was like a croak.

Wrapped in my towel, I went to the living area and grabbed my phone. I opened my music and hit shuffle. LP's "Tightrope" came on, like some sort of gift.

I stood in the middle of my little studio, listening to her achingly beautiful voice that said, with every soaring syllable, that she knew exactly what longing was.

Just look out into forever.

My hands balled into fists and tears stung my eyes.

Don't look down, not ever.

"Don't look down," I said. "Just keep going."

I sucked in deep breaths. My hands unclenched.

And when the song ended, I put on some clothes and went into the kitchen to make a tuna casserole.

Chapter 11

Sawyer

I set down my pen and bent my fingers back to stretch the stiffness out of them. My latest notebook was nearly full, every page covered in my 'translations' of California Family Law code. I felt pretty confident about the final next week. Not so confident about Judge Miller's latest assignment.

Beside me, my trashcan was brimming with snowballs of paper. Rough drafts of the brief I'd started and stopped a dozen times when the pain threatened to bubble up and spill out onto the page. He wanted life and I saw only death.

Red and blue flashing lights colored my memory and I blinked them away.

I stretched and rubbed my aching neck. The clock read eleven-thirty. Above me, a floorboard creaked.

Darlene.

I wondered what she was doing tonight. Earlier, I'd heard the faint sounds of a song she was listening to. Did she dance to it? Was she wearing that tight black dance top with the crisscrossing straps? The top that accentuated the lean muscle of her arms and shoulders in the back, and highlighted the small perfection of her breasts in the front. Was she smiling that smile of hers that made it seem like nothing in the entire fucking world could possibly be bad?

You're getting loopy. Time to call it.

I started to pack up my materials into my briefcase. A soft knock came at the door.

I opened it to Darlene.

She wasn't wearing that dance top, but a peach-colored sundress, no shoes. The dress skimmed her breasts and flared out at her narrow waist. Her hair fell over shoulders, dark with dampness from a recent shower. Oven mitts covered her hands to protect them from the glass pan she held. The delicious scent of tuna casserole wafted up from underneath the tinfoil. It smelled warm and good in a way my TV dinners never did.

"I know it's late, but I took a chance that you were up," she said. "I made another casserole. Mostly because it's the only thing I know how to make. And to keep myself out of trouble."

She seemed on the verge of tears for a second, but blinked them away to smile brightly. "Anyway this is for you. Can I just drop it off? Then I'll go."

"Uh, sure," I said, opening the door for her. "Thanks."

"I don't want it to go to waste." She breezed past me and set it on the kitchen counter. "You can return the pan whenever."

"Are you okay?" I asked.

"Sure. Great. I don't want to bother you. I should go back..." She headed for the door, head down and her voice thick. "Livvie's asleep? Of course, it's late..."

"Darlene, what's wrong?"

"It's nothing. Stupid, really." At my door, she took off the oven mitts and tucked them under her arm. "I just had some kind of good news today and I wanted to tell somebody. At 11:30 at night," she said with a small laugh. "Sorry, never mind. I don't want to bother you."

She turned to leave and I knew I'd never sleep that night if I let her.

"Don't go," I said. "I could really use some good news right about now."

"Oh, did you have a bad day?" Darlene said softly. Her beautiful face that had been wrought with inward pain, instantly opened with outward concern. For me. "You can talk about it. If you want."

Talk to her. Such a simple concept, but I didn't do this. I didn't let women into my place. I didn't talk about my day. Except with Olivia, I was on auto-pilot, slogging through the hours to get to the finish line. But Darlene kept slipping in and I couldn't keep her out.

Maybe I don't want to keep her out.

I cleared my throat. "You were going to tell me *your* good news."

She put one bare foot on top of the other, her smile tentative. With her face scrubbed free of makeup, she was impossibly beautiful. I crossed my arms over my chest, a flimsy shield against her.

"It's so weird, but I feel like I need to tell someone or I'll burst or cry, or I don't know what."

"Tell me."

"Okay, well…" She heaved a breath. "I auditioned for this little dance company earlier today and they gave me a small part. It's the first time I've danced in a while so it's kind of a big deal to me. And my place is so quiet…" She tucked a lock of hair behind her ear. "My friends and family are all asleep on the East Coast now. I called my sister earlier but it's not the same thing, talking on the phone. Silly, I know."

"It's not," I said, moving to the kitchen, grateful for an excuse to put some space between us. For a second, she looked so small and vulnerable, my arms wanted to go around her. "That's awesome. We need a celebratory piece of tuna casserole."

I pulled two plates from the cabinet, and two forks, and a serving spoon I'd never used, from a drawer.

"I don't want to keep you up."

I turned with a small smile. "But I'm already up."

"Thank you," Darlene said softly. She joined me at the kitchen table. "I'm not used to living alone. The quiet gets to me and I'm not a fan of TV."

I cut two squares of the casserole, and ladled one onto her plate, one onto mine. I took a bite.

"Holy shit, this is better than the first one."

"Yeah?" Darlene's smile brightened. Her light was always on but now her internal dimmer switch was turned up higher.

"I put peas in it. I thought you might want to give Livvie some tomorrow." She took a taste. "Not bad, eh?"

"Not bad at all." I watched her mouth as the tip of her tongue touched her lower lip. "It's fucking perfect."

She raised her eyes to meet mine. I went back to my food.

"So, what's the show?" I asked. "Anything I would've heard of?"

"God, no," she said. "It's a tiny little dance troupe doing a revue. Independent. But even so, it's the first time I've danced in about four years."

"Really? Why the long break?"

She shifted in her seat and poked her food with the fork. "I got distracted by... other things. And it's really easy to let something go if you don't let yourself *be* that something. Do you know what I mean?"

I did, but I shook my head no. I wanted to hear Darlene talk. Now that she was here, I realized my place had been damn quiet too.

"I always danced but I didn't call myself a *dancer*," Darlene said. "I still don't. I feel like I haven't earned the title, but maybe this little show is a good step towards something bigger."

"I think it's fucking awesome that you took a shot and it paid off," I said.

Darlene looked at me through lowered lashes. "You do?"

"Yeah. You put yourself out there. You faced rejection."

The bitterness of my meeting with Judge Miller crept into my voice. I could hear it and Darlene did too.

"Did something happen today?" she asked.

"Nah, nothing," I said. "We don't need to talk about it."

"We don't *need* to, but you can if you want. I'm here."

You sure as hell are.

I shifted in my chair. Talking about myself was like trying to get a rusted engine to turn over.

"I'm trying to win a clerkship with a federal judge after I graduate. It's between me and another guy, and I'm just stressed out that the judge is going to choose my competition. If he does, I'm fucked. And on that note..." I went to the fridge. "I need a beer. You want one?"

"No, thanks," she said. "What's a clerkship?"

"It's a job in which you act as a sort of assistant to a judge." I popped the cap off an IPA and rejoined her at the table. "A Clerk of the Court advises them on codes and precedents and procedures during a trial."

I took a pull off my beer. The cold ale went beautifully with Darlene's casserole.

"Sounds like an important job," Darlene said.

"It's a vital stepping-stone on a path to a career as a federal prosecutor. To have a clerkship on your résumé, especially for a judge

90

like Miller, is a big deal." I took my last bite of casserole and pushed the plate away. "Moreover, I need the salary. I'm on a scholarship that's going to run out right about the same minute I'm handed my law degree. If I don't have this job waiting for me, I'll have to find something else."

"So what makes you think you're not going to get this job?" Darlene asked. "Doesn't this judge know about your mega-mind?"

"Maybe. But the competition isn't just about academics."

"No? Is there a talent portion, too?" Darlene speared the last pea on her plate with a grin. "Does your opponent look better in a bathing suit?"

My thin smile morphed into a full-blown laugh. "Probably."

"I find that impossible to believe," she said. Darlene's cheeks turned pink and her eyes widened. "Why yes, I did say that out loud..."

She shook her head at herself. The nervous sadness was gone from her now that she'd shared her news

I did that. I made her happy.

I took another sip of cold beer. A long one.

"But for real," Darlene said, "why on earth wouldn't he pick you?"

"He's eccentric," I said. "Hard to know how to please him sometimes."

I took another sip of beer to wash the lie from my tongue. But talking about Miller's assignment would lead to talk of my mother, and that wasn't going to happen.

A short silence fell that lasted as long as Darlene could tolerate—all of three seconds.

"So Elena says you're about ready to graduate."

"Yeah, I have finals over the next two weeks, then the bar exam. I think I'm good with the finals, but the bar," I shook my head. "The pass rate is only 33% right now, which is pretty fucking scary."

"What does that mean?"

"Only 33% of everyone taking the test will pass. The state puts a cap on how many lawyers will get a license per year. The cut score is 1440 out of 2000, which is insanely high. So I could answer all the multiple choice questions correctly and write essays that show I know my shit and still not 'pass' the exam on paper. If my work isn't first rate, it'll get tossed in the fail bin."

Darlene's eyes widened. "So it's not even a matter of your

mega-mind getting most of the answers right?"

"It's a matter of getting *all* of the answers right and writing the most exceptional essays. And that," I said, leaning back in my chair, "is what keeps me up at night."

"Wow, I've never heard of a test where you could be good enough to pass and still fail."

"Well, it's technically a fail if you score below the cut, but the cut score has never been this high. The standards have risen. Which is a good thing—no one wants a bunch of shitty lawyers running around—but it's still fucking scary. My buddy, Jackson, took the exam last quarter and barely passed with a 1530. And he was top of his class."

Darlene toyed with her fork, scraping it lightly on her empty plate. "So you have Judge Miller's decision, finals, and a bar exam with a crazy low pass rate, all the while taking care of a one-year-old."

I nodded with a small smile. "When you put it that way…"

"And yet, you still find time to comfort your neurotic neighbor over her dance audition news." She rested her cheek on her hand. "Elena was right about you after all."

Another flood of warmth suffused my chest, and I knew it was Darlene, slipping past the defenses I'd built around my heart. The moment held, wavered, and then broke when the baby monitor on my desk lit up. Olivia began to stir.

Darlene straightened. "Shit, did we wake her up?"

"No," I said. "She wakes up once or twice a night, like clockwork."

We both listened for a moment. Olivia fussed sleepily and then the baby monitor went quiet.

"She went back to sleep," I said. "Sometimes that happens too, but around three a.m. she'll wake up and I'll have to hold her for a bit. Most of the baby books I've read said to stop indulging her in it, but I'm not going to just let her *cry*." I shrugged, rubbed my neck. "So I'm a big pushover, I guess."

"No, it's sweet," Darlene said. She had a soft smile on her face that I didn't like because I liked it too much. "You take good care of her."

"I try. She probably doesn't even remember her mom. But what if she does?" I glanced over at the monitor, quiet now. "Those baby books don't cover what to do if your kid's mom abandons her. Livvie might know that deep down. She might not. But I sometimes think she wakes up just to make sure she's not alone."

I blinked and tore my gaze from the monitor to Darlene. She was watching me, her eyes soft and shining, and I realized what I'd said. How much I'd said.

"Shit, sorry. I don't… I'm so tired, I just started rambling."

"You weren't rambling," Darlene said, then added in a brighter tone, "But you do look really tired. And stressed. And I happen to be a certified massage therapist." She held up her hands. "It's like, fate, or something."

"No, no, I'm fine, thanks."

"Are you sure? Because your shoulders look like they're growing out of your ears."

"I'm used to it."

"You can get used to a lot of things," Darlene said. "Doesn't mean they're good for you."

I hesitated. I hadn't had a beautiful woman's hands on me in ten months.

This is bad. Or really fucking good, which is also bad.

"Aren't you tired after massaging people all day?"

Darlene grinned, seeing victory at hand. "I think I have one more left in me. My shoulders hurt just looking at you. Five minutes and then I'll leave you in peace."

Without a word, I sat ramrod straight while Darlene rose from her chair to move behind me. I could feel her all up and down my spine. I was in the soft cloud of her space, and the scent of her— shower soap and her warm skin—fell over me. The light weight of her hands on my shoulders sent little shocks coursing straight down to my groin.

See? Bad idea.

Then Darlene's thumbs dug into my shoulders with an exquisite pain, and all rational thought fled. A small groan of relief was pushed out of me with her digging fingers.

"Holy crap," Darlene murmured. "Your knots have knots. I have never, in all my weeks of professional massage, had anyone as tense as you."

I murmured something intelligible. My words were turning to mush in my brain. Darlene's hands were merciless and my eyes fell shut. Tight fists of muscle unclenched in me, and sleepy warmth flooded in.

"You're going to knock me out," I said.

"You should be lying down," she said. "I can work much better that way."

"If I fall out of the chair, does that count?"

She murmured a small laugh, and then her fingers sunk into my hair, grazing my scalp, and sending gentle currents down my back. I felt drunk.

"Darlene," I said, my chin sinking to my chest. "You're really good at this."

"Thank you."

Her small hands were stronger than I expected, and she slid them down over my shoulders, to press into my solar plexus. Stiff knots loosened, and as the relief flooded me, the dormant physical needs I'd been denying myself began to wake up under her hands. Blood flowed and as muscles loosened, my own hands clenched to keep from reaching up to touch her.

The air between us felt thick and charged, and I knew Darlene felt it too. Her hands stilled. I felt her stiffen behind me.

"Darlene," I said, my voice gruff and thick.

"I should go," she said, her own voice hardly more than a whisper. She gave my shoulders a final, stiff little pat, and moved to the door.

I moved sluggishly, like an animal coming out of warm hibernation into cold, harsh light, to open the door for her, but she was already there.

"You should get some sleep," she said. "I have to be up super early for the spa, then rehearsal. Thank you for listening to my news. You're a good neighbor, Sawyer. Good night."

And then the tornado that was her, swept out of my place just as fast as she'd swept in, and I was alone.

Chapter 12

Darlene

I practically ran upstairs to my studio, and shut the door hard, as if I could barricade my feelings and aching want on the other side.

I'd massaged male clients—handsome ones, even— at Serenity, and it was nothing to me. Part of the job. I'd never felt like this.

I leaned with my back to the door and looked down at my hands. They were warm and I could still feel Sawyer's hard muscle under them; the impossible softness of his hair; the warmth of his skin through his undershirt. I'd wanted to pull that shirt off of him, touch his skin with mine, and then…

"No, no, no, you do this *every* time," I hissed.

I let physical attraction pull me under and the next thing I knew, I wouldn't be working on me; I'd be losing myself in the touch of a man, the pleasure, the attention that came from feeling wanted.

And with Sawyer, it felt a hundred times more dangerous, because he wasn't like any other guy I usually associated with. He was a law student with a real career ahead of him, and a little girl.

I shut my eyes. *This is bad. So bad.*

Except it didn't feel bad.

"It will, if he finds out where you go three nights a week," I said aloud, and my words were like a cold bucket of water, dousing the pleasant warmth and washing away the memory of his skin under my hands.

Tears stung my eyes but I blinked them away.

For the next two weeks, my days became a sameness of work at the spa, NA meetings, and rehearsal. The dance troupe paired me up with a guy named Ryan Denning who, I could only guess, made the cut because he looked ridiculously hot in guy's dance shorts and no shirt. Hot, but a total klutz; I spent most of every rehearsal sidestepping his crushing feet, and subtly correcting for his bad positions and holds.

"Sorry about that," Ryan said one day, after he mistimed his cue and we smacked heads on a close turn. "Paula's my cousin, so here I am. I'm not a professional, that's for sure."

You've got that right.

I rubbed my head where a lump was forming and forced a smile. "No problem. The show must go on, right?"

Ryan wasn't the only one. The whole troupe was barely professional—I felt like I'd joined an after-school club in high school doing black-box theatre. Greg, the director, was overly pompous about his 'vision', and aside from flyers on lampposts, there was no marketing of any kind.

But I showed up to every rehearsal and gave it my all, even though the other dancers—especially the other three women—hardly spoke to me. The lead, Anne-Marie, wouldn't even look my way, unless giving me the stink-eye counted. When rehearsal was over they hustled out to drinks without me.

"*Darlene,*" I once heard her whisper. "Sounds like a truck-stop waitress."

I fled the tiny theater with their tittering laughter chasing me.

Saturday morning, and I woke up with the dawn. My work schedule had drilled it into me and now I couldn't sleep in. An uncommon heat wave made my third-floor studio feel stifling. I lay on my loveseat in my underwear and watched the sun fill the sky with white, gauzy light as it rose. A mug of coffee cooled on the table beside me as I wondered just what in the hell was supposed to come next.

I hadn't missed a single NA meeting. Granted, I wasn't talking as much or as deeply as Max wanted me too. But talking felt like giving a eulogy, over and over again, for someone who had died a long time ago. I didn't want to resurrect that addict-self. That girl was gone and I wanted her to stay gone.

I was working hard—my arms and back ached after every day of work, only to be worked harder at rehearsal.

I was doing everything right.

And still, the other ache was there. The emptiness.

I watched the sun rise from my loveseat, and remembered my favorite poem by Sylvia Plath, "Mad Girl's Love Song." I wasn't much of a book-reader; the long blocks of text couldn't hold my attention. I loved songs. Lyrics. Poems. Where a writer has the entirety of the English language to choose from and she picks only a handful of words.

I was the Mad Girl. Lying on my couch that morning, I closed my eyes and made the world vanish.

I haven't seen Sawyer in two weeks.

"I think I made you up inside my head," I murmured.

My hands tried to remember his skin, and crept down my thighs, brushing the edges of my underwear. A tingle of electricity shot through me, and I bolted off the couch.

"No, that's cheating."

I balled my hands into fists and sucked in several deep breaths. I couldn't cool my heated blood, I always ran hot. My only cure was to set fire to the passion, to feed it until it burnt out. But I still had hours until rehearsal where I could channel my restless want into dance.

I threw on jogging shorts—green with white stripes along the edges—a white T, and my running shoes, socks pulled to my knees. I grabbed my phone, ear buds, water bottle, and headed out.

Two blocks north of the Victorian was a park with large expanses of green grass, surrounded by more beautiful old houses. A path ran around the perimeter and I set out to do laps.

At only nine in the morning, it was already warm. From all I'd heard of San Francisco, this heat wave wasn't just rare, it was unheard of. The city dwellers were taking advantage. There were already couples and families gathered, enjoying the sun. Some people were alone, stretched out on the grass, an open book acting as a sun shield while they read.

I did a loop around the perimeter of the park, Madonna's "Open Your Heart" playing in my ears. On my second pass, I saw Sawyer.

He stood about twenty yards away from the jogging path in jeans, a dark blue t-shirt and a Giants baseball cap on backwards. Olivia's stroller was beside him; I could just see her little feet kicking to get out.

I slowed to watch Sawyer lay out a blanket, then extricate his daughter from her stroller. She immediately started to toddle away. My heart felt too big for my chest as Sawyer laughingly scooped her up and planted her on the blanket, then gave her a snack to keep her occupied while he finished setting up. A zwieback biscuit.

My feet wanted to turn in their direction, as if my inner compass was pulling to Sawyer's magnetic north. I kept on the path, running faster.

On my next loop, Sawyer was playing catch with Olivia as best as one could play catch with a one-year-old. Olivia, dressed in pink overalls, held her biscuit in one hand and spastically chucked a small yellow ball in Sawyer's general vicinity. He laughed and bent to retrieve it, then rolled it across the grass toward her.

My head was craning to keep watching, and I turned my attention forward before I crashed headfirst into someone. I felt like a stalker, spying on them, and had to remind myself I was there first, taking a jog and minding my own business.

Working on me.

On my third lap, two young women were with Sawyer. One was laughing way too hard at something he said, while the other was kneeling at eye-level with Olivia, smiling and talking to her. A crazed urge to run straight at the women and tackle them both to the grass came over me.

I wrenched my gaze away just as a stitch in my side stopped me short and bent me double. I wheezed for breath, hands on my knees. I hadn't realized how fast I'd been running but my face was covered with sweat and the pain in my side was like a little knife stabbing me.

When I was able to stand straight I sucked in deep breaths, and glanced over at Sawyer. My breath stuck all over again.

Sawyer was looking right at me, his expression unreadable from this distance, though I thought I caught a glimpse of a small smile on his lips.

I watched, rooted to the spot, as he picked up Olivia and headed toward me without so much as a word to the two women. They watched him walk away, twin expressions of confusion and disappointment morphing to disdain on their faces before they gave up.

"Are you being chased?" Sawyer asked with a small smile. On his hip, Olivia beamed and bounced to see me.

"Ha ha, no," I huffed. God, I must've looked like a mess. My face felt red and puffy from running so hard and sweat made my shirt stick to my skin. "I got confused for a second and thought I was Usain Bolt."

Olivia reached her little hand out to me.

"Hi, sweet pea," I said, giving her hand a gentle squeeze. "Are you being good?"

"Always," Sawyer said with that smile he reserved just for her. He plucked a blade of grass off her overalls, not looking at me. "So, haven't seen you in a while."

"Yeah, I've been busy. Job, rehearsals." I dug my toe into the dirt. I'd caught my breath but my heart was still pounding loudly. "How are your finals going?"

"Good. Finished two. Two more to go."

"And then the bar exam?"

"Yeah, in Sacramento in a few weeks. Three days of motel living." He made a face. "Can't wait."

"Three days? Will Elena be watching Olivia?" I asked. "Because I can help. If you need it."

"Maybe," Sawyer said. His dark brown eyes were soft as they met mine. "Thanks."

"Anytime."

A silence fell and then Olivia squirmed. "Down. Down."

"Well, we'd better get back before someone steals our wheels." Sawyer nodded his chin at the bulky, second-hand stroller. "It's such a beaut."

I smiled and tried to think of something witty to say but my brain was addled by the V of Sawyer's tanned chest revealed by his shirt, and the flexing muscles in his arms as he set Olivia down.

"Yeah, I'd better get back...to...more running."

More running? Seriously?

I felt a tug on my hand. "Ball, Dar-een?" Olivia pulled me toward their blanket. "Ball?"

A joyful laugh burst out of me, erasing my nerves. "Oh my God, she just said my name." I knelt down beside her. "Did you just say Darlene?"

"Dar-een," Olivia said, and pointed toward her yellow ball sitting on the green grass. "Play?"

"Well, if it's okay with your daddy?"

I looked up to see Sawyer watching his daughter.

"I didn't know she knew your name," he said quietly.

"I didn't either," I said. I got to my feet. "I'll play with her if you want. Or if you'd rather I not..."

"No, that'd be great. If you don't mind."

"Not at all."

I joined Sawyer and Olivia on their patch of grass and played three-way catch—Sawyer threw to me, I rolled the ball to Olivia, and she threw it to Sawyer who inevitably had to go chasing it down or pick it up when she torpedoed it straight into the grass.

Olivia's thirteen-month-old attention span wore out five minutes later, and she dropped the ball, game over.

"Snag? Snag, Daddy."

He scooped Olivia up. "Do you want a snack? What about a swing first?"

"Swing!"

Sawyer swung her down and then tossed her up in the air in the way that guys did that made babies squeal with laughter, and made every human with ovaries in a twenty-yard radius inwardly panic.

"Oh jeez," I whispered.

I peeked at them through my fingers, but Sawyer caught his little girl smoothly and planted her on his hip.

"Okay, snack time." He looked to me and laughed. "It's safe to come out now. Do you want to join us?"

"I don't want to interrupt your private time..."

"Nah, we do this every Saturday," Sawyer said. He set Olivia down on the blanket—where she found her half-chewed biscuit—and rummaged in the stroller. He held up two pieces of fruit. "Apple or banana?"

"Apple," I said.

He tossed it to me and I caught it and sat with them on the

blanket. We ate and talked, and Olivia helped to give us something to focus on when the air between us seemed to thicken. It had been too long since Sawyer and I had been in the same space. Since his skin had been under my hands. My face felt perpetually hot, and I turned my eyes to Olivia whenever I found myself staring at Sawyer for too long. Twice I thought I caught him staring at me before doing the same.

An elderly couple, strolling arm in arm, veered our way.

"We just had to tell you, that you are such a beautiful young family," the woman said. "Just beautiful."

I glanced at Sawyer. "Oh, um...we're not..."

"Thank you," he said. "Thanks very much."

The couple beamed and moved on.

"It's easier than explaining," Sawyer told me.

"Oh. It's happened to you before?" I asked lightly.

"Yeah, with my friend, Jackson," he said. "He joined us one Saturday and an entire bachelorette party surrounded us, thinking that we were a couple and that Olivia was our adopted daughter."

I took a long pull from my water bottle. "That's too cute."

"I didn't bother to tell them the truth, though Jax hitting on the Maid of Honor the entire time must've been confusing."

Sawyer was good at making me laugh, and I vowed to relax and enjoy the day, instead of crowding it with silly, impossible thoughts. I leaned back on my hands, let the sunshine spill over me.

"Jackson's a lawyer, too? I think you mentioned that."

"Yeah, practicing. So he's an *attorney*," Sawyer said with a grin. He smiled fondly at Olivia who was eating bits of strawberry, alternating with bites of biscuit. "He does tax law at a big firm in the Financial District."

"Tax law. God, I'm getting sleepy just thinking about it." I started to take a bite of apple, then froze. "Oh shit. I just realized I never asked you what kind of law you're studying."

"Tax law," Sawyer deadpanned, but the glint in his eye gave him away.

"Liar," I laughed, and crunched my apple. "What is it, for real?"

"Criminal justice. I want to be a federal prosecutor."

"Oh," I said, and it seemed as if a cloud had crossed the path of the sun. My skin broke out in gooseflesh and I swallowed my lump of apple like it was a rock. "That's the kind of attorney who works to put people in jail, isn't it?"

I knew perfectly well that's what it was, because I'd had one standing across from me in a courthouse three years ago. He helped get me sentenced to three months in jail for misdemeanor drug possession.

"There's more to it than that," Sawyer said. "A federal prosecutor represents the state or federal government in criminal cases, argues before grand juries…"

"But is that why you want to be a lawyer? To punish those who have broken the law?"

He frowned as if the question didn't make any sense. "It's not only about punishment, it's about justice." A smile softened his face. "It's not like the Pirate Code. The laws aren't there to serve as *guidelines*. They're meant to be followed."

I nodded faintly. "Yeah, they are."

A short silence descended. Livvie was turning the heavy cardboard pages of a book about a hungry caterpillar. The sunlight made her brown hair gold at the edges.

I cleared my throat, determined to keep my spirits up. "What made you decide to practice?"

He gave me a smile but it faded as he spoke. "I like the law. I like how black and white it can be. Words on paper that last and have power." He plucked a few blades of grass, tearing them from their roots. "I want that power to protect people from what happened to my family."

"What happened?"

Sawyer seemed to be struggling to find the words, or whether to speak them at all.

"No, you don't have to tell me," I said gently. "I do that. I pry."

"You're not prying," Sawyer said. "You're making conversation. Something I'm not very good at lately."

I smiled. "You're doing fine."

He smiled back but it was flimsy and faded quickly. "I don't talk about this very much. Or ever, actually."

I itched to touch him. "You don't have to."

"No, I should, I guess. For her sake. My mom died in a car accident when I was a kid," he said all at once, then swallowed. "She was killed by a drunk driver."

My hand flew to my throat. "Oh my God, Sawyer. I'm so sorry. How old were you?"

"Eight," he said. "My little brother, Emmett, was four. Worst fucking day of our lives."

My eyes stung with tears at the sudden image of two little boys learning they no longer had a mother. "I don't know what to say. I'm so sorry."

He shrugged, as if he could minimize the whole thing, but I could see the pain behind his deep brown eyes. A muscle in his jaw ticked.

"Anyway, the guy who killed her had been arrested twice before," he said, his voice hardening. "And both times he pled before a judge he wouldn't do it again, that he'd cleaned up his act. The prosecutor was weak. He didn't push hard enough. Three weeks after his latest release from jail for DUI, the guy drove his truck—on a suspended license—into my mom's car as she was coming home from work."

I shook my head. "That's so awful."

"I don't like talking about it, and I don't want to write it about it, either, but I don't know what else to do."

"What do you mean?"

"Judge Miller has asked us to write a brief about a personal incident in our lives and how we'd handle it as prosecutors."

"Judge Miller, this is the guy you're trying to have a clerkship with?"

Sawyer nodded. "And I plan to write about my mother, but it makes me so fucking angry and..."

"Hurt?" I offered gently.

Sawyer shrugged. "I don't have time to hurt. Maybe that's my problem. Miller told me I lack feeling." He scoffed. "I have no idea what that means. Law doesn't have feelings. It has direction. It tells you where to go and what comes next."

"But that's not how life is," I said.

Sawyer's head shot up. "What did you say?"

"Life has no guide map. Things happen and people react, and no two people will do the same thing." Now I plucked at the grass at the edge of the blanket. "Some people are beyond saving, like that asshole who...killed your mom. But not everyone is like that."

"He was given plenty of chances," Sawyer said darkly. "He threw them away."

"So you don't believe in second chances anymore?" I asked, my voice sounding high and tight in my own ears.

Sawyer watched me for a minute, his dark eyes full of thoughts. Then he shook his head. "I don't know. It shouldn't be about what I *believe*. It should be about what I can do. The law failed my mom. I'm going to make sure it doesn't fail anyone else."

"He sounds nice, this Judge Miller," I said after a moment. I plucked another blade of grass.

Sawyer nodded. "He is. Sometimes I wonder why I'm in the running for a clerkship with him in the first place."

"Because you have plenty of feelings," I said, shocked at my old boldness but it was too late now. The words had come flying out and there was no taking them back. "And he probably sees it."

Sawyer looked at me from across the blanket. Between us, Olivia dozed. He covered her eyes with a little sunhat. "I do believe in second chances. For her, I do. For criminals like the guy who killed my mom?" He shook his head. "Once a person crosses over the line, it's too easy do it again and again."

"What line?"

"Breaking the law," Sawyer said. "Falling back into drugs and alcohol, or stealing or murder or…any criminal act."

I nodded and looked away, into the gulf of sadness that opened between us. The idea of telling him about my past felt even more impossible.

He won't see me anymore, only my record. A criminal.

I cleared my throat. "Tell me about your brother, Emmett. Where is he now?"

"Good question. Last I heard he was heading toward Tibet. He travels all over. Doesn't have a permanent address. After our mom died, he ran away a lot. He always came back but when he got older, he stayed away longer. Dropped out of school, even though he has a genius IQ. Or maybe because of it."

A quiet, proud smile touched Sawyer's lips. Then it faded.

"I've always felt like the world can't contain Emmett. Or he's too smart to deal with it. Like he can see all of its moving parts, and it's too much for him. He has to keep going. To outrun it, maybe."

"Do you miss him?"

"Yeah, I do. I don't have much family left. Dad remarried and now they live in Idaho. Patty—his wife—has her family there, so I never see my dad. Birthday cards and the occasional phone call."

He glanced at me, took in my darkened expression. "Hey, sorry for dumping all that about my mom on you. I don't normally talk about my shit. Not to anyone."

"I'm glad you told me," I said, smiling faintly. "I'm glad you feel like you can."

"It's not a pretty story."

"Not many people's are, I think."

"What about you?" he asked. "I don't mean you have to tell me your not-so-pretty story, if you have one. I meant, you mentioned you had a sister?"

"One sister, back in Queens," I said. "She's older. And married. Perfect husband, perfect house, perfect everything."

"And you didn't get the perfect gene?" Sawyer asked lightly.

"Oh no, I'm the fuck-up," I said.

Sawyer frowned. "You don't seem like a fuck-up to me."

If you only knew.

"My sister went to college, I didn't. She pursued a 'real career' in interior design. I didn't. I wanted to be a dancer, which everyone knows is no way to make a living. So speaketh my parents, away."

"Is that why you moved out here? To do your own thing?"

"Yes," I said. "A fresh start."

He nodded. Smiled. "Fresh starts are good. Emmett makes one every day," he said. "Once I get this clerkship, *if* I get this clerkship, I'll have one too."

"You will get it," I said. "You'll pass the bar. Your brother isn't the only one with the genius IQ."

Sawyer waved a hand. "Nah. He's the real deal."

"But you have a photographic memory, right?" I blew air out my cheeks with a laugh. "I can hardly remember what I wore yesterday."

"You wore jean shorts over ripped black tights, and a black, satiny-type blouse with gold flowers and skulls on it," Sawyer said. "And combat boots."

I stared, a blush creeping up my cheeks. "How do you know that?"

"I was getting off the Muni last night when you were getting on. You didn't see me."

"I was on my way to rehearsal," I said automatically.

And an NA meeting after that.

But that part I kept to myself. I wanted to put as much distance between myself and the kind of person he imagined an addict could be. I cleared my throat.

"Okay, Mega-mind, what did I wear when I babysat for Olivia on the fly?"

"You wore black leggings, a long white shirt. And combat boots."

"What was I wearing the day we met?"

"A beige skirt—linen, maybe—with a men's jean button down shirt, and maroon socks pulled up to your knees." He grinned. "And combat boots."

"God, hearing it like that, I sound like a slob."

"You don't look like a slob," he said quickly, his gaze intent. "You look like you. I've never met anyone who looks and acts and dresses one hundred percent like themselves."

My blush deepened. "Thanks."

The moment caught and held, and the entire city went silent. I could hardly blink, I wanted to hold on to every second of that moment. The way the sun glinted off the burnished gold of his hair, and how his dark brown eyes were looking at me.

Olivia stirred in her sleep.

"She got up super early this morning," Sawyer said, "which means I got up super early this morning. I should get back."

"Yeah, me too. I have rehearsal."

We packed up the mini-picnic, and Sawyer gently laid his daughter in the stroller. We walked back to the Victorian in silence, and for once I wasn't tempted to fill it with talk. I didn't know what to say anyway. Half of me felt devastated by Sawyer's ideas about addicts being beyond redemption, and the other half was floating over the rest of the morning, and how he looked at me in that one, perfect moment in the sun.

"So this rehearsal," Sawyer said as we entered the Victorian. "It's for the dance show you auditioned for?"

He unlatched Olivia from her stroller and lifted her gently in his arms. I folded the stroller and followed him up the stairs as if we'd been doing it like this for ages.

"Yeah, at the American Dance Academy, until five."

He unlocked the door to his place and I followed him in, and left the stroller by the door. He went to put Olivia down in her bed, and came back with his hands jammed in the pockets of his jeans.

The silence that fell was different now. Olivia wasn't here to act as a buffer between us. It was just Sawyer and me. I didn't know what to say, so I blurted the first thing that came to mind.

"Is it hard having a memory that doesn't let you forget anything?"

"Sometimes," he said, and the word felt loaded.

"I'd think it would be annoying, remembering things that have no meaning. Like what your neighbor wears every time you see her."

His gaze held mine. "It's not all bad." He glanced away for a moment. "I remember what you were wearing the night you came over to tell me about your audition."

"What was I wearing?" I asked softly.

"A dress. You were wearing a pink-ish, orange dress that looked like a slip." He glanced at me and there was something in his eyes that hadn't been there before. "And nothing else."

"You remember that?"

"I remember everything about that night, Darlene."

"Oh." I swallowed hard. "That's nice."

That's nice?

I winced. "Well, okay, I should go."

"Let me get the door."

He moved to me, leaned over me to reach for the handle, but somehow we ended up face to face, my back to the door. My heart clanged madly and my eyes felt fixated on his, unable to tear away.

Sawyer's expression was anguished, unsure. "Darlene..."

"Yes?"

Oh my God, he's going to kiss me.

The need tore me in half again; to run away before we did something we couldn't undo, and to let him kiss me until I could hardly remember my own name.

Sawyer's gaze moved from my eyes, to my lips, to my forehead, and for a crazy second, I thought he looked straight into my mind where all my secrets were laid bare. His brows furrowed.

"What is it?" I asked.

He frowned and his hand came up to brush a wisp of hair from my temple. "You have a bruise there." His eyes dropped to mine. His fingertips were still resting on my cheek.

"Oh, that," I said, with a nervous, whispery laugh. My heart was now pounding so loud I could hardly hear myself. "My dance partner in the show? He clobbered me."

Sawyer's expression hardened. "What does that mean?"

"Oh, no, it was an accident," I said. "We bonked heads. He's kind of a klutz."

Sawyer lifted his chin, and took a step back. "Tell him he'd better be more careful."

I nodded. "I will. Okay...bye."

I reached behind me for the door and slipped out, into the empty hallway where the only sounds were my shallow breaths and the blood rushing in my ears.

Chapter 13

Sawyer

"Holy shit, I almost kissed her."

My discipline had nearly gotten away from me, but Darlene was so beautiful and full of light and life, who the hell could blame me? Her tornado-like ability to sweep people up was so potent, it drew me in so that I wanted to kiss her and touch her and tell her everything.

I told her about my mother.

It had been years. And while I hated to see the story cloud Darlene's light, I felt better for sharing it with her. My mother was gone, but instead of turning that horrible memory over and over in my mind, like a bad song stuck on repeat, she'd become a real person again with Darlene.

I wanted to kiss Darlene for that, too. When she was at my doorway with her chin tilted up, it was almost impossible not to. Until I saw the bruise on her forehead. Anger that some careless asshole hurt her—accident or not—surged through me with a different kind of heat. I was glad that my anger had pulled me out of the moment because it reminded me that I couldn't start something with her. Not now.

I was so close to the end. A few more weeks and I would be done with law school and the bar exam.

Maybe then?

I had a purely selfish moment where I felt as if maybe, if I kept my head down and worked my ass off, I'd have this beautiful, vibrant woman waiting for me on the other side.

I went to my bathroom and took a very long, cold shower.

I spent the rest of the day without my studies, focusing only on Olivia as I did every Saturday. We read books and ate lunch and I let her watch Sesame Street. As usual, when it was over, she asked for more.

"Elmo?"

"You want more Elmo?" I asked, and tickled her until she was squealing. I was paranoid about too much TV, but it was hard to resist her baby voice and wide blue eyes. She was smart and I loved watching her blow past the milestones like a champ.

A month and a half left to go to the biggest milestone.

I'd had Jackson, acting as my attorney, draw up the petition for a Voluntary Declaration of Paternity. As soon as it had been a year since Molly left us, I could petition to have my name put on Olivia's birth certificate.

"She should have done that before she gave her to me," I muttered, watching my daughter watch her show. But instead of the thought irritating me, the tension I perpetually carried around with me on my shoulders relaxed a little bit and I was almost surprised to find I was in a really good mood. It was easy to do around Olivia but now that I had Darlene my life too…

"Settle down, Haas. Go take another cold shower."

Around six, I was putting Olivia's and my dinner dishes in the sink when there came a knock at the door. My heart stuttered to think it might be Darlene, maybe this time with a chicken pot pie, or some other concoction she wanted to share.

I opened the door to Jackson and his mother, Henrietta.

"Sawyer, my man," Jackson said. He was dressed to go out in a dark blazer, white button down, and black pants. We clasped hands and he pulled me in for a half-hug. "Are you ready?"

"For what?" I moved to hug his mom. "Hi, Henrietta. Are you dropping him off? Because I don't want him either."

Henrietta Smith looked like a younger version of Toni Morrison; heavyset with graying dreads down to her shoulders. She always dressed in billowy, silky clothes and large jewelry that Olivia loved to play with whenever she babysat.

She chuckled and took my face in her hands to kiss my cheek. "Hey, baby boy. How've you been? You look tired."

"I'm well," I said, pulling away from her embrace with a small ache in my chest. With my own mother gone, my brother trekking around God-knew-where, and my dad in Idaho with his wife's family, Henrietta and Jackson were the closest I had to family.

"What are you guys doing here?" I asked, shutting the door behind them.

Olivia bounced and squawked from her highchair, her arms reaching. Henrietta freed her from the highchair and gave her a squeeze. Olivia hugged her back and immediately reached for the bulky necklace around Henrietta's neck.

"This," Jackson said, "is an intervention. Get dressed, you're going out." He held his arms out and did a Michael Jackson-esque turn in my living room. "Dancing."

"Say again?"

Jackson pointed one finger to the ceiling. "Is the lovely Darlene home?"

"I have no idea. I think she had rehearsal until five so yeah, she should be…hey, where are you going?"

Jackson had made an about-face, and strode out the door.

I looked to Henrietta who laughed heartily, Olivia secure in her arms, and I chased Jackson upstairs.

I caught up to him just as he knocked on Darlene's door. He jerked his jacket down to straighten it and smoothed his short hair that didn't need smoothing.

"What are you doing?" I hissed.

"I told you," Jackson said. "It's an intervention. You're off your game and what kind of wingman would I be if I—why, hellooo," he said smoothly as the door opened.

A cloud of clean scents, daisies, soap and warmth, billowed out with Darlene. She was fresh from the shower and wrapped in a silky robe. Her hair fell around her shoulders in damp, dark waves. Her brilliant blue eyes took in Jackson and me and lit up from within. She crossed her arms, a laughing smile on her lips, and leaned against the doorframe.

"If you're here to sell me a set of encyclopedias, you're too late."

Jackson threw his head back and bellowed a laugh.

I rolled my eyes. "Sorry, about him, but—"

"You must be the lovely Darlene," my friend cut me off, holding his hand out. "Jackson Smith, Esquire."

Darlene's grin widened and she gave me a raised-eyebrow-look as she shook Jackson's hand. "Nice to meet you, Jackson. Sawyer has told me so much about you."

"Has he? What a coincidence. Sawyer has told me quite a lot about you, as well."

I shot my friend a death glare, which he completely ignored.

"One of the *many* things Mr. Haas has told me about you, Darlene, is that you are dancer. Therefore, I am here to extend an invitation for you to come dancing."

Darlene's arms dropped. "Really? Oh my God, yes, please. I just moved here a few weeks ago and I don't know anyone. I'm dying to go out."

Jackson shot me a dirty look and whacked me in the chest. "Are you hearing this? This beautiful woman—who lives right above you— is new to the city and you haven't even taken her out to show her the town?"

The blood rushed to my face on a heated current of embarrassment that left me tongue-tied. "I don't...I..."

"There's a bunch of us going to Café du Nord on Market Street. Have you been?"

"Never heard of it," Darlene said.

"It's a throwback, speakeasy kind of scene," Jackson said. "Is swing dancing part of your repertoire?"

Darlene's grin widened. "It's been a while, but yes."

Jackson clapped his hands together once. "Great. We're meeting some friends at Flore for dinner and then walking up to the club. You're officially invited to come with us."

Her glance darted to me. "I'm trying to imagine Sawyer the Lawyer dancing."

Jackson laughed again. "Sawyer the Lawyer? Holy hell, I love this woman already." He clapped me on the shoulder and gave me a fond look while I glared daggers. "He can't dance for shit but I'm convinced it's only because he doesn't have the right instructor."

I rolled my eyes as if his comments were no big deal, but the blood was leaving my face, heading due south at the idea of dancing with Darlene.

"It sounds awesome," she said. "Thank you so much for inviting me. Give me half an hour?"

"Of course," Jackson said. "Head down to Sawyer's place when you're ready."

"Thank you," Darlene said. She glanced at me almost shyly, her cheeks pink, before shutting the door.

Jackson turned to me with a triumphant look on his face that morphed into confusion at my hard stare.

"What?"

"What the hell, man?" I dragged him away from Darlene's door.

"I'm just being a good friend," Jackson said as we took the stairs down. He stopped at the bottom and turned, put his hand on my shoulder. "I appreciate your dedication to your work, but I cannot let you turn down the chance to see that woman—" he pointed a finger at Darlene's door— "dressed up to go out and dance. You going to say no to that? And Ma's been dying to see Olivia again." His eyes widened with mock alarm. "You going to say no to *Henrietta*?"

I laughed despite myself. "I can't dance for shit, remember? Not exactly the best way to impress a woman."

"Details, details." He waved a hand. "You'll thank me when a slow song comes on."

In my place, Henrietta was sitting on the floor with Olivia, playing with blocks. She looked up when we came in, the same conspiratorial smile on her face as her son's. "Well?"

"It's on," Jackson said.

Henrietta laughed and clapped her hands together. "Oh baby, you should see your face," she said to me. "Go on now, get ready. This little angel and I have some catching up to do."

It was useless to argue, and part of me realized I had no intention of arguing at all. I took a quick shower and then dressed in black slacks, a dark gray dress shirt I hadn't worn in a year, and a jacket.

Twenty minutes later, Darlene knocked on the door. Jackson opened it and a low whistle issued from between his teeth. "Darlene, you're a vision," he said "Don't you agree, Haas?"

He stepped aside to let Darlene in, and closed the door behind her. My heart nearly fucking stopped beating in my chest; I don't think I'd ever been so glad for my photographic memory in my entire life.

I took her all in, every detail. Her sleeveless dress hugged her slender body in black silk, then flared out at the waist. Instead of her usual combat boots, her shoes were the black, low-heeled, strappy kind dancers wore, and she carried a black coat in her arms. Her dark hair was pulled back from her face on the sides and curled softly down over her shoulders. She'd done her eyes in smoky shadow; and the dark of her clothing and makeup left me transfixed by her translucent skin and fire-engine red lips that stood out, like white and red slashes of paint in a dark masterpiece.

I blinked from staring at her to realize she was staring at me.

"Hi," she said, a nervous little smile. "You clean up good, Sawyer the Lawyer."

"Ha!" Henrietta cackled and slapped her thigh. "Haven't heard that one in a while." She got up and came over to Darlene and took both her hands in hers.

"Why, aren't you an angel?" she said. "I'm Henrietta, Jackson's mother."

"So nice to meet you. Your son is quite a charmer," Darlene said warmly.

"That's one word for him," I muttered.

"Dareen!" Olivia said, reaching a hand up.

Darlene knelt beside her. "Hi, sweet pea. Are you playing with your blocks?"

"Bocks."

I wrenched my gaze from her and my daughter to see Jackson watching me with a shit-eating grin on his face. He held his hands up like a circus ringmaster for whom everything was going precisely as planned.

"Shall we?"

We met some friends of ours I hadn't seen in a long time at Flore restaurant. Twelve of us crowded around the long table by the window that afforded a perfect view of bustling Market Street.

Jackson sat next to Darlene and directed me to sit across from her. For a split second, I wondered at my friend's actual motives, but Jackson wasn't a dick. As soon as I sat down, I understood his plan; I had a full view of Darlene sitting across from me, looking stunningly gorgeous in the amber light of the restaurant.

Our friends took to her immediately. Even the most outgoing

women among them seemed reserved compared to Darlene. She wasn't loud or obnoxious, but laughed and talked easily with no self-consciousness about being amongst a group of new people. Now and again, her eyes stole glances at me, and as the dinner plates were being served, she leaned over the table.

"How am I doing?" she asked. "It's been a while."

"You're fucking perfect," I said, but the noise and clatter of silverware on dishes was so loud, she didn't hear me.

"What? Say again?"

I shook my head with a smile, and we both were pulled toward other conversations.

After dinner, the group of us walked down Market Street. I'd forgotten what it was like to hang out with friends, to be part of the city's energy. Darlene linked her arm in mine as we set out.

"Is that okay?" she asked, when I stiffened.

"Yeah, sure," I said. Her sudden touch on my arm had sent a current shooting through me and I cursed myself. Jackson was right; I was completely off my game. I'd forgotten what it was like to flirt with a girl.

Because you always flirted with an agenda, a voice whispered. With Darlene, just being with her, having her hand on my arm, was enough.

Café Du Nord was a small, former speakeasy underneath an actual restaurant. We walked down the short stairs into the windowless, oval-shaped room. At the far end was a place for a band, but tonight the red curtains were closed and swing music came in from the sound system. We passed pool tables on the left, and Jackson led us immediately to the bar on the right.

"The first one's on me," he told Darlene, and clapped his hand on my shoulder. "The rest are on him."

She laughed. "I'll take a Coke with three cherries."

The music was loud. Jackson craned in. "A what? Rum and Coke?"

"No, a Coke with three cherries in it." Her smile tightened. "I don't drink...when I dance."

"Fair enough." Jackson turned to me. "What will it be, slugger? The usual?"

"Just one," I said. "I don't want you taking advantage of me later."

Jackson ordered Darlene's soda, and two Moscow mules for him and me. Big Bad Voodoo Daddy blared overhead, and dozens of dancers were swinging on the dance floor, ringed by onlookers. Old-fashioned lamps on the walls cast a golden light.

The bartender set down Darlene's soda and two copper mugs, brimming with vodka, ginger beer, and ice—each with a lime perched on the rim.

Jackson tossed down a twenty, and then lifted his drink in a toast. "To interventions."

"To interventions," Darlene echoed, her voice low.

We clinked classes and I watched, mesmerized as Darlene plucked a cherry from her drink and put it to her lips that were painted just as red. She held the cherry with her teeth to pull it free from the stem, and then it vanished into her mouth.

"My God," Jackson murmured to me under his breath. "Did you see that?"

"Hell yes, I did."

"She's the hottest woman in this joint."

"I know," I said, watching as Darlene struck up a conversation with Penny, one of our friends from Hastings. "And she has no idea."

That's part of what makes her so damn beautiful.

Jackson nudged my arm. "What the hell are you waiting for? Ask her to dance."

"I can't fucking dance," I said. "You know that."

Jackson heaved a sigh. "You leave me no choice. Hold this for me?"

I gritted my teeth as Jackson handed me his cocktail like I was a freshman at a hazing, compelled to do his bidding. Jackson took Darlene's hand and gave an exaggerated bow.

"Care to dance?"

She shot me a glance and a smile, then nodded her head. "I'd love to."

He led her to the dance floor with a parting glance at me. Jackson, that smooth bastard, had taken a ballroom dance class as an undergrad. I watched him spin Darlene expertly across the floor, and goddamn, watching her dance...

Her dress whirled over legs that seemed to go on forever, and her body moved through complex steps effortlessly. She was better than Jackson, but they looked good together. Watching them, I suddenly felt ravenously hungry. I took a long pull of my cocktail.

It had been ages since I'd drunk anything—the vodka went straight to my head. I started to order another and drank Jackson's instead. By the time the second copper mug was drained, the room's muted light had taken on a pleasantly fuzzy glow, and I watched my best friend dance with Darlene with a small smile over my lips.

He met my eye several times, eyebrows raised to his hairline, and inclined his head at his dance partner as if to say, *What are you waiting for?*

I only grinned back. I was content now to wait. I'd been off my game, true, but I realized with Darlene I didn't need one.

The song ended and Jackson bent Darlene over his knee in a deep dip. Her back arched as if she had no bones, and when he hauled her up, her face was radiant.

A slow song began, "Cheek to Cheek" sung by Ella Fitzgerald, and I pushed myself off the bar, through the crowds.

"May I?" I asked, cutting in before Jackson could answer.

"It's about damn time," he muttered under his breath.

"You're going to need a new drink," I told him as he slipped away, and then I was holding Darlene.

I slipped an arm around her slender waist, and held her other against my chest. Her body radiated soft warmth through the silky material of her dress, and I imagined her lean muscles moving under my hands. Her face was flushed from the dancing, and her eyes were crystalline blue over her red lips.

"I wondered if you were ever going to come over here," she said.

"I don't dance," I said. The vodka had stripped my words down to the bare bones. "I liked watching you."

"Jackson is very good."

"You're better."

"Mmm, now I know what you were doing instead of dancing," she said with a small smile. "Are you having a good time?"

"I am now." I couldn't take my eyes off of her.

She held my gaze for a moment, then laid her head against my chest.

"I'm having a good time too," she said. "Maybe a better time than I should."

"I know."

"I'm supposed to be working on me."

"I know," I said again. "I can see my finish line from here. I should keep going but..."

"But what?" she asked against my heart.

"I don't want to kiss you drunk, but I want to kiss you."

Her breath caught and she raised her head to look at me, her lips parted. It took everything I had not to kiss her anyway, but it felt wrong; with vodka on my breath and my thoughts clouded and dizzy. I'd kissed a hundred women drunk or tipsy, but something stopped me with this woman.

She deserves more.

"You want to kiss me?" she asked.

I tilted her chin up with a loose fist, and my thumb brushed the skin just beneath her lower lip. My mouth was clumsy with the alcohol, but the booze had freed my emotions that I'd kept on lockdown, always, and I was helpless against her beauty to keep them in.

"I think about you," I said. "A lot."

"I think about you, too," she whispered, and I smelled the sweetness of Maraschino cherries on her breath. "And Olivia."

Instantly, my arms held her tighter at those words. "You do?"

She nodded. "And I know it's fast, but I feel like," she swallowed. "I don't know what I feel. Like I'm supposed to be getting myself together and not getting swept up in all the things I usually get swept up in. I keep saying I need to work on me, but I'm doing everything right and I still feel like something's missing." Her eyes were impossibly blue as they gazed up at mine. "Is it you?"

"I don't know," I said. *But maybe it could be.*

I held her and turned a slow circle, possibilities whispering in my ear.

"What do you want, Darlene?"

"I think I want you to kiss me, too. No, I know I do. More than anything, actually."

Hearing her say the words conjured something deep in me. Not sex or lust. What I wanted with her went beyond that. And deeper, somehow.

"But Sawyer, there's something I have to tell you."

"Anything."

"I wish it were that simple."

Her beautiful face morphed into anguish, and then the song ended. "In the Mood"—the quintessential swing song—came on and the crowd filled the floor in a mad rush.

The heat and depth between us vanished and it felt like I'd been thrust up from somewhere hot and dark, into bright, cold light.

Darlene was asked to dance by some other guy but she declined and walked with me back to the bar where Jackson was watching us, a new Moscow mule in his hand.

He opened his mouth to make a joke, but snapped it shut again.

"Are you having a good time?" he asked.

"I'm having a great time," Darlene said, not looking at me. "I'm so happy to have gotten out into the city."

"Glad to hear it," Jackson said, his gaze landing on mine. "I thought it was about overdue."

The three of us said goodbye to our friends and Darlene exchanged phone numbers with Penny. I hoped a friendship would come out of it.

Anything, if it makes Darlene happy.

Jackson, Darlene and I, took an Uber back to the Victorian. There, Darlene gave Jackson a peck on the cheek.

"Thank you so much. I had such a good time." Her glance landed on me then darted away. "It was a lovely night."

Then she hurried upstairs in a cloud of soft perfume and cherries.

Maybe it was the vodka, but a sense of certainty and peace settled over me.

Jackson was staring at me. "Well? What the hell happened?"

I smiled like an idiot but I wasn't trying to be smooth; I didn't have game, or moves, or an agenda anymore. I pulled my bewildered friend in for a sloppy hug.

"Thanks, man," I said.

"For what?"

"For tonight."

For her.

Chapter 14

Sawyer

Tuesday afternoon, in study group, I stared absently at the notebook in my lap. Andrew's voice droned in the background of my thoughts like a mosquito as he pestered Beth and Sanaa to quiz him. He monopolized the group, in a panic over the American Legal History final this week. Our last final, and, as with the others, I was confident I was going to pass. My eidetic memory had gotten my tired ass through so many late nights, not only would I graduate, but I'd do it with honors. But three days of grueling testing in Sacramento loomed ahead for the bar exam, and I was no closer to finding an angle for my brief to Judge Miller.

I can't get distracted now.

But I was. I tapped my pen on my knee, determined to focus, as visions of red lips and a cherry; a black dress and long legs; a heated body pressed to mine wafted into my thoughts like a delicious scent to a starving man.

I was hungry for Darlene, in every way.

Henrietta once told me that it was hard for a person to imagine a better life than the one he had; to really know and feel that it was possible. It was the reason, she said, so many people worked so hard just to stay where they were. They never reached out for what they really wanted because they believed what they wanted was out of reach. But it wasn't. Like words written on a mirror: *Objects may be closer than they appear.*

I still had so much work left to do, and even if I passed the bar and Judge Miller hired me, I'd have to work my ass off just as hard to keep that job, to keep providing for Olivia on my own. There would always be another finish line to cross. Was it stupid of me to not reach a little more for what I wanted? To imagine a life with something more than what I had?

My pen rattled against the denim on my knee.

The law that I had taken such refuge in for being black and white, was cold compared to Darlene's smile. The sanctuary I had found in the codes and sections was an empty place. She was life, and maybe, if I didn't screw it up, I had something to offer her too.

How about you start with a first date?

A slow smile spread over my lips. I shut my notebook with a snap, startling the others, and packed up my stuff.

"Where are you going?" Andrew demanded.

"Home."

"We're one final away from graduation."

I clapped him on the shoulder. "I have no doubt you will pass with adequate colors."

Andrew shook me off. "Asshole."

I grinned. "Ladies. It's been real."

Outside, I fished out my cell phone and called Serenity Spa. The snobby sounding woman at reception told me that Darlene had already left for the day.

"Early," she added with a sniff.

I had Darlene's phone number programmed into my photographic memory, but I didn't want to call or text her. I wanted to see her, to talk to her in person when I took the monumental, earth shattering, life changing step of actually asking a woman out on a date.

Jackson will shit his pants.

I laughed at myself, and called Elena. After asking about Olivia, I tried my best to sound casual as fuck. "Has Darlene come home by any chance?"

"She did," Elena said. "She dropped off more chocolate chip cookies for the kids on her way out. Such a sweet girl."

"Do you know where she was going?"

"No, but she looked dressed to practice her dance."

"Right. Okay, thanks, Elena. I'll be home on time tonight."

"No rush, querido. No rush at all."

Quickly, I recalled Darlene and my conversation at the park. She'd said she rehearsed at the American Dance Academy. I looked up the address on my phone for directions and headed to the Muni.

There was no one manning the front desk at the Academy, but a layout of the building on the wall guided me to the practice rooms. I headed down the pristine white hallway, passing open doors of ballet dancers at a barre, a jazz class for older couples. I expected to find Darlene with her dance troupe.

She was alone.

My breath caught. My heart stopped. Every part of me froze as I watched her from the doorway. She was wearing that damn black top with the crisscrossing straps along her back that made it hard for me to think. Her long legs were bare but for tight spandex short-shorts. Her dark hair spilled out of a high ponytail. A New Age-sounding instrumental played over the sound system, and Darlene folded and unfolded herself across the wooden floor in a series of flowing movements.

I was mesmerized, my eyes tracking her and when she stopped short, I flinched.

She tossed her head from side to side, as if her neck was stiff and rubbed one hand, then shook out her arms. She listened to some internal count in the music for a moment, then continued the dance.

Twenty seconds later, she stopped again, and she shook her arms, frustrated, and crossed to a small sound system against one wall. The music went quiet, and that was my cue; I'd lurked long enough.

"Hey," I said, stepping into the room.

She turned around and the surprised smile that flitted across her face was like a gift.

"What are you doing here?" she asked.

"I needed to talk to you," I said, "but I got side tracked watching you. Sorry, I don't mean to come off like a creepy stalker. You're really good, Darlene. Incredible, actually."

She shook her head, her cheeks turning pink as she walked to meet me in the center of the room. "It's not a good show," she said. "Or maybe it could be but..." She sighed and rubbed her fingers.

"What's going on here?" I asked, indicating her hands.

"God, it's my job at the spa," she said. "My supervisor told me turnover was high when I first started working there. Now I know why. My hands hurt all the time."

"You need a massage for yourself," I said. "Don't they give employees a discount?"

"They do, but I don't like being there," Darlene said. "No one is friendly. It's not my scene. And all of the employees are stressed out and sore. The last thing we want to do is give a discount massage to one of our own."

I reached out and took her hand in both of mine before I could talk myself out of it. Her hand was soft skin and delicate bone, and I gently rubbed circles into her palm with my thumbs.

"How is your show going?" I asked. "Has your partner learned to watch himself?"

"No," she said, with a small laugh. "He's a menace, as always, but I think I've learned to dance around him. Some added choreography. That's why I'm here, rehearsing alone. Safer that way." She glanced down at her hand in mine, then back to me. "That feels nice," she said softly.

I nodded, and let go of her hand to take the other one, gently massaging and squeezing the tension out.

"I had a really good time the other night," she said.

"You were an incredible dancer then, too," I said. "With Jackson."

"I wanted to dance with you."

"I'm no good."

"I'll bet that's not true."

I smiled, concentrating on her hand. If I looked up at her beautiful face this close to mine, I wouldn't do what I came here to do. "I'm pretty sure the only move I could pull off is the dip."

"A dip is easy," Darlene said. "All you have to do is be there for the woman. Hold her. Make sure she doesn't fall."

Slowly, I raised my eyes to meet hers. "I want to try."

Our gazes held for a moment, the air thick between us. Darlene moved close into my space, and my senses were overwhelmed by the heat of her body and the perfume of her skin; daisies tinged with the salt of her sweat.

Her mouth was inches from mine, as she ringed her arms around my neck. Her breasts pressed against my chest.

"Hold your right arm out at an angle," she said. Her breath was sweet against my cheek.

I did as she said and, effortlessly, she hooked her leg over so that my arm held her under the crook of her knee.

"Make a right angle out of your other arm," she said.

I did, creating a stiff-armed frame around her.

"You got me?" she asked.

"Yeah," I said, daring a glance at her eyes. "I got you."

A smile spread over her lips, and slowly, with precise yet fluid movements, she bent herself back over my arm, her hands reaching for the floor, while her leg, hooked on my other arm, anchored her. I watched her bend, watched her breasts strain against the black material of her shirt as she flowed backward like water. She stretched her other leg behind her in a split, and her reaching fingertips grazed her foot.

Instinctively, I bent my knee to dip her lower, keeping my arms stiff like scaffolding while she flowed and ebbed around me.

I held her securely for a long moment, then slowly straightened. She came up with me, graceful in my arms, our gazes locked. Her leg came down but her arms were still around my neck. Mine slipped around her waist.

"How was that?" I whispered my mouth inches from hers.

"Perfect," she said.

I watched her form the word. Her teeth grazed her lower lip over the 'f' and then I had to have her. Without thought or hesitation, I laid my mouth to hers.

She gave a little gasp and her lips parted for me. I deepened the kiss, while wondering how I'd lived twenty-four years without having kissed her before.

Kissing Darlene was kissing all of her. I tasted the sweetness of her, the energy she put into her art. Her breath suffused my mouth and I inhaled her.

This is life.

My tongue slid against hers, and the taste of her went straight to my head like a shot of whiskey. She moaned—not quietly—and I swallowed that, too.

Our gentle kissing turned harder and needier. I wanted to devour her, every breath, every touch…my hands skimmed down her back, to her ass, to fill my hands with her. Her fingers slid down my chest, then back up around my neck and into my hair, to pull me closer. Her leg hooked around my waist this time, and cinched tight, pressing herself against the erection that strained against my jeans. In every electric inch of her body, I felt how badly she wanted me too.

I kissed her until I was nearly biting her, and my fevered imagination wanted to know what it would be like to have her—this woman—in my bed, under me and naked. I wanted all of her skin on mine, and the soft little moans she was making now would turn to screams under my hands, my mouth, every part of me touching all of her.

"God, Darlene," I ground out between kisses. My hands tangled in her hair, to angle her head, to kiss her more. "I want you, right now."

She nodded against my lips. "Yes, me too. So much," she breathed.

Voices sounded in the hallway outside the open door, prying the moment apart. With effort, I broke from her but stayed close, feeling her breath on my lips that were wet with her kiss.

"We should stop," I said, striving to catch my breath. "This is not why I'm here. To hook up. I don't want to just hook up with you. I want you. Fucking hell, I've never wanted anyone more. But I want to take you out. A real date. It sounds insane, but I've never done that."

Her eyes were glassy and bright with desire. "Neither have I. Not at first, I mean. It always starts with this. But Sawyer—"

"I want you to have more," I said. I pulled away, and sucked in a breath. "Will you have dinner with me? Tonight, if you can. Or tomorrow?"

"I can't tomorrow," she said, and the brilliant light in her eyes sparked with something like fear. "But tonight is short notice. What about Olivia?"

"I'll take care of her," I said.

The urge to touch her again was like a hunger in my entire body. But if I did, we wouldn't make it out of this room.

"I'll make reservations," I said. "Someplace nice."

"Not too nice," she said quickly. "I don't want you to spend a lot of money on me."

"I do. I want to take you to a place nice enough where you can wear another dress like the one you wore on Saturday," I said. "Something that will make every man in the room seethe with jealousy."

Darlene's smile was tremulous. She opened her mouth to speak and I dared to take her face and kiss her again.

"Tonight. Seven o'clock? A real date. Okay?"

She nodded, and with supreme effort, I pulled myself away and went home, toward something more.

Chapter 15

Darlene

On the way home from the Dance Academy, I opened the contacts in my phone a hundred times to call Max. Each time, my thumb hovered over the call button, and each time I chickened out.

You know what he'll tell you to do. He'll say you have to tell Sawyer the truth.

I squeezed my eyes shut as the Muni train rumbled and swayed beneath me.

With every passing block, my resolve waxed and waned. Yes, Sawyer deserved the truth, and I started to call Max for moral support in that endeavor. The next instant, the thought that Sawyer would hate me filtered in, and I shoved the phone away.

Instead, I let my fingers touch my lips, where I could still feel Sawyer's kiss. Our first kiss. My heart crashed against my chest at the sense memory.

Sawyer's mouth on mine was exactly as I had imagined it and nothing I had ever prepared for. Soft and hard. Sweet and masculine. Demanding and generous at the same time. I wanted more of his kisses, his body holding mine tightly to him. I thought of how he looked at me…

He won't look at me the same way if I tell him.

By the time I'd arrived at the Victorian, my stomach was a knot of nerves, worry mixed with butterflies of excitement. I dashed up the two flights of stairs to my place, hoping the exertion would burn off the anxiety and I'd know what to do.

"Why do I have to tell him at all?" I asked my empty studio. "There's no reason! It's in the past and that's where it should stay."

I took a hot shower, scrubbing my skin with a loofah, as if I could scrub out the whispers of memory imbedded there; of nights spent on a jail cell cot, or on a hospital bed with an IV drip in my arm to flush out the heroin…

Even though the drugs were long gone, the shame they left behind hurt in so many ways.

I stepped out on a cloud of steam, wrapped myself in a towel, and grabbed the phone. Before I could stop myself, I jabbed Max's number.

"Hello, Max speaking."

"Hi, it's me."

"Hey, Me. What's up?"

"Sawyer kissed me," I blurted. "And we have a date tonight. I just thought…as my sponsor, you should know that."

A silence.

"Are you there?"

"I'm here," he said slowly. "Processing. Is there anything else you want to tell me?"

"Nope. That's it." I wrapped a lock of dripping hair around my finger. "He's taking me out to dinner. Oh, and we went dancing on Saturday night too. It was fun. No big deal."

See how well I'm handling this? I wanted to shout.

"Okay."

Max hadn't been able to get out of a shift on Monday night and had missed the NA meeting with me. I'd considered that lucky at the time, but now I wished he'd been there. I wished I'd talked.

I wish I could talk.

A small sob tore out of me, and the pretend bravado gusted out with it. I sank onto my little loveseat. "Fucking hell, Max, this sucks."

"I know," he said. "Tell me."

"I want to. I want to be honest. I do. That's why my stomach is in knots, isn't it? Sawyer isn't like any other man I've ever been with. I'm not just attracted to him, Max. I like him. A lot. In a different way than I've ever… *liked* a man. And his little girl…" Tears sprang to my eyes. "I like her, too. So much. And I want…"

"What, Dar?" Max asked gently. "What do you want?"

Everything.

"I don't know," I said. I wiped my eyes irritably. "I hate that no matter what I do, I'll always be *that girl*. The girl who was weak and sad. Who had this big yawning hole of *want* in her, and filled it up with terrible shit. And you know what? The drugs are gone but the *want* is still there, and the good things I want to fill it with are right in front of me but I'm scared to grab for them." My voice turned small and watery. "I'm scared, Max, that he'll hate me."

"If he's any kind of a good guy, he won't hate you, Dar. But you have to tell him. Not just so he lives with your truth, but so that you do too. That's fair to him and it's fair to you. You deserved to be loved as you are, Darlene. Not in bits and pieces."

I sniffed. "How come you're not telling me to cancel the date? To forget about all of this and stick to my year-long men boycott?"

"Unreasonable expectations..." he said gently. "Besides, telling you not to love is like depriving a flower of sunlight. You aren't meant to be contained, Darlene. It would be a crime against humanity. Just do it honestly, okay? And then tell me all about it. Then tell the *group* all about it at tomorrow night's meeting."

I nodded against the phone, my tears burning hotly down my cheek. "God, this is so hard." I huffed a sigh. "Can't I sleep with him first?"

Max laughed. "You're going to be fine, I promise. Okay?"

"Okay. I should go. I have to get ready for this dinner. What does one wear to tell a future criminal prosecutor that you're a former criminal?"

"Something with bold patterns. Maybe ruffles..."

I sniffed a laugh.

"Call me later, Dar."

"I will."

I hung up and stared at the phone. Then I got dressed for my first—and probably last—date with Sawyer Haas.

I chose ruffles after all. I put on a soft, prairie style blouse-dress in light beige with tiny pink and green flowers. It had puffy sleeves and a high collar, but barely skimmed the tops of my thighs. I paired it with white ankle boots, and piled my hair on my head in a loose, messy bun with tendrils falling down, to frame my face and show off my lucky gold hoop earrings.

I glanced at myself a final time in the mirror as the clock read seven.

"You can do this," I told my reflection and heaved a sigh. I plastered on a wide smile. "Hi, Sawyer! Guess what? I spent three months in jail for misdemeanor drug possession. I just wanted to do the responsible thing, and tell you that before you let me *babysit your daughter again*."

I covered my eyes with my hand.

"He's going to hate me."

The doorbell rang.

"Oh, God."

I sucked in deep breaths and smoothed my dress.

"Okay, here we go."

I mustered a pitiful amount of mental fortitude, and it all fled the exact second I opened the door.

Sweet Jesus, no fair. No fair at all.

I forgot how to breathe and my heart sent rushes of heated blood throughout my entire body. Sawyer was dressed up as he had been on Saturday night, only this time he was dressed up just for me. He wore a black jacket, white dress shirt—unbuttoned at the top—black slacks and a stylish leather belt with a sleek silver buckle around his slender waist. He looked casually elegant—like a Best Man at a wedding after the ceremony was over; where every bridesmaid was ready to drop her panties for a stolen moment with him in a closet during the reception.

"I…oh my God," I stammered, my eyes drinking him in. "You are…so hot."

I cringed at my clumsy words but Sawyer didn't seem to have heard.

"Darlene…" he said. "You're…" His words tapered to nothing as his gaze swept over me unabashedly.

"Take a picture, it'll last longer," I joked weakly.

"Oh, I did," he said, and gave his head a little shake. He withdrew a bouquet of three white roses from behind his back. "It's the best I could do on short notice."

"They're beautiful," I said.

"You're beautiful," he said. "You're stunningly beautiful, Darlene."

"Thank you, Sawyer," I said, and my cheeks warmed at the lovely compliment even as my anxiety deepened into a deep blue of sadness for how I was going to ruin the perfection of this night. "I'll just put them in some water."

He waited by the door as I scrounged for a vase. A tall drinking glass was all I could find. I put the flowers in it with shaking hands, and grabbed my black coat. Sawyer helped me into it.

"Where are we going?" I asked in a small voice, as we headed down the stairs.

"A restaurant called Nopa," he said, his own voice sounding thick. "Jackson said it's a good one."

At the bottom of the stairs, in the entry of the house, Sawyer's hand snaked out to grab mine. He pulled me close, and his hands slipped around my waist. I melted against him as he hauled me in for a deep kiss. His tongue slid against mine, then swept through my mouth. I clung to him, the clean taste of him, the scent of his masculine cologne, the softness of his lips, the intense want that coiled in his muscles under my hands...they all bombarded my senses and threatened to melt me into a puddle at his feet.

"The kiss is supposed to come at the end of the date, but I can't help myself," he said, his voice gruff, his eyes dark and so beautiful in the dim light.

"You don't have to stop," I whispered, kissing him again. "We don't have to go out. We can stay here. Go upstairs and..."

Not say a word.

"God, you have no idea how badly I want that." He kissed my neck, my cheek, just under my ear. He pinned me to the wall with his body and my hips adjusted to him on their own so that he fit so perfectly against me. His erection brushed me between my legs.

"Or maybe you have some idea..." he said hoarsely.

I pressed my body into his as his hand slid up my thigh, to the lacy thong I wore beneath the dress. One more moment, one more touch and he would take me upstairs, and it would be too late to tell him. I wouldn't have to. It would be so easy...

"Jesus," Sawyer whispered. He backed off so that the only place we touched was his forehead pressed to mine, and his hands on my hips, bracing himself. "Okay, wait," he said. "I want to take you out. I'm *going* to take you out." He grinned sheepishly. "Just give me a minute."

My heart ached at that grin, one that I don't think many people saw. He was so serious, so stressed, all the time. But with me he smiled and made jokes and let himself be a little bit vulnerable.

And once I told him what I'd done, it would all go away.

I took his handsome face in my hands. "Do you ever wish you could take a moment and keep it forever? Like right now...how you taste on my mouth, and your hands on me, and your eyes...God, Sawyer, the way you're looking at me... If I could have just one moment, one feeling, and live in it forever, I would choose this one."

Sawyer's brows came together, his smile tilting. "No one's ever said anything like that to me before." His hands came up to take mine. "But you look...sad. Is everything okay?"

The words came to my lips and I nearly let them out. I drew in a breath...and let that out instead.

"Yes, sure. Sorry, I don't know what came over me. I'm hungry, I guess. We can go. We should go."

Sawyer held the door for me, and I walked down to the street, wishing for San Francisco's allegedly famous cold wind to slap some sense into me. But the heat wave was lingering long enough that I hardly needed my coat.

"The restaurant isn't far," he said. "We could walk or Uber. Up to you."

"Let's walk," I said. Maybe, I thought, if I kept moving my body, I could work out the nerves and be able to talk. "So...where is Olivia tonight?"

"Jackson took her over to Henrietta's," Sawyer said. "Olivia knows her. Before I moved to the old Vic and was blessed with the miracle of Elena, Henrietta did all my babysitting."

"Have you lived in the Victorian long?"

"Almost a year now. When Olivia's mom left her with me, I had to move there."

"Why?

"Jackson and I, and some buddies of ours, had a killer place on Stanyon Street. Big parties every month. Not a place to raise a baby."

"No, I guess not," I said.

His expression took on a tint of faint wistfulness, as if he were talking about something he'd had that was gone forever.

"All of UC Hastings showed up at our parties. They all had costume themes, like Marvel heroes, favorite musicians, evil-doers. No costume, no admittance."

"Evil-doers?"

"Yeah, you had to dress as a villain. From anything; movies, comics, TV, books...It was awesome." He chuckled. "One time, a chick showed up dressed as Lizzie Borden and brought her own axe."

"A real axe?"

"We confiscated that pretty quickly. Axes and tequila do not mix." The wistful look came over his face again. "Yeah, those were fun times. Seems like a lifetime ago. *Olivia's* lifetime ago."

"Do you miss it?" I asked.

"Yeah, I do," he said. "But she's worth it. No more parties for me."

"Yeah, me too," I said, keeping my gaze firmly on the sidewalk sliding under my boots. "I used to party pretty hard."

There. That was the truth. Ish.

"Yeah?" Sawyer asked. "If I had an Evil-Doer party next weekend, who would you come as?"

A convict.

"I don't know," I said. "Catwoman, I think. Michelle Pfeiffer's version."

Sawyer's grin turned sly. "I wouldn't mind seeing you in that costume."

I managed a smile.

"She's not truly evil though," I said. "She's vulnerable too, which is why I like her. But I think it would be nice to maybe not care so much about everything all the time. It's not always easy being the good guy, especially when being good or nice is so often mistaken for being weak."

"What do you mean?"

I shook my head. "I'm nice at the spa, I'm nice with the dance troupe, but I can't seem to do anything right with either group."

Sawyer scowled. "Why not? Are they being assholes to you?"

"No, just...indifferent."

His scowl deepened. "I find it hard to believe that anyone could be indifferent where you're concerned."

His hand closed around mine, holding on to me just as tightly as

I held on to him, and maybe I was weak and cowardly, but it felt too good to let go.

The street around us had changed from rows of old houses to a bustling city. The restaurant, Nopa, was a squat building that looked somewhat plain on the outside, but I could tell even before I saw the menu on the outer wall that it was a 'nice place,' as my Grandma Bea would say. The kind where your food didn't come with a side of vegetables; you had to order them separately.

I turned to Sawyer.

"Hey, how about pizza and a walk along the Pier? And ice cream sundaes after?"

Sawyer's smile tilted again. "You don't like the menu...?"

"It looks amazing. But...I don't want you to spend a lot of money on me."

"The reservations are made," he said. "And I told you, I want to. I don't want to be cheap or...tacky. I want to take you out and have a nice dinner. I want to talk and then maybe take a walk somewhere, and kiss you goodnight at your door, and leave it at that." He brushed the backs of his fingers down my cheek. "You're not like any other girl, Darlene. I'm not...indifferent about you."

I swallowed and blinked hard. "You don't have to prove anything to me, Sawyer."

"Maybe not, but this is for me too. I've never been on a real date, remember?" His charming grin reappeared. "You going to deprive me of the experience?"

I managed a smile. "How could I do that?"

He held the door open for me. "After you."

The interior of Nopa was industrial chic, with cement floors and elegant booths in gray leather. Amber lights cast a golden hue over the crowds that talked and laughed over pork chops or roasted salmon.

A host ushered us to a table for two, and I sat across from Sawyer, a candle flickering between us. We opened our menus and my stomach dropped. The prices weren't outrageous but this was definitely a 'nice' restaurant. Even the beers were expensive and had eccentric names.

A waiter in a black apron approached us. "Something to drink?"

Sawyer looked to me. "Would you like wine?"

My gaze darted to the wine list and the double-digit—and triple digit—numbers beside the bottles.

"No, thank you," I said and smiled weakly. "Not a fan."

Sawyer smiled back. "A Coke with three cherries, maybe?"

"I'll just have water for now."

"I'll have a Death and Taxes Lager," Sawyer told the waiter. "I don't think I have a choice."

"Inevitable," the waiter agreed, and the two men chuckled at the joke.

Inevitable, I thought. *What a horrible word.*

It was inevitable that Sawyer would have to know about my past. If we continued seeing each other he'd have to know where I went three nights a week. If he needed me to babysit on a Monday, Wednesday or Friday, I couldn't do it, and he'd want to know why.

And then there's the whole 'being your honest self' thing. You might want to try that.

I looked over at Sawyer, devastating in black and white, and the inevitable felt impossible.

"God, you look…so handsome right now," I said.

"Thank you…"

"I'm not kidding. Your mouth…God. You have the most beautiful mouth."

Sawyer shook his head, laughing. "Okay, wow. Every time I think I'm used to how direct you are…"

"I'm not always direct. Not when it counts. But I'm very serious about your mouth. And when you kissed me…I've never been kissed like that before. I've never been smiled at by a man the way you're smiling at me now. It's almost too much."

Sawyer's smile froze on his face then wilted as tears filled my eyes.

"Darlene, what's wrong?"

"It *is* too much." I set my menu down. "This place. It's too nice. Too much for you to spend on me."

"It's not…"

"It is, because…" The words choked my throat. "It's not fair to you."

Sawyer frowned. "What are you talking about? I want to be here with you. I want to spend money on you and—"

I shook my head vigorously, my tears falling faster now. "No. No, you shouldn't. You work so hard and you take such good care of Livvie, and I'm just…I'm not what you think, and I'm sorry. This was a mistake. I'm so sorry, but I have to go. I have to…"

The waiter returned. "Are you ready to order?"

"No, I have to go."

I rose to my feet, and my chair scraped loudly. Diners at other tables were looking at us. The waiter's eyebrows rose.

"Darlene…" Sawyer leaned over the table. "What's going on?"

"I can't do this. It's not right and I just… *can't.*"

I grabbed for my purse on the back of the chair but the damn thing was snagged.

The nearby diners were snickering and murmuring now.

"No, no, it's not him," I said loudly. "It's not him. He's wonderful. He is…" I looked to Sawyer who was staring at me in a kind of mild shock. "You are, Sawyer. You're wonderful, and I'm so sorry."

I yanked my purse off, knocking my chair over, and stumbled out of the restaurant.

"Darlene, *wait.*"

Outside, I walked faster, my boots clopping on the cement, and then a hand closed around my arm.

"Darlene, come on." Sawyer pulled me to a stop and turned me to look at him. "You're scaring me. What just happened?"

"Nothing," I said, and that was so obviously a lie, I cringed at my own cowardice. "I can't tell you. I can't. Please…I need to go."

"No," he said, his dark eyes hardening. "You need to tell me what the hell is going on." His expression softened slightly. "Are you okay? Tell me."

"I…I can't…" I whispered. "I don't want to…"

Sawyer's jaw clenched and he looked away for a moment. "Is there…another guy?" he asked tightly.

I froze, the absurdity of it shocking me. "What? *No…*"

"Is it what's his name? Max?"

"No, nothing like that."

"Are you sure? You mentioned him a couple of times and he's always texting you…"

Sawyer bit off his words, and carved his hand through his hair.

"Dammit, Darlene, I don't want to be *that guy*. The jealous asshole. So I never asked about Max or where you go some nights. It wasn't my place, but then our moment in the dance studio happened, and now it feels like it *is* my place. I mean…I'm not saying you can't see other people. We haven't figured anything out. But I have to be honest, if you are seeing other people, it would fucking suck, okay? And I think you should tell me, so I know the score." He held his hands out, a hard, joyless smile playing over his lips. "So there. I guess I'm a jealous asshole after all."

The tears blurred my eyes so I almost couldn't see him. "You...you would be jealous if I were seeing someone else?"

"Jesus, do I have to say it again?" Sawyer gave an incredulous shake of his head. "What the hell, Darlene, just *tell me*."

"I'm scared," I whispered. "I'm scared that if I tell you what I need to tell you, you'll never look at me like you looked at me tonight." My lips trembled over a teary smile. "I just wanted that for a little bit longer, you know? That feeling…?"

Sawyer held my gaze a moment, and then swallowed hard. "Darlene," he said gruffly. "I haven't so much as touched a woman in almost a year. You're the first. Because I care about…I think about you…"

He clenched his teeth and carved his hand through his hair again.

"Fucking hell, I can't talk about what I feel. I don't. I never do. My life has been Olivia and law school and keeping my goddamn head above water. And that's it. And then you came along and now everything's different. It's better. It's *better,* Darlene, when I'd sort of given up on being happy."

"Oh, God, don't say that," I whispered. "Or no, I want you to. Part of me wants you to keep talking because it's incredible to me that I could…*be* that for someone. For you. But it makes this so much harder."

He looked to the ground and planted his hands on his hips, bracing himself. "Just tell me the truth. Are you seeing someone else?"

"No," I said. "I—"

A text came in on my phone, and I knew without looking it was Max. He'd gotten the news about his transfer. I froze and Sawyer's expression hardened to stone. The rare vulnerability in his eyes vanished. He was walling himself up, second by ticking second. Another chime came, and then my phone rang.

"It's him, isn't it?" Sawyer said.

"Yes. But he's not… I'm not dating him. I'm not dating anyone."

"Then who is he?"

"A friend, I promise. He's… not what you think."

Sawyer held up his hands as he walked backward a few steps. "I don't know what to think." My phone rang on and on. "You should get that," he said, then turned and strode away.

I watched him go, the words to call him back stuck in my throat. My phone went quiet, then started ringing again. I fished it out of my bag.

"Hi, Max," I said softly.

"Hey, Dar." He sounded breathless and exhilarated. "I'm calling you first. Before my other friends or anyone…I had to tell you. It doesn't feel real until I tell you."

"You got the job."

"I got the job. They say I might have to leave at any time. Whenever the paperwork is finalized and something about a contact in Seattle, but holy shit, I got it."

I sagged against Nopa's wall, my shoulders hunched against the world. "I'm so happy for you. I'm so happy and yet completely crushed at the same time."

"I know," he said. "I'm sorry and yet I have to thank you."

"Thank *me*? Why—?"

"Oh *shit*, wait. You're on your date with Sawyer the Lawyer, aren't you? Oh my God, I'm such an idiot. I got so excited and completely forgot everything else. Fuck, I'm so sorry…"

I shook my head. "It's okay. It's over now."

It's all over.

"What's wrong? What happened?"

"I can't tell him, Max," I whispered. "I can't. I try and the words stick. He'll look at me like everyone else in my family does, and I'll die a little inside." I huffed a breath, wiped my nose on the back of my hand. "He thinks you and I are dating."

"You *wish*," Max said, coaxing a small laugh out of me. His voice softened. "Dar, you have to tell him the truth. You know you do."

"I know," I said. "You're right. You were right about everything."

"Of course I was, but it's so hard to keep track. What else was I right about?"

"You know that emotional rock bottom you keep talking about?"

"Yeah."

"I'm standing at the edge of it, staring right down into it. Teetering," I said, my voice hardly a whisper. "It'll just take one push and…"

"And?"

"I'm going to fall in."

Chapter 16

Sawyer

I walked back to the Victorian alone, cursing myself for letting the whole night fall apart; the ruination of what had the makings of a perfect night was a bitter pill I couldn't swallow. I'd never let myself care about a woman before. My mother's death made caring too much seem like a dangerous proposition. I already lived with the constant fear Molly would show up any minute and try to fight me for Olivia. That kind of strain on my heart was already too much, but Darlene...

"Fuck," I muttered.

She'd gotten past every one of my usual defenses so now the mere idea of her with another man felt like a goddamn knife in my chest.

She was upset and you walked away.

Like an instinct, the steely cage around my heart was resurrecting itself, reforming minute by minute. I'd been stupidly optimistic, I told myself. Taken my eye off the prize and got knocked on my ass for it.

Henrietta had planned to keep Olivia all night, but I went and got her, muttering some excuse about Darlene being under the weather and having to cancel.

I took my daughter home, fed her dinner, and put her to bed.

"Just you and me," I told her, brushing the brown curls from her eyes as she drifted to sleep. "I'm going to take care of you, Livvie.

We're almost at the finish line, aren't we?"

I put on sleep pants and a T-shirt, and sat at my desk, my study materials arrayed in front of me. I had one last final, Judge Miller's assignment, and the damn bar exam. I didn't need any more distractions.

I tried to focus on my studies, but my stupid heart felt bruised, and when I heard her footsteps on the stairs going up, I fought the urge to bolt out of my chair and confront Darlene. Or comfort her. I didn't know which.

I did neither.

"Fuck me," I muttered.

I opened my laptop to the document I'd begun for Judge Miller's assignment when writing by hand wasn't working. Typing didn't work either.

He wanted life. The brightest burst of life I knew was right above me, and I was down here, afraid of how much I wanted to be with her, knowing all too well how the things—and people—we care about most can vanish right before our eyes.

I went to bed and tossed all night.

The next morning, I dragged myself through the motions of getting Olivia and myself ready for the day.

"Everything all right, querido?" Elena asked when I dropped Livvie off.

"Fine," I said. I kissed my daughter. "Be good. I love you."

"Wuv, Daddy," Olivia said. From Elena's arms she pressed her palm to her mouth and then flung her arm spastically to blow me a kiss.

My stung as I turned to go.

She's the most important thing in the world. Focus on her.

The idea of having more happiness than that would have to wait.

I stepped outside the front of the Victorian and started down the stairs. A silver sedan was parked at the curb in front. Before I took one step, the door opened and a man looking to be in his early fifties stepped out. He straightened his pale blue, seersucker suit jacket. He looked like he just stepped off a yacht.

"Sawyer Haas?"

I froze. "Yes."

"A moment."

The man opened the back door of the sedan and an older couple, both looking to be in their mid-sixties stepped out. The man wore khaki pants and a white button-down shirt, the woman in a lavender dress. The June sunshine glinted off his gold Rolex and sparkled in diamond studs in her ears. They stood hand in hand on the sidewalk, nervous smiles on their faces.

"Hello," the man said. "My name is Gerald Abbott and this is my wife, Alice. We're Molly's parents."

The blood drained from my face.

Molly's parents. Molly. She's here. She's back and now—

"This is our attorney, Mr. Holloway," the woman, Alice said, indicating the man in the suit.

"Mr. Haas." Mr. Holloway extended his hand to me.

They stood at the bottom of the three stairs, me at the top. I stared back without taking it.

"What do you want?"

Gerald and Alice exchanged grief-stricken looks, a shared pain that only they knew. They couldn't speak, so their attorney spoke for them.

"Molly has unfortunately passed way," Holloway said.

I went cold all over while breaking into a sweat at the same time, as my body tried to process the thousand conflicting emotions that shot through me at those words.

"She's...dead?"

He nodded. "Yes."

Alice slipped her hand into Gerald's and they exchanged a pained look that was brief but went miles deep.

"What happened?"

"Car accident."

"When?" I choked out.

"Six months ago."

My eyes darted between Gerald and Alice Abbott, and I felt like I couldn't move; *shouldn't* move, from the front stoop of the house. I had to guard it. Because Olivia was inside and they were here.

"We're here," Holloway said, each word like a knife in my chest, "to talk about the custody arrangements for Molly's daughter— my clients' *granddaughter*—Olivia Abbott."

Chapter 17

Sawyer

Jackson hung up the phone and tossed it on the coffee table. "Not the best news. The officer said since Molly is an adult and left of her own free will, she's not technically 'missing.'"

I looked up from the baby in my arms taking a bottle Molly had left in the gigantic diaper bag. "She abandoned Olivia," I said. "That has to be illegal. You've finished the Family Law section. Tell me. They'll track her down for child abandonment, right?"

Jackson rubbed his chin. "Safe Haven laws protect her. She can't be arrested. If she leaves the baby with a parent—you—it's considered legal abandonment after six months. If she leaves her with a non-parent—maybe also you—it's one year."

"I can't do this alone."

"You might not have to do it at all," Jackson said, his Mac open on his lap. "They sell paternity tests at the Walgreens. It's non-legal for any official capacity, but accurate. You'll at least know if Molly was telling the truth. And if she was lying, you take the baby to CPS and go back to your life."

I glanced down at Olivia. Go back to my life, *I thought.* Like nothing happened. *I swallowed the sudden lump in my throat.*

"How long does the test take?"

"Three days from the time you mail it to the lab," Jackson said. "Simple enough."

"The test won't hurt her, right?" I asked. "If I have to draw her blood or prick her finger, forget it."

"Nah, man, cotton swab to the cheek."

I nodded. The baby stirred, made a little sound as she ate. I settled her better in my arms. Around me—us—the detritus of the party lay scattered across the coffee table and on the floor. Olivia's bottle from this morning stood next to an empty pilsner.

I was still in my Man in Black costume. I'd had to sleep with Olivia on my chest, propped on my bed and surrounded by pillows, paranoid she'd roll out of my arms, and woke up every time she moved. I had no place to put her down.

I didn't want to put her down.

Jackson shut his laptop. "I'll go get the test. There's no point in panicking until we know for sure what the deal is."

"Three days until results?" I said. "What the hell do I do in the meanwhile? I have nothing."

"We'll take her to my mom," Jackson said with a grin. "Henrietta will set you up." He clapped a hand on my shoulder. "Everything's going to be okay."

I stared at the people in front of my house.

Everything's going to be okay.

Except at that precise moment, the words felt laughably weak. I tightened my grip on my briefcase.

"Mr. Haas," the lawyer, Holloway, said. "We'd like to have a sit-down with you. The four of us."

My gaze darted to the Abbotts, who were watching me with a strange mixture of sadness, fear and hope in their eyes and painted over their features.

"I have a final this morning," I said. "My last final for law school. It's kind of important."

The Abbotts stiffened at my sarcasm. Holloway was unperturbed. "Perhaps, after?"

"After, I have a meeting with my advisor to sign off on my graduation requirements. My schedule is full."

"Please," Alice said. "We only need a little time. An hour?" Her glance darted to the house behind me. "Is she there? We'd like to see her…"

"Not going to happen," I said, making her flinch, and despite my bone-numbing fear, I felt a little sorry for her.

Fuck that, they want to take her away from me.

I straightened my shoulders. "How do I even know you're who you say you are?"

Gerald reached into pocket for his wallet to show ID, while Alice pulled a small stack of photos from her purse.

"Mr. Holloway said to bring these. Here's Molly as a little girl, and one as a teenager." Her voice thickened with tears. "Here she is at her Sweet Sixteen birthday party…"

She held the photos to me while Gerald flashed his driver's license. I barely glanced at them and I didn't move any closer. They exchanged troubled looks again, their arms slowly lowering. Holloway cleared his throat.

"We need to sit down, Mr. Haas. Today. I advised the Abbotts to limit all contact with you for the hearing before the court, but they insist on speaking to you first."

A hearing. There's going to be a hearing…

My heart dropped to my stomach, but outwardly my armor was on, my face impassive. "Three o'clock," I said stiffly. "At the Starbucks on Market and 8th. One hour. I'll be bringing my attorney."

I said all this as if I were calling the shots, while inside I felt like I was disintegrating.

"Very good," Holloway said. He opened the back of the sedan, and indicated for the Abbotts to get in.

They did so, reluctantly, both of them looking like they wanted to say more. Both of them giving the Victorian a final, longing glance. After his wife was in the car, Gerald Abbott fixed me with a stern look.

"Good luck with your test," he said, then climbed in.

I watched the sedan drive away. The instant it rounded the corner, out of sight, I sank to the steps, my briefcase scraping along the cement beside me as I dropped it to cover my face with my hands. I sucked in deep breaths, grasping for calm when panic was tossing me like a tiny ship on a vast ocean.

Holy fuck, it's happening. And I was so close. A few more weeks…

Defeat tried to drown me, but I shrugged it off. I had rights. If the Abbotts were here for a fight, I'd give it to them. I'd give everything until there was nothing left of me.

Livvie…

I fished my phone out of my jacket pocket. "Jackson," I said, my voice hoarse. "I need you."

I'd never been more grateful for my eidetic memory in my life. The American Legal History exam was all names and dates, statutes and by-laws, ground-breaking precedents and Founding Fathers. I scanned my mental database for the answers, and finished the exam in record time.

At the meeting in my advisor's office, she asked me twice if I needed a glass of water and once if I wanted to reschedule when I was 'feeling better.' I pushed through, pushed my emotions aside where they sunk their claws in my back and shoulders. Under the conference table, my leg wouldn't stop bouncing.

The day crawled and yet flew by, and at a quarter to three, I met Jackson at the Starbucks.

"Jesus, will you calm down?" he said while waiting in line to order. "I'm getting an ulcer just looking at you."

"I have a bad feeling about this," I said. "A fucking horrible feeling. I have *rights*," I spat. "They can't just take her from me…"

"Whoa, whoa, slow down," Jackson said. "We have no idea what they want yet."

"They want a hearing, Jax," I said, glancing over my shoulder at the front entrance. "It's already set up."

"We'll see," he said.

"Do you know what you're doing? It's a far cry from tax law…"

Jackson fixed me with a raised-eyebrow stare. "You have the money to retain someone else? 'Cause if you do, I'll give you my phone to call him right now. I'm taking time out of my work to be here."

"I'm sorry," I said, sucking in a breath. I clasped his hand. "God, I'm sorry, man, really. I trust you. I'm just scared shitless."

"I know you are. Go ahead and be an asshole to me if it helps, but as your attorney, I'm officially advising you to *not* be an asshole to these people, okay? They're Olivia's family, for one thing. For another, you catch more bees with honey, or some shit."

I nodded absently. My mind was reeling, going in a thousand different directions. One thought stuck out from the rest, in bold type.

Molly is dead.

I'd spent the last ten months praying she wouldn't come back to try to take Olivia from me. She'd obviously been a mess the night she gave her to me; drunk and disheveled, and looking as though she lived out of her car. Maybe that wasn't the real her, or she'd had a bad night, but that was the mental snapshot she'd left me of her as a mother.

But she *had* been Olivia's mother, and in the back of my mind, I'd always assumed she'd be in our daughter's life somehow. Now that was over. I would never have to explain to Olivia that her mother had left her. Instead, I would have to tell her she died.

She has no mother, either.

A deep pain for my little girl that I added to the noxious concoction of emotions swirling in my guts.

It was my turn to order. "I'll take a tall coffee."

"*Decaf,*" Jackson told the barista, and shot me a wink. His reassuring smile faded as he looked over his shoulder. "This must be them."

I looked to the front where the Abbotts were coming in, Holloway holding the door for open.

"That's them," I said.

"They look like money," Jackson said.

The knot of fear twisted tighter. The Abbotts had money. Enough to fight me. Enough to tell a judge they had the means to provide Olivia with a life I couldn't afford.

Jackson sighed and elbowed me in the arm. "Hey. You're jumping to conclusions in that big brain of yours. Cut it out. Nothing's happened yet."

"*Yet.*"

We took our coffees to a table in the corner that was big enough for five and waited for the Abbotts to join us. My leg bounced under that table too.

"Mr. Haas," Holloway said, extended his hand.

This time I shook it, and gave the Abbotts a small nod in greeting.

"This is Jackson Smith, my attorney," I said.

Jackson offered his hand and a bright smile. Introductions were made all around and then the five of us sat with drinks in front of us that only the attorneys touched. The Abbotts studied me with that same mix of hope and fear in their eyes. They had nice faces. Kind. They weren't monsters, but a grandma and a grandpa. *Olivia's* grandma and grandpa.

I tried to loosen my clenched-jaw and unfurrow my brow to look less like an asshole next to Jackson's friendly smile.

"I'll get straight to the point," Holloway said. "Mr. and Mrs. Abbott were only recently made aware of their daughter's passing six weeks ago."

"She'd always been on the run," Alice said in a shaky voice. "We tried to give her everything but it wasn't enough."

Gerald covered his wife's hand. "We hadn't seen her in so long. We had no idea she'd been in an accident. Nor did we know that she'd had a baby."

"We knew nothing," Alice said. "So much joy and sadness all at once…"

Jackson nodded sympathetically. "And when, exactly, were you made aware that you had a granddaughter?"

"Two weeks ago," Holloway answered. "Through a friend of the late Miss Abbott's."

Alice sat straighter, imploring me with her eyes as she spoke. "As soon as we knew, we wanted to see Olivia. To be a part of her life."

"In what capacity?" Jackson asked. He looked to Holloway. "What's this I hear about a hearing?"

Holloway folded his hands on the table, his gold watch glinting in the sun in tandem with his gold pinky ring.

"The friend of Molly's informed us that Olivia's birth certificate is most likely in your possession. Is that true, Mr. Haas?"

My heart did a slow roll in my chest. I nodded.

"And is your name listed as the father?"

"No, it is not," I said slowly. "There is no name there. It's blank."

Holloway nodded. "I presume you have taken a paternity test?"

I glanced at Jackson. He nodded his head. Once.

"Yes. A few days after Molly left Olivia with me. She's my daughter. And I'm not saying another word until you tell me what you want."

Holloway opened his mouth to speak, but Alice put her hand on his arm.

"Wait, please. This is not going at all as I'd hoped. Perhaps it was a mistake to bring our attorneys into this so quickly." She looked to me. "Can we see her? We'd like to see her." Her voiced teetered on the edge of breaking. "Our daughter is gone. Our only daughter. All we have left of her is Olivia. We'd like to spend some time with her and maybe…get to know each other better. And you, but in a warmer setting."

She looked to Jackson when my hard stare shut her out. "Is this possible?"

"Let me confer with my client."

Jackson ushered me onto the sidewalk outside.

"You're not making a great impression."

I gritted my teeth. "Jackson…"

"I know. We'll deal with *that* later. For now, let them see Olivia. Do what she said; get to know them. They don't seem like bad people." He cocked his head. "Don't you want a family for Olivia?"

"Yeah, I do, but on *my* terms," I said. I took my friend's arm and gripped it tight. "She stays with me, Jax. You do whatever you feel is right. If they want to come see her, fine. But I want full custody. I'm *keeping* full custody. They can visit, they can have a weekend, maybe a week in the summer, but they're *not taking her from me.*"

Jackson's expression showed no trace of his usual cheerful self. He gripped my shoulder and met my eyes with an unwavering, intense stare.

"I'll do my best, Sawyer, but it might not be up to us," he said. "And you know it."

The Abbotts took the sedan, and Jackson and I took an Uber back to the Victorian. Four o'clock on a Wednesday. Where was Darlene, I wondered as I climbed out of the car. Rehearsal? I would've given my right arm to see her smile just then. Her smile that made all the bad shit in the world seem far away.

But I fucked up. The thought of her with someone else hurt more than I was prepared for. Instead of talking to her, I renamed that pain *jealousy*, and shut down. Walked away.

Maybe I've lost her too.

I gave myself a shake.

Get a grip, you haven't lost Olivia. This isn't over. It hasn't even started.

But unlocking the front door of the Vic for the Abbotts and their lawyer felt like inviting the dragon straight into the damn castle.

"This is quite a lovely old house," Alice said in the entry. "I just love San Francisco architecture."

"Are you not from this area?" Jackson asked.

"Huntington Beach, in southern California."

The night Molly and I hooked up in Vegas whispered in my memory; Molly in a pale dress in the dimly lit bar. *I'm from So Cal, originally. My folks are still there in their huge, white bread mega mansion...*

"Jackson can take you to my place," I said, my voice wooden in my ears. "I'll get Olivia from her sitter and bring her up."

I waited until they were upstairs, then knocked on Elena's door.

"You're early today," she said with a smile. It faded at once. "But you're so pale, my dear. Is everything okay?"

Everything is going to be okay...

I nodded. "I got finished early."

Elena's mouth turned down in concern. "Come in. I'll just get her bag."

I stepped inside Elena's place. Olivia was on the floor in the living room with Laura, Elena's two-year-old, playing blocks. Olivia looked up and her little face broke into a smile.

"Daddy!"

Oh Christ...

My chest constricted and goddamn tears stung my eyes. With trembling arms, I picked her up and held her tightly, my hand behind her little head. Her arms went around my neck. I closed my eyes and fought to contain the maelstrom of emotions, to push them down, lock them up. If there was a battle to be fought, I needed to be strong.

Elena's hand on my arm and her voice gentle. "Sawyer."

I sucked in deep breaths, still holding Olivia tight to me. When my exhales were no longer shaky and I opened my eyes.

"Thanks for watching her," I said, shouldering the bag Elena handed me. "I'll see you tomorrow."

"Bye-bye," Olivia said to Elena. "Bye bye bye bye…"

I took Olivia upstairs on leaden legs.

In my place, the Abbotts were seated at the small kitchen table with Jackson, glasses of water before them. Mr. Holloway was standing with his hands clasped behind his back in front of the wall near my desk, eyeing my degree from UCSF with Honors; my Valedictorian certificate; my award for a full scholarship at Hastings that had been like winning the lottery.

He turned and all conversations ceased as I stepped inside and set my daughter down at my feet.

"This is Olivia."

Alice's hand flew to her heart, and Gerald's jaw clenched as if fighting back some strong emotion.

"Oh my heavens, she's beautiful." Alice rose slowly and approached Olivia who stood clinging to my pant leg. "Hi, sweetheart. I'm your Grandma Alice."

"Hey, there, angel," Gerald said gruffly, joining his wife. "I'm your Grandpa Gerry."

My own jaw tightened. *I want this for her.* I felt like I was in a dream and I didn't know if it was going to turn out to be everything I wanted or a nightmare.

Olivia pressed herself closer to my pants.

"She likes blocks," I said, indicating the pile on the floor. "Can't get enough of them."

Alice clapped her hands on her thighs. "Would you like to show us your blocks, Olivia?"

Alice and Gerald sat down on the floor with no aching or complaining about joints or bad knees. They were fit, strong, good people, with a lot of money, and their DNA in Olivia's veins. My little girl babbled in a baby talk/English hybrid, and plopped down beside them.

I moved to the kitchen for a glass of water and Jackson joined me.

"Not so bad, right?" he said in a low voice.

I poured a tall glass with a shaking hand. "I'm going to puke."

Jackson chuckled. "Be cool. I have a good feeling about this."

Jackson and I joined the others in the living room, sitting on my small couch while Holloway took the chair. The Abbotts stayed on the floor with Livvie, playing and chatting and making her smile.

"She looks just like Molly, doesn't she?" Alice said, and her smile wavered. I reached for the tissue box beside me and handed it over. "I'm sorry," she said, dabbing her eyes. "It's still so new, losing her."

"What happened?" I asked in a low voice.

Alice smiled sadly.

"Molly was always the rebellious girl but when she turned eighteen, she began to drink pretty heavily. It was like she'd been stricken with a disease. That's what they say it is, don't they? A disease."

I shifted in my seat, blue and red lights dancing across my vision.

"She had a happy childhood, or so we thought," Gerald said.

Alice smiled weakly. She handed Olivia a block and Olivia stacked it on top of another. "Did she mention us at all?"

I shook my head slowly. "I did not know Molly very well."

She and Gerald nodded in silent understanding.

"We did our best," Gerald said, "but whatever was driving her away from us got worse. She called and texted us occasionally, but we didn't see her for two years. She never said anything about a baby or even being pregnant."

"A friend of hers got in touch with us," Alice said. "She told us about Olivia and gave us your name. I guess Molly had told her about you."

My cold silence created another look between them, and then Gerald continued.

"We're renting a condo by the Marina. We've talked about retiring to the Bay Area."

"We've always loved San Francisco," Alice said, "and when we found out you were here it seems like the right thing to do."

I swallowed hard. "What was the right thing to do?" My voice sounded cold and hard but I couldn't help it. The fear had tightened me up inside so I could hardly breathe.

"To be a part of Olivia's life. An important part."

There was pity in Alice's eyes, which scared me more than anything else.

"We want to make sure she's provided for," Gerald said. "And ensure she has everything she needs for a happy and healthy life."

"Well, she does," I snapped. "I'm giving her that."

Jackson put a hand on my arm. I fought for calm, and tried to see these people as something other than the enemy. "I'm sorry, but I've been raising Olivia on my own for the last ten months and I'd begun to believe it was always going to be just her and me."

"But it's not," Gerald said, in a low voice. He stood up and put his hands in his pocket and looked at Holloway. "We have rights. And some information…"

My gaze jumped to Holloway who was making a negating motion with his hand.

"What kind of information?" Jackson asked.

Holloway reached into his jacket and pulled out an envelope. Now we were all on our feet but Alice who clapped hands with Olivia, tears in her eyes.

The Abbotts attorney handed Jackson the envelope. "Now, I really must insist we depart," he said to his clients. "Everything will be elucidated at the Family Court in two days' time."

Gerald helped Alice to her feet.

"Bye-bye, sweetheart," Alice said to Olivia. "We'll see you again."

"Bye-bye," Olivia said and babbled in a sing-song voice. "Bye-bye-bye-bye…"

"She's darling," Alice said to me, and that pitying look was there again. She opened her mouth to say something more, and her husband gently took her by the shoulders and guided her toward the door.

I shut it after them while Jackson opened the envelope.

"What is it?" I asked. I could hardly hear my own words for the blood rushing in my ears.

"A hearing notice. For Friday." He raised his eyes to mine. "They've filed an Order to Show Cause for custody of Olivia."

"Based on what?" I asked. "What cause?"

But of course, I already knew. The Abbotts had plenty of cause and if they didn't know it yet, soon they would.

I turned the letter over and over in my hand, the Sensaya Genetic Lab address disappearing then reappearing with every rotation. Beside me, Olivia slept in the middle of my bed. I had barricaded the three-month-old in a ring of pillows to keep her safe but I was still paranoid she'd roll off. I sat beside her, watched her sleep. Watched the shallow rise and fall of her chest, and her rapid pulse beat in her neck.

Was it my blood that flowed in her veins?

Slowly, so as not to wake her, I tore the envelope open. Inside were the test results that would tell me probabilities. The probability that my life would change forever, or that I would turn this baby over to the proper authorities and my life would continue on, as planned. But a whisper in the back of my mind told me my life was already changed— probability 100%—no matter what the test said.

I unfolded the paper with shaking hands, and scanned the columns of numbers; they meant nothing to me. It was the conclusion at the end that mattered.

DNA Test Report

For Personal Knowledge Only

Case 8197346		CHILD		Alleged FATHER	
Name		**Olivia A**		**Sawyer Haas**	
Test No.		8197346-20		8197346-30	
Locus	PI	Allele Sizes		Allele Sizes	
D3S1358	1.91	16		15	16
vWA	0.00	18		16	17
D16S539	3.86	10	11	10	11
CSF1PO	0.00	10		12	
TPOX	0.96	8	11	9	11
D8S1179	0.00	11	12	13	15
D21S11	0.00	28	29	30	32.2
D18S51	0.00	14	18	12	20
D2S441	1.02	12	14	14	15
D19S433	0.00	12	14	13	16.2
TH01	0.97	8	9.3	8	9.3
FGA	2.67	19	25	22	25
D22S1045	0.70	15	16	12	15
D5S818	1.43	12		10	12
D13S317	0.00	11		10	12
D7S820	0.91	10	12	9	10
SE33	0.00	20	22.2	13	17
D10S1248	0.00	15	16	14	
D1S1656	0.00	12	17.3	16	16.3
D2S1338	0.00	21		17	23
Amelogenin					

Interpretation: RN: 1248396

Combined Paternity Index: **0**   Probability of Paternity **0%**

0% probability.

A burden had just been lifted. Eighteen years and more. My life could carry on as it had. On track. Law school, clerkship, federal prosecutor, District Attorney...

I waited for the relief to hit me.

It never did.

I shook myself from the memory. It felt like a bad dream that had been on hold for ten months, and now was picking up where it left off.

Jackson was shaking his head, and his gaze dropped to Olivia. Mine followed. To my little girl, because why did I need a piece of paper to tell me what I felt in my heart? In my goddamn soul?

Olivia looked up at me from her pile of blocks on the floor and smiled. "Bye-bye!"

Forever (adv.): for all future time

Now (adv.): at present time

Chapter 18

Darlene

I wiped a rivulet of sweat off my brow, and then planted my hands on my hips to catch my breath. Ryan, my partner, was bellowing beside me, and I fought a wave of irritation. He had mistimed three cues during the run-through—nearly head-butting me, *again*—and with the show a week away, his clumsiness wasn't just annoying, it was going to make the rest of us look bad.

We already look bad.

I hated to even think it, but the show completely lacked inspiration and in my humble opinion, Anne-Marie, the lead dancer, was wooden and mechanical. Worse, she was the kind of person who thought she no longer had anything left to learn in dance, or life in general. The kind of person who began almost every sentence with "I know."

Greg and Paula had watched from foldout chairs at the head of the practice room at the Dance Academy. They shifted in their seats like they were sitting on splinters. There should have been a palpable air of excitement this close to opening night. Instead, the six of us dancers were like humming electrical posts, filling the room with nervous tension.

The director and stage manager put their heads together for a moment. Anne-Marie tossed her blonde ponytail over her shoulder.

"Well?" she demanded. "Are you going to give us notes, or

what?"

Greg and Paula murmured and nodded, having come to some sort of agreement.

"It's...good," the director said. "It's coming together well. But it's short, even for a showcase."

"We timed it at twenty-seven minutes," Paula said. "Thirty would be better."

"We need one more act to fill out the time," Greg said. "Darlene."

My head shot up. "What?"

"We'd like you to perform your audition piece. As a solo."

My glance immediately shot to Anne-Marie who audibly gasped.

"We're a week out," she said. "You can't just change the whole show."

"We're not changing the whole show," Greg said. "We need one more act. A time filler, really."

Oh, is that what I am? I wanted to say. Truthfully, between the menace that was my partner, and the cold shoulders from the rest of the troupe, the words *I quit,* were teetering from my lips. But I was trying to be professional and not quit something just because it wasn't what I'd hoped. And I wasn't about to leave them in a lurch so close to opening night.

"Darlene?" Greg asked. "Can you?"

"Umm," I glanced at Anne-Marie who was glaring poison-tipped daggers at me. "Are you sure?"

"We'll put it between *Entendre* and *Autumn Leaves.*"

"Okay, I guess I could do that."

"This is ridiculous," Anne-Marie said. "Who cares if we're three minutes short?"

Greg pretended not to have heard her. "Take your positions for the finale of *Entendre,* and then Darlene—"

"Rehearsal is over," Anne-Marie said. "I have somewhere else to be."

She flounced to the wall to grab her stuff and headed out. The other dancers shuffled their feet until Greg dismissed them too.

"Right, time's up. We'll have the music cues set up for tomorrow's rehearsal then," Greg said stiffly, trying to hold on to his authority. "Will you be ready?" he asked me, and I saw the spark of nerves dancing behind his eyes.

"Sure, no problem," I said. "I'll just stay here for a little bit and put in some extra time."

And try to turn my improv into a routine.

Greg eased a sigh. "Good. That's fine then."

He left and Paula sidled up to me. "Anne-Marie *really* wanted to be the only soloist."

"I noticed."

"Thank you for stepping up."

I smiled. "Doesn't suck to have a solo on a résumé."

"Yeah, well, we need it. The show needs it. A spark. Having just watched the whole run-through." She bit off her words with a sigh. "Anyway, thanks."

"No problem."

After everyone had gone, I stood in the center of the room, and stared at the girl in the wall of mirrors.

"Persistence," I murmured.

I didn't quit, and I got a solo out of it.

If I told Sawyer the truth.

What would I get out of that? I wondered. Recriminations or acceptance?

I hit 'play' on my music app and Marian Hill asked her question. But I couldn't answer. I wasn't down or up. I was in limbo, unable to move. My body suddenly stiffened by all the words I needed to say, and I began to see why I'd quit dancing when the drugs started; when I'd begun to lie to my family and friends about what I was doing and where I was going. Dancing was my honest self. My body speaking the truth of the music, and I couldn't *be* that while stuffed with lies.

I was probably just as stiff and mechanical in the run-through as Anne-Marie.

I took the Muni home, showered, made dinner. Always doing something, never letting myself stop and think. While doing the dinner dishes, a text came in on my phone from Max.

Well?

I bit my lip and typed, **Not yet.**

When?

Tonight. After his daughter goes to bed.

Shit. There it was, in black and white.

There was a short pause and then Max wrote back, **"Don't ever regret being honest. Period."** –Taylor Swift

I laughed, and it was like a sigh of relief.

You can't argue with T-Swift, I typed.

No you cannot. Max wrote back. **Call me any time if you need to.**

I smiled at my friend, who was going to move to Seattle any minute and leave me alone. **I will. <3 you**

Love you, D.

I held the phone to my chest. It wasn't a hug, but it was the next best thing.

At eleven-thirty, dressed in soft shorts and a white T-shirt, I headed down to Sawyer's. I was going to bring some food for him and Livvie, but changed my mind. I wanted no pretense; there was no other reason for me being there than to tell him the truth.

My pulse was jittery as I tapped lightly on his door. It opened after an agonizing thirty seconds in which I almost ran away. Twice.

Sawyer was there in what I called his jammies—V-necked T-shirt and plaid flannel pants—though it didn't look as if he'd done any sleeping in them. Dark circles ringed his eyes that were bloodshot. For a split second, the dark pools of them lit up to see me, then faded again.

"Hey," he said.

"Hey. Is this a bad time?"

"You can come in." He shoved the door open and then turned his back to walk inside. "You want anything? Something to drink?"

"No, I'm fine." I shut the door behind me. "I came here to tell you what I should have told you the other night." I heaved a calming breath and started with the easy part. "I'm not seeing anyone else, I promise. Max is only a friend."

"Okay," he said. Sawyer moved slowly to his desk. He slumped in the chair, and covered his eyes with his hand.

Is he this torn up about our failed date?

A selfish part of me would like to think he cared that much about me, but no, it had to be something big, like he failed a final or that judge picked someone else for the clerkship he needed. It suddenly seemed horribly out of place to talk about myself when he was so obviously upset.

Not just upset. Devastated.

My fear for myself reshaped itself into fear for him.

"Sawyer, are you okay?" I moved to stand on the other side of his desk. "What happened?"

Sawyer dropped his hand from his eyes like it was too heavy, then reached over his desk to take a folded piece of paper. He tossed it closer to my side of the desk and slumped back in his chair.

I snatched it up and read it, my heart clanging harder with every word, then stared at him, incredulous.

"A hearing? For custody of Livvie?" The paper trembled like a leaf in my hands. "Who…who are these people?"

"Olivia's grandparents." Each sentence came out dull and staccato. "They were here with their lawyer. They have money. Lots of it. They met Olivia and they want custody."

I let the notice of the hearing fall back to the desk. "But they can't do that," I said. "You're her father. They can't just…take her from you."

Sawyer covered his eyes again and I rushed to him, behind his chair and wrapped my arms around him. He didn't move but let me hold him and I fought not to burst into tears.

"It's going to be okay," I whispered. "It has to be. You're so good for her."

I straightened and without thinking—my body charged with panic I needed to channel—I rubbed his back, talking and kneading his muscles that felt like rocks under my hands. "There has to be a law, right? They can't just barge in here and take her away from you."

"It's not that simple," Sawyer said, his voice gruff.

"But it doesn't make any sense—"

"There are circumstances, Darlene."

"What kind of circumstances let the grandparents take a baby away from her father?"

"I'm not her father."

I reeled, his words pushing me back a step from his chair. It felt as if the air had been sucked out of the room.

"What…what are you saying? Of course you are."

Sawyer looked around at me, shaking his head miserably.

"I'm not. I took a paternity test when Molly first left her with me. I'm not a match, but it doesn't matter. Even after only a few days of having her in my life, she was mine. I tried to take her to CPS with Jackson. He tried to convince me it was the best thing, that I was crazy to try to raise her on my own. But I couldn't do it. Molly told me she was mine and that's how I thought of her. I still do. In my heart and fucking soul, she's mine and I love her."

He bit off the words, fighting for control.

"It doesn't matter to me what some stupid fucking test says. It only matters what I feel." He shook his head, a harsh, bitter laugh breaking free. "But turns out, that doesn't matter either. The court is going to order another paternity test. The Abbotts will demand one, and when the results come out, I'm going to lose her."

I put my hands back on his shoulders, shaking my head. "No. They can't do that. Not after so long. She calls you Daddy," I bit back my own tears. "Because you *are* her daddy and they have to see that. They *have* to."

He shook his head and a small silence fell. I pulled myself together and Sawyer's shoulders rose and fell under my hands as he took deep breaths to compose himself.

"Do you have help? A lawyer?"

"Jackson."

I bit my lip. "He does taxes…"

"I can't afford anyone else. And I trust him."

"Okay. Okay good."

I kept massaging Sawyer, working at his shoulders; the coiled knots of worry that his deepest fear was coming true. His entire body hummed with tension and I felt so helpless to do anything for him but this. I dug my thumbs into the hard muscles of his back, working circles over his shoulder blades, then back up, over his collar bone.

For long moments, there was silence. I didn't know what else to do or what to say. I could only try to ease his pain somehow, because I had nothing else.

Sawyer didn't move and I wondered if he'd fallen asleep, chin to his chest. Then his hand rose to take one of mine. He pressed my palm to his lips and I sucked in a breath as the kiss slipped up my arm, raising goosebumps, then spread over my shoulder and chest like a flame.

Sawyer turned my hand over and kissed the back, then held it to his cheek, still saying nothing. My heart thumped hard as he pulled me around in front of him, and then sideways onto his lap.

Face to face, and so close, he was breathtaking, but his eyes were so heavy. I lifted my hands and continued the massage, pressing circles on either side of his face, at the hinge of his jaw, below his eyes, his forehead. Then I grazed my fingernails along the sides of his head, just above his ears, over and over.

Our gazes never broke, we shared a breath, and then his hand was on my thigh. The other slipped up to hold my cheek, and even that small touch I felt everywhere. It scared me how much I wanted him.

"Did it help?" I asked. "I want to help."

He nodded. "You're the best thing in my life right now, Darlene," he said hoarsely. "The only good thing."

And then he kissed me. Like a drowning man needing a breath, he kissed me hard and desperately, his brows furrowed as if he were in pain. His hand found the back of my head, and he made a fist in my hair, gently but urgently, pressing me closer, deeper; holding me to him when I felt weightless. My mouth opened for him; Sawyer holding me to his kiss was the only reason I didn't float away.

A little moan of want fell out of my mouth and he took it in his. The kiss deepened as I came back to myself, wanting to feel every second, every sensation. His tongue ventured into my mouth and another little sound escaped me. My arms went around his neck, my fingers slid into his hair, nails grazing as our kiss intensified.

Sawyer's breath rasped in his nose as he kissed me harder, his arms wrapped around me now, both hands in my hair now, angling my head to take him deeper. The bite of his teeth on my lower lip made me dizzy and the chair was suddenly too small to contain us.

But Sawyer wrenched himself away from me, shocking me with the sudden break. He gently but quickly moved me off his lap and strode to the kitchen where he stood with his back to me, head bowed, hands resting on the counter.

"I'm sorry," he said. "Shit, I'm sorry, Darlene, I shouldn't have done that. Everything is so fucked up right now, and kissing you is like stepping outside of a nightmare."

I nodded quickly, thinking of my original reason for coming here tonight. "Me too. I'm sorry. I didn't mean…"

"We can't do this. *I* can't. I can't do this to you." He turned to face me, carved his hand through his hair. "Goddamn, Darlene, *now*? Why is this, why are *we* happening now? My whole life is about to implode. I have *nothing* to give you. Nothing."

"That's not true."

"It is," he said tiredly. "You deserve someone who's not stretched to the goddamn breaking point every second of his life." His jaw clenched and his dark eyes shone. "I was close to being done and now this hearing..."

"I know," I said in a small voice.

"I have to fight for her," he said, his tone hardening. "I have to put everything I have into that. No, not just that. I have to pass the bar, and get the goddamn clerkship so that I can prove I can provide for her. *Fuck.*"

He rubbed his eyes and my heart broke for him, for the weight that was pressing down on him, trying to crush him.

"I know it's so hard for you right now..."

"Too hard. I feel like my fucking heart is being torn in half. I'm scared shitless about losing Olivia, and yet when I'm with you, I see something real. For the first time in my life, I want whatever we have to be real."

Real. But I'm a liar. A fraud. He doesn't know me, I haven't told him anything.

He shook his head. "But I can't give you anything right now but stress and pain. When all this shit blows over..." he said hoarsely. "If I still have her when it's done..."

"You will. You will, Sawyer."

His jaw worked and for a moment he said nothing. "I don't know, Darlene. I've never been so terrified in my life. But when it's all done and if I have Olivia," he swallowed hard. "Then I can really be with you, if you still want that. Or at least we can try. Until then..." He let his hands drop to his sides. "I have nothing."

"That's not true," I said. "But I understand. I do. And I'm supposed to be working on myself, and God knows there's still so much left to do. To say to you."

I wiped my eyes with the heel of my hand.

"But I can be here for you," I said. "As a friend. Or to babysit Olivia if you need me to. Whatever you want, okay?"

He nodded. "Thank you."

I moved to the door, feeling like I was running away, but God, how could I tell him anything when he was about to face the fight of his life? Keeping Olivia was the most important thing right now, but it still felt like a cop out.

"Tell me how the hearing goes," I said, opening the door. "Tell me if you need anything. Anything at all. Tell me…"

Tell me you'll forgive me when you know the truth.

The words stuck in my throat, and I flew out of his place, tears spilling over.

I guessed not being so much of a coward was something I still needed to work on.

Chapter 19

Sawyer

I didn't want to—seeing her was too painful now—but I needed Darlene sooner than I'd expected. The day before the hearing, Elena told me she had a family emergency in the East Bay, and couldn't babysit. Henrietta was out of town for a wedding so I had no choice but to ask Darlene.

She agreed readily, even though it meant taking the day off her work. I added her lost wages to the tally of things I owed all the people who helped me during these last ten months.

And maybe it was all for nothing.

Friday morning, Darlene came downstairs to watch Olivia in my place. Her eyes were heavy and warm, and she hugged me tight.

"We're just friends right now," she said. "This is a friendly hug, but I'm putting every bit of my positive energy and best thoughts into it that this hearing goes how it's supposed to. For you."

I held her tightly, feeling her dancer's body mold to mine. I closed my eyes, my cheek against her hair, and inhaled her so I could keep some of the light and life she was giving me.

God, you're turning into a sap.

But I needed all the damn help I could get.

Jackson met me at the Duboce Muni, and we took a train to the Civic Center at eight a.m. Outside the Superior Courthouse, my friend stopped me with a hand to my arm.

"You ready?" Jackson asked.

"No."

"That's the spirit!" He chucked me on the arm. "Come on. Let's do this."

I smoothed down the lapel of my best suit—a slate gray jacket and pants with a white shirt, and ruby-colored tie. Jackson looked impeccable in blue and beige, a briefcase in his hand. We climbed the steps—me on wooden legs—and into the courthouse where we followed the signs for the Family Court. Jackson spoke in a low voice as we walked.

"This might be a bit of a battle but I've done my homework and I'm sure you've got the entire Family Law Code memorized."

"Section 7611, subsection D," I said.

"Exactly. Additionally, we can show removing Olivia from your custody would be detrimental to her. You're providing for her in a safe environment and have been for months. Courts don't like taking children out of good homes."

"They're her family, Jax." I rubbed my tired eyes. "Fuck me, I was so close. A few more weeks and the year would have been up."

"We can't worry about that now. Fight the fight in front of us, okay?"

I nodded. We'd arrived at the designated room on the hearing notice. "Breathe. Stay calm. Think positive."

"Thank you doing this," I told him. "For taking time off work…"

"Forget it," he said. "You're my family, too. And so is she."

"Jesus, don't say shit like that," I said with small laugh. I blinked my eyes hard.

"I'm trying to wipe that serial-killer look off your face," he said.

I tried to loosen the stiff expression, but I was fighting for my kid. My life. I left the smiling to Jackson.

Inside, the Abbotts were on their side of the courtroom, at a table with Holloway. They turned to watch me come in and the small smiles on their faces faded at my glare. I tore my eyes away. Instinctively, I liked them. Down deep, somewhere beneath the fear, I wanted to know them.

That's just your shitty childhood talking. They're here to take Olivia away from you.

I sat down stiffly at the table with Jackson, eyes forward, and didn't look their way again.

"All rise."

We got to our feet as the bailiff announced Judge Allen Chen, a stern-looking man, with dark hair that was graying along the sides. He put on glasses as he inspected the paperwork in front of him.

"In the matter of Olivia Abbott, a minor child, there is an order before the Court to show cause for custody filed by Gerald and Alice Abbott, maternal grandparents." He glanced up at Jackson. "I've read the preliminary facts of the case and I'm familiar with the position of Mr. and Mrs. Abbott. I'd like to hear from Mr. Haas, please."

Jackson stood. "Your Honor, my client has been raising Olivia since her mother disappeared ten months and two weeks ago. At that time, she made it clear that Sawyer was the father of their child. Pursuant to 7611 of the Family Law Code, section one, subsection D, Sawyer received Olivia into his home and openly held out that she was his natural child. He has provided a home, food, safety; healthcare via his university, and has been a devoted and loving father. The law clearly grants therefore, in black and white, that he is her natural father and should retain full custody." Jackson held out his hands. "Honestly, I don't even know why we're here."

Mr. Holloway rose to his feet. "That is a very narrow reading of the law," he began. "Molly Abbott did leave Olivia with Mr. Haas, though what she told him with regards to his paternity is a matter of hearsay. The birth certificate, of which we have retained a copy, lists no father. Additionally, neither Mr. Haas, nor his attorney, have provided us with a copy of the results of any paternity test."

Jackson was back on his feet. "Uniform Parentage Act, Your Honor?"

Judge Chen nodded. "Quite so." He turned to Holloway. "The State of California is not in the habit of tearing children from a secure home environment without cause. The Court will determine whether a paternity test is warranted based on the evidence presented."

"I understand, Your Honor, and to that end, we would like to read a notarized statement from Karen Simmons—friend to the deceased Molly Abbott—and to enter said statement into the record of proceedings here."

"Objection, Your Honor," Jackson said, but the judge held up a hand.

"This is not a trial, but an evidentiary hearing. I'll allow it." He nodded at Holloway. "Proceed."

Holloway set a pair of glasses on his nose.

"'I, Karen Jane Simmons, do swear under penalty of perjury that the following is true and correct: Molly Abbott was a close friend of mine since we were thirteen years old. After high school, Molly began to drink pretty heavily, and traveled place to place, hooking up with different boyfriends. But we always managed to stay in touch. She told me when she got pregnant, and I met up with her in Bakersfield after the baby was born. She told me the baby's father was a guy named Ross Mathis but that he wanted nothing to do with Olivia. Molly said she'd hooked up with another guy around the same time named Sawyer. He was studying to be a lawyer and that meant he was going to be well off. She said that her current boyfriend wouldn't stay with her if she kept the baby so she was going to drive to San Francisco where Sawyer lived, and tell him it was his baby. I didn't see her or hear from her again after that and was saddened to learn of her death. She was my best friend and I miss her.'

"Signed," Holloway concluded, "Karen Simmons." He took off his glasses. "Miss Simmons has provided text exchanges between her and Miss Abbott around the time in question that verify her statement, and has agreed to testify, either in deposition or in open court, should the Court desire it."

Ross Mathis. Olivia's natural father. Hearing the name brought bile to my mouth. He didn't want his own child, but I did. I would fucking die for that girl, but instead I was, fighting to keep her. Under the table, my hands clenched into fists.

"Your Honor," Holloway said in a closing-statement kind of tone, "Alice and Gerald Abbott are loving, devoted people who lost their daughter to the terrible disease of alcoholism. They had no idea they had a granddaughter, and the instant they learned of her existence, they set about taking the steps to see her, to be with her, and to provide for her the kind of life she needs and deserves. At this time, they request weekend visitation rights, and that a paternity test be administered, to either establish or refute Mr. Haas's claim that he is Olivia's father, before any further steps are taken toward granting permanent custody. Thank you."

I couldn't move. Couldn't breathe. Even my pounding heart slowed to a heavy clang.

The judge nodded. "Supervised weekend visitation is hereby

granted, and a paternity test shall be administered at the Health and Human Services department on Monday of next week."

Jackson was on his feet again. "Your Honor, my client has just completed the requirements for graduating UC Hastings law school, and is set to take the bar exam in Sacramento the week after next. We request a postponement of all proceedings until the completion of the exam, to give him time to focus and prepare without the threat of this outrageous and callous attempt to separate a loving father from his daughter hanging over his head."

The Abbotts visibly flinched at this. Judge Chen fixed me with a scrutinizing look. I probably looked like nothing like a 'loving' father, but I remained still as stone, afraid I'd shatter if I moved.

"There is one other issue we feel is of interest to the Court," Holloway said.

"Jesus, now what?" I whispered to Jackson.

He made a silencing motion with his hand.

"Mr. Smith has stipulated that his client has provided safe and adequate care for Olivia, yet a rudimentary investigation reveals that his childcare provider, Elena Melendez, is not licensed to run a daycare. She is merely a neighbor who babysits Olivia for eight hours a day while also taking care of her own two small children."

Jackson shot to his feet.

"I believe the obvious health and happiness of Olivia speaks for itself. This is irrelevant, Your Honor, and frankly, it's insulting to the good work and kindness of Ms. Melendez whom Mr. Haas pays appropriately for her excellent care."

"I am merely speaking to the general environment in which the child is raised," Mr. Holloway said. "Mr. Haas relies on unlicensed childcare from Ms. Melendez and occasionally from Darlene Montgomery, his upstairs neighbor."

Jackson held up his hands. "Again. Relevance?"

"It's relevant," Mr. Holloway said, "as Ms. Montgomery was incarcerated for drug possession three years ago and spent three months in a New York County jail."

It felt as is the air in the room had dropped twenty degrees, as I went cold all over.

"What'd he say?" I blurted stupidly. The words fell out of my mouth. I had to have misheard…

"Is this true, Mr. Haas?" the judge asked.

Jackson looked to me, eyes full of questions.

I shook my head. "I don't...I never..."

Darlene. Jail. Drug possession.

The words went around and around in my head individually but I couldn't get them to make sense all together.

"This was three years ago, Your Honor?" Jackson asked, still looking at me. He tore his gaze to stand and face the Court. "Do we punish people for the rest of their lives for mistakes that are years old?"

Mr. Holloway smiled placidly. "We wanted to ensure the Court had all of the information before making any rulings. In light of these revelations, we feel a speedy resolution to this matter is in the best interest of the child."

Judge Chen pursed his lips at me. "Agreed. We will reconvene next Thursday to read the DNA test results, and to make a further determination as to custody of Olivia Abbott. This hearing is adjourned."

Alice and Gerald should have been victorious, but both wore concerned expressions on their faces when they looked in my direction. I stared back in a daze. Jackson had to haul me to my feet when the judge left the room.

I loosened my tie but it wasn't what was strangling me.

"You didn't know about Darlene?" Jackson asked.

"I had no clue," I said. "She told me she had something she wanted to tell me." I gripped my friend's arm as the enormity of what had happened hit me like a punch in the chest. "Jesus, Jax. What do I do now? It's over. Isn't it?"

"Don't think that way," Jackson said, though his pre-hearing optimism had all but vanished. "The Abbotts did their homework, I'll give them that, but the stuff about Elena and Darlene is bullshit. They're throwing anything at the wall to see what sticks."

"It doesn't feel like bullshit," I said.

But truthfully, I didn't feel anything at all. Numb. Like how I felt when that cop told us my mother was dead. I had to feel nothing or else I'd feel fucking everything and collapse under the weight of it.

"It's the test results that we need to deal with," Jackson said, walking us out of the courtroom. "But it's not over. You have rights. Molly left her with you. She wanted you to be Olivia's dad. We'll make a game plan. We'll prove how well you've taken care of Olivia, we'll get character witnesses…"

Jackson kept talking as we stepped outside into the overly warm summer heat. The bright sun was muted now. Thick storm clouds were brewing overhead, turning the sky gray. My entire world had caved in, and everything was gray, as if all the color and light had been drained out until there was nothing left.

Chapter 20

Darlene

"Dareen!" Olivia kicked her feet in her high chair and pushed at the tray.

"All done, sweet pea?" I wiped her mouth of the strawberry residue, then *booped* her nose with the cloth. She laughed. "You want to get down?'

"Down," she agreed. "Bocks."

"Jeez Louise, girl. You're all about the blocks, aren't you?"

I took off the tray and set Olivia down on the floor. She immediately toddled to her pile of wooden blocks with the letters and numbers on the sides, and started stacking.

I watched her for a moment, my smile fading, my heart aching. What was happening at the hearing? Surely, a judge wouldn't just rip a child from the man who'd been taking care of her as his own just because the grandparents had more money. There had to be some rule or law that protected Sawyer.

"There is, and he and Jackson know about it," I murmured.

But worry laced the blood in my veins and wouldn't leave. I sat down with Livvie on the floor and played blocks with her, then read her a story. When she began to yawn and rub her eyes, I put her down for a nap in her little room and left the door open a crack.

The house felt quiet. Waiting. Outside, thunder boomed distantly, ominously. As if something terrible were on the horizon, rolling this way.

"Oh stop. It's just weather."

I paced around a bit, shaking out my stiff arms from yesterday's spa work. I couldn't afford to miss any more shifts, I was glad I took the day off to babysit for Sawyer. It wasn't the same as being with him, but taking care of Livvie made me feel good about myself in a way I hadn't felt in a while.

And maybe, after all is said and done, the three of us...

I shut that thought up quick. In my experience, holding on too tightly to something I wanted was the surest way to lose it.

I wandered around Sawyer's living area, taking him in through his degrees and awards; his messy desk covered in his study materials he worked so hard on. I missed him. He wasn't really gone, but I missed him anyway.

And you still have to tell him...

"I should've told him at the beginning," I muttered, my fingers trailing over his pen lying on a stack of notebooks.

But if I had told him, maybe nothing would have happened between us. The Small Something we had was better than Nothing, wasn't it?

I could practically see Max roll his eyes at that one.

"I know, I know, I'm supposed to be working on being honest and responsible," I said. "On that note."

I plopped on the couch and fished my phone out of my purse, to make the call I'd been putting off for days. I opened my contacts and scrolled down to the H's.

Home.

I breathed out and hit 'call.'

My mother picked up on the second ring. "Montgomery residence, Gina speaking." Her Queens accent was pronounced, so it came out 'Geen-er speakin'.'

"Hi, Mom, it's me."

"Hello, baby, what's wrong? Is everything okay?"

I flinched at her standard opener. "Everything is fine. Really good, in fact. Did Carla tell you I got a spot with a dance troupe? I didn't even have a planned routine, I just winged it and got in."

"She didn't mention it, but that's wonderful, honey. But how's the spa job? You keeping up over there? You need money?"

"What? No, I'm fine."

"Keeping your nose clean?"

"Yes."

"Good girl."

"So listen, Ma," I said, my own accent coming back as if she were drawing it out of me from across the country. "The dance show isn't a huge deal. It's in a small space in the city, but they just gave me a solo, and I'd love for you guys to see it."

"I don't know, Dar," Mom said. "That's a lot of travel for a show that's what? An hour?"

Thirty minutes. I thought. *She's right. This was a dumb idea.* But persistence had paid off for me before, and hearing my mom's voice awakened in me how much I missed her.

"Not to mention, Grandma Bea's hip is acting up," she said. "She can't travel so good anymore."

"I know, Ma, but I haven't danced at all in four years. And anyway, the show would only be one part of it. You could come visit me, and see where I live—in this really cool, old Victorian house. And I could show you around San Francisco. It's such a beautiful city."

"When is this show?"

"Next weekend."

"Oh honey, I can't wrangle your father into something like that in a week."

I nodded, trying to ignore the relief in her voice.

"You know how he is," she said. "Work, work, work."

I knew how he was. My dad owned a successful auto body shop. He made good money and could take time off whenever he needed to. Or wanted to.

"No, you're right," I said softly. "It's a huge expense to fly all this way, and the show isn't a big deal. Next time."

"Absolutely."

"Give Daddy a kiss for me," I said.

"I will, baby. Take care, now, and call if you need anything."

I just did.

"Sure, Mom." I wiped my cheek with the heel of my hand. "I'll talk to you soon. Love you."

"Love you too. Bye, now."

I let my hand fall in my lap.

"Stop feeling sorry for yourself," I muttered, but the ache in my heart wouldn't go away.

A text came in on the phone in my lap from Max.

I need to see you. Work, home, or dance?

Home. Second floor, I typed back, and my heart sank even lower. **You'd better not be coming over here to tell me what I think you're coming over here to tell me.**

I'll tell you when I get there.

Smartass, I tapped, but the ache in my chest deepened.

Twenty minutes later, a soft knock came at the door.

I opened it to Max, and stepped into the hallway, leaving the door ajar.

"The baby's sleeping," I said. "And you're leaving, aren't you?"

He nodded. "I got the call. My flight leaves in a few hours."

"I'm so proud of you, Max."

"Are you?" The softness in his voice and the tears in his eyes shocked me. "I may have been your sponsor, but you've also been a friend. It means a lot to me, what you think."

"Thank you," I said. "No one's said anything like that to me in a long time."

I put my arms around him and held him tight. He held me tighter.

"You're going to do great," I said. "Going back to Seattle's going to be the best thing for you. You can maybe reconcile with your parents, and you'll definitely meet some hot doctor who is going to love you. How could he not?"

Max kept hugging me. "You're going to be okay, too. I know it."

"I don't. I feel like everyone I care about is moving farther and farther away and I can't hold on to anyone. My family, Sawyer, you. And I feel that other rock bottom coming. I wish you could be here when it does."

He pulled away to look at me, concern heavy in his light blue eyes.

"I hate that I'm leaving right now. Maybe I should postpone…"

"Don't you dare," I said. "I need to deal with this on my own, I think. Maybe that's why you got the transfer now. Everything happens for a reason, right?"

"It does," he said. "And you're so much stronger than you know. You've come far, Darlene. Hold on to *that*. And call me. Any time." He gave me a stern look. "And don't skip any meetings. Not one, or

I'll have to fly back, away from my hot doctor boyfriend."

I laughed. "I'm going to miss you."

"Miss you too."

I hugged him until I heard footfalls on the stairs. Sawyer stood at the end of the hallway. He stared at me in Max's arms, and his hand resting on his shoulder bag dropped to his side.

I took a step back from Max. "Hi, Sawyer."

Max whipped his head around and the action prompted Sawyer to stride up to us, eyes forward, his face unreadable. Blank. And that worried me more than anything else.

"Hey, man," Max said, offering his hand. "Max Kaufman. Good to meet you."

Sawyer stopped in the door. He stared down at Max's offered hand, then met my eye for one blood-curdling second before pushing past us into his apartment.

"He had a very important hearing," I whispered. "I don't think it went well. God, I'm so scared for him."

"I hate that I have to leave you like this," Max said. "I'll call you when I land."

He kissed my cheek and I watched him until he was down the stairs and out of sight. I suddenly felt like a tightrope walker strung up between two high-rises.

And my safety net just left to get on a plane to Seattle.

Inside Sawyer's place, he was shaking off his suit coat that was smattered with rain. He tossed it on the back of his chair, then loosened his tie.

"Where is Olivia?" he asked. No, demanded.

"Sleeping. She's fine. She's…sleeping."

"You can't just bring strangers into my place. With my kid. You know that, right?"

"I know, I'm sorry," I said. "He didn't come in, I promise. He's—"

"He's what?" Sawyer asked. "Your drug dealer?"

The blood drained from my head, leaving me dizzy. I reeled. "My…what?" I breathed.

"Were you ever going to tell me?" Sawyer demanded.

"Tell you…?"

"About your criminal record?"

There they were, those three words in all their ugly glory. My criminal record. But how was it coming up *now*?

"Yes, I was going to tell you," I said, my voice weak and watery. "I wanted to, so many times but I was scared. But how...how did you find out?"

"I found out at the *preliminary custody hearing* for my child," Sawyer spat. "The Abbotts investigated this entire fucking building. Now, in the eyes of that judge, I'm the kind of guy who leaves his kid either with unlicensed childcare all day or drug addicts."

I stiffened all over. "I'm not a drug addict," I said, my voice quavering. "Not anymore. I'm recovering. I don't even drink. Max isn't a *drug dealer,* for God's sake. He was my NA sponsor. That means—"

"I know what it means," Sawyer said. "I just have no fucking clue what I should think about it. Jesus, Darlene."

He shook his head and the stony exterior started to shatter; I could feel the tension radiating off of him as he tried to hold himself together.

"Did you lose her?" I asked, my voice hardly a whisper. "Because of me?"

"It doesn't matter. It's over." He shook his head, then planted one hand on the wall as if it were the only thing keeping him standing. "It's all over."

And I knew he meant me, too. Whatever we had had, it was gone now. I'd tried, once again, to hold on by not telling him, and it all was wrenched out of my fingers.

"I'm sorry," I whispered. "For so much. For everything."

Sawyer raised his eyes to mine and for a split second the hard, stony exterior cracked and the pain flooded out. He opened his mouth to speak, and at that moment, lightning flashed and a booming thunder followed after. Rain lashed the windows in a sudden deluge, as if the sky had cracked open.

The sound woke up Olivia; the baby monitor chirped with her fussing. Neither of us moved and that ugly feeling of wanting to escape everything I was and all I had done came over me. I hurried to Olivia's room.

She was standing in her crib, and her sleepy little face broke into a smile to see me.

"Dareen."

She held her arms to me and I picked her up; held her close for a moment, breathing in her sweet, baby powder smell. Her arms went around my neck, squeezing tears from my eyes in her little hug.

It felt like goodbye.

Back in the living room, Sawyer stood with his arms crossed, his gaze cast down and his expression hard again.

"Look who's awake," I said weakly.

"Daddy," Olivia said, her voice still cloudy with sleep.

Sawyer looked up at Olivia and me, his face a blank mask. And then he strode forward and took the baby out of my arms.

My skin went cold all over; I felt where Olivia's warmth had been, and a goose bumps raised on my skin. Sawyer took his child a few steps away and turned his back on me.

"Okay," I said, my voice barely a whisper. A thousand more words rose up behind that one: how I'd been clean for almost two years, the progress I'd made, how proud Max was...

Max. He was gone. That pain hit me in the chest to join that of Sawyer's silent rejection. Tears drowned every other word I had, and I grabbed my bag off the kitchen chair.

"Okay," I managed again. "Okay."

It was all I could say and yet nothing was okay. Not one thing.

I went to the door and opened it. Sawyer stood in profile to me, his gaze over Olivia's head, full of thoughts but none for me. His silence was worse than a thousand condemning words.

"Goodbye."

My voice broke and Sawyer's head whipped toward me, his hard features morphing into pain and regret, and his mouth opened as if he might finally have something more to say, but I shut the door between us.

Outside in the hallway, I leaned my forehead against the cool wood. Rain smattered the small window in the hallway, and lightning lit up the night sky. I pushed off the door, and headed out instead of up. Out into the cold wind and rain that had doused the summer heat. It tore through my clothing. I was drenched immediately and shivered hard enough to rattle my teeth.

There's a bar two blocks down. Someone there will know someone. Know where I can score. Whiskey sour and a pill, and who gives a shit what Sawyer thinks of me.

"Max," I whispered, like a cry for help. The wind tore the word and drowned it in rain. I looked up and down the street to see if I could still catch him, but there was no Max. No help, save what I gave myself.

The bar was two blocks away.

The Y with tonight's NA meeting was six.

Backward or forward.

I stood on the empty street, and the rain came down.

I pulled my phone from my purse with shaking fingers and shielded it from the downpour. My finger hit the Uber app and I waited. I'd had no words in Sawyer's apartment but they were coming back to me now. So many of them, filling me up, filling that emptiness that lived within me that I'd tried to fill with drugs. Filling me with the truth, that I was not the sum of my criminal record; I was not words on paper, black and white.

I was everywhere in between.

At the Y, there was an NA meeting already in progress. It wasn't my group, but it didn't matter. It was my community.

A woman stood at the podium, but she fell silent when she saw me come in. The rest of the group turned in their seats to follow her jaw-dropped stare, to me, dripping rainwater and shivering.

I strode to the front of the group and the woman wordlessly gave up the podium. I met the gazes of those assembled. My lips trembled with cold. All the words I'd wanted to tell Sawyer but couldn't were boiling up now, and I wished, more than anything, that Max was here one final time, to hear them. Because if he could have, he'd be getting on that plane knowing he had done his job. And that he didn't have to worry about me. Not anymore.

I faced the assembled group, my hands clutched the side of the podium.

"Hi," I said. "My name is Darlene and I'm an addict."

My voice was strong despite my trembling jaw, and the voices that answered were just as strong, lifting me up and carrying me on a simple, two-word current of acceptance.

"Hi, Darlene."

Chapter 21

Sawyer

I soothed Olivia back to sleep. The thunder quieted so that she was nodding off on my shoulder within minutes. I held her for a long time, my eyes closed, feeling her little weight and warmth against my chest.

Is this one of the last times?

I fortified myself against the thought, but hope was draining out of me, minute by minute. It didn't matter how much I loved her and that I thought of her as my own. The paternity test would read **0% probability**, in black and white, and the judge's ruling would be final.

The impassivity of the law I'd taken such great comfort in was now a faceless stranger turning its back on me, uncaring that my heart was breaking.

I set Olivia gently down in her bed and went out. Outside the living room window, rain was still falling in sheets and Darlene was out in it.

Her heart was broken too, and I'd broken it. Shattered it into tiny pieces when I'd taken Olivia out of her arms.

"Fucking asshole," I muttered, but my voice cracked at the end, my throat thick.

I'd been holding on to anger at the revelation of her past; using it to keep the pain at bay, but it hit me hard like a heavy fist to the chest. Darlene wasn't why I was going to lose Olivia, but—Jesus Christ—my life was infused with addictions. My mother, Molly, and now Darlene?

Was I destined to lose her too?

The fear, anger, confusion all swirled in me like a tornado, and at its center, in the calm eye, was what I felt for her.

"What the fuck do I do now?"

I sank into the chair at my desk and pulled out my phone for the hundredth time. No messages or texts, but why would there be?

"There won't be. Because I broke her heart," I muttered and felt each syllable stab me.

I typed a text.

Tell me you're okay.

I backspaced it away. She didn't owe it to me to make me feel better.

Are you okay?

I deleted that too. Of course she wasn't okay. I'd seen to that.

I'm sorry.

My thumb hovered over the send button but I was too chickenshit to push it. And too ashamed.

Another voice whispered in my ear, like the proverbial devil on my shoulder. *What if she was doing hard stuff? What if she associated with felons or owed money? Maybe she moved clear across the country to escape bad people? You want that kind of stuff around Olivia?*

My excuses about what I didn't know about Darlene fell apart under the sheer weight of all that I did know about her.

And what I felt about her.

I hit 'send.'

I sat at the desk, listening to the rainfall and waiting to see if she'd read the message. Waiting for her to answer. Waiting for her to tell me that she was okay. The thought flitted into my head that she might be doing something to herself that she shouldn't, but I swatted it dead.

You know nothing about her situation because you didn't ask. You shut down on her.

That was one truth. The other was that the image of Darlene, standing in a doorway, being held by another man, was an added layer of misery. Another crack in my stony heart that was already on the verge of shattering, and the emotions that seeped out weren't any I recognized.

"That's because you're a fucking asshole," I said, dully.

I tossed the phone on the desk and rubbed my face with both hands. The clock ticked the hours away. Olivia woke up from her nap. I fed her, played with her, read to her, cherishing each second with her and trying not to imagine the internal countdown in which she'd be taken from me.

Every other moment, I felt something different; the mind-numbing pain that I'd already lost her, followed by the red-hot anger that I'd fight for her until I didn't have a breath left in my body.

And when I put her down for bed that night, I was wrung out, and my anguish turned back to Darlene.

"Jesus Christ," I muttered, staring at my haggard reflection in the mirror after I changed into sleep clothes and brushed my teeth. "You're a fucking mess. Pull your shit together, Haas."

I made a pathetic attempt to study for the bar, and gave up after a minute. What was the fucking point?

I sat and stared at nothing. I was so exhausted I could hardly move, but my phone was still silent. My agonized mind wanted to know which would come home first: the blue and red silent sirens? Or Darlene, safe and well?

The rain kept falling but the wind quieted enough for me to hear the door shut below and footsteps on the stairs.

Panic and relief sent a jolt through my bones, and I bolted out of my chair for the front door. I threw it open just as Darlene went past.

"Darlene."

She stopped and turned to me, and I hated myself even more for taking note of her eyes, that were clear and sharp. Rainwater dripped off the end of her nose, and her clothes clung to her lithe body as she looked at me, waiting.

"Come in," I said. "Please."

She shook her head, her damp hair falling over her face. "I don't think that's a good idea."

"Please, come in. Please," I said again, and the word was the start to every thought in my head.

Please don't hate me.

Please forgive me.

Please.

"Please," I said. "Stay. Talk to me."

"No, I shouldn't," she said. "I'm cold and tired and it's been a really long day. For both of us. I'm going to take a hot bath and get some sleep." Her smile was gentle, sad. "You should try to, too."

"Darlene," I said, my voice thick and frayed at the ends. "It's the paternity test that's going to ruin me. Not you. I just…My mother…Molly. I don't know what to do. Or what to think."

"I know," she said. "But the idea that I could, in some way, jeopardize your situation with Livvie makes me sick inside, and it was stupid to try to hide the truth. There is no hiding it. Not from you, the court, or myself. It's on my record."

"In black and white," I muttered.

She nodded. "I thought about going to a bar to get drunk or high tonight, because if people are going to look at me like a drug addict, I might as well act like one. But the truth is, people will always look at me like that, no matter if I've been clean for one year, or two, or ten. It's a part of my past and a part of who I am. Sliding backwards because I got hurt doesn't solve anything. But being proud of what I've accomplished does."

Tears filled her eyes, but there was a blue flame burning behind them I hadn't seen before, and her tears didn't douse it.

"I will always be an addict even if you put the word 'recovering' in front of it. I will always have to work ten times as hard to be trusted, to be trustworthy but that's the price I have to pay for my mistakes."

I clenched my teeth; tossed on a sea of emotions I had no idea how to navigate.

"I'm sorry I took Olivia away from you," I said. "That was…a shitty, shitty thing to do."

Darlene leaned against the doorframe. "I get it. I really do," she said and even then, shivering with cold, she found a smile for me. "I totally understand, and it totally sucks. It's amazing how two opposite things can be completely true at the same time, isn't it?"

"I don't know what to say," I said. "Or what to feel. I don't feel…anything. To keep myself safe. And when I saw you with Max…"

She drew her old man's sweater, damp with rain, around her shoulders.

"He's my friend. My best friend. And I'm sorry he showed up at your apartment. He jumped on a plane tonight to Seattle, which is too bad because everything I told you is what I said at my NA meeting tonight. I think he would've been happy to hear it, and know that I'm going to be okay. Because I am. I'm going to be okay for me."

Darlene reached out and cupped my cheek in her hand. "If there is anything you need, tell me. I don't know what I can do, but I'm here."

I couldn't speak; I only nodded, and it sent a tear sliding down my cheek, to her hand.

"See?" she said with a quavering smile. "You feel so much, Sawyer. So much." She wiped the tear into her palm. "I'm going to keep this," she said, then turned and walked away.

Chapter 22

Darlene

The hours of the weekend dragged me behind them. I didn't see Sawyer at all, at least not up close. I watched from my upstairs window as the Abbotts came to pick up Olivia. Elena had told me they'd won supervised weekend visitation at the condo they were renting in the Marina.

I watched, my heart in my throat, as Sawyer helped them put Olivia in a sleek, white BMW SUV and drive off. He sat down on the front steps and was still sitting there long after they'd gone.

Every part of me ached to go to him, but after the other night, my mind felt as if it had been scrubbed free of the nagging whispers and doubts that always plagued me. I could think clearly. Sawyer had so much to contend with already. He didn't need me adding to the storm of his turbulent emotions. If he wanted to talk to me, he knew to call or visit, and I'd be there for him.

He didn't.

After work on Monday, I rehearsed with the dance troupe, dodging both Anne-Marie's stink-eye and Ryan's clumsy feet the entire time. But Greg loved my solo, even if he wouldn't say it out loud.

"Saturday night, we open," he said, as if we didn't know that. "Take some of these flyers to pass out to your friends and family. "It'd be good if each of you brought at least two people to the show as your guests."

"How many tickets have been sold?" Anne-Marie asked.

"We're doing okay," Greg said. "We could use a few more."

Glances were exchanged among us. That was code for "hardly any" and my heart sank a little. I wasn't doing the show for fame or fortune, that's for sure, but it would be nice if someone other than Anne-Marie's bitchy friends witnessed my first dance in four years. I took a handful of the Xeroxed papers and posted a few of them on my way home.

My phone rang after dinner, while I was curled up on my loveseat. I picked it up and a smile burst over my face.

"Maximilian," I said. "Just the person I wanted to talk to."

He told me about his new job at a Seattle hospital, and I told him about my emotional rock bottom and the NA meeting after.

"It was like taking a *Silkwood* shower," I said.

"What does that even mean?" he asked with a chuckle.

"You haven't seen *Silkwood*? That old movie where Meryl Streep works at a nuclear plant or something, and she gets irradiated? So these guys in Hazmat suits blast her with water hoses—in her eyeballs, gums, and everywhere—to decontaminate her?"

"That's what your NA meeting felt like?"

"Yes. Being brutally honest in front of God and everyone feels like a *Silkwood* shower." I smiled against the phone. "Put that in your Sponsor's Manual."

"Maybe, I will." Max laughed. "Or you could put it in yours."

I snorted. "Ha. I'm a long way from that."

"Maybe. Maybe not," Max said. "I'm so fucking proud of you."

"Thank you. Me too. And I'm proud of you. Seen your folks yet?"

"Not yet. I have tentative dinner plans with Mom on Saturday. I'll see how that goes before I tackle The Dad Situation."

"Let me know how it goes. I'm always here for you."

"Ah, and the student has become the master," Max said.

I laughed. "Oh, stop." My smile faded, and Max read my silence.

"How is Sawyer?" he asked gently.

I curled up on my loveseat, making myself into a ball. "Not good. He's fighting for custody of Olivia and I'm scared he's not going to win."

"God, that's awful. And what about you two?"

"There isn't much to say," I said. "I don't want to add to his problems."

"Darlene..."

"No, I mean that honestly. He has so much to contend with right now. I don't want to pressure him and I told him if he needed me, I'd be there."

"Sawyer the Lawyer, in the brief moments of our acquaintance, didn't strike me as the kind of guy who goes around asking for help or comfort when he needs it."

"Maybe not," I said softly. "And he definitely doesn't want it from me."

The week felt as slow as the weekend, and yet was rushing up to meet me at the same time. Saturday was opening night. On Thursday, we rehearsed in the actual theater space for the first time. My heart sank a little at the shabby little place—the Brown Bag Theatre—with black walls and floors that needed paint, and fifty seats facing a tiny stage.

But my fellow dance troupers were getting excited. Anne-Marie was bringing a bunch of people, apparently.

"Who's coming to see you?" Paula asked as we cleared out after dress rehearsal.

"Oh, it's bad timing for me all around," I said with a small laugh. "My family is in New York and can't get over here, and my best friend upped and moved to Seattle on me, the bastard."

I realized then, that my other best friends, Zelda and Beckett, would've dropped everything to fly out and see me, but I never asked. It had felt like too much. Now that I had begun to grow some semblance of a backbone, it was too late.

Paula gave me a gentle smile. "That's too bad," she said, and leaned in to whisper, "You're the best part of this thing."

I watched her go and stood in the black box, alone.

"If a dancer dances for the first time in four years and no one sees it, did she actually dance?" I murmured under my breath.

I wiped a tear away. I should've called Zelda and Becks, but I was too scared of coming off as weak and needy. Again. But I *did* need them, and I realized—too late—that being with the people who love you isn't weak. It's how you stay strong.

"See, Max?" I sniffed. "I still have a long way to go."

Back home, I showered, changed, and set about to make another tuna casserole. It was the only thing I could think to do and I had to do something. Sawyer's hearing was tomorrow, and Max's words about him never asking for help wouldn't leave my head. I could drop off the casserole and let him decide if he wanted my company.

A knock came at the door just as I was pulling the finished casserole from the oven. My pulse fluttered, and I took the oven mitts off my shaking hands.

But it was Jackson at my door, looking casually elegant as usual, in slacks and a dark sweater over a blue dress shirt. His handsome features were drawn together with worry and his dark eyes were heavy.

"What happened?" I blurted, my pulse hammering in my chest.

"Nothing yet," Jackson said. "Can I come in? I told him I was stepping out to make a phone call."

I blinked, shook my head. "Sorry, yes. Come in."

Jackson was at least six-feet-three and seemed like a towering presence in my small space. I was suddenly glad Sawyer had this imposing and charismatic guy on his side.

"Would you like anything? Something to drink?"

Jackson shook his head.

I braced myself. "The paternity test...?"

"He and Olivia took it on Monday. The results are sealed until tomorrow at the hearing. Unless there's been a miracle of science since he took the first test, it's not going to go well."

I sagged against the counter. "I don't know what to do. I feel so helpless." I waved a hand at the pan. "I made a casserole..."

"Come with us to the hearing."

I jerked my eyes up. "What? No...I'm the drug addict neighbor, remember? I didn't help his cause at all."

"That was a low blow by their attorney," Jackson said. "If the judge sees the real you and not the image Holloway tried to plant in his mind, it'll help. And frankly, we need all the help we can get."

"Can they really just take Olivia away?"

Jackson rubbed the back of his neck. "The system's improved for fathers' rights in the last ten years, and courts never want to pull children out of good homes. There's a statute about Sawyer acting and providing for Olivia as if she were his own, which gives him some claim to her, but it's all we have. I don't know that it's going to be enough. Especially since Molly gave the baby to Sawyer but never bothered to put his name on the birth certificate," he added bitterly. "If she had just done that…"

He broke off and shook his head.

"I'll go if you think it will help," I said, slowly. "Of course, I will. But are you sure that's what he needs?"

Jackson nodded. "Yeah, I do. Sawyer needs you. He needs…" He blew air out his cheeks. "God, he needs something and I don't know what to do for him. He's like a robot these last few days. Hardly talks except to Olivia and even then it's like…"

"Like what?" I whispered.

"He looks at her like, inside his mind, he's already saying goodbye."

My hand flew to my mouth. "Oh no."

"I know he'd fight for her with everything he has, but that's just it. We don't have much to fight with. At least not as far as the law goes." Jackson put his hands on my shoulders. "Sawyer needs you. You do something for him I've never seen before. You make him happy."

Tears filled my eyes. "I don't know, Jackson."

"I do. The judge needs to see Sawyer as something other than cold and stiff. I think you're the only person who can bring that out of him."

"I'll try," I said. "But what if Sawyer doesn't want me there? What if…"

"He doesn't have a choice," Jackson said, his old smile coming back. "He has to take the advice of his attorney—me—and I say I want you there."

I smiled and hugged Jackson. "Okay, I will."

"Thank you, Darlene." Jackson gave me a final squeeze and let me go. "I'll have a car out front at nine o'clock."

"I'll be there. Oh, wait! Come here."

Jackson followed me to the kitchen area and I put the oven mitts on his hands.

"Take the casserole to him. It has peas in it. For Livvie."

Jackson smiled. "He *might* guess that I didn't step out to make a phone call."

I grinned. "Your cover is blown."

I opened my front door and craned up on tiptoe to give Jackson a peck on the cheek. "Thank you for helping him."

"Right back at you, Dar," he said, and went out.

The next morning, I put on my best I'm Not A Junkie outfit—a flowing, white dress with colorful flowers that brushed my knees. I usually paired it with my combat boots to give it some edge, but today I wore my low-heeled dance shoes, and toned my usually heavy eye-makeup down. I piled my hair on my head in a loose bun and put on my lucky gold hoop earrings.

I was downstairs at ten minutes to nine, my stomach twisting itself in knots. Sawyer and Jackson were at Elena's, giving Olivia over to babysit. I slipped past them to wait outside. If I talked to Olivia for even a second I was going to burst into tears.

The front door opened behind me a few minutes later. Sawyer stopped short. He was devastating in a dark blue suit and paler blue tie. I could swear I saw the stoniness of his eyes melt a little as he took me in.

"There she is," Jackson said, his smile brilliant. "Our secret weapon." He kissed my cheek. "You're a vision. Everyone in that courtroom will be helpless not to fall in love with you."

My face flushed red up to my ears. "Oh my God, stop." I looked to Sawyer. "Jackson said I should come. That it might help…"

"Don't you have to work?" Sawyer asked dully.

It was going to put a dent in my bank account to miss another day, but what was that to what Sawyer was facing? I'd worry about it later.

"This is much more important," I said.

Sawyer held my gaze a moment more, then nodded and moved to the sedan idling at the curb.

"See?" Jackson murmured in my ear as we followed him down. "He's shut down."

"No," I said, my heart heavy. "He's just scared to death."

In the car, I sat wedged between Sawyer and Jackson in the backseat. Sawyer propped his chin on his hand, his gaze on the streets outside. His other hand was in his lap. Without giving myself a chance to outthink it, I reached over and took it in mine. Sawyer stiffened and didn't pull his gaze from the window. But after a moment, he sighed; a little tension left his body and he laced his fingers with mine.

I eased a sigh of relief too and glanced over at Jackson. He gave me a surreptitious a-okay sign. But as the car rolled up in front of the Superior Court, Sawyer's body tensed all over again. He let go of my hand and got out of the car without a word.

Inside the courtroom, the Abbotts were already there. My immediate reaction was confusion; I'd imagined them as heartless monsters, but they looked put together and wealthy with their pastel clothing and silver hair.

They look like nice people.

Both of them turned in their seats when we came in, their eyes searching to meet Sawyer's, both wearing hopeful smiles. But he refused to look at them, and their gazes landed on me.

I smiled brightly at them, almost like a reflex. I couldn't help myself, and besides, I figured it couldn't hurt if someone on Sawyer's side acted as a goodwill ambassador.

The Abbotts' attorney frowned at me, whispered something to his clients. They turned back to me as I took a seat in the audience, directly behind Sawyer and Jackson's table, wary now.

Yes, that's me. I'm the recovering drug addict, I thought. But I kept my chin up and smile friendly. A few minutes later, the bailiff told us to rise and the judge came in.

He settled his glasses on his nose and took up an envelope in his hand. "In the matter of the custody provisions for Olivia Abbott, a minor child, the Court has received Mr. Haas' paternity results." He fixed his stern gaze on Sawyer. "Mr. Smith, does your client have anything to enter into the record at this time?"

Jackson rose to his feet. "Your Honor, we'd like the Court to recognize Darlene Montgomery." He turned to gesture to me. "The last time we met, Mr. Holloway tried to cast aspersions on those who have helped Sawyer take care of Olivia, and we would like the Abbotts, and the Court, to hear a few words from Ms. Montgomery herself."

My eyes widened and I shot Jackson a panicked look.

No one said anything about talking!

But I sucked in a breath to calm down. Hell, I'd already taken the *Silkwood* shower. What was saying nice things about Sawyer compared to that?

But the judge shook his head.

"There will be time enough after the test results are read for any character statements, though if Mr. Haas himself has anything he'd like to say, he is free to do so."

From my vantage behind them, I saw Jackson nudge Sawyer under the table, but Sawyer remained still as stone. My gaze darted to the Abbotts. Both looked on the edge of their seats, craning in with hopeful expressions on their faces.

The judge sighed. "Very well. The Clerk of the Court shall now read and enter the DNA test results into the record."

He handed the envelope to a young woman in a sharp navy suit. The courtroom went silent but for the soft tearing of paper. My imagination told me that was the sound of Sawyer's heart tearing in two.

He lifted his head, and the sudden movement drew everyone's attention.

"Please don't."

The words hung in the air and it took me a second to realize Sawyer had said them. A collective gasp whipped through the courtroom. My own breath stuck in my throat to hear the pain that saturated every syllable; he sounded exhausted down to his soul.

"Please don't read that," he said.

Sawyer rose to his feet. His shoulders were rounded, as if he carried the weight of the universe in every pore and sinew of his body. But I watched him unfold, stand straighter, his voice strengthening but still soft with pain and hope and love.

"Olivia is my daughter," he told the courtroom. "She is, no matter what that test says. And in a few weeks, none of this would have mattered. I would have crossed that arbitrary finish line the law has drawn in the sand, and petitioned to have my name put on her birth certificate. And it would've been done, no matter the test results. But there *is* a line, and simply because we're on this side of it, I could lose her."

I was riveted to Sawyer, but out of the corner of my eyes, Holloway whispered frantically to the Abbotts. They shushed him with shakes of their head. Everyone in that room hung on Sawyer's every word.

"I have raised Olivia since she was three months old. She calls me Daddy." His voice cracked and my heart cracked right along with him. "That test? It doesn't mean anything to me. I don't need it to tell me how I feel, or how much I should love that little girl. I love her with every molecule in my body, and it doesn't matter that none of mine match any of hers. I don't care that they don't. I never did."

He heaved a steadying breath. "I took a paternity test before. Ten months ago, after Molly left the baby with me. That test didn't matter, either. It had only been a few days but it was still too late. Since the minute Molly put Olivia in my arms and said she was mine, she was."

I bit the inside of my cheek, but tears streamed down my face anyway. Mrs. Abbott dabbed her eyes with a tissue and her husband pressed his fist to his mouth, listening.

Sawyer turned to them, his eyes full. "I know you don't know me, but Olivia does. Please don't take her from me. Please. She's my daughter. She's my little girl. Thanks…thank you."

He slumped back down and it took everything I had not to jump out of my chair and go to him, to hold him. Jackson gripped his shoulder and said something but Sawyer only shook his head, covered his eyes with his hand.

Judge Chen looked to the Abbotts who were talking in hushed, urgent voices at their attorney, who whispered and gestured back in a mess of confusion.

"Mr. Holloway," the judge said, "is there something your clients would like to say?"

Reluctantly, the lawyer got to his feet. "Your Honor, we'd like a conference in chambers."

Judge Chen's face remained impassive, but I could swear I saw relief touch his features. He nodded.

"Granted."

I watched as the bailiff led the court reporter, and both parties to the judge's chambers at the rear of the courtroom. Jackson put his arm around Sawyer, who moved like a sleepwalker carrying a thousand pounds on his back. Just before he stepped into the chambers, he turned and our eyes met. His beautiful face was painted with anguish and hope. I smiled through tears and gave him two thumbs up.

The smallest twitch of a smile touched his lips, and stepped inside. The bailiff followed him and shut the door behind him.

I let my hands drop and my tears fell with them. I felt like fool for giving him such a silly gesture but it's all I had. That and hope, because it was so apparent that if he lost Olivia, nothing would ever be okay ever again. And I realized with a horrible pang that added to the already heavy anguish in my heart, that losing Olivia would hurt me too. More than I realized.

Minutes ticked by. I was the only person in the gallery besides the Clerk who sat at her desk, shuffling papers. She had the results of the DNA test. I wanted to hurdle the rows of benches, tear it from her hands, and rip it to pieces so no one could ever know what it said.

Finally, the chambers' door opened and a jolt of panic and hope jerked me ramrod straight. The judge emerged first, his face impassive as ever, followed by the Abbotts, who exchanged nervous smiles with each other. I craned my head, practically jumping out of my seat, until I saw Jackson's wide smile and Sawyer…

I love him.

The thought tore through me with heat and electricity both.

Oh my God, I love him. I'm in love with him.

I was in love with Sawyer, because in that moment, his happiness—the wholeness of his heart—was the only thing that was important to me. And I realized too, that all times I'd thought I'd been in love before were nothing. Infatuations of my lonely heart. I had no thought for myself in that courtroom. Only love for Sawyer and the fervent hope that nothing would ever hurt him.

I drank him in, searching for a sign of what happened in that meeting. His eyes were red-rimmed but and he looked shell-shocked; heaving a sigh—of relief?—and answered Jackson's smile with a wan one of his own. As he crossed the courtroom, his eyes found mine. His smile widened a little, and then he turned to take his seat.

I sucked in a breath. The judge cleared his throat.

"The Petitioners have requested a motion to delay reading of the order for paternal DNA results until the Respondent has completed his bar exam for the State of California, scheduled to be begin on Monday of next week. The motion is granted. The test results will remain sealed until that time as this Court reconvenes on the following Friday. Plaintiffs, in addition to their prearranged weekend custody, are granted temporary, supervised custody of Olivia Abbott, the minor child, for the three-day duration of Mr. Haas's bar examination. Hearing adjourned."

He banged his gavel and Sawyer slumped in his chair. The Abbotts approached and words were exchanged. Jackson shook Mr. Abbott's hand. Alice Abbott moved to Sawyer and it looked to me like she was trying not to touch him or hug him. She looked like a mother regarding her son, and hope took flight in my chest. A few more words were passed between them, and then the Abbotts left, both giving me a nod as they did.

I hurried around the partition to Sawyer and Jackson.

"What does this all mean?"

"It means the Abbotts didn't want to tank Sawyer's bar exam with bad results," Jackson said. "We haven't won, but this delay gives me hope that no matter what happens, the Abbotts are flexible." He elbowed his friend. "Either that, or susceptible to your manly displays of emotion."

Sawyer heaved a ragged breath. "Now what do I do?"

"They take Olivia tomorrow morning through Wednesday," Jackson said. "You have this weekend to study, and then the Big Test, which you are going to kill."

Sawyer nodded. "So we can go? Right now I just want to get back to Olivia."

We left the courthouse. The sun was high and golden, and almost as bright as Jackson's smile as we walked to the sedan he said his company had given him to use. It seemed the entire world was different from the one we woke up in this morning.

"So, Darlene, what's going on with you?" Jackson asked as we walked to the parking lot. "Have any fun plans this weekend?"

I gave a small laugh at his infallible humor and optimism.

"Uh, yeah, I have a dance thing Saturday night."

In my peripheral, Sawyer raised his head. With effort, I kept my eyes on Jackson. "It's totally no big deal, though. Tiny little show in a nothing theatre. Like, fifty capacity." I laughed nervously. "If we fill ten seats I'd consider it a success."

"Damn, my brother's got a graduation party tomorrow night in

Oakland, or I'd totally show up," Jackson said. "I didn't know you were part of a dance company."

"I wouldn't call it a company," I said. "It's super small. I just auditioned to dip my foot back in the waters, you know?"

We arrived at the sedan and the driver opened the door for us. "Well, break a leg," Jackson said. "Wait, am I supposed to say that for dancers, or just actors?"

"If you're wishing me luck, I'll take it."

We climbed in and once again, I was wedged between Sawyer and Jackson. My thigh pressed against Sawyer's and I felt every place where we touched, just the same as we had on the way over.

Except now I know I'm in love with him.

The car dropped us off first. Jackson climbed out to say goodbye. He pulled Sawyer into a hug.

"I'll drive you to Sac on Sunday, but just know you're going to kill it. You're ready."

"Thank you," Sawyer said. "For everything."

"You did all the heavy lifting." Jackson turned his smile to me. "And you go bring that fifty-seat house down with your dance, okay?" He raised his eyebrows meaningfully. "Where is it again? And what time? Just in case I can sneak out of the party early."

"Um, eight o'clock at the Brown Bag Theatre, off Capp Street? But really, it's cool. You don't have to. It'll take longer to find parking than to watch the actual show."

"That's what these babies are for," Jackson said and tapped the roof of the car. "Or Ubers. Or cabs. Or trains. Or buses," he said at Sawyer, then grinned. "Take care, you two."

Outside our house, Sawyer carved a hand through is hair.

"Thank you for coming today."

"I didn't do anything…"

"You did," Sawyer said. "It was good to have you there. I think it helped me to find the words when I needed them most."

A warmth spread through my chest. "I'm glad I could help," I said in a small voice.

Sawyer turned his gaze to the Victorian. "I don't want to go to Sacramento," he said. "I feel like I'm losing whatever time I have left with her. I'm too scared to let myself think today was anything but a stay of execution."

I touched his hand. "The Abbotts are good people. Even if they get custody, I feel like they won't cut you out. You'll have partial custody, or visitation…"

"I don't want that," Sawyer said, his eyes hard. "I want full custody. All the time."

"I know you do. But I think, somehow, it will be all right. In a way that we can't see yet."

He nodded. "I can't fall apart right now. Or at all, I guess. Not until after the exam." He looked up at me suddenly, the anguish pulling at him again. "Five days, Darlene. Jesus, I wish…"

"What?" I asked softly. "Tell me."

His jaw clenched and anger hardened his features in a way I recognized; when he was overcome with emotions and didn't know what to do with them. The anger was directed inward, as if he thought he was a failure for having them.

His dark eyes caught and held mine. "I wish Olivia was staying with you."

I reeled at the words. Words that meant he trusted me. That my past didn't scare him. It was like a gift of hope, that maybe there was still a future for us too, even if we couldn't see that yet either. Hot tears sprung to my eyes.

"Me too," I said.

Chapter 23

Sawyer

The front door buzzed promptly at eight a.m. I had Olivia bathed and dressed, and her bag packed until the zipper looked ready to burst.

Like the bag Molly gave me the day she left.

"I'm not giving her up," I muttered, jamming her sippy cup into a side pocket. "It's just for five days and then..."

I couldn't see anything after that. All the prepping and studying and planning ahead wasn't going to get me out of the unknown. I was that kid again, standing in the foyer of my house, blue and red lights flashing, waiting with a horrible anticipation for what was to come.

The buzzer sounded again. I picked Olivia off the floor. "Come on, baby. Time to see Grandma and Grandpa."

I took Olivia down to the Abbotts, into the morning's amber light. The smiles on Gerald and Alice's faces were genuine and it felt impossible to hate them.

But if they take Olivia from me, how could I help it?

The court-appointed supervisor, a kind-faced woman named Jill, waited by the BMW, as the Abbotts and I stood in a tense silence.

"Good morning," Alice said as I came down the steps with Olivia in my arms. "How are you, little one?" Olivia rested her head on my shoulder. "Tired, honey?"

She wasn't tired. Olivia wasn't a complainer; she was resting her head on me to stay close. I tightened my hold on her.

"And how are you, Sawyer?" Alice asked quietly.

"Fine. Why did you ask for a delay on the DNA results?"

She and Gerald exchanged glances.

"As we stated at the hearing, you have your big exam," Alice said. "We…didn't want you to be distracted any more than you probably are."

"We didn't realize you had so much going on right now," Gerald added.

Newsflash, folks: there is no good time to rip apart a guy's life and take his kid away.

The words were on my lips but I swallowed them down. Animosity wasn't going to get me anywhere, and I didn't want Olivia to feel it and be wrapped up in it.

And you like them, a voice sounding like Jackson spoke up.

"Thank you for that," I said grudgingly.

Alice smiled nervously. "We hope you do well on your test, and when you get back, maybe we can all have lunch?"

"Alice," Gerald said in a mild tone of warning.

"Just a thought." Alice smiled.

"Sure. Lunch," I said, trying not to sound like a complete asshole, but goddammit, they were going to take my daughter and drive off with her and the pain was squeezing my heart so I could hardly breathe.

It's just five days…isn't it? Please, God, I can't do more than that.

Jill approached. "Can I help put her in her car seat?"

I nodded slowly. It was time to go. I wanted to hold Olivia forever; or grab her and make a run for it… I kissed my girl on the cheek.

"I love you. I'll see you soon." I put Olivia in Jill's arms. "Be good, honey."

"Be goo, Daddy."

My chest tightened and I busied myself with fishing a piece of paper out of my pocket while I pulled myself together.

"This is the name of the hotel I'll be staying at in Sacramento," I told the Abbotts. "This is my cell phone number. This is Darlene's number—my upstairs neighbor, and this is Elena, my sitter's number."

You remember them? My unlicensed, irresponsible babysitter and my drug addict neighbor?

I bit back those words too, hid them behind a stiff, expressionless mask.

"If you need anything and can't get a hold of me, call one of them," I said.

"Will do," Gerald said.

They both seemed to be waiting for me to do or say something more.

"Okay, so…that's it, I guess," I muttered.

Apparently that was the wrong answer. Gerald pressed his lips together, and ushered his wife to the car.

Alice gave me a final, small smile. "Good luck."

I watched them climb in and the engine roared to life.

"God help me walk away," I whispered.

I couldn't move. As with last weekend, I stayed rooted to the curb until their SUV, with Livvie safely buckled inside, drove down the street and around the corner. It wasn't possible to walk away, but if the court gave full custody to the Abbotts, I'd chase their car down until I hadn't breath left in my body. A dumb notion. It wouldn't do me any good if the law sided with them.

Fuck the law.

I couldn't help but feel it had betrayed me when I was trying so hard to be its agent and advocate. And now I had to devote three full days to proving I had what it took to do just that.

I dragged myself up to my place.

Inside, it was quiet; the silence amplified my aloneness. No sound of Olivia or her baby babble that was fast growing into language; no wooden *clunk* of her blocks coming together as she stacked them. The baby monitor was silent; her crib empty. I refused to believe this was a preview of my future, but it was hard. So damn hard.

I put on a pot of coffee and while it brewed, I slumped at my desk and pulled my study materials around me. But they blended together in a mash of words that were already familiar to me. I knew this stuff, forwards and back. All those endless nights hadn't been for nothing. I was as ready as I ever could be for this exam.

I shut my books and sat in the quiet of my place. My stomach growled loudly in that quiet, and I shuffled to the kitchen for something microwavable. I found Darlene's latest tuna casserole in the refrigerator.

I pulled it from the fridge and set it on the counter, staring at the tinfoil-covered pan. My stomach was still complaining, but another hunger grew and spread, upward and out, like a strange fire that had nothing to do with food.

I needed to see Darlene; my hands wanted to touch her, my overworked brain needed to laugh with her, and my stony heart wanted to be with her, and give whatever we had between us an honest chance.

How? How can I be with her when my heart could be shattered with one bang of a judge's gavel?

"Fuck," I said, shoving the tray away.

Above was quiet too. No creaks. Darlene might still be sleeping or maybe she was out taking a run, or getting ready for her dance that night.

Jackson, with all the subtlety of an elephant on roller skates, had gotten the theater address from Darlene and now it was in my brain forever. She'd tried hard—too hard—to minimize it, but I knew the truth. She hadn't danced in four years. This was a big deal to her.

My phone rang, and I looked at the number.

Speak of the devil...

"What's up, Jax?"

"Just calling to make sure you didn't beat up two nice old people, and were now racing toward Mexico in their white Bronco with Livvie."

"It's a white Beemer," I said dully. "And the thought crossed my mind."

A bunch of clicking and shuffling sounds came over the line.

"What are you doing?" I asked.

"Driving to my bro's grad party in Oak-town," Jackson said. "I put you on speaker. So listen. Darlene's show."

"What about it?"

"You're going, right?"

I glanced at the tuna casserole. "I don't know."

"Goddammit, Haas," Jackson said, nearly shouting. "What the fuck is wrong with you?"

I blinked, shook my head at the sudden volley, then fired back. "What is wrong with *me*? Where should I fucking start? You think it's easy sitting down here when she's up there, ten steps away?"

"Then get your ass up there."

"And do what? Sleep with her? Start a relationship with her? And what happens after the hearing next Thursday? If I lose, I'm not going to be good for anyone, Jax. It's going to fuck me up. Hard."

"You're so sure you're going to lose…?"

"I'm not super optimistic," I said snidely. "I don't know what else I can do."

"You can start but not being a colossal asshole to the Abbotts. They *want* to like you, Sawyer, but you are making it so easy for them not to. And furthermore, they want *you* to like *them*. The delay in the test results? That was a gift. Did you even thank them for it?"

"Yes," I spat. "I did. But what the fuck, Jackson? Should I send them a gift basket too? 'Thanks for not ripping my daughter away from me… *yet?*' Like that's some kind of huge favor and I should be kissing their ass? If they want me to like them so fucking much, they can leave Olivia and me alone. I'd let them see her. Be a part of her life. I want that for her, but I want it on *my* terms."

"You might not get that, but you could get *something*, but not if you throw it all away by shutting them out. Stop fucking shutting people out."

I gaped. "Who have I been shutting out?"

"How about every single one of our friends? When was the last time you spoke to any of the guys from our old group?"

"I've been a little bit fucking busy taking care of Livvie and trying to get through law school," I said through gritted teeth. "This isn't exactly news."

"Mmkay, how about Darlene?"

I rubbed my eyes with my free hand. "What about her?"

"You shouldn't throw away a chance at happiness with an awesome chick because everything else is shitty. Or is it her drug history freaking you out? Because I know that's not easy for you. I get that, but—"

"But what? Suddenly you're an expert at this shit because you've had *how many* long-term relationships? Oh that's right, *none.* Get off my back, Jackson. I don't care about her past. I trust Darlene, and I know she deserves a lot better than me."

"That's a fucking cop-out. She cares about you. She might even love your dumb ass, and you're just going to let her go?"

The fire in me died at his words, at the possibilities behind them. I sank into my desk chair.

"Got your attention, did I?" Jackson said with a small laugh, the warmth returning to his voice immediately.

"I don't want to hurt her, Jax," I said quietly. "I don't know what I'm doing, and all this custody shit just makes everything a million times harder. It's not a cop-out to want everything good for her. She deserves to be happy."

"So do you, man," Jackson said in a low voice. "That's all I'm saying. You do too." There was a pause. "And Henrietta agrees with me. Hold on, she wants to say something."

I jerked up straight. "What?"

More shuffling sounds and then I heard Jackson's mother's muffled voice. "I want to talk to him off the speaker. Is it this button? Hello?" Then loudly, "*Hello?*"

I winced and held the phone away from my ear, a smile I couldn't keep back spreading over my lips. "Hi, Henrietta."

"Hello, Sawyer," she said. "How are you doing, baby?"

"I've been better."

"I know it, but listen to Mama. I know what you're trying to do, and it's sweet. You're trying to protect that girl because you're going through some hard times, and they might get harder, right?"

"I don't have anything to offer her, Henrietta."

"That's where you're wrong, honey. No one expects you to be okay through this situation. It could get rough, no lie. But when things get rough, that's when you draw people to you. You don't push them away. And the lovely Darlene? She can take all your rough times. She's been through rough times of her own, I've heard. She's not expecting you to get it all right the first time because she won't either. But reach out, baby. Reach out and hold on to those you need, because they need you too more than you think. And that's how you get through the rough stuff. You hold on and don't let go. Okay?"

I nodded, my jaw clenched. "Okay."

"Good," Henrietta said. "Now you go be with your woman. Don't worry about what to give or not give. Just be with her. Sometimes that's more than good enough."

"Thank you, Henrietta."

"Any time, baby. I'm going to give you back to Jackson and you two had better watch your language this time. You sound like a pair of fools with all that swearing."

I grinned. "I didn't know there was a lady present."

"Well, now you know."

"Yes, ma'am."

More scuffling and muffled talk, then Jackson put me back on speakerphone.

"Hello? Who's this? Sawyer? Are you still there?"

I laughed. I didn't think it was possible, but I laughed. "I'm going."

"Good."

"Hey, Jax…" My damn throat closed up. "I…"

"I know," he said. "Love you too, bro."

I hung up and heaved a sigh that felt miles deep. And though it felt a little bit like lowering my guard, I decided to do something I hadn't done in almost a year. I crawled into my bed without setting an alarm, and tried to take a nap.

But as exhausted as I was, sleep eluded me. I tossed and turned on cold sheets. My bed had always been empty. Even in the past, when I'd had a woman in it, it was only for a few hours. No sleep, just sex and then the woman left. I made sure of that.

I closed my eyes and used my infallible memory to recall Darlene, in perfect detail. A few tricks of mental Photoshop, and she was lying next to me, her dark hair splayed across my pillow, her mouth inches from mine—laughing and smiling…

I slipped into the twilight world between sleep and awake, and the image of her wavered like a mirage, just out of reach.

When I finally did fall asleep, it was fitful, skimming above the surface of deep rest, and when I awoke, the bed was still empty.

Chapter 24

Sawyer

The afternoon sun was high when I climbed out of bed, and I was hungry as hell. I heated up a huge portion of Darlene's casserole and ate every bite. After, I took my best gray suit to the dry cleaners and told them to rush it. While it was being cleaned, I wandered into Macy's on Union Square and bought a new tie.

After, I picked up my dry cleaning, showered, changed, and at a quarter to seven, I headed out. At the florist on 14th, I started toward the red roses, but a stand of daisies in brilliant yellow and orange caught my eye.

"Gerber daisies," said the florist with a smile. "In Egyptian times, the *gerbera* daisy represented light and sun. In the Victorian era, they came to represent happiness."

"In the *Victorian* era…" At the word, my photographic memory conjured my house; Darlene's house too.

The florist smiled. "They're my favorite."

I touched one of the soft, bright petals. "Mine too."

With a bouquet of two-dozen Gerber daisies wrapped in green tissue paper under my arm, I jumped on the Muni for the Mission District; an artsy, bohemian part of the city.

I walked along a busy street lined with shops and cafés, and one too many new condo complexes. The tech industry was sucking some of the life out of the old San Francisco. The Brown Bag Theater was a hole in the wall; a holdover from before the tech boom, and that still existed by the city's sheer force of will, though I wondered for how much longer.

I paid a $10 ticket at the rickety box office and stepped into the shabby interior. The wallpaper was faded and covered in posters from previous shows. The lobby was nonexistent; a small space where one wall was heavy with black curtains. A handful of people loitered in the space, talking and drinking wine from a tiny bar stand. I was the only one wearing a suit.

At ten to eight, a nervous-looking guy in black passed out programs and told us to take our seats. I filed in to the fifty-capacity space with the rest of the audience; we filled maybe twenty seats.

I laid the flowers across my knee and watched the stage—a small rectangle of scuffed black illuminated by a single light in the center. My stomach twisted as if I were the one about to perform, and I scanned the program—a smudgy Xerox folded in half.

Most of the dances were as a group, but Darlene had a solo, halfway into the show.

She never told me.

Then the house lights dimmed and the show began.

It wasn't good.

I was no dance connoisseur but every number felt amateurish and overly dramatic. Trying to make a statement, somehow. Except for Darlene. My considerable bias aside, she was riveting. Stunning. I couldn't take my eyes off of her. The dumbass director shoved her in the back of every ensemble dance, and still she shone brighter than the lead dancer we were supposed to be watching.

Three routines later, and Darlene took the stage. She moved gracefully into a cone of light in a simple black dancer's dress with billowy material that floated around her long legs. Her hair was tied up on her head in a loose ponytail, revealing the long lines of her neck and shoulders. Like my favorite shirt of hers, the back of her dress crisscrossed her shoulder blades—highlighting the lines and lean muscle. The sleeves were long but sheer, also giving elegant definition to her arms.

God, she's so beautiful.

The program said she'd be dancing to a song called "Down." I'd never heard it before, the first notes—a lone piano—descended like downward steps. Darlene remained frozen until a woman began to sing. A lonely voice, yet bright and clear.

I stared at Darlene, watched the play of her muscles under her skin as she moved, filled the small space with her presence, flowing like shadows and light; slow with the piano, fast and precise with the techno beat.

As the song came to an end, Darlene collapsed onto her back, braced on one elbow; the other arm reached for the unlit space above her, her hand grasping at nothing. On that final note and last haunting lyric, her back arched and her head fell back, as if she were being pulled upward by an unseen force, and then left there, suspended in the silence.

The moment hung and then the meager crowd caught their breath. I broke free from her spell and my hands slammed together over and over. A few other audience members whistled or whooped where they had only politely applauded every act that had come before.

My chest swelled with pride. She was the best and they all knew it.

Then the next and final dance came, and Darlene was once again relegated to the back of the stage. I didn't know what kind of hierarchy this dance troupe had but it was painfully obvious Darlene deserved to be the lead.

I watched her make-do in the back with her partner—the clumsy schmuck who'd bruised her head in rehearsal a few weeks ago. She struggled with him now. I saw her correct mistakes, or cover for him when he was off-time. A sneer curled my lips, and I tried to focus on her. Just her.

And then it happened.

The pairs of dancers in the back came apart and then flew together, and Darlene's klutzy partner stomped on her foot with his heel. I shot halfway out of my seat as Darlene's face contorted in sudden pain. No one else seemed to have noticed—the lead dancer had executed some sort of gymnastic feat to capture their attention.

Darlene put on a stage face and I sank down slowly, watching in awe as she powered through the rest of her dance—about ten more seconds. She favored her right foot, but subtly, and the only real sign of her pain was the sweat the glistened across her chest.

As soon as the dance ended, the dancers bowed, and Darlene's partner shot her an apologetic look. She stared straight ahead, into the lights that blinded her to the audience, but I saw the tears in her eyes and the clench of her jaw. She kept her right foot behind her left as she bowed to the smattering of applause, but as soon as the black curtain began to drop, she limped off.

The lights came up and while everyone else filed toward the exit, I raced down the small aisle with the flowers and jumped onto the stage. I had to paw at the heavy material for a moment but I found the split and stepped through it.

It was dim, but backstage lights guided me to a small anteroom where the dancers were laughing with post-show nerves and being congratulated by their director.

"Where's Darlene?" I demanded.

They all stopped and exchanged glances. Her asshole partner had the good graces to look chagrined but said nothing.

"Probably in the dressing room," the lead dancer said in a bitchy tone I didn't like. "She kind of...does her own thing."

I remembered how Darlene had told me they didn't welcome her with open arms, but made her feel like an outcast.

Even though she's the best of them. Because *she's the best of them.*

I snorted in disgust and turned back the way I'd come. I found the tiny dressing room. Empty. A short corridor led behind the stage. I heard the muffled crying first, and followed it to her, picking my way carefully through the dimness.

Darlene sat on the floor, her back against one of the movable backdrops that had been used in show. Her right foot was propped up on a coil of rope and even in the dark, I could see the swelling and bruising around the last two toes.

"Darlene."

She lifted her tear-stained face, taking in me and my suit, and the flowers in my hand. And in one glance, I felt how she appreciated all of it more than she had words for. More than I deserved. Because her every emotion lived in her body, in her eyes, and beautiful face that couldn't keep anything a secret.

She smiled through her tears, her voice whispery and tremulous. "You came."

I knelt beside her, examined her foot to conceal the sudden rush of emotions that swept through me. I had too many and didn't have the first clue what to do with them all.

I've never felt this way about a woman before...

And she was hurt. That clumsy asshole hurt her. I channeled my feelings into anger at him and felt more in control.

I set the flowers down, and carefully pulled her foot onto my lap. Her last two toes were swollen, and the bruising was spreading down the outside edge of her foot and across the top in purple splotches. "This isn't my specialty, but it looks broken."

"I think so. It's hurts. A lot." She sniffed and shook her head. "So much for my dance comeback."

"For now," I said fiercely. "You'll heal and get out there again. You have to. You were the best damn part of that show."

Darlene smiled, or tried to, for me. But it crumpled under the weight of her tears.

"I try so hard...and it all just slips out of my grasp. My best friend...now this job..." She tilted her head up to look up at me, her blue eyes brimming and her cheeks stained with the trails of dark makeup. "I can't hold on to anything..."

I swallowed hard, Henrietta's words filtering into my thoughts. I put my arms around her.

"Not this time." I said, gruffly. "Hold on to me."

She raised her eyes to mine, uncertain. "Sawyer..."

"And I'll hold on to you, okay?" I said. "Just as tightly."

A little sob escaped her and she wrapped her arms around my neck. I held her for a long, selfish moment, until her body in my arms tensed with pain, pushing a little whimper from her. I set the flowers in her lap, and lifted her off the ground carefully, holding her around the back and under her knees.

"The daisies are beautiful," she said, with a sniff. "They're so bright and cheerful."

I nodded. In the dark, and in pain, Darlene was still giving, still generous and vibrant. I held her closer, and carried her through the theatre, her head tucked under my chin and her hand on my chest. We passed through the green room, and the troupe stopped their small celebrations.

"You broke her damn foot," I snapped at her partner.

"It was an accident," Darlene said, clinging to me tighter.

"Accident or not, he should have known better. *Been* better to her," I said, still pinning the guy with a hard stare, then sweeping it over the room. "You all should have. You should have taken care of her."

I should have taken care of her.

I gritted my teeth. "Whoever you find to replace her won't be one tenth the dancer she is." I looked down at Darlene. "You have stuff here?"

She nodded. "In the locker."

"I got it." A small woman in glasses brought Darlene's bag and her ratty old gray sweater. Darlene added them to her lap, beside the flowers.

"You were great tonight," the woman said, her eyes darting to mine and back. "He's right. I hope you get better quick. Some other company's going to be lucky to have you."

"Thanks, Paula," Darlene whispered.

I carried her out of the theatre, onto the street, where the night was cold and the wind made Darlene's black dance dress slide up her legs. She shivered, and then let out a little cry.

"God, it hurts," she whispered.

"Do you mind calling me an Uber or a cab?" I said, trying to take her mind off of it. "I'd do it, but my hands are tied."

She smiled and fished her phone from her purse. "You can put me down. I must be heavy."

"You're not," I said.

I'm not letting you go.

An Uber arrived within minutes, and I was glad the driver had the heat turned up. In the backseat, I kept her against me, holding her. And the way she molded herself to me, I felt like she was mine, and never in my life had I known such happiness. A bruised happiness, given what I faced with the Abbotts, but a happiness I hadn't ever experienced. It felt like too much to ask for more, but in my mind's eye, I tentatively reached for a future that had both her and Olivia. A real life.

A family?

"Thank you for coming to the show," Darlene said, pulling me from my thoughts. "It meant so much to me, I can't even tell you."

Shame ripped through me at how I almost hadn't. At how close I came to letting my own fear keep me home. I wouldn't have been there to witness her dance, or be there for her when she got hurt.

I said nothing but held her tighter.

"I called my parents a few days ago," Darlene said against my chest. "I waited so long to tell them about the show because what if I gave them plenty of notice, and they still said no? I thought it would hurt less if I told them at the last minute. Then they could say no, and it would make sense. Kind of like insurance, you know?"

"Yeah, I know."

"And I didn't even tell my best friends back home at all. But I wished I had. I wish I'd been braver."

"You are brave, Darlene," I said. "You're braver than anyone I know."

"My best friend Beckett told me that once, too. I don't know if I believe it but I feel like I'm getting closer. This may not be the best show, but it was my first since I started using. My first since I'd been clean."

She craned her head to look up at me. "Tonight was a disaster, but it was also better than anything I could have imagined. I needed someone there." Her eyes shone. "You were there."

"It wasn't a disaster. You were incredible." I swallowed hard. "And I showed up, yeah, but I should've been there for you a hell of a lot sooner."

She shrugged and smiled, her fingertips touching my cheek. "You're here now, Sawyer. That's all that matters."

Chapter 25

Darlene

Sawyer directed the Uber driver to take us to the ER entrance at UCSF medical center. A team approached with a gurney. Sawyer helped me out of the car, and held me gently, reverently, as if he were reluctant to let me out of his arms. He set me down on the gurney and I bit back a cry at the pain when my heel touched down. But I couldn't hold the next little moan in as we went over a bump. Sawyer grabbed my hand and I squeezed. He squeezed back.

The ER was bustling with nurses, doctors and people in pain; the air a sterile cold. They wheeled me into a space and closed a curtain around me. A nurse tucked a pillow under my foot, and then laid an ice pack on it. I clenched my teeth as the pain turned icy and bit deep. Under the bright glare of the hospital lights my foot looked awful; swollen and wearing a bouquet of purple, red, and blue bruises. My last two toes throbbed dully; a terrible just-stubbed-my-toe pain that wouldn't fade.

Sawyer pulled up one of the two chairs in the little space, and took my hand, wrapping his warm fingers around my cold ones.

"A doctor will be in shortly to examine you," the nurse said. "It looks like you've broken a toe or two. He'll want x-rays to confirm. In the meanwhile, I can give you something for the pain."

"Advil," I said.

"Are you sure you don't want something stronger?"

"No, just your strongest Advil, please."

She smiled. "My strongest Advil is called Percocet, honey, but you're the boss."

I took the little pills and the glass of water, not looking at Sawyer.

"I try to stay away from anything that alters my mental state," I said in a quiet voice when the nurse had gone.

"You don't have to explain," Sawyer said.

"I feel like I do," I said. I forced my eyes to find his. "I hate how you learned about my past. I'm sorry it came out like that—at the worst time and place for you."

"It's not what's going to hurt my chances with Olivia."

"I would never, ever bring anything bad near her." Tears stung my eyes again. "I promise you that. I never would."

"I know you wouldn't," he said. "I freaked out about your record because of what happened to my mom. And Molly, too. And because I had my own ideas about what justice means. But what I believe has been turned up on its ass, and the only thing that matters right now is you."

I sniffed and wiped my eyes. "It's a good feeling."

"What's that?"

"Being trusted."

Sawyer took my hand and pressed it to his lips just as a young doctor with a bald head and warm smile stepped into the space and examined my foot.

"Looks like a few breaks, judging by the swelling and bruising," he said. "Let's get you to x-ray and see what's what."

They wheeled me to the radiology department where it was determined I had hairline fractures of the fourth and fifth middle phalanges. I breathed a sigh of relief. As far as breaks went, I could do worse than hairlines.

Back in the ER space the doctor was all smiles. "You'll live to dance another day,"

"Are you sure?"

"If you rest well, you should be ready to roll in six weeks."

"Six weeks," I said. "What about work? I have to stand for my job."

The doc wrinkled his lips. "Better if you didn't. We'll get you a walking boot but the more you can stay off it, the faster it'll heal. A nurse will be in soon to wrap you up, and give aftercare instructions."

He went out, but no nurse made an appearance. I was obviously a low priority in an ER filled with more serious injuries and illnesses. I shivered in the cold, sterile air, and sharp pain shot up my foot at the movement, making me wince.

"Will you hand me my sweater?" I asked.

"There's something I've been meaning to tell you," Sawyer said, reaching at his feet. He came up with the old, ratty thing with holes at the cuffs. "This is the ugliest sweater I have ever seen in my life."

I giggled then winced again. "Don't make me laugh. It hurts."

Sawyer tucked the sweater around my shoulders. My eyes closed and wanted to stay closed. The exhaustion of the dance performance and the pain were dragging me down.

Sawyer brushed a lock of hair from my forehead. "You should try to get some sleep, if you can. We might be here awhile."

"What about you? You should go. It's so late and you have studying to do…"

He shook his head, his chin rocking on the back of his hand. "You've been taking care of me for ages," he said. "It's my turn."

I smiled and my eyes started to close against the bright lights glaring down over us. No sooner had I begun to drift, then the nurse came back. She wrapped my foot, put a heavy walking boot on it, and gave me a cane.

"A cane to go with your granny sweater," Sawyer said, pushing me to the front of the hospital in a wheelchair.

"Ha ha. Sawyer the Comedian."

"I'm here all night, folks."

I hoped that was true.

We took a cab home and Sawyer carried me up the two flights of stairs like it was nothing. He set me down in my place, and I gave a cry as I tried to put weight on my foot. "They said I can walk in this," I said, holding on to his shoulder. "Do you think they lied to get me out of there?"

Without hesitation, Sawyer picked me up again, cradling me. He carried me to my bed in a corner alcove between the kitchen and the loveseat under the window, and gently set me down.

"Do you want anything?"

"Maybe some water? And then you can go and study. I don't want to keep you."

He shot me a small grin. "What if I want to be kept?"

"Then stay," I said. "I *do* want to keep you. And I don't want to sleep alone."

"Me neither. I'm tired of it. And I'm just…tired."

"Come here," I said. "Actually, take off your suit and then come here."

"If I take off my suit will you take off that sweater?"

"Will you stop? I love this sweater. I wear it all the time."

"I know," he said, bringing me the glass of water.

"Your mega-mind remembers everything I wear, doesn't it?"

"I remember more than what you wear, Darlene," he said, loosening his tie enough to take off. "I remember many things about you."

"Like what?"

He removed his jacket and tossed it on the loveseat. "I remember you in the grocery store the day we met, and how you smirked at me like I was an idiot for not wanting you to cook dinner for me."

I grinned. "Stubborn man-pride."

Sawyer took off his pants and dress shirt, leaving him in his boxers and undershirt.

"I remember how your hands felt on my shoulders the first time you massaged me. I remember how red the cherry was that you ate at the club that night. I wanted to kiss you so badly; more than I'd ever wanted to kiss anyone. I remember how you tasted the first time I did kiss you, and secretly wondered if you'd ruined me for all other women."

He climbed into bed beside me. Instantly, I curled into him and he wrapped his arms around me. We held each other close, my face nestled in the crook of his neck, and his chin on my head. My heart pounded to be this close to him. In bed with him, even if all we did was this.

"Why are you telling me all this?" I whispered.

"I'm trying to be romantic. How am I doing so far?"

I smiled. "Not bad. But you'll have to continue for me to know for sure."

Sawyer chuckled and pulled back to look at me. His eyes softened as they swept over me, like he was memorizing me over and over again, only because he wanted to. His fingers drew my face as he spoke.

"I remember every time you made me laugh when it felt like it had been ages since I'd even smiled," Sawyer said, and his voice turned gruff over his next words. "And I remember how you held my daughter like you'd been doing it forever, and that was the first time I imagined having something more than what I had."

Tears filled my eyes. "Sawyer..."

"Darlene, I don't know what I'm doing. I don't know what's coming around the corner and I'm fucking scared to death. But the half of my heart that isn't banged up from this fight for Olivia is all yours. It's not much but it's all I got right now."

"I'll take it."

"Are you sure? Because I'm scared I can't give you what you deserve. I'm living partially in the real world, and partially in a future that's a handful of days away. Jackson—and his mother—think otherwise, but dammit, Darlene, it's not fair to subject you to the shit storm that might be coming."

"I can take it, Sawyer," I said. "I want to take it. I'd rather be here for you, if it helps at all."

"It does," he said. "So much."

I snuggled closer to him, ignoring the throbbing of my foot. That pain was a much weaker echo of the one that lived in my heart, for him.

He stroked my hair. "I've never slept with a woman before. Just sleep, I mean."

"Neither have I," I murmured against his neck. "I've never just...been held. It's nice."

I felt him melt around me, the tension seeping out, at least for now. For a few precious hours, we slept deeply, tangled together. I held on to him, and he held on to me, just like he promised.

The following morning, I woke to sunlight streaming in from the window above the loveseat and Sawyer standing, looking out, his eyes full of thoughts.

"Hey," I said softly. "Sleep well?"

He nodded. "It's nearly ten o'clock. I haven't slept this late since the summer before I started Hastings." He turned to me, and I could see the weight of his exam, and the fight for Olivia were back, pushing him down again. "How's the foot?"

"Hurts, but I'll live."

"I wish I didn't have to leave you," he said, coming to sit with me on the bed.

I turned him so I could rub his back, keep the tension from digging deep, but I was too late. "What time is your bus to Sacramento?"

"One o'clock," he said. "I'll get you some groceries or…anything else you need before I go."

I turned him to me and cupped his cheek. "You're good at taking care of people."

His smile wilted a little and I knew he was thinking of Olivia. He patted my arm and rose quickly. "I'll make you some coffee."

Sawyer made the coffee, then left to shower, change and pack. He came back afterward and sat with me, hardly saying anything. I let him have his silence, and just held him, our fingers laced together.

At noon, Jackson arrived to take him to the bus depot. His suit looked slept in, and he kept sunglasses over his eyes, even indoors. He propped one hand against my doorway.

"I am…so hungover." He craned his neck forward, then took his sunglasses off to blink blearily at me. "I was going to ask how you dance show went. Judging by that boot on your foot, I'd say either really badly, or you slayed so hard, you up and hurt yourself."

"The first one," I said, with a smile.

"The second," Sawyer said.

"Thatta girl." Jackson shuffled into my place, and clapped Sawyer on the shoulder.

"You ready?"

"As I'll ever be."

"My man. Let's roll."

I got to my feet and hobbled on my cane. The pain wasn't as bad though the notion of a six-hour shift at the spa the next day made me vaguely nauseated.

"Are you sure you want to come?" Sawyer asked. "Maybe you should rest."

"Shush, I'm coming."

"Shush, she's coming," Jackson said. He jerked a thumb at

Sawyer. "This guy, am I right?"

The guys helped me down the stairs and into the car Jackson had waiting. I guessed he was doing really well at his firm. I wanted that for Sawyer; to get his clerkship and the career he dreamed of. But he needed to pass the bar first, and in the car ride to the bus depot, he was silent. Preoccupied. His eyes were full of thoughts he didn't share with Jackson or me.

I held his hand the entire time and he held mine, but he hardly spoke. I hoped Jackson would get him talking with his usual jovial humor, but Jackson was nursing a hangover and when I looked over at him, he was snoozing against the window.

At the bus depot, we roused Jackson, and Sawyer got his bag from the trunk. We stepped outside into the brilliant sun, and I recognized this spot as the place where I got off the bus after my trek from New York.

"Jesus, the sun hates me," Jackson muttered, shielding his eyes even though his sunglasses were back on. He clapped his hands together once, winced at the sound, and then turned to Sawyer. "This is it. The big one. How you feeling, champ?"

Sawyer shook his head. "I don't know. My head's not in the game."

"Get your head off the bench and onto the field," Jackson said. "It's fourth-and-one. Ten seconds left on the buzzer. Hail Mary pass. Slap shot from center line, and other assorted sports metaphors."

Sawyer rolled his eyes. "You watch too much ESPN."

"No such thing."

The two men clasped hands, then pulled each other in for a hug.

"You got this," I heard Jackson say in a low voice. "I know you do."

"Thanks, Jax," Sawyer replied.

He turned to me, his eyes still so heavy. Jackson shot us a small smile, and took a few steps back to give us privacy.

"I gave the Abbotts your number in case Livvie needed anything," Sawyer said. "I didn't think to ask you. I hope that's okay."

"It is," I said. "You're going to do great."

"We'll see."

"I'd tell you to break a leg, but the last time someone said that to me I wound up in the ER."

He smiled thinly and I didn't know what else to say or do to make this easier for him. The pressure was sitting on his shoulders, pressing him down.

What would Max say to make me feel better?

Max. He was like a guardian angel, watching over me. From Seattle.

I smiled to myself.

"You see that pillar over there?" I said, jerking my chin to the white column of cement. "When I first got off the bus from New York, Max was standing right there. I'd just left my home and traveled three thousand miles away from friends and family to a brand new city. But he was there, waiting for me. We didn't know each other, but it didn't matter. Just the fact he was there for me…that made all the difference in the world."

I put my hands on Sawyer's shoulders and kissed him softly on the cheek. "I'm going to be waiting for you right there when you get back. Okay?"

Sawyer nodded, his eyes sweeping over my face. Then he abruptly took my face in his hands and kissed me. Hard. A kiss I felt in every part of me, like a sudden rush of electricity, surging through me and leaving me breathless.

He kept his forehead to mine after he broke apart, his own breath coming hard.

"A tornado, Darlene," he whispered. "I'm swept up."

Then he pulled away, shouldered his bag, and got on the bus.

Jackson drove me back home, and helped me inside. He gave me a hug and one of his trademark, brilliant smiles.

"You call if you need anything," he said. "I'm at your beck and call."

"Thank you, Jackson."

"Anything for you, Darlene."

He turned to for the door.

"What are his chances?" I asked before he could turn the handle.

Jackson stopped, shrugged. "He's got that freakish memory. That'll get him through the multiple choice—"

"No, I meant what are the chances he's going to keep Olivia?"

He blew air out his cheeks, and ran a hand over his close-cropped hair. "I don't know, Dar. We just have to hope for the best."

I shook my head incredulous. "Jackson, how do you stay so positive? My stomach feels like it's going to turn itself inside out."

"Well, according to Henrietta, the universe is listening."

"What's that mean?"

"You get back what you put in. Negative shit gets you negative shit. Positive energy begets positive energy. Whatever you put out there in the universe…it listens. And then it answers. So when I talk, I try to give it something it wants to hear and hope it answers with something *I* want to hear." He shot me a wink. "Now if you'll excuse me, I'm going to go lay down. I put in too much vodka last night and my body has answered." He rubbed his temple. "Loudly."

I watched him go, and heard voices on the stairs after he shut the door. A knock came, and Elena peeked her head in.

"I saw you come in with the boot and the cane," she said. "Poor dear, is it broken?"

"Just two toes. The little ones. I'll be fine."

She nodded, her hands turning over and over in front of her. "Henrietta tells me the hearing was hard on Sawyer." She leaned in, as if she were afraid the universe was listening too. "They can't take her from him, can they?"

"I don't know," I said. "There's a law. A deadline, of sorts. If he'd had Olivia for a year, with no help, he'd have been able to put his name on her birth certificate."

Elena scoffed. "A year? That's weeks away! What difference does a few weeks make?"

I shrugged helplessly. "That's the law."

Elena shook her head and then reached to pat my cheek. "We will tell the judge. I'll come to the next hearing too. Character witnesses. Whatever he needs."

Acting on pure instinct, I threw my arms around her. She hugged me back in a motherly embrace I was loathe to leave, and I smelled cumin and a light perfume, and over that, the clean baby scent of Olivia. She was still there, in Elena's clothes and in her skin.

When I pulled back, the woman had tears her in eyes.

"I love that little girl. And I love him, the sweet boy."

"I do too," I said. "Both of them."

Elena's face burst into a smile like a sun from behind dark clouds. "See? What did I tell you," she said, moving toward the door. "This is no house. It's a home."

Elena left and the quiet of my place descended, leaving me with a thought that sunk its claws into me and wouldn't let go; if Sawyer lost Olivia, I'd lose them both, and this home would be empty.

Chapter 26

Darlene

The next day, Monday, I struggled through my shift at Serenity. My foot throbbed with a second heartbeat and by three o'clock, I was fighting back tears. Whitney, my supervisor, was more concerned that my boot was 'unsightly.'

"If it's too much, maybe you should stay home tomorrow," she said in the break room as I readied to head out.

I took up my cane and limped past her, my chin up. "I've dealt with worse."

The Muni home was blessedly empty. I put my aching foot up on the seat beside me and fantasized about three Advil, my bed, and maybe a Sylvia Plath poem or two.

As I was making the arduous block-and-a-half trek to the Victorian, my phone rang with a number I didn't recognize. I rested on someone else's front stoop and answered.

"Hello?"

"Darlene Montgomery?" an older woman's voice asked.

"Yes…?"

"This is Alice Abbott."

I froze, a bolt of anger-laced fear ripping through me. "Yes? What is it? Is Livvie okay?"

"She's…upset. She didn't sleep well last night. Or at all, really."

"Why not?"

A pause.

"She misses Sawyer. I wondered if we might come over to his place for a bit? So that she can play with her toys there and maybe sleep in her own bed."

I pressed my lips together. The poor woman sounded tired and more than a little sad, though she tried to hide it. I was caught between wanting to comfort her and wanting to chew her out.

"Come over," I said. "I think I can get a key from Elena."

"Thank you, Darlene," Alice said, and I heard Olivia's plaintive cry in the background. "Thank you so much."

Elena gave me Sawyer's spare key, and I waited in his place. I scattered a few of Olivia's blocks out on the floor in case she wanted to play with them.

Twenty minutes later, the door buzzed and I limped over to let them up. I left the door ajar, then started the journey back to the sofa. Footsteps, voices, and Olivia's little cries stopped me. She pushed the door open first and my heart broke at her distraught expression and tear-stained cheeks.

"Where Daddy?" she cried, looking around her home. Her blue eyes, shining with tears, found mine. "Dareen. Where Daddy? Where Daddy?"

"Oh, honey, come here."

She hurried to me, bypassing the blocks on the floor, and I picked her up and held her close. Her little body shuddered with sobs, and I glared daggers at the Abbotts coming in the door behind her.

But my anger burnt out with one glance at their kind faces. They both looked exhausted and worn out; identical defeated expressions of the best intentions gone awry.

"We didn't know what else to do," Alice said, and Gerald put his arm around her.

"She's very…astute for such a young child," Gerald said. "None of the diversions our supervisor told us to try have worked."

"She doesn't want a diversion," I said in a low voice. "She wants her daddy."

I limped to Sawyer's chair at his desk and sat with Olivia against my chest.

"Where Daddy?" she sniffled against my neck. "Wan' Daddy."

"I know you do. He'll be home soon, sweat pea. Soon."

I rubbed her back and rocked her as best I could. The Abbotts sat at the kitchen table, watching me as if I were a lion-tamer or magician. Olivia's crying tapered away to hiccupping sobs, and then she fell asleep.

"Should I put her down in her bed?" Alice whispered, rising from her chair.

"No, I want to hold her," I said. "I don't know how much longer I'll be able to."

Gerald and Alice both stiffened, looking both chagrined and defensive at the same time. Alice sat back down.

"I'm just being honest," I said. "I know you're doing what you think is right, but it's hurting people I love."

"I know," Alice said tiredly. "We're the bad guys, aren't we? But Molly…she was our only daughter. And Olivia is our last tie to her. She's our family."

"She's Sawyer's family too," I said.

"Are you sure about that?" Gerald asked.

I didn't answer. I held and comforted Olivia for long moments in the strange silence between the four of us, until my arm—already sore from massaging all day, began to complain.

"My arm's getting numb," I said. "I'm going to put her down after all."

With effort, I hauled myself out of the chair and carried Olivia to her bed. I set her down and she whimpered and stirred like she was going to wake up. But within moments, her little chest rose and fell, and the splotchy red of her cheeks from crying had faded.

I limped back to the kitchen and sat down at Sawyer's table, with the Abbotts. The air between us was thin and tight, and I, who usually burst out the first words that came to mind, knew that I had to choose them carefully. To help Sawyer if I could.

Don't fuck this up, don't fuck this up, don't fuck this up…

"How did you injure your foot?" Alice asked.

"It wasn't from chasing my next high," I said, and inwardly winced.

Good start, Dar. That should do the trick.

Gerald bristled. "Our attorney suggested we find out precisely who is living in the same house as our only granddaughter."

"You have to understand," Alice said. "We hadn't seen her in two years. Her calls and texts became more sporadic and then stopped altogether. We lived in fear of one of those visits from the highway patrol, or the phone call in the middle of the night."

"And then we got one," Gerald said. "Our baby was gone, but her friend told us she'd had one of her own."

Alice's eyes filled with tears. "I've never been so scared and…lost. Our only child was gone and her baby—a helpless, little baby—was in the hands of a complete stranger." She composed herself and met my gaze steadily. "We had to act. To find her and protect her."

"We thought Sawyer would be happy to see us," Gerald said. "Or at least friendly enough that we could get to know each other. To work together and…maybe build something."

"But he thought you were coming to tear everything down," I said softly. "Aren't you?"

Alice's hands twisted on the table, her brows drawn together. "I hate that I feel this way. That we're trying to do the right thing for Olivia, as we should, and yet it feels wrong too."

Gerald covered her hand with his.

"We were prepared to let the judge read the paternity test results," he said. "In fact, we were fairly certain, even before Sawyer spoke, what the outcome would be."

"But then Sawyer spoke," Alice said, picking up where her husband's thought left off with the ease of two people who have been married for decades. "He spoke and I had hope that he was the sort of man who would let two strangers—family and strangers both—share Olivia's life. But after the hearing, he was cold again. So cold."

"He's not cold," I said. "If he's an asshole it's because he's scared you're going to take Olivia from him. Doesn't he have every right to fear that?"

"Is he her father?" Gerald asked, with a directness that said whatever his occupation had been, he was used to being in charge.

I lifted my chin. "Yes," I said. "He is. By every standard that matters."

They exchanged pained looks. "I just wish we'd seen more of him as he was at the hearing. If we had assurance that he…was loving and kind, that Olivia felt cherished by him…"

"She is," I said softly. "God, she is. I wish you could see them together when he thinks no one is looking. How he smiles at her, or makes her laugh; how he cooks her healthy food and makes sure she eats her peas, while he heats up a frozen dinner for himself because he's working so damn hard to create a beautiful life for her."

I wiped my cheek, and shook my head. "How you saw him at the hearing is who he really is. Underneath the prickly armor, he's full of love and humor and goodness, and he would never let anything hurt that little girl." I inhaled a ragged breath. "He wants to protect her because he knows what it's like to not have a mom."

Gerald sat up straighter, and Alice's hand went to her throat. "He does?"

"He got the same visit from the highway patrol that you did. A drunk driver killed his mother when he and his brother were little. His entire world fell apart. His family fell apart, and I know that he wants Olivia to have more than he did." I leaned my arms over the table toward them. "He wants you in her life, I swear it. He won't shut you out, but… he wants full custody too."

They bristled at this and I ventured to touch Alice's hand. "Isn't that a good thing? He doesn't want to be a part-time dad. But that doesn't mean he wants to do this alone, either."

"Olivia seems quite fond of you," Alice said. "Will you be a part of her life too?"

"I'd like that," I said. "I'm quite fond of her too. And I know what you must be thinking about me. What Holloway dug up on me is true. I was arrested and did time in jail. But what his investigation didn't show you was how hard I've worked to get past that. I've been clean for a really long time, and I'm never going back. Not only for the people I love, but for me too. Especially for me."

The Abbotts were quiet, though it seemed as if they exchanged a thousand thoughts with one look.

"Does that couch fold out?" Gerald asked after a moment, nodding at the sofa.

Hope bloomed in my chest. "Only one way to find out."

The couch did fold out and Gerald went back to the condo to pack a few things for Olivia and Alice to stay through until Wednesday.

"Do you think Sawyer will mind?" Alice asked. "We're

invading his space…"

"He won't mind," I said, "because Olivia is home."

Alice met my eye. "I think it's important you know that our being here doesn't mean we're giving up our petition, necessarily."

"I know," I said. "But I'm glad you're here."

Her eyes widened and a small smile lit up her face for a fleeting moment. "Are you? I've been feeling like the evil witch in a story."

Her pain was there, just beneath the surface of her coiffed and elegant exterior and I realized that on top of everything, she was mourning her child.

"I'm sorry about Molly," I said.

Tears filled her eyes at the name; the name that she'd said a million times over her child's life, and was now imbedded in her soul. It had meaning and conjured memories only she could know.

"Where did we go wrong?" she whispered, more to herself than me. "We did everything right. Good schools, opportunities, and we loved her. God, we loved her."

In my mind, I saw Max leaning against a pillar, arms crossed, smiling at me expectantly. I drew in a breath.

"When I was sixteen, I was in the running for a dance scholarship to an academy in New York. My parents weren't one hundred percent on board, but a scholarship meant something to them. They were proud of me, in their own way. And my teachers and friends were sure I'd get it. But I was petrified. I felt like I was so close to catching something I'd wanted even before I had a name for it."

I toyed with the cuff of my ratty gray sweater.

"The night before the audition, I went to a party. Some guy offered me Ecstasy and I took it, even knowing it would keep me up all night and wreck me for the audition in the morning. I took it because that euphoria was right there and I didn't have to do anything but take a pill. I wasn't scared any more. I didn't have to care so hard about…*everything*. The desire I had in me to be, and do, and dance…I filled it up with that drug. Of course, I blew the audition, and once the X wore off, the pain of that failure swooped in. So I did the only thing I could think to do to make it go away." I shrugged my shoulders. "I took more."

I looked up to see Alice watching me with a mother's eyes; full of concern and care, and I wished, just then, she'd had the chance to talk to her own daughter like this.

"I can't speak for Molly, but maybe she was chasing something too. Something in her she couldn't catch and she filled that emptiness the best she could."

"We could have done more," she said. "We should have tried harder to find her."

"Addicts don't always like to be found," I said. "Sometimes it's just as simple and awful as that."

Alice stared at me a moment, then wiped her eyes. "Darlene, I'd like to hug you right now. May I?"

A sudden warmth spread through every part of me. My head bobbed. "Sure, yeah," I whispered.

She pulled me into a warm embrace full of her expensive perfume, but beneath that her arms were soft and I held her tight.

She hugged me for long moments, then pulled away, laughing sheepishly. "Well. I'm suddenly very hungry. Shall we have dinner?"

I grinned. "How do you feel about tuna casserole?"

Chapter 27

Sawyer

I typed the final sentence on my second of two Performance Tests. I was instructed to research, analyze, and support a solution to the case as if I were a practicing attorney. Earlier that day, I had written three essays, each requiring a demonstrated knowledge of law and relevant precedents. The day before that I had written three others. Monday, I had answered two hundred Multistate Bar Exam questions over the course of six hours. My brain was fried, but I was done.

I read over the final draft of the PT, my eyes burning. I made a few changes, and then, with aching fingers and my stomach twisting in knots, I hit 'save.'

Done. There's no going back now.

A red light on the specialized testing computer lit up. In another room, the test proctor's computer lit up with the same light, and the guy arrived at my closet-sized test space a few moments later.

"Finished?"

"That's the exact right word," I said.

"Yeah, you look pretty done," he said. He checked my area one last time for any contraband items—especially those of the digital persuasion—but all my stuff was locked away in another room, including my cell phone, wallet, and even my watch.

I shuffled out of the testing center in the Sacramento Hilton, and through the lobby. Other potential attorneys had gathered in the bar for drinks at three in the afternoon. Their laughter was loud; years of study, stress, and long hours were over, for better or worse. 33% of us would pass. The rest would put in more study and stress to come back next year and try again. Or quit. I prayed to whatever god would listen that I was not one of them.

I veered away from the bar, and headed to the elevator bank. An attractive young woman in a black skirt and white blouse got into the elevator with me. Her blonde hair was up in a twist and her perfume filled the small space.

"Bar exam?" she asked.

"Yep."

"Me too."

I was facing forward, but I felt her eyes rake me up and down. She shifted an inch closer to me.

"Why don't sharks eat lawyers?" she asked.

I smiled faintly. "I think I've heard this one before."

"I'm sure you've heard a million of them," she said. "So? Why don't sharks eat lawyers?"

"Professional courtesy," I said.

She laughed. "Indeed. Your turn."

I scrolled through my mental database. "How do you save a drowning lawyer?"

"How?"

"Take your foot off his head."

The woman laughed again, and the elevator *dinged* her floor. She stood with her back against the door to hold it open, affording me a full view of her slender body and her breasts pushing against the silk of her blouse.

"So listen, that exam was a monster," she said. "Want to have a drink with me? To celebrate? I may have already started a little bit at the bar," she said with a small laugh, "but you can catch up."

God, here it was; one of my oldest fantasies since I decided to become a lawyer come to life. A previous version of myself, the kind that had parties and never went on dates—only hookups—would've taken this woman up on her offer without a second thought. Hell, I would have *made* the offer.

And now...

I smiled thinly. "No, thanks. I'm with...someone."

"Someone?" the woman said. "Girlfriend?"

I tried the thought on for size.

Darlene's my girlfriend.

It didn't fit. One failed date and a few kisses did not a girlfriend make. We hadn't even slept together, yet I felt closer to her than I'd ever had to a woman; my feelings for her ran so deep they scared me. But she wasn't my girlfriend. The word was both too strong and not enough at the same time.

"Darlene is someone special," I said.

"Oh God, say no more," the woman said. "I was hoping I'd caught you early, but the way your entire face changed when you said her name..." She shook her head with a rueful sigh. "I'm too late."

She shouldered her purse and let the doors close, giving me a little knowing smirk and a small wiggle of her fingers goodbye.

The shiny silver doors shut, leaving me to stare at my own reflection. A blurred face of exhaustion, and a smile that I hadn't realized I'd been wearing.

I'd planned to take the bus back in the morning in the event the test ran late, but as I got back to my hotel room, I was torn. My exhausted brain cried out for sleep, while my heart demanded I jump on the next bus back to Olivia and Darlene.

I picked up my phone and punched in Darlene's number.

"Hi," she said softly when she picked up. "Done?"

"Yeah, I'm done," I said. I hadn't called her or Jackson while in Sacramento in an effort to stay focused. In two syllables, how much I missed her came roaring back.

"How do you think it went?" she asked.

"I did my best," I said, and a ragged breath gusted out of me. I lay back against the pillows on the bed as one part of the tremendous pressure I'd been carrying, lifted off. "Yeah," I said, wiping my eyes in the crook of my elbow. "I did my best for Olivia. And for you. For us. Whatever we are after the hearing on Friday."

"Oh, Sawyer," she said, her own voice tremulous. "I'm proud of you. And I know someone else who is proud of you too. Want to say hello to Olivia?"

I sat up. "She's there? Where are you?"

"I'm at your place. I've been staying here the past couple of days with Olivia. And the Abbotts."

"You have?" I shook my head. "What...why? What's happening?"

"Olivia missed you too much. Being here in her home has helped. And being with me has helped too," she added in a small voice. "It's kind of amazing, but this little human likes being with me. I feel...honored, if that makes any sense."

I had to clench my jaw for a moment. "It makes perfect sense," I said, gruffly. I swallowed hard, and took a breath. "But...the Abbotts? They're there?"

"They've been camping out on your sofa, and that lady, Jill, from CPS, pops in and out to make sure everything's kosher. I hope that's okay."

"I...don't know what to think," I said. "But it feels like that's a good thing. Is it?" A sudden, genuine laugh of happiness burst out of me. "Holy shit, Darlene, what have you done?"

She laughed too with happy tears. "I don't know, Sawyer, but I'm just trying to be as positive about this whole situation as I can. Because the universe is listening."

"And it will answer," I murmured. "Jackson told me that once. Or maybe it was Henrietta."

"Yep. He told me the same the other day, and I think he's right." Darlene's sigh gusted over the line and when she spoke again, her voice was cheerful and strong. "Olivia wants to say hi to you now."

"Okay," I whispered, and heard Darlene calling Olivia to her.

"You want to say hi to Daddy?"

A muffled sound came and then I heard little breaths. I could see it so clearly; Darlene holding the phone to Olivia and my little girl not having any idea what to do.

"Hi, honey," I said, my voice thick. "It's Daddy."

"Daddy?" Olivia said, and my goddamn heart cracked in two. "Where Daddy?"

"I'm right here, honey, and I'll be home soon."

Olivia babbled a little. She sounded good. Happy and safe.

"Say, 'love you, Daddy,'" I heard Darlene say. "Say, 'see you soon.'"

"Wuv, Daddy," Olivia said, and then there was more breathing and babbling. Darlene came back on.

"We haven't yet grasped the concept of the phone but she heard you," Darlene said. "She's back to playing blocks. And Alice and Gerald want me to tell you that they hope your test went well. They—"

"Darlene?"

"Yes?"

The words bubbled up from my heart, scraping and bumbling their way up my throat where they got stuck.

"I…I…Jesus, I can't speak."

"I hate the phone, don't you?" Darlene said, quickly. "It's so lame. Even babies don't like it." She heaved a tremulous breath. "Come home, Sawyer. Tomorrow? Your bus arrives at eight?"

I nodded. "Yeah," I managed. "Yes. Eight."

"Okay, get some sleep. You need it. And I'll see you then, Sawyer the Lawyer."

"See you then, Darlene." *My tornado.*

I hung up with her, and sat with the phone in my lap. She'd swept me up, then Olivia and Jackson, and now the Abbotts too.

And now, thanks to her, I might have a chance.

I ordered some dinner through room service, then crashed at nine o'clock. I slept almost as deeply as I had when wrapped in Darlene's arms, in her bed.

Almost.

The hour and a half bus ride took me from the dark of dawn to a rising sun. I got off at the depot and, just as promised, Darlene was there, at the white pillar. Standing beside her were the Abbotts, looking as nervous and hopeful as I probably did. Olivia was in Darlene's arms, and she squirmed to get down as soon as she saw me.

I set down my bag, willing myself not to cry like a baby in front of God and everyone at the bus depot as Olivia toddled her little legs as fast as she could straight for me. I scooped her up and held her tight, my face pressed against her hair.

"Hi, honey," I whispered. "I'm back."

"Daddy back!" Olivia said, and jounced up and down in my

arms. She pulled away and her blue eyes—sharp and clear—studied my face. She put her little hand on my chin, and I struggled mightily to hold it together.

"Wuv, Daddy," she said, almost solemnly, and I could feel that my absence perplexed her.

"I love you too, Livvie." I hugged her again, as Darlene hobbled over with her cane. She was wearing that ugly old sweater that I loved so much. Because I loved her.

Oh Christ, I do...

Her smile was brilliant as she joined Olivia and me. "The conquering hero returns," she said. "We missed you, didn't we, Livvie?" She gave my daughter's hand a little tug, then raised her eyes to mine. "I missed you. A lot. And Sawyer—"

"I love you," I said. Still holding Olivia in one arm, I reached over and cupped Darlene's cheek, and kissed her softly. "I love you, Darlene. No matter what happens, I know that's true."

She stared at me in shock, then her entire being seemed to grow brighter, blinding in her beauty. "I love you, too," she whispered, kissing me again. "I do. No matter what happens, I love you." She turned her face to Olivia. "And you too, sweet pea. I love you, Livvie."

I held them both tightly, and this time I couldn't keep a damn tear from escaping. But through my blurred vision, I saw the Abbotts, standing in front of that cement pillar, hands clasped together. And they were smiling.

"All rise."

The courtroom got to its feet, as Judge Chen entered from his chambers to take a seat at his desk.

My heart thundered in my chest, and Jackson gripped my arm under the table, reassuring. I glanced behind me at Darlene. Her smile was shaky but she gave me two thumbs up, and that little gesture sent a small flash of warmth through me. Then the judge cleared his throat and I was stiffened by fear all over again.

"This hearing, in the matter of custody and establishment of paternity for Olivia Abbott, a minor child, the Clerk of the Court will now read the DNA results as subscribed in our last hearing that was since delayed."

He nodded his head at the clerk, and she started to rise.

Mr. Holloway, sitting beside his clients on the other side of the courtroom got to his feet first.

"Your Honor, before we begin the Abbotts have requested I read a statement to the Court."

Judge Chen frowned and peered over his glasses. "I hope this isn't yet another delay in proceedings, Mr. Holloway?"

"No, Your Honor."

I nudged Jackson. He shrugged back.

"Very well," the judge said. "Proceed."

Holloway cleared his throat. "It is the wish of my clients, Gerald and Alice Abbott, that they hereby rescind their petition for custody of Olivia Abbott. With this statement, they do intend to terminate their Order to Show Cause, and request that the paternity test results remain sealed in perpetuity and/or destroyed. Furthermore, they, as the parents of the deceased Molly Abbott, wish to sign on her behalf a Voluntary Declaration of Paternity, naming Sawyer Haas the natural father of Olivia Abbott and inscribing his name on her birth certificate as required by law."

The words rolled over me like an avalanche. I'd hardly grasped one revelation of what the Abbotts had done before Holloway read another. Dazed, I glanced up at Jackson who looked like he was trying his best not to jump out of his chair. I turned to Darlene, sitting beside Henrietta. She had her fingers pressed to her mouth, tears streaming. Lastly, my robotic movements brought my gaze to the Abbotts. Alice's kind face was tear streaked and Gerald's lips were pressed tight. Their hands were clasped on the table, tightly.

I opened my mouth to speak, not quite sure what would come out, but Holloway wasn't finished.

"It is the Abbotts' further wish to pay child support in the amount of five thousand dollars per month until such time as Mr. Haas's bar exam results are known and his employment secured. This support comes with no conditions or caveats." Holloway flashed a pleased smile my way. "That is all."

The judge's eyebrows came together. "Are your clients aware, Mr. Holloway, that rescinding all claims to custody—permanent or partial—means that any visitation or contact with Olivia Abbott will be left to the sole discretion of Mr. Haas?"

"They are aware, Your Honor. But they have hope that Mr. Haas will honor the faith the Abbotts have in him as Olivia's father, and do what is best for all parties."

I nudged Jackson but he needed no prompting. He shot to his feet.

"He will, Your Honor," Jackson said, and I was shocked to hear my friend's voice crack a little. "In the eyes of the law, a judge's ruling carries more weight than one's word, but in this situation, I know that this man's honor and duty to his daughter run deeper than any order...or blood test." He turned to the Abbotts. "And on a personal note, thank you. Thank you very much, on his behalf and mine."

"And mine too," Darlene said in a small voice from her seat in the gallery.

"Amen," Henrietta intoned, as if we were at church.

The judge sighed, though the hint of a smile pulled at the corners of his mouth. "Well, this is the most unorthodox custody hearing I've ever presided over, but if the Abbotts are withdrawing their petition, I have no reason to deny their request. The paternity test results will be destroyed and Mr. Haas, you are free to file a Voluntary Declaration of Paternity. That is all."

He banged his gavel, and it was like a door slamming shut on one terrible future and opening on another. I stood on shaking legs as the Abbotts approached.

"I...don't know what to say," I said. "Thank you doesn't seem strong enough."

Alice tentatively reached out and touched my cheek. "Olivia loves you, and more than anything, that's what we want. What we've always wanted. For her to be happy. She wouldn't be, without you."

I nodded, my teeth clenched. "I love her," I said. "So much. I promise I'll do right by her for the rest of my life."

"We've finalized the purchase of the condo in the Marina," Gerald said gruffly. "It has a spare room that we will keep for her. For when she visits Grandma and Grandpa?"

It was like a question and I wanted to erase all doubt in their minds. "Just make sure it has blocks. You know how she is about her blocks."

Gerald held my gaze a moment, then burst out laughing. He

shook my hand and then pulled me in for a hug. Alice joined, and I felt like some huge, empty space in my life I didn't know was there, was filling up with everything I'd ever wanted.

My eyes found Darlene over Alice's shoulder, and she gave me two thumbs up, tears streaming.

She's everything I've ever wanted.

I made a motion with my hand to wave her over. She started to hobble, but Jackson was quicker. He scooped her up and carried her to our little group. Our family, and the last piece fell into place.

Chapter 28

Darlene

We picked Olivia up from Elena's, and then she and her children, Jackson and Henrietta, the Abbotts, Sawyer and I went to brunch at Nopa. We gathered in the front, Olivia squealing with laughter as she was passed around from hand to hand, to keep her occupied while we waited for our giant group to be seated.

"I hope we get the same waiter as our first non-date," I told Sawyer. "He'd go crazy trying to figure out how we went from that to the Partridge Family."

Sawyer smiled but his eyes were dark as they gazed down at me. He bent to kiss my cheek and whispered in my ear. "I need to be alone with you. Badly."

A flush of heat swept through me, and I tightened my hold on his arm. "Me too," I whispered back. "Do you think they'd notice if we ducked out?"

"Not me," Sawyer said, "but you, mostly definitely."

"That's sweet but—"

Sawyer silenced me with a kiss that I felt down in the deepest part of me. I kissed him back as much as was appropriate in a restaurant, and then swatted his arm. "You can't kiss me like that in public," I teased. "I have to stay away from mind-altering substances, remember?"

He chuckled but over the course of the meal—as we sat beside each other at one long table—our eyes kept finding one another, and our hands were clasped under the table. Mostly to keep the other from exploring, as I longed to touch him and be touched.

I looked around at the table full of faces we loved and thought of what was to come after, and it was almost too much.

Oh my God, this is happening. All of this…

Jackson noticed me surreptitiously dabbing my eyes with a napkin, and leaned in. "The universe listened," he said, "and then it answered."

"Big time," I said with a laugh. "Huge."

"It listened to you, Dar," he said. "What you did? With the Abbotts? You saved him."

I shook my head. "Noooo…They were right there. They just needed a little push."

"And you gave it to them," he said. He inclined his head at Sawyer who was talking animatedly with Gerald about Gerald's former profession as a broker for a large accounting firm. "We might be in a world of hurt had it not been for you."

"That's giving me too much credit," I said. "But this, right now? This is a good feeling. The best."

And I want it to last forever.

We ate and talked, and then said goodbye to everyone. Sawyer made plans with the Abbotts for them to come over tomorrow, Saturday, and play with Olivia at the park.

"It's our Saturday ritual," Sawyer said.

"We'll be there," Alice said, her smile beautiful. She pulled me in for a hug. "And will you be there, my dear?"

"Wouldn't miss it."

We said our goodbyes and headed back to the Victorian with Elena, her kids, and the Smiths. Everyone stayed and chatted and played with Olivia. Sawyer's hungry expression when his eyes met mine never left, and he pulled me into the short hallway between the living area and bedrooms.

His kiss sent currents of electricity shooting through me, and I had to cling to his shirt to keep upright. My need to be with him was a physical ache in my body, but I caught my breath and pushed gently back.

"If Henrietta catches us now, we'll be in big trouble," I said.

"The second everyone leaves…" Sawyer said, pulling me close

again. "You're mine."

"I want that," I said. "So badly, but...I have to go out for awhile."

Sawyer frowned. "Go? Where?"

I dropped my gaze to his shirt, smoothed out a wrinkle I'd made, clutching him during our kiss. "I have an NA meeting. I have one every Monday, Wednesday and Friday."

It still felt a little bit strange to say it out loud, but then I mustered my courage and raised my eyes to meet his head-on. My breath caught to see Sawyer looking down at with me with such a potent mix of love and pride, it brought tears to my eyes.

Acceptance, I thought, *is a kind of love too.*

"Dammit, Sawyer, I've cried all my makeup away today because of you."

He smiled and cupped my cheek in his hand. "Go to your meeting," he said, his lips brushing mine. "I'll be here for you when you get back."

I pressed myself into his touch. "You might not believe this, but that's the sexiest thing I've ever heard in my life."

He chuckled and kissed me again. "I think I can do better...tonight."

At my meeting, I told the group everything. I watched, with joy in my heart, as the faces of the attendees—who looked tired in a way that had nothing to do with sleep and everything to do with internal battles that never ended—filled with hope.

Afterward, Angela, the program director, approached as I was making plans to have coffee with some of the group members sometime next week.

"Wonderful share tonight, Darlene," she said.

"Thanks," I said. "It felt good. But I'm Max-less. Any word on a new sponsor for me?"

"I've been talking with Max by phone, as a matter of fact," she said. "And we feel that, given your two years' sobriety, and your amazing progress, that you would be an ideal candidate to sponsor someone yourself."

I scrunched up my eyes. "Come again? You want *me* to sponsor someone?"

"You'd still be required to attend the meetings, but you'd be doing it in a more supportive capacity to one of our own." She smiled a gentle smile. "Do you think you'd be up for that?"

I tried to envision it. Me, as a sponsor, helping someone else. The call-ee, not the call-er.

"Yes," I said. "I'd love to help. Any way I can."

The warm fuzzy feeling in my stomach was burnt away on the way back to the Victorian, as I thought about Sawyer, waiting for me.

I snuck past his place, and went up to mine to take a shower. It took me forever, since I had to move so slowly with my broken foot. The swelling had gone down and the bruising had faded from purple to ugly green, but it still didn't look pretty.

"Suck it up, foot," I murmured as I dressed in a thong, sleep shorts, and t-shirt; no bra. "If all goes as planned, it's going to be a rough night for you," I said and laughed nervously.

I'd never been nervous before. I'd never waited this long to consummate an attraction.

"I'm in love with him," I told my reflection. "This is sort of a big deal."

It was also sort of crazy to talk to an empty studio, but I was so nervous, words popped into my brain and out of my mouth before I could stop them.

I put the boot back on my foot.

"Oh yeah, that's sexy," I muttered. Then heaved a breath and headed down.

I knocked on the door softly, but I heard Olivia's little voice crowing excitedly on the other side. Sawyer answered the door with a smirk on his face, looking sexy as hell in his pajama pants and V-neck undershirt.

"Parenthood," he said. "Destroyer of evening plans." His eyes softened as he looked down at me. "God, you're beautiful."

His hands slipped around my head, to bury themselves in my hair as he kissed me deeply, with intention. I melted into his kiss, until Olivia surrounded by blocks on the floor, saw me.

"Dareen!"

I smiled against Sawyer's lips. "To be continued."

We stacked blocks with her, Sawyer and I lying on our sides with Olivia in the middle. I watched him smile and laugh with her easily, none of the terrible tension weighing him down. She was his and the joy of it was practically radiating out of his skin.

When Olivia started to fuss, Sawyer took her into her room to read her a story and put her to bed. My nervousness had long vanished, leaving me with a pleasant, heady anticipation of what was to come.

Sawyer emerged from Olivia's room and smiled at me from across the living area where I was sitting on the sofa with my foot propped, flipping through an issue of *The Harvard Law Review* I'd found on his desk.

"She's asleep," he said. "Finally."

I shook the magazine at him. "Have you been rethinking actual causation in tort law? Because according to this article, you really need to."

He grinned and sat with me on the couch. "I'll keep that in mind. How was your meeting?"

"Fine," I said. "Really fine, actually. They want to make me a sponsor for someone, but I'm not sure…"

"I'm sure," he said. "You should. You'd be amazing at it."

"You think?"

"You saved my life, Darlene," he said. "In more ways than one."

He leaned in and kissed me then. A sweet, deep kiss that asked for nothing in return. But it woke that hunger in me for him, and I kissed him back, with tingles of anticipation shooting down my spine.

"Sawyer," I breathed.

He nodded and I saw that same need darkening his eyes. I kissed him again, hard, opening my mouth for him, my tongue sliding against his. We fell into each other on the couch, hands roaming, getting acquainted, until I moaned when his hand found my breast over my shirt.

"We should move this to the bedroom," Sawyer said, breathing hard. "If she wakes up right now, I'm going to fucking die."

Sawyer stood up and gently pulled me to my feet, then lifted me under my arms and knees. He maneuvered carefully down the hallway so as not to crash my boot into the wall.

"That's some sexy footwear right there," I said.

"I love your sexy boot," he said. He set me down in front of his bed. "I love you, Darlene. All of you."

"I love you too, Sawyer," I said, kissing him between words. "And it feels so…real. So unlike anything I've ever felt before. And it's making me crazy to have you right now."

He nodded. "Me too." He kissed me hard, his hands in my hair again, angling my mouth to take him deeper. "I want you so fucking bad," he whispered. "But your foot… I don't want to hurt you."

"You won't or…God, I don't even care. Touch me, Sawyer. Please…"

He didn't need more than that. He kissed me again, his tongue sweeping into my mouth, his hands in my hair, gripping. I tasted him, felt the soft, warm wetness of his tongue, the sharp bite of his teeth, the sucking of his lips. And then the sweetness of his breath, like resuscitation, breathed into me and I came alive. More alive than I'd ever felt before. My arms came around his neck and I kissed him back, touched him and pulled him to me.

"Sawyer." My hands clasped his face, then I snaked my fingers through his hair at the back of his head. "Is this happening?" He nodded, breathing heavily, then kissed me again, kissed me like it hurt him to stop. "I need you," he whispered against my lips, then plunged in again, talking and kissing between words. "Wanted you… for so long…"

"You have?"

He pulled back then to look at me, his dark eyes searching and full of want and gentle reverence. "Haven't you?"

I nodded, pressed my cheek into his hand that touched my face. "No man's ever looked at me the way you are right now."

His brows came together for a moment and then he said fiercely, "Good."

"Good?"

"Yeah, good. I'm the first to see you, Darlene," he said, the intensity of his words, his look, making my heart pound. "I'm the first to have you like this. All of you. As you are, and you are…so fucking beautiful."

His eyes glistened in the dimness and mine blurred and stung with tears.

"Sawyer…"

"I'm glad it was me, Darlene," he said, his voice gruff. "Me. And no one else."

I nodded, blinked hard. "No one else," I whispered back. "I don't want anyone else but you, Sawyer. Only you…"

His jaw clenched for a moment and he held my face in his hands, then kissed me with hard sweeps of his tongue. "You're mine. Let me have you…"

God, the possessiveness in his voice and the hunger in his eyes. I'd never felt so wanted, in every way, in my life.

"Yes," I whispered. "Sawyer…."

His mouth on mine was everything, an ecstasy of taste and sensation. But then his hands slipped from my face, needing my body. He stripped off my shirt, and my hair fell down around my shoulders, above my naked breasts.

"Beautiful," he said, trailing kisses down my neck as he took one small breast in each hand. "So beautiful."

I fit perfectly in his palms, and my eyes fell shut when his mouth went to one nipple, sucking and teasing. His hair on my bare skin sent shivers up my shoulders, and I raked my hand through his blond curls. His mouth worked over the other nipple. Electric currents fanned across my chest and down my back, over my spine.

I lifted his shirt off the moment he came up for air, and gaped at his body.

"Jesus, Sawyer," I said, trailing my fingers across the smooth planes of his pecs, down to the hard lines of his abdomen. "Hastings has a gym, I see."

I didn't wait for an answer, but took my turn putting my mouth on one small nipple, biting and nipping, and reveling in the masculine sounds I elicited from him, while my hands slid up and down the hard muscles in his back.

My mouth trailed its way up his chest, his throat, to kiss him again.

"I'm obsessed with your mouth," I told him, taking his lower lip in my teeth and grazing it softly.

"Darlene," he said, his voice rough with need. "Turn around. Want to kiss you everywhere."

I heard the restraint in his voice. If I weren't hurt, he would have manhandled me into any position, and I would have let him; would have let his hands mold me however hc wanted, because what he wanted was all of me.

I turned around, and he sat down on the edge of the bed and pulled me on to his lap, my back to his chest. I gasped at his first touch at the nape of my neck. His mouth was soft and wet, his breath hot, and I couldn't contain the little moans that escaped me as he kissed and caressed me until I was writhing.

"Sawyer…" My head fell back. "What are you doing to me?"

"Exploring."

"God…"

This wasn't just sex or lust. It was him touching and tasting me, becoming acquainted with my body. Sawyer knew me—my heart that beat for him and my soul that understood him—and now he wanted to know my body. In the past, it had always been the sex I'd given first, never thinking a man would want me for much more, not right away, if ever. Sawyer took it last, and his every touch and kiss and desperate groan to have me was the completion of us, not the beginning.

"God, right here," he whispered, his mouth trailing wetly between my shoulder blades while his hands came around my breasts, squeezing and pinching until I was half out of my mind. "I've had fantasies about kissing you here."

"You have?" I breathed. My ass ground against his thighs, my body pressing itself into every place he touched me; a contortion of my dancer's sinews and ligaments to be everywhere at once—on his lap, in his hands, against his mouth.

"Fuck, yes," he groaned, and everything tightened; his hands squeezed, and his teeth grazed my flesh. "I have to have you. Now. Are you ready for me?"

I nodded mutely, and bit back a cry as his hand slipped down, below my navel, and then under the hem of my thong. His fingers found me, rubbing a slow circle. I gasped and arched into his hand, and he went inside, two fingers delving into me.

"God, Darlene," he hissed, scraping his teeth along my back. My hips bucked into his hand again and again. "So wet. I want you to come…"

He withdrew his hand and I gave a little cry at the loss. He stood me up and stripped my panties off, careful around my injured foot. He gently laid me on the bed, and then wasn't careful at all as he put his mouth between my thighs. Ravenous.

"Ah, God," I cried, one hand snaking into his hair, the other up and onto the headboard, holding on as his tongue swirled and then plunged, his groans adding vibrations of sensation. My hips undulated; I made a fist in his soft curls and pressed him harder as my legs fell apart, wide and open.

"Yes, yes, *yes...*"

The word came out of me in hissing whispers, then moans, then screams I had to bite back, as Sawyer drew from deep inside me, a heavy ache of ecstasy so strong I became lost in my own body. I felt only that searing, beautiful agony and Sawyer's mouth, his tongue and lips, and his hand on my thigh, squeezing and pressing me open to him, not stopping until my cries filled the room and then tapered to whimpers as the orgasm swept through me.

I sank back against the headboard, after the currents of that first orgasm streaked through me. My legs were boneless. My arms dropped to my sides, my head lolled.

Sawyer wiped his chin with the back of his hand and went crawling back up my body.

"Not done with you yet," he growled in my ear, and then I gasped and sat up straight as his mouth on my neck sent reviving currents through me. The desire for him—to have all of him, naked and inside me—surged through every part of my body.

I reached to pull the drawstring on his pants as my mouth found his. I kissed him hard, with gnashing teeth and a tongue that explored every inch of his luscious mouth that had just unraveled me. My hand slipped inside his pants to find him huge and hard.

"Oh my God," I hissed against his mouth, stroking him. "This. You...I need you."

He nodded, and bent to reach for the nightstand drawer.

I scooted back against the headboard to watch Sawyer strip out of his pants, then his boxer briefs. Another flush of heat swept between my legs at the magnificent sight of his nakedness; defined arms, pecs, abs, under smooth, tanned skin, and then the V that led down to his pure masculine beauty. My hand went to my own wet desire, needing the touch until he finished rolling on a condom.

"Yes," I whispered, as Sawyer knelt over me, kissed me, then lifted me so he could kneel under me, sitting on his heels. I rested on his thighs for a moment, my back against the headboard and Sawyer in front of me, his beautiful dark eyes full of hard want and reverence; gentle care and heated need all at once.

"I don't want to hurt you," he said again with a soft voice, even as his hands gripped my hips painfully. "But Darlene…"

"You won't," I said. "I don't care if you do. I need you…God, Sawyer, please. Please…" I craned my mouth to him and his lips met mine just as he lifted me over him and slipped inside me as I sank down.

"Oh God," I hissed, as the huge, heavy pressure of him filled me, stretched me.

"Jesus," he groaned, his forehead on mine. "You feel…fuck, you feel so good…So…"

"Perfect," I whispered, tears stinging my eyes and then burning away. "This is perfect."

Sawyer lifted his head to look at me in the dimness, and I saw everything I'd ever wanted to see in a man staring back at me.

The moment of stillness caught and held, and then the need in our bodies became ravenous and couldn't wait one second more. His hands on my hips gripped harder, lifting me and then bringing me down on him. I wrapped my arms and legs around him, kissing him at first as the heaviness of him pushed into me, touching deep, and I undulated my hips to bring him deeper, to take his every thrust harder.

Kissing became impossible, and Sawyer reached above me to grip the headboard with both hands, caging me in his arms. I reached up too, held on and lifted into his thrusts, to meet his every movement. My soft breasts brushed against the hard muscles of his chest, while the intense pressure of him inside me grew and tightened, coiled into something ready to explode. I couldn't get enough of him. His warm scent, the taste of his kiss when our mouths clashed frantically, the feel of his powerful body pinning mine against the headboard.

"More," I whispered. "Sawyer… I want more." I could barely speak, barely comprehended the words that fell from my mouth. "Take me…"

Though it didn't seem possible, Sawyer's hips moved faster and harder at my words. He reached one hand down to hook my leg onto the crook of his elbow, to cradle my injured foot, while taking him somehow deeper into me with every thrust.

I could barely hold on as the tight coil he'd been brushing and coaxing and touching inside me came apart like an explosion. My

250

entire body stiffened; I arched into him, opened my body to him, a scream wrenched out of me as the orgasm rocketed up from where we were joined.

"Yes," he groaned, his thrusts slower now, hard and deep. "Come for me, Darlene. Just like that...Christ, you're so beautiful."

And in my ecstatic delirium, I realized I was going to be his first orgasm in almost a year.

He waited until me.

I held his face in my hands reverently, kissed his broad mouth deeply. "Now you," I whispered against his lips. "Come for *me*, Sawyer. Come inside me."

I felt his own body tense, every one of his taut muscles drawing tighter. His hipbones ground against mine, he was so deep in me. I pressed myself into his last thrusts, nails digging into his ass to hold him tight. He let go of my leg to brace himself on the bed, his other hand gripping my hip to push into me. His mouth found my neck, and he bit down, danced the line between pleasure and pain, and came against me, inside me, the masculine sounds of his release breathing hotly against my throat.

I wrapped my arms around him as he shuddered, wound my fingers in his hair, and held him as the tension in him ebbed and our chests met and retreated, over and over, like a tide, as we caught our breaths together.

"Holy hell," Sawyer groaned into my neck.

"I know," I said. My fingers curled in his hair. The aftershocks of the orgasm made me shudder against him. "Oh my God, feel that?"

He nodded against my shoulder. "Everywhere. I feel you everywhere."

I held him tighter, his beautiful body that was warm, soft skin, over hard muscle and power he had unleashed against me so magnificently.

After a time, Sawyer lifted his head to look at me blearily, drunk with the pleasure and utterly spent. I was sure I looked the same—my hair a tangled mess with strands falling over my face and billowing with my breath. Sawyer's eyes sharpened as his hand came up to brush them away.

"Darlene..."

He fought for more words but found none.

"Just kiss me," I said, and he did.

And in that kiss, I felt his emotions he still hadn't found the words for, but knew that he would. We had time now, and the freedom to be happy. His heart that he had kept locked away for so long was mine. He gave it to me in every soft look, and touch, and in the trust he placed in me to care for his little girl.

And in return, I gave him my entire self; I didn't know how to give less. I loved him with all of me, even the tarnished parts that would always bear the bruises of my past.

"I love you, Sawyer." I stroked his cheek. "Always. I won't ever stop loving you."

"I love you," he whispered. "I love you, Darlene. God, I love you. I don't want to stop saying it. I can't say it enough."

His eyes were dark and beautiful in the dimness, and I loved how I look reflected there. And it was real, his love; not something my lonely heart had manufactured to hold on to, and I knew I'd feel this way, like I did in that moment, forever.

Chapter 29

Sawyer

Again and again, I had her.

We spent the night making love, or going at each other like wild animals, and everything in between. We stopped to catch our breath; I brought us water, we talked a little and laughed a lot, but inevitably, the gentle touches of Darlene's hand in my hair, or mine gliding down the softness of her skin would make us greedy. Like a flare sparking to life, we'd fall back in a sweaty tangle of arms and legs, grasping at skin, her nails raking down my back, my mouth kissing her everywhere. I couldn't get enough of touching her body or listening to her come undone beneath me, over and over again. It was a celebration of our victories that lasted long into the night, and finally ceased when dawn's first light filtered in through the window.

And, miracle of miracles, Olivia slept through the whole thing.

As we lay in the drowsy silence of the morning, my body heavy and spent, I heard Olivia make a little sound in her sleep, through the baby monitor, but she didn't wake.

"She usually wakes up at least once per night," I said. "This is a first. Not to mention," I added with a grin, "you were loud as hell. We probably woke up *Elena's* kids."

Darlene swatted my arm. She lay curled against me, her leg slung over my hip and her booted foot resting on my thigh.

"That's all your fault, not mine." She nestled closer to me. "You told me you thought Olivia woke up because she was afraid she was alone," she said after a moment. Her fingers trailed over my chest. "Maybe she senses the tension has been lifted and she gets to stay where she belongs. And with whom she belongs."

"Maybe so," I said. "But there's still a little tension. One last hurdle."

"Your meeting with Judge Miller?"

I nodded. "Monday. I have not written a word of that essay he wants."

Darlene propped her chin on my chest. "Are you worried?"

"I should be, but I don't know. So much has happened, I feel like what I need to say to him will come to me."

"It will," Darlene said. "I know it will."

"Well, it had better get here quick. It only has two days."

The baby monitor lit up with Olivia stirring.

"She's so cute when she wakes up," Darlene said.

"I'll get her."

Darlene pushed me back. "Let me."

She drew on her underwear and found one of my dress shirts on the floor. It came down to her thighs, and made her legs look like they went on forever. Her hair was tousled—my hands had been buried in it all night—and her lips were swollen from my kisses.

"God, you're sexy," I murmured as she buttoned up the shirt, leaving the top three undone.

She grinned. "You're only saying that because we just had sex for six hours straight."

"I don't think it's subjective," I said. "But I'm willing to put in more time. Just to be sure."

She laughed as she limped to Olivia's room. I slipped on my boxers, then sat against the headboard, listening over the monitor as my daughter crowed 'Dareen!' and Darlene answered with sweet words and silly noises to make her laugh.

They came back into the bedroom, Olivia on Darlene's hip. My little girl blinked sleep out of her eyes; a lock of Darlene's hair was curled around her fingers.

"Look who's awake," Darlene said, bouncing her lightly. "Say, 'good morning, Daddy.'"

"Daddy," Olivia said, and something caught her eye. "Birr. Birr…" She reached her hand and Darlene moved to the window.

"What do you see? Is that a bird?"

"Birr."

The light streamed in, slanted over Darlene holding my baby, and I drank in every detail. The blue of her shirt against Olivia's pale yellow jammies; the sunlight turning strands of Darlene's brown hair gold with hints of red; Olivia's blue eyes as she pointed and babbled at only something she and Darlene could see.

I saw only them; filled my eyes with them and my photographic memory captured every nuance of that moment, and saved it forever.

Monday morning, I arrived at Judge Miller's office promptly at eight a.m. Roger was already there, naturally. He gave me a short glance.

"How did your brief turn out?" he asked.

"It didn't," I said.

His eyes widened slightly, and a small smile tugged the corners of his lips. "What does that mean, exactly?"

It means I'm taking a colossal chance, and possibly throwing away my dream job.

I shrugged. "We'll see."

Roger pressed a smile between his lips and his fingers smoothed the cover of a sleek portfolio that no doubt held his perfectly collated and annotated brief inside.

My hands were empty.

Judge Miller arrived. "Gentlemen."

We followed him into his office and waited at attention until he sat behind his desk.

"You may sit. So. The bar exam," he said, without preamble. "I know results are weeks away, but how do you feel it went?"

"Very well, Your Honor," Roger said. "I feel good about it."

The judge turned to me. "Mr. Haas?"

"I don't know, Your Honor," I said. "I did my best. I'm proud of my work." I shrugged. "That's all I can say at this point."

Miller nodded. "Indeed. Your briefs, please?"

Roger perked up and handed his portfolio to the judge, who flipped through it to give a cursory glance, then looked to me.

"I don't have a brief written."

Judge Miller's thick white eyebrows shot up. "I see."

Beside me, Roger shifted in his chair, sensing victory.

"And for what reason were you unable to complete the assignment?"

"In part, I'm not prepared because I became locked in a custody battle for my daughter."

The judge sat back in his chair. "And did you prevail?"

"I did," I said, "but I shouldn't have. Not under the law."

The words that had been tangled in knots and locked in my heart, unraveled. Finally. Not on paper, in black and white ink, but in words spoken from one man to another.

"I won custody of my daughter, except she isn't technically my daughter. Under the law as prescribed, I came up just short of the year deadline under which she would have been mine. And without my blood in her veins, I was going to lose her to her grandparents who can provide her with everything she could ever want."

I could feel Roger's eyes darting back and forth between us, watching intently to see how my words landed on Judge Miller's face.

"I did try to write your brief," I said. "About my mother. She was killed by a drunk driver, and I was going to write how I wanted to do a better job than the prosecutor who plea bargained, and put her killer back out on the street. He let him go, my mother died, and my family was ripped apart. My father, brother and I were flung far away from one another because of an addict, and that addict became the standard by which I judged all other addicts."

Judge Miller laced his fingers together and rested his chin on them, listening intently.

"I had facts and figures memorized; recidivism rates, and the statistics that painted a bleak picture for drug-and-alcohol-related crimes. Had I written that brief with those facts and figures, you would have given the job to Roger. But I met a woman who is fighting the same battle as the man who killed my mother. The only difference is that she never gave in, even when no one believed in her. When *I* didn't believe in her. This woman…she showed me life. Not the rules and the laws, but everything in between."

Judge Miller's eyes never left mine, and I drew in a shuddering breath, endeavoring to be professional.

But this is life. Sometimes it's messy.

"I made a promise to my daughter's grandparents that wasn't sealed by law," I said. "They accepted knowing they had no legal recourse should I renege. But they trusted me because Darlene showed them—and me—what a second chance truly means. Thanks to her, my daughter has a father and grandparents, both. Family. I have a family for the first time in fifteen years."

I fought for control, as the enormity of what Darlene had done for me swept through me. I blinked hard, and swallowed harder.

"As a federal prosecutor, I'm going to fight to uphold the law one case at a time. One individual at a time. I want justice for victims, no question; but I will have the evidence in front of me, instead of my anger and rage behind me. That's gone now, and I have one amazing, strong, brave woman to thank for that. My career will be forever aimed at making her proud and doing right by her. All else, including this job, will come second. Thank you."

I slumped in my chair feeling as if I had just purged myself of something heavy and black that had been weighing me down. I wondered if Darlene felt like that, standing in front of her meeting group, telling the absolute truths of her heart, and a wave of pride swept over me. It didn't even matter what the judge decided. I could go home to Darlene and Olivia and be the kind of man they both deserved, with or without this job.

The room grew quiet. Judge Miller was looking at me the way my father once did when I'd come home from school with all A's or after I'd hit a home run in Little League. Before my mother was gone and he was still able to be Dad without it hurting so damn much.

Roger glanced at me, then at Judge Miller's expression. A small smile flitted over his face and he rose to his feet. He straightened his jacket, picked up his briefcase and offered his hand to the judge.

"Your Honor, it's been a pleasure," he said. Then he turned to me and offered his hand. "Congratulations."

Roger walked out the door and closed it behind him. Judge Miller did not call him back.

At the Victorian, I stepped inside my place. Darlene was at the kitchen counter, nervously flipping through a magazine. She stopped when she saw me; searched my face for clues. I fought to keep my expression neutral.

"Olivia's taking a nap," she said in a low voice. "So?"

"Well…" I rubbed the back of my head, keeping my gaze cast down.

"Holy hell, Sawyer Haas, I love you, but I'm going to kill you if you don't tell me right now. Did you get it?"

A smile spread over my face in tandem with love for this woman spreading in my heart. "I got it."

Darlene squealed then covered her mouth. She hobbled over to me and threw her arms around my neck and I lifted her up, holding her tight to me.

"It's not official; I have to have passed the bar. But now that I can look at it without being scared to death with custody hearings, I think I passed that bastard."

"I'm so proud of you," she said kissing me over and over. "But I'm not surprised. Not in the least." She held my face in her hands. "My Sawyer the Lawyer."

"Sawyer the Clerk of the Court."

She pretended to think about that a moment. "Doesn't have the same ring to it, but I'll take it."

"I'll take *you*," I said, carrying her to the bedroom. "Again and again and again…"

"Until the baby wakes up," she said, kissing me hotly.

I set her down and she reached for me, but I held her hands in mine. "Everything good in my life is because of you. How do I thank you for that?"

She smiled and traced the line of my jaw with her finger. "You don't. Just love me, Sawyer."

I nodded wordlessly and kissed her. Of course that's all she wanted. Only love, because that's who she was, and as I took her to bed, touching her gently and slow, I vowed to always be worthy of her, right now and forever.

Epilogue

Darlene

One year later…

"How many in your party?" the hostess at Nopa asked us.

I glanced at Sawyer with Olivia on his hip. "Oh gosh, there are… sixteen of us?" I said. "We have a reservation for brunch. Under Montgomery?"

The hostess smiled and checked her book. "We're setting that up now. When your entire party is here, we can seat you."

"She might want to rethink that," I said to Sawyer. "We're going to clog up the works in the front here."

"Probably," he said absently, hoisting Olivia higher. She looked like a cream puff in a ruffled yellow dress. Sawyer looked devastatingly handsome, as always, in a dark gray suit and ruby red tie.

"Every time we come here, our crowd is bigger," I said, smoothing the front of my own black dress. "They're going to have to build an addition for next time."

Sawyer smiled but didn't reply.

I smiled reassuringly. "Hey, if you're nervous about meeting my parents, don't be. They're going to love you. All of my friends are going to love you." My eyes widened over his shoulder. "Speaking of friends…"

I let out a little squeal as Beckett held Nopa's front door open for Zelda.

"Oh my God, you're here!" I hugged them both at the same time. "You smell like New York."

"Like urine and cement?" Zelda asked with her usual sarcasm.

"Like a thousand lights and warm rain," I said, pulling her in for another hug. "I missed you."

"Missed you too, Dar," she whispered. "So much."

"Ten bucks, please," Beckett said, holding his hand to Zelda, which she swatted away. "I bet her ten bucks she'd be tearing up within the first five minutes," he said to Sawyer, and offered his hand. "I'm Beckett and this is my emotional fiancée, Zelda."

"Oh shut up," she said, but I saw something warm and deep pass between them.

"Good to meet you both," Sawyer said. "Darlene's told me a lot about you."

Zelda's green eyes stared at Sawyer, and I could tell the sketch she'd made of my boyfriend in her mind didn't match the one standing in front of her.

"Sawyer, hi," she said, shaking his hand. "Nice to meet you." She turned her head to me so a curtain of her long black hair shielded her from Sawyer, and mouthed, *Are you kidding me?*

I mouthed back. *I know, right?*

They both cooed over Olivia, who immediately grabbed for Zelda's hair.

"Are you nervous about the show?" Zelda asked, gently extracting Olivia's little fist. "*Chicago*...I mean, that's huge, Dar. I'm so excited for you."

"Thanks, yeah, I was nervous at first, but now that we're settling into the run, it's easier."

The San Francisco Repertory was doing six weeks of Kander and Ebb's *Chicago* at the Orpheum Theater. I auditioned for one of the Merry Murderesses—the prison inmate who shot her husband for popping his gum. It was my dream role, though I would have been happy just to be ensemble in such a big, elaborate production.

But I got the part and had done a week's worth of shows to find my groove, and now my friends and my parents had flown from New York to see a Sunday matinee.

They filtered in, in pairs: Henrietta and Jackson, Elena and her husband, Alice and Gerald, my sister Carla and her husband, and my mom and dad. A tingle of nerves shot through me when my family arrived that was more potent than the nervousness I'd felt on opening night.

"Darlene, my God, girl! You look like a million bucks." My sister enveloped me in a perfume and hairspray cloud as she hugged me. "Look at you, I can't get over it. And you must be Sawyer," she said, staring. "Wow. Dar. Just wow. And this peach...this must be Olivia."

Carla introduced her husband, Stan, and then Mom and Dad were there, hugging me.

"She's right," my dad said. "You look like a million bucks, kiddo."

"Thanks, Daddy." I heaved a breath. "Mom and Dad, this is Sawyer and Olivia."

The men shook hands and I thought I saw a glimpse of nervousness dance over Sawyer's brown eyes. Then my mother smacked a kiss on his cheek, and the entire front area dissolved into laughter and loud talk.

The hostess came back and offered to take us to our table. I lingered behind, looking to the front entrance that was crowded with brunch customers. And then I saw him—tall and with the summer sun glinting off the gel in his hair.

I pushed my way through the crowd, and threw my arms around my friend.

"Max," I said against his leather jacket.

"Hey, Dar," he said, holding me tight. "Sorry I'm late."

"You're not late, you're right on time. And I don't even care; you're here, and that's all that matters."

He glanced down at me. "Look at you. A Merry Murderess. Holy shit. Did you know *Chicago* is one of my all-time favorite musicals?"

I made a gun with my index and thumb, and sneered, "If you pop that gum one more time..."

"Jesus, Dar, you gave me the chills." He held out his shaking hands. "Look at this shit? Christ, I can't wait to see you in this."

My murderous expression vanished. "Thank you, Max. Now come on, I need to share the awesomeness that is you with the rest of my people."

I brought Max to our table that was already seated and embarrassed him by making a show of introducing him to everyone. I sat him down with Beckett and Zelda at one end of the table. Sawyer sat across from me. I was beside Olivia, who was scribbling with crayon on a sheet of coloring paper. On the other side of her highchair was my sister, Carla and her husband who was on his phone watching baseball, until she smacked his wrist and told him to put it away.

The waiter came to take our drink order, offering mimosas. Most of our party took her up on that but I abstained, as did Max.

"None for me," Sawyer said, giving me a smile.

"None for me either," Zelda said.

"And I'll abstain too, out of solidarity," Beckett said, and they shared another look over the table.

"Solidarity for what?" I asked.

They exchanged another glance. "Nothing," Zelda said quickly, and they both looked like they were biting back smiles.

My eyes widened and my heart felt like it would burst. "Oh my God...Zelda? Are you...?"

Zelda flapped a hand. "No, hush, this is your day."

I ignored her and turned to Beckett. "Well?"

His proud grin told me everything. "Yes. She is. We're going to have a baby."

"Holy shit!" I screamed and nearly toppled my chair to get to her as the table raised their glasses in cheers. I hugged her and tears were shed all around.

"How far along?" I asked.

"Ten weeks," Zelda said. "We weren't going to say anything until after your show, but this one—" she tossed her napkin at Beckett—"can't keep a secret to save his life."

Beckett held out his hands. "What can I say? I'm too damn happy to keep it quiet."

"You should be," I said. "I'm so happy for you both."

I chatted with them for a while, then sat back down in my seat, flushed with happiness and found Sawyer looking at me from across the table with an expression I couldn't identify.

"It's such great news, isn't it?"

He nodded. "Absolutely."

The food orders were taken, and talk and laughter rolled over the table in waves and swells. Olivia entertained everyone with her ability to count to twenty and recite her ABCs. At one point, Sawyer moved to sit at an empty chair near my dad, and I heard them talking about my dad's business and Sawyer's job as Clerk of the Court for Judge Miller. Of course, Sawyer had passed the bar with an outrageous score of 1990 out of a possible 2000. He was modest as all heck about it, but he'd worked so hard for so long and I was so proud of him. And proud of myself, for being here. For making it to this moment, with these people I loved best.

I bent my head to find Max and met his eye. I didn't have to say a word. He nodded once, and smiled, and I knew he understood.

After we ate, dessert was offered and Sawyer was back in his chair across from me.

"You're so quiet today," I said, leaning toward him and taking his hand. "Everything all right?"

He nodded. "It's perfect."

The desserts were served but I abstained from them too. The last thing I needed before the show was a sugar rush.

"Ma! Hey, Mama," Carla called to our mother over a table of talk. "You have to split this tiramisu with me. I can't do it alone."

"Where Mama?" Olivia asked.

"What's that, hon?" Carla said, leaning sideways to Olivia while she prepped her coffee.

"Where Mama?"

"Oh, she's my mama." Carla pointed at our mother with her spoon. "That's my mama, right there."

"Ohhh," Olivia said. "Das my mama righ' dare!" she said, and she pointed straight to me.

The whole table stopped, conversations ceased. I felt warm all over, as if a ray of sunlight suddenly fell over me, turning everything gold and soft.

My gaze jumped to Sawyer. He gave a short, disbelieving laugh, his mouth open in shock but wanting to smile.

"What did you say, honey?" he asked Olivia.

"Mama," Olivia said, hooking a little chocolate-covered finger my way again. "Darlene my mama." She said as if this were common knowledge and went back to eating her cake, completely unaware of the knowing laughs and teasing that swept through the rest of the table.

The Abbotts stared in surprise, and a pang of fear shot through me, certain they must be saddened for Molly, that she wasn't here to share in this happiness, and that Olivia had given her title to someone else. To me.

"I didn't tell her…" I said. "I mean, she's never called me that before…"

I held my breath until they both smiled, Alice with her hand over her heart. "It's okay," she told me. "It hurts and yet it's perfectly right. Does that make sense?"

I nodded, tears in my eyes. "Yeah, it does."

"Oh jeez, Dar," my sister said, breaking the solemn moment. She spooned sugar into her coffee. "A mama. You ready for that?"

Jackson was less subtle. He bellowed a great laugh and clapped his hands. "Thatta girl, Livvie! Up top."

He reached across the table to high five the two-year old. Henrietta swatted his arm down.

"You hush. This is personal between them, and you have no cause to say a word."

Henrietta's word was law, and everyone went back to their conversations.

Jackson chuckled and shot me a wink, but I didn't feel like laughing. I leaned over the table to Sawyer.

"I didn't say a word, I promise. She only ever calls me Darlene. I—"

"It's okay," he said, a strange smile on his lips. "We live together. It was inevitable that she'd bond with you even more than she had already.'"

"I know, but I know you don't want to confuse her…"

"Darlene," Sawyer said. "It's fine."

I nodded and sat straight in my chair, the beautiful happiness I'd felt at Olivia's words fading to leave my stomach twisting in knots.

The last few days Sawyer had been acting funny. He was in his head a lot, and not talking as much as usual. And today, he'd been so quiet and subdued. As the others ate their dessert and drank their coffee, I found myself going back over the last few days trying to find something that could be amiss. But I had to keep going, back and back, as this year had been the most incredible of my life.

I'd been able to find big parts in small shows so that my massage work was mostly freelance to make extra income. And now I'd had a small-ish role in a really big show. And the day I told Sawyer, his eyes had widened and the pure joy and happiness for me felt as good as getting the part.

Rachel had returned from her Greenpeace tour wanting her apartment back. After many long talks, I moved in with Sawyer and Olivia. We both wanted to protect Olivia, but we were so much in love, the idea of something going wrong between us seemed impossible. We were happy. I wondered sometimes how it was possible to feel so happy with Sawyer and Olivia, and building a life with a man and his little girl was something I'd never imagined I wanted, and now couldn't imagine living without.

I glanced at Sawyer across the table. Jackson leaned in to tell him a joke but Sawyer only smiled, a far-off expression on his face. My stomach twisted a little more. Was this the slow fade I'd seen before? No big drama, no blow up fights...

You're being ridiculous, I told myself, but I'd seen it too many times. And that impossible happiness...maybe it was just that. Too impossible to last.

I got up from my seat and moved down the table to where Max was talking with Beckett.

"Excuse me," I said, "but I need to borrow this guy for minute."

I tugged Max to his feet and drew him away from the table, to the bathroom alcove.

"Help! How do you shut down overthinking?"

Max looked dashing in a suit he wore with a black leather jacket instead of a coat. "That's the secret to life," he said with a grin. "If I knew that, I'd be on Oprah right now."

I bit my lip.

His teasing smile fled. "What is it?"

"It's nothing. I'm jumping to conclusions...or, not even that. I don't know what to think." I looked up at him, tears coming to my eyes. "I've been so happy and that stupid little voice is back. You know the one? It whispers in your ear that everything good is going to go away soon."

He nodded. "I know the voice. That little fucker talks to me. Frequently." He smiled gently at me. "But don't talk back. Don't feed it. That'll get you nowhere. If you're concerned about something with Sawyer, talk to Sawyer."

I nodded. "You're right. I know you're right." I sucked in a breath. I was stronger than this. I'd come so far, and I couldn't let nagging doubt get the best of me. I wasn't the girl who thought a man being upset with her meant the end.

"You're still as wise as ever," I said, as we walked back to the table. "I just…got scared."

"That'll happen. Just don't let it stay."

I kissed his cheek and sat back down. Sawyer was watching me.

"You okay?" he asked.

"I wanted to ask you the same," I said. Jackson laughed loudly at something Gerald said, and I flinched. "But not here. After lunch?"

He smiled warmly and nodded, and I felt a little better.

At the Orpheum theatre, outside the back entrance, I hugged and kissed everyone and they all told me to break a leg.

"Hey, Dar," Jackson said. "You know that's just a figure of speech, right?"

"Such a comedian," I said with a laugh and a roll of my eyes.

I hugged Alice who was holding Olivia. "I'm going to keep her occupied until your big number," she said, "then come out and watch."

"Thank you," I said. "Just cover her eyes over the naughty bits." I bent to kiss Olivia's cheek. "Bye-bye, sweet pea."

"Bye-bye, Mama."

My heart clenched again.

"She's a smart cookie, this one," Alice said with a knowing smile. "Once she gets a notion in her head, it's hard to get it out. Just like her daddy."

She inclined her head at Sawyer who was last to wish me luck before the show. The rest of our people moved away and we were alone.

"She did it again with the Mama, thing," I said. "Sawyer…"

Without a word, he slipped his arms around my waist and kissed me, the kind of kiss that never failed to steal the strength from my legs so that I melted against him. I did then, my arms ringing his neck to keep upright as his hands slid up into my hair, and then down to my cheek. He held my face and broke the kiss, his eyes so beautiful and dark as they bored into mine.

"I love you, Darlene," he said.

"I love you too," I whispered. "And I'm so happy with you. And with Olivia."

"Are you?" he asked, a ragged breath chasing his words. "Truly? I know it's a lot to take…living with a kid…"

"No, I love her to pieces, and I love you so damn much, I feel like my heart's going to burst. But I get scared sometimes."

"I do too," he said, his brows furrowed. "I worry that it's all going to go away...this happiness."

"Yes! Me too," I said, clutching the lapels of his jacket. "What do we do?"

He smiled, his thumb running over my bottom lip. "We make sure it doesn't. We hold on, right?"

I nodded through tears. "Yes. We do."

"*We* do," he said. "Together." Sawyer kissed me again, then inclined his head at the stage entrance door. "I don't want you to be late. You're amazing, and I'm so damn happy your friends and family are here to see this. You deserve it all, Darlene. All of it."

I threw my arms around him and kissed him hard, then swept into the theater, my heart full, and a huge grin on my face.

There is no slow fade. What we have is real.

I went to the dressing area, where the rest of the cast greeted me with cheerful smiles and high fives. The other Merry Murderesses—six of us who performed the Cell Block Tango to tell the story of how we ended up in jail for murdering our husbands—were like sisters to me. I belonged here, just as much as I did in my NA meetings where I was attendee and sponsor, both.

I changed into my costume—tight black dance shorts, black nylons, black knee boots, and a black halter top that left my midriff bare. I put on my dark eye make up and red lips; then a hairdresser brushed out my hair and tousled it so it looked like a man's hands had just been in it.

The show began and I waited for my number. The Cell Block Tango. I had the first line, "Pop", that began a series of key words from each of the Merry Murderesses, and if I didn't hit my cue every time, the entire song would be off tempo.

But everyone I knew and loved was watching me. I didn't want to disappoint them, and as the emcee announced the song, I felt a glowing well of strength in me. Not stiff and unbending, but molten and hot so that I could dance. So that I could tell the story with my body, and give everything that I had to it. Because I had a lot to give, and I'd finally found it.

The energy was running high for a matinee, and we danced the hell out of Cell Block Tango, and after the sound effect of a prison door slamming shut boomed across the stage, the crowd erupted into cheers that carried me on a tide of joy to the end of the musical.

As the last number ended, the crowd grew thunderous—a rolling swell of appreciation and excitement that barreled through the theatre with whistles and applause and hollering.

I stood just offstage with my other Merry Murderesses, waiting for our cue for the curtain call. "Standing O," one said. "Not bad for a matinee."

When it came time for our curtain call, we slunk onto the stage languidly; long-legged steps in our high heels. I slung my arm on my co-inmate's shoulder and tried to look sexy and tough in our curtain-call pose, but the lights had come down and I found my people in the audience.

They were all there, and I wished I had Sawyer's photographic memory; I'd have taken a thousand photos of my parents looking proud of me; my mother dabbing her eye.

Of Max clapping his hands so hard, I was afraid he'd hurt himself.

Of Beckett trying to be stoic as he fought back strong emotion, but the shine in his eyes gave him away.

And Zelda who didn't bother to hide her tears.

And Sawyer…

Sawyer's seat was empty.

My heart dropped but before I could contemplate it, the Merry Murderesses had to relinquish the stage to Mama Morton, and the rest of the *Chicago* cast that had become a second family to me.

After Velma and Roxie took their bows, the entire cast stormed the front of the stage with clasped hands to bow. The energy surged through us, hand to hand, and now we were free to break character and smile. But Sawyer still wasn't there.

Maybe he had to use the bathroom, or Alice needed help with Olivia.

Ushers passed out bouquets of flowers to the dancers from audience members, as the emcee strolled onto the stage. He held a microphone in one hand and a bouquet of Gerber daisies in another, all white.

"Now, hold on folks," the emcee said. "Before we wrap this up, we have a very special little guest who wants to say something to one of our Merry Murderesses. Darlene…? Would you step forward, love?"

I stared for a moment, unable to breathe or move until one of the dancers nudged my elbow. I came forward and the emcee put the bouquet in my hand.

"You have a fan, Darlene," he said, then looked stage right. "Come on out here, little sweetheart."

Olivia toddled out from stage right with Sawyer holding her hand as she raced toward me. The audience cooed at the cuteness before them, Olivia in her puffy yellow dress, her little legs working.

"Here," Olivia said, holding a black velvet box in her hand. "Is for you."

I had no words. The crowd reacted for me, gasps and murmurs and a few *ohhhs*.

"That was supposed to come last," Sawyer said, moving to stand before me. "I was freaking out that doing this here was a bad idea," he said and glanced nervously at the crowd. "Now I'm sure of it. How do you do this every night?"

I shrugged and laughed. My heart was pounding in my chest, I could hardly hear myself talk.

"Here go, Mama," Olivia said, still trying to give me the box.

I bent to touch her cheek, then stood to face Sawyer. "She keeps calling me her Mama."

"Would you...?" His voice cracked and he tried again. "Would you want to be her mom? Because what I'm about to ask...I'm asking for her, too. For both of us."

I nodded, tears spilling down and the audience took a collective intake of breath.

"I would be honored to be her mommy," I whispered.

Sawyer's jaw clenched and he got down on one knee, next to Olivia. The audience *oooohed* and *awwwwed,* but I hardly heard them.

Sawyer put one arm around his daughter. "Give it to her now, honey."

"Here go!" Olivia said, and offered me the velvet box.

"Thank you, baby," I managed. I took the box, but couldn't open it. "My hands are shaking," I whispered to Sawyer.

"Mine too." He took the box from my hand and opened it on a small, square-cut diamond solitaire in a ring of white gold.

My hands flew to my mouth and I felt the energy of the audience wrap around us in joyful anticipation.

"Darlene Montgomery," Sawyer said, his voice ringing out into the auditorium, clear and loud. "Will you marry me?"

I could only nod at first, my voice silenced by happiness and tears, and the future that was waiting on the other side of this question.

"Yes," I whispered, and got to my knees too. "Yes," I said, louder. "Yes, I'll marry you. Of course, I will."

The audience went crazy. Underneath the noise and lights, I kissed Sawyer, and tasted his tears that mingled with mine. Then I turned to Olivia and held her close.

"Can I be your Mommy, sweet pea?"

Olivia gave me a perplexed baby look that said, *I believe we have already established this, silly woman.* Aloud, she said. "You my Mama."

Sawyer looked about ready to fall apart, and I knew that the last thing my stoic man wanted was to burst into tears in front of fifteen hundred people. I hugged Olivia, and we got to our feet. Sawyer slipped the ring on my finger, and held my hand tight as he kissed me again. The crowd swelled with applause and cheers.

In that perfect moment, Olivia slipped one of her little hands into mine, the other into his, and she held on. And we held on to her—and each other—just as tightly.

The End

Sneak Peek

The worlds of a poor, aspiring actor and a well-to-do, but troubled girl collide in a small Midwestern town.

In Harmony, coming February, 2018

Add to your Goodreads TBR here: http://bit.ly/2yxJZtI

More From
Emma Scott

How to Save a Life (Dreamcatcher #1)
Let's do something really crazy and trust each other.

"You're in for a roller coaster of emotions and a story that will grip you from the beginning to the very end. This is a MUST READ…"—
Book Boyfriend Blog

Amazon: http://amzn.to/2pMgygR
Audible: http://amzn.to/2r20z0R

Full Tilt
I would love you forever, if I only had the chance…

"Full of life, love and glorious feels."—**New York Daily News, Top Ten Hottest Reads of 2016**

Amazon: http://amzn.to/2o1aK1o
Audible: http://amzn.to/2o8A7ST

All In (Full Tilt #2)
Love has no limits…

"A masterpiece!" –**AC Book Blog**

Amazon: http://amzn.to/2cBvM26
Audible: http://amzn.to/2nUprDQ

Printed in Poland
by Amazon Fulfillment
Poland Sp. z o.o., Wrocław

70126457R00161